D0581399

Undone

KRISTINA LLOYD

BLACK
LACE

1 3 5 7 9 10 8 6 4 2

Published in 2014 by Black Lace, an imprint of Ebury Publishing
A Random House Group Company

Copyright © Kristina Lloyd, 2014

Kristina Lloyd has asserted her right to be identified as the
author of this Work in accordance with the Copyright,
Designs and Patents Act 1988

This novel is a work of fiction. Names and characters are the
product of the author's imagination and any resemblance to actual
persons, living or dead, is entirely coincidental

All rights reserved. No part of this publication may be reproduced,
stored in a retrieval system, or transmitted in any form or by any
means, electronic, mechanical, photocopying, recording or
otherwise, without the prior permission of the copyright owner

The Random House Group Limited Reg. No. 954009

Addresses for companies within the Random House Group can
be found at: www.randomhouse.co.uk

A CIP catalogue record for this book is
available from the British Library

The Random House Group Limited supports The Forest Stewardship
Council® (FSC®), the leading international forest-certification
organisation. Our books carrying the FSC label are printed on FSC®
-certified paper. FSC is the only forest-certification scheme supported
by the leading environmental organisations, including Greenpeace.
Our paper procurement policy can be found at:
www.randomhouse.co.uk/environment

Printed and bound in Great Britain by Clays Ltd, St Ives PLC

ISBN 9780352347268

To buy books by your favourite authors and register for offers visit
www.randomhouse.co.uk
www.blacklace.co.uk

For Ewan, for being generous with the measures.

Part 1

Monday 30th June

I can't recall my first thought that morning: that I was in a strange bedroom; that an unfamiliar man was naked beside me; or that a woman was screaming somewhere in the distance.

The scream filtered into a hung-over dream so I couldn't be sure if it was real or imagined.

'You hear that?' I asked him. My mouth was bone dry.

He said nothing, his slow, sleepy breath rattling in his throat. 'Hey.' I nudged him and he rolled on his side, the muscles in his back slipping and shifting as if his body were liquefying, man becoming river. He grunted as he turned, dragging the sheet so it twisted like a toga, flashing that distinctive tattoo.

His breath grew quiet. I tried to piece him together. Broad, bronzed shoulders. Scruffy dark hair. I looked at his back, as big and silent as a continent, his spine a groove swooping down to the furred cleft of his buttocks. What was his name? Hell, what had we done together? A solid

thrum between my thighs responded before cognitive
memory could answer.

I flopped away from him, squinting. The room was
cream and gold, its walls slanted, the curtains glowing
with light as pale as honeydew melons. I licked my teeth.
Outside birds trilled and chattered, and I couldn't hear
even a murmur of cars. I must have imagined the scream,
the noise an echo escaping from a dream. Dravendene
Hall was too tranquil for drama. Even a bad dream seemed
out of place.

Pleasure bubbled as snatches of the night before
returned to me. Forty-one years old and my first threesome. Go, Lana Greenwood, go! Work that bucket list! I
smiled and stretched, feeling fucked, messy, glorious and
alive. I tried to ignore the dull sense of disquiet threatening to upset my happiness. A forgotten nightmare, that
was all. Beneath the bed sheet, I rubbed my foot against
his, just making contact and saying, 'Hi there, relative
stranger.' His foot edged away, avoiding mine. Ah, I
thought. One of those. Shuns affection. Well, I could
handle that for a one-night stand.

That's when I realised a third person should have been
in bed with us: Misha, the Russian guy. Oh boy, the things
we'd done together. The things *they* had done. Images
rushed in of bodies slamming, of sweat-damp hair, limbs
entangling and mouths gaping. I'd watched them as if in a
fog, my perception misted by thwarted desire. What was he
called, this guy lying next to me? He had a freshly bust-up
lip when I'd first met him. Damn. Embarrassing if I couldn't
recall his name. Should I rummage through his wallet?

Sol, that was it. Sol Something-or-other. Dangerously
attractive and charmingly cocky. An ex-New Yorker with a

dirty smile and an introductory handshake that had turned my knees to mush. It wasn't one of those concerted, hefty handshakes taught in business schools to suggest sincerity. It was a grip from a man who liked to tease but didn't know his own strength. There's not a lot I wouldn't do to bed someone like that. As I later demonstrated.

And Misha was a customer from The Blue Bar. Ack, I should not have fucked a customer and crossed that professional boundary. Jeez, but the guy was hung. How awkward was *that* going to be when he next stopped in for a drink? All I'd be able to think about was his ginormous schlong. Already I was itching to tell Katrina. I could picture her laughing as I relayed the highlights. 'I swear, Kat, his cock was so huge he nearly passed out when he got hard! You could practically see the colour draining from his face! Couldn't even form a sentence. No blood supply to his brain!'

I glanced around the room in search of water. I'd packed coconut water, good for rehydrating. Sensible me. The smooth beige carpet was littered with bondage gear, condoms, beer bottles and tissues. Well, maybe not so sensible. But, oh, what a night.

Misha's absence didn't concern me until the scream rang out again.

'We need help!' yelled a male voice from far away. A door banged.

My heart speeded up, nausea clutching. Don't ask why, but a gut instinct told me this was related to Misha. I stood and slipped on my dressing gown, a 1950s wrap in pistachio green silk and sprigged with dusky roses. Does it seem shallow of me to mention details of my clothing when a tragedy was unfolding? It's an impulse I can't resist. If I'm to tell my story to these pages, I need to visualise myself and how I acted, otherwise I risk vanishing into the words, disappearing in the slippage between my outsides and insides, between the sound of language and the meaning.

I parted the curtains, fingertips trembling on gold brocade. Far below, beyond the tiny, diamond-paned window, the calm of striped green lawns and orderly flowerbeds rolled towards surrounding woodland. I picture the scene now and I'm a character in an Elizabeth Bowen novel, albeit without the youthful innocence.

We were high in the West Tower, having opted to use my room because I'd brought Clejuso handcuffs and a bottle of Belvedere Unfiltered to the party. The American had been impressed by the cuffs; the Russian, by the vodka. Personally, I'd been impressed by their eagerness for a post-Cold War ménage but then neither guy had turned out to be as straight as I'd imagined.

The silk belt to my dressing gown lay on the cluttered floor. I grabbed it, picking hurriedly at knots as I remembered how Sol had used the silk to tie my legs to the chair. I threaded the smooth length through the loops of my gown, fastening a limp bow as I swished from the room, leaving Sol asleep. I descended the steep spiral staircase to the second floor of the west wing to find doors opening along the corridor. A pyjama-clad woman with bird's-nest hair and grumpy, kohl-smudged eyes glared at me, as if I were to blame for the disturbance. 'What the fuck's going on?' she growled.

'Search me.' I strode quickly, holding my gown to my groin for decency's sake, hung a left, and then took the stairs down to the next level. I found myself on the balcony floor overlooking the oak-panelled entrance hall with its chequerboard floor, tall Chinese urns and trophy stag heads. Since my arrival the day before, I'd grown better at navigating the higgledy-piggledy gothic monstrosity that was Dravendene Hall.

Below, a guy stood in the centre of the tiled hallway, arms wide, appealing up to the balcony.

'Swimming pool, anyone?' he called. 'Best way to the swimming pool? Didn't even know there was one.'

I trotted down the staircase like a poor man's Scarlett O'Hara, thinking the owners were crazy to allow random party-goers free rein in such a spectacularly grand manor house. Their insurance must be sky high. Half-dressed people flitted and flowed, some alert to the sense of urgency, others bleary-eyed and reluctant. A lanky guy in droopy blue boxers descended one step at a time while rolling a cigarette. A woman with tears streaking her face ran in the opposite direction, elbowing people aside as she stumbled up the stairs. 'He's dead,' she was sobbing. 'He's dead.'

People exchanged glances, some stopping in their tracks, others springing forwards. 'Who's dead?' 'What's happening?' 'Has anyone called an ambulance?' 'Oh, fuck, keep calm.'

Two guys were having an animated discussion in the entrance hall, one pointing ahead, the other to the right. In the chaos, someone decided it was easiest to reach the pool via the gardens so I followed while others ran deeper into the house. Outside, the grass underfoot was cool and moist, and the morning sunlight hurt my eyes. I'm too pale and blonde for summer, even a British summer.

The pool was at the rear of the pointy, redbrick hall, housed in glass like a Victorian conservatory. Gravel pinched my feet as we hurried along a path flanked with regimented box hedge. Ahead, a huddle of people gathered on the poolside, some crouched low. A palm tree behind the conservatory glass obscured my view and it wasn't until we were at the sliding patio doors that I saw the splayed bare feet and hairy shins of a figure on the marble floor. Two guys knelt over him, one pumping his chest.

A burly guy with a phone to his ear gazed down at the men, his crimson face filmy with sweat. 'Anything?' he asked.

To enter the poolhouse was to slam into a wall of tropical humidity. An acrid scent of chlorine tainted the heat, and silver reflections shimmered on the rectangle of blue water. Alabaster nymphs gazed impassively from slender plinths, their nipples round enough to pluck. The potted palms were lush and tranquil, and a faint mechanised hum hovered around us. My back was slick with sweat, the dressing gown sticking to my skin. I was panting, the air so dense I felt as if I were trying to inhale fabric. My legs quivered, my head booming, my skull like a vice. This sudden shortage of breath, damn it. I half-feared I might collapse. Too much late-night sex and alcohol.

'No, nothing, mate. I think we should give up. There's no pulse.'

A man kneeling by the body sat back on his heels.

A woman's sob erupted as if from a trapped, primitive place.

People swung around to look at me.

The sound hung, a blood-curdling cry muffled and held by glasshouse echoes.

My hand was clamped to my mouth, my eyes fixed on his grey, bloated, froth-smeared face.

'Lana.' The voice was gentle. A woman moved towards

me. She seemed to glide on the periphery of my vision; then she clasped me in her arms, so strong and solid. 'Hush, babes.' I let her hold me, hiding in the comfort of her hair, wanting to unsee what I'd just seen. 'I think he must be a friend of Rose's,' she said. 'Do you know him?'

Far away, coming from another world, the anguished wail of sirens slid over the countryside.

I nodded into the woman's neck. Her hair smelled cold, like starlight and outer space. For a long time, I couldn't form the words. Then, croakily, 'Misha Morozov. A customer at The Blue Bar.'

'I'm sorry,' she said, rubbing my back. 'Sweetheart, I'm so sorry. But I don't think we can do anything else for him.'

I'm too raw. My head's jangling with sex and death. I wish I could turn back the clock.

I can't write any more today. I need to try and sleep.

Tuesday 1st July

I have decided this journal will have a therapeutic function. It will help me regain the sense of control I've lost in these last few days. If I don't get back on track, I may fall apart. I need to record events in detail in case I'm called in for questioning. I am liable to forget things when my mind is overburdened.

My writing will not be comparable to unfettered, adolescent self-expression. I will pay attention to my prose style. I will narrate both the surface and the depths. I will adhere to chronology as far as I can.

Last night, I woke from a fever dream of jackboots thumping down a corridor, black, glinting, vicious. They were coming to get me as I lay in my own bed, alone in the dark. When I opened my eyes, I was desperately confused because I *was* lying in my own bed, alone in the dark. Fact and fantasy swam in a whirl. I strained to listen above the pounding of my heart. I was wet with sweat. At the juncture of my thighs I was wet too because I knew that when they found me my oppressors would be merciless.

All these men are Sol, and Sol is all these men.

I fear authority and I crave it.

I can't allow the truth to rise up like this. This diary will help me stay sane.

I've been trying to identify the point where I began losing it. The death disturbed me, of course, but that wasn't the start. I think it was later, in the woods, when Sol climaxed with a cry that haunts me even now.

When I was younger, I was a sucker for the romantic notion of not knowing where I ended and where the object of my affection began. Now, I want to know exactly where I end, thanks very much, and I'll erect barriers should anyone attempt to trespass. Sol threatens my boundaries but I can't yet pinpoint how, nor can I fathom why I've become so permeable and desperate.

The moment I met him seems a lifetime ago but, in real terms, it was a matter of days. For the first time this year, the sky was the rich, saturated blue of high summer. I'd driven to the party on my own, windows down, great music, winding country lanes, scarlet poppies blazing in the hedgerows. The breeze whipped at my hair, and I couldn't stop grinning. I felt on the brink of newness, as if this was destined to be a weekend of change.

I'd been in two minds about attending because at the last minute we were short-staffed at the bar. Perhaps Misha would be alive now if I'd decided not to go, but madness beckons if I start thinking along those lines. When I'd paid my deposit, the weekend had looked perfect: the fortieth birthday party of a former work colleague from my days of working in a design practice in central London. A chance to breathe some country air, relax and hang out in the fabulously grand manor house they'd hired. There'd be al fresco dining, tennis, woodland walks, croquet, dancing and drinking. I'd meet some old faces and, more importantly, some new ones, which I still needed to do since the break-up of my marriage.

Technically speaking, it was a joint party: Zoe's fortieth and the thirty-fourth of a friend of hers, Rose, whom I'd never met. What else? My first holiday since opening the bar, if you can call a couple of days off a holiday. And our decree absolute had come through so a celebration seemed in order.

Damn. Already I'm guilt-tripping myself, trying to justify my presence at Dravendene Hall. Spot the workaholic.

On arrival, I'd unpacked my case in my adorable little turret room, and then joined a couple of ex-colleagues, Trish and Abbi, in the sprawling garden at the rear of the house. The trees were hung with inert balloons of colour, Chinese lanterns waiting to be enlivened by darkness. Two conical canvas tipis, connected at the centre and trimmed with bunting, offered shade from the sun but few people seemed to want it. There was no bar or waiting service because this wasn't a wedding or a high-society do. We were a bunch of people sharing a space for a couple of days and hoping to keep the costs relatively manageable.

After a short while, I went to fetch another bottle of chilled rosé from the utility room, as directed by Abbi.

'Fuck, I need to pace myself,' Trish had said from her deckchair, her cigarette hand rocking as she brought it to her mouth. You could tell it was already too late but nobody minded.

Guests were arriving in dribs and drabs while those already present were scattered around the grounds, doing their own thing prior to the evening celebrations. The weekend was a child-free zone and the atmosphere buzzed with a readiness to party. I passed a small raised lawn, edged by a stone balustrade and spiky, architectural plant-ing. Silvery plumes of pampas grass fluttered against the blue sky. The breeze could barely be felt. Three men were playing giant-sized Jenga, hands on knees as they studied the precarious tower. A nearby field had been set aside for camping, and Zoe and Mike had driven off in search of a supermarket. There weren't as many familiar faces as I'd been anticipating. I experienced a brief tug of yearning for the old, comfortable days when I'd belonged to a couple, and never had to feel alone at social occasions. I pushed the thought aside, knowing I was better off now than then.

The stone utility room was cool and shadowy, an Aladdin's cave of alcohol. Sunlight filtered in through a small, grimy window, casting a meagre sheen on kegs, crates and exotic, multi-coloured bottles. I blinked as my eyes readjusted, goosebumps stippling my bare arms.

In the veiled light, a shirtless man stood before a tall American fridge, head bowed. He rested one hand on the matte silver door, while the other angled a pint glass at the ice dispenser. He wore canvas knee-lengths, slung low on his hips, and his dark, sweat-soaked hair was hooked behind his ears. He was powerfully muscular but not unnaturally chiselled, and a small roll of softness edged his waist. Ice cubes clattered into the glass. The bars of his ribs pumped below wet spikes of hair in the pit of his raised arm. His torso glistened, a soft curve of light resting on one shoulder. Beads of sweat trickled down his chest. A couple of droplets fell, making dark spots on the flagstones.

I shivered. Laughter and the clink of glasses from outside grew faint, as if I were sinking under water, the world fading out of reach. He stood straight, glancing at me. For an instant, the light around him was magical, a diaphanous haze pricked with glittering motes. His chest hair was plastered to his body, and his lower lip was smeared with blood, a glossy violet bulge distorting its shape.

'You see any cloths around here?' His accent was American, a sexy, sonorous drawl, and a slight slur marred his words. He stepped into shadow and slid open a flaky, wooden door beneath an old Belfast sink. He bobbed down to peer in, holding the sink above for balance. Down his left side, from underarm to hip, was a tattoo unlike any I'd seen before. To be accurate, there were several tattoos but they formed a picture, or a panel, depicting a stemmed dandelion head gone to seed. The images were as delicately rendered as etchings under tissue paper in a botanical encyclopaedia. Single, fluffy orbs drifted from the spiky round flower, as if a breeze were blowing tattoos across his body. I half wanted to reach out and catch one so I could make a wish.

The man stood, glancing around the dimness. I grabbed a folded tea towel on the counter-top.

'Here,' I said. I caught a waft of fresh sweat as I handed him the cloth. The heat from his body pressed on my chilly skin. An image hovered in my mind of him shoving me up against the rugged stone wall and destroying my nice, neat tea dress with his hard, ruthless hands.

It's fair to say, I hadn't seen much action for a while. Bitch-on-heat had become my default setting. I'd been hoping the weekend might offer some respite from my dry spell. If he were available, a guy like this would suit me fine for a fling.

'You OK?' I asked. 'What happened?'

'Got whacked in the face with a tennis racquet.' He spread out the chequered cloth on the wooden drainer by the sink and tipped ice into the centre. He cupped the tumbling cubes with one hand, muscles shifting in his shoulders as he moved, his breath puffing fast. 'My backhand, his forehand.' He twisted the cloth into a bundle and gingerly pressed the ice pack to his lip.

'Ouch,' I said. 'Can I do anything? Does it need stitches?'

He tugged open the fridge door with his left hand and snatched a large bottle of mineral water. 'Take the top off that, would you?' he said, proffering the plastic bottle.

I did as asked. 'Are your teeth OK?'

He nodded. 'He just caught me. I was lucky.' He transferred the ice pack to his left hand, taking the opened bottle with his right. 'Cheers.' He tipped back his head, his mouth open wide, and poured in a stream of water. His Adam's apple bobbed in his stubble-shadowed neck as he glugged, liquid bubbling from his mouth and spilling down his front. He stopped drinking, laughed and shook his head like a wet dog, showering me in droplets of sweat and water. 'Whoa!' he said, eyes popping.

'You want to sit down?' I said. 'I could try and find some antiseptic. You should probably—'

'You kidding me?' he said. 'It's break point!' And he bounded out of the room, ice pack in one hand, bottle in the other. He streaked past the window in a blur. I leaned forwards, hands on the drainer, watching him through the dirty, cobwebbed glass. He upended the bottle, emptying its contents over his head. Water coursed down the wedge of his back, pinging off his body as if a halo of diamonds were shattering around him.

Outside, a distant roar erupted amid a bang and rattle of wood. The Jenga tower had collapsed.

I watched him disappear from view. I was in control then, I'm sure of it. Lecherous? Interested? Oh, without a doubt. But I don't fall that easily. I'm like the Jenga tower. I need to be studied and carefully dismantled by a man with skill and patience; by a man smart enough to recognise my own smartness and complexity. This sexy guy with the broken lip, he was sporty and he looked like fun. He'd never be up to the task.

You'd think, wouldn't you, that people can't help but reveal themselves in bed? That they're made vulnerable by their nakedness and admission of desire. That when you tacitly agree to trust each other by sharing the space of sex, there's a truth in what you do. The barriers are down.

But it's not always the case. Sol gave away so little that night. He was an artful performer keeping his distance. Only later, after Misha died, when he fucked me on the forest floor, did I see Sol for who he was. Or, at least, I'd thought so at the time. Because, ironically, I'm starting to suspect I saw his true colours when he was lying. Fucking and lying. Fucking with such abandon I thought we might disintegrate; thought we might crumble into ancient earth and tremulous ferns, pulling each other

down into the disappearance of old bones and deep-
diving tree roots.

I'm afraid Sol is too much like me. He longs for the
edge but a fear this would destroy him curtails his compulsion to know that dark delirium. I don't know how
close to ruin he allows himself to get but I know he is not
merely fun. He's more than the sunny, sociable, game-
playing Sol he makes himself out to be; so much more.
And I'm glad, and I'm scared. He has a hiddenness I want
to find, but I'm terrified I might regret it. I expect the feeling's mutual.

So he watches me. I watch him. And I do not know who
will win.

Wednesday 2nd July
Time's ticking on. It's been three days now, and I still
haven't recorded the events of day one at Dravendene
Hall. I'm being too cautious with my words, too reflective
in my thoughts. I've been swimming too much as well,
upping my daily quota of lengths by two then four. Last
night, after closing the bar, I fell into an exhausted sleep,
assisted by a large brandy and soda. I wish I didn't dream.

It's nearly 2 a.m. now. I'm sitting in bed with my journal propped on my knees, ink-blue handwriting making
veins on the page as if I'm bringing something to life.
Monsters and magic. Dr Frankenstein, I presume. I've
tilted the slats of the bedroom blinds so stripes of silver-
white light from the lantern in the courtyard pattern the
room. The noirish illumination is negligible but at this
brandy-steeped hour, writing by the glow of my reading
lamp, the reminder of the ordinary outside world brings a
comforting stability.

I take comfort too from being analogue. I feel more truthful when writing longhand, forming shapes on the page unique to me, the words flowing from my fingers rather than appearing on a screen in the tap-tap uniformity of Calibri or Times. And a brandy and soda, for shame! I ought to be wearing a Vanity Fair bed jacket in peach chiffon and lace while sipping champagne from lead crystal. But I'm distilling my story, and the drink matches my mood: a sparkle of alertness with an undernote of hot, sweet darkness.

To get to the point: Sol called in at The Blue Bar this afternoon, and I am all undone.

After Misha's death, I wasn't sure I'd ever see Sol again. Wasn't sure I wanted to, either. But when he sauntered into the bar today, scruffy, dirty and hot, I wanted him so badly it hurt. He won't be good for me, I'm sure of it, yet I'm tormented by thoughts of him and of the things he might do to me. Obsession starts this way. I fear we are doomed. There is no going back.

'Let's be in touch soon,' he'd said when we were finally allowed to leave Dravendene Hall. That afternoon, black tarpaulin sheets had shrouded the glasshouse of the swimming pool. A barrier of tape stating POLICE LINE DO NOT CROSS encircled the building. Detectives and uniformed officers busied themselves indoors and out, asking questions, taking notes. The detectives looked so clean-living; pleasant, patient people in good shoes and crisp shirts, not the scotch-sozzled cynics of legend.

I hadn't contacted Sol since then. Back in Saltbourne, back at work, the weekend's events became a nightmarish limbo to which I was loath to return. So many questions remained unanswered: How did Misha die? Does he have family? Who did he know at the party? What happens next? Are we under suspicion?

I had an urge to keep talking about it, to straighten out the chaos and make a coherent narrative in an attempt to get a handle on it all. But I knew that was dangerous, hence this journal. Damn, I'm going off track again.

To go back to the party. After meeting Sol in the utility room at Dravendene, I later saw him several times that day, always talking to someone, his aviator shades giving him silver-black, shellac eyes. He felt dangerous to look at because if he were mutually curious, I'd be none the wiser.

I was interested in talking to him but didn't get the chance until the evening. I'd napped, bathed and changed, and was feeling nicely buzzed. I was wearing a 1960s mod dress, cut just above the knees, in navy blue cotton with a white Peter Pan collar and large, white buttons down the front. On my feet were strappy, Lola Ramona wedges in red, white and black. As I said before, when I picture myself from the outside, the nightmare feels more manageable. The events become discrete, strung neatly and evenly across a timeline of the weekend, rather than swirling in a maelstrom of upset. If I order them by clothing, we have: Day time: tea dress. Evening: mini-dress. Night time: handcuffs.

I spotted him alone on the fringes of the party, beyond the hubbub of the garden, where glowing Chinese lanterns now hung from trees like strange pastel moons. He was leaning against an enormous horse chestnut tree, smoking, and gazing out across undulating countryside to a mauve-blue sky shot through with streaks of pink. Swifts swooped high above, their screams trailing. Long shadows slanted across the landscape.

Emboldened by a couple of glasses of sangria, I approached, heels a touch wonky on the grass. 'Hey, how's the lip?' I called.

He turned, giving me a quick up–down assessment, and smiled tentatively. 'Yeah, good thanks.' He took a last drag on his cigarette, tapped it against the trunk, and then dropped the butt to the ground, swivelling his heel where the end fell among tree roots.

His bottom lip, although less swollen and raw, was still marked by a ruby-purple lump, sagging and splitting like an overripe fruit. The wound had a lascivious quality, as if the man were melting from an excess of sensuality; as if the private hollow of his mouth were bursting out in a shameless display of wet, pouting obscenity. I wanted to suck him there, to carefully place my lips on the tenderness and taste the point where he was too much for himself. His broken flesh and blood would tingle on my tongue in a concoction tasting of velvet and copper, and I'd drink him down.

'Did you win your match?' I asked.

He tucked a thumb in his belt loop, and crooked his knee against the wide tree trunk, all cool and laid-back like a beat-up cowboy. Outdoors, he seemed older than he had done earlier, high on endorphins in the utility room. His hair was thick, as dark as bitter chocolate, and his brown eyes were set in warm, crinkled rays. He smiled as if he found me amusing, his mouth lopsided from the injury. It was a sexy smile, arrogant, jeering and playfully calculating; a smile which suggested nothing would stop him from taking his pleasures as he preferred them.

'Certainly did,' he replied, as if it were never in doubt because he always wins. I cast my eyes up and down his body, checking him out because two can play at that game. He wore jeans, a leather belt and a checked shirt unbuttoned over a tee.

'You look as if you're auditioning for the role of Marlboro Man,' I said.

He laughed; then dabbed his lip. 'Yeah? So do I get the gig?' He checked his fingertips.

'Well, I'd hire you.' I smiled and stepped closer, offering him my hand. 'Lana. Lana Greenwood.'

He wiped his fingertips on his jeans and shook my hand, his big, firm grip threatening to crush my fingers. 'Sol Miller. Apologies. My lip bleeds when I smile.'

He held the greeting for a fraction too long, preventing me from withdrawing at the natural end-point of the handshake. I felt a tiny jolt in my shoulder, and my blood raced in nervous excitement. His palm was warm against mine and the bones in my hand felt as fragile as a bird's. We locked eyes as the handshake extended into uncomfortable territory. A smile lifted on his lips, presumably in response to the sight of my discomposure. That smile made me weak in the knees.

Asshat, I thought, amused. He released my hand and I wondered if his blood were on my skin. 'Nice to meet you, Sol.'

He smiled more broadly, watching me all the while from under heavy brows, his eyes as dark as old oak casks in a shadowy bodega. I held his gaze, determined to meet his flirtatious intimidation with a refusal to succumb.

I nailed him as the toppy type straight away. He had that playful superiority, that bad-boy swagger, and my Domdar's pretty reliable these days. Admittedly, his Attitude (upper case) was a touch off-putting. My preference is for

men with quiet confidence; the ones who can be straight-
forwardly decent, kind, and aren't scared to convey their
desire for you. Men who brandish their sexuality like a
weapon aren't to be trusted in the realm of BDSM. I ran
into to a couple after I split from Jonathan. Their arrogance excited me, but I've learned not to mess with guys
who have something to prove. They're not dangerous, just
disappointing. They peak too soon.

I figured that even if Sol weren't au fait with reef knots
and tawses, he'd have an instinct for raw, rough sex. That
would suit me perfectly for a one-off at a party. Again, I
was convinced I was in control at that point. Our exchange
by the tree was scarcely more than a brief flirtation, an
opening gambit that might have come to nothing.

Except it did come to something, because later that
night, I found myself sprawled on a bed of cushions in the
double tipi, disco lights swirling as I chatted to my new
acquaintances, Sol and Misha. The wooden beams of the
tipis were wrapped with fairy lights, so strings of stars
appeared to be scrawled across the dark, pointed skies of
the canvas. People danced, clustered around the makeshift
bar, chatted at tables or, like us, lazed around on cushions
and rugs.

Earlier in the evening I'd recognised Misha as a customer from The Blue Bar. We'd expressed small-world
surprise at bumping into each other at a place like this. He
looked different. I was used to seeing him in his steel-
rimmed glasses, reserved and unsmiling, a smartly dressed,
self-contained man who rarely engaged in small talk. He
had sandy hair, cropped around the sides but topped with
short, soft curls, and there was an unfortunate echo of the
nineties about him.

He wasn't wearing his glasses for the party, and I found the transparent vanity of that touching. Turned out he knew Rose, Zoe's co-host at the party. I was privately intrigued because I was starting to realise Rose had a number of openly kinky friends. They weren't strutting around in latex and leather but the clues were there if you knew what to look for: a few unusual piercings, interesting tattoos, a touch of geekishness, a polyamorous triple, a leather choker that could double for a collar.

Was Misha part of that scene? He always seemed kind of buttoned-up when he visited the bar, a creature of habit sitting there with his tablet and Long Island Iced Tea. He rarely stayed for more than an hour, only occasionally being joined by a companion. But then I wouldn't be the first to observe that some of the most ostensibly straight-laced people turn out to be the wildest perverts.

I knew him as Mikhail Morozov, the name on his credit card. But here at the party he was Misha, the name his friends call him, he'd said, except the two friends he was supposed to be meeting had failed to arrive. Like me, he didn't know many other people.

Talking to him and Sol on the cushions put me in an awkward position. Misha, with his smart blue jeans and crisp lilac shirt, made me feel I ought to behave nicely. I was the proprietor of The Blue Bar. I had professional responsibilities.

Sol, on the other hand, made me want to misbehave in ways I hardly dared contemplate. I kept imagining him naked in bed, energetic, hard and controlling. He'd be the sort who'd grab your hair or pin your arms to the pillow and whisper in your ear that you were his dirty little slut. And afterwards he'd come on your face without even asking, and he wouldn't feel guilty because it never occurred to him his dominance was gendered and potentially problematic. And I figured I could cope with that blindness for one night if it meant I was then spared from having to assuage his liberal guilt for having treated me like a whore.

I was hoping we might slip away from Misha, or Misha might sense a spark between us and retreat. The problem was, Sol appeared far too interested in Misha. Had I misread his sexuality?

'Man, I'm sure I know you from somewhere,' Sol had said. But Sol's face was new to Misha, and neither man could suggest how Sol might know him.

I was considering leaving the two guys to their blossoming bromance, or whatever it was, when a young couple canoodling nearby started to ramp up their action. The DJ stuck on some sleazy, trippy beats, the sort of music that makes you feel as if a nightclub's melting into your veins and you could fuck until you died of bliss, intoxicated by a sly, dangerous eroticism. Misha was talking in that clipped way of his, and we all conspired in pretending not to notice the amorous couple. But our feigned unawareness soon became too embarrassing to sustain. The couple began grinding their hips together, squirming and caressing in an apparent attempt to have fully clothed sex in front of dozens of party-goers. Shifting light cast colours over their writhing bodies.

Sol raised his brows in wry acknowledgement. 'Get a room already, people,' he murmured.

Misha laughed, and so did I.

'Hey, we've all been there.' I tried to sound casual but the music was getting to me, making my hips syrupy, my body loose. I watched sidelong as the woman rubbed her partner's crotch, his hand snaking beneath her halter-neck top. Jeez, she was bra-less. That was seriously hot. I imagined being in her place, feeling fingers land precisely where you wanted them, no clothes to disrupt their passage. And I imagined those grubby feelings of shame and excitement arising from being lewd in public, half wanting your audience to leer and urge you on; half wanting them to vanish and leave you be.

I'm reminded now that most of my fantasies centre on being both lusted after, and being scorned for 'sluttish' behaviour, even as I offer resistance. It's fucked-up, I know. But then I was raised in a fucked-up culture.

My fucked-up hunger swelled as the couple groaned into each other's mouths, smearing each other with drunken kisses. I wanted to look away but couldn't, nor, apparently, could my two companions. What a thrillingly sexy car crash this was. A languid pulse thickened low in my body as the woman flopped onto her back, spine arching, tits thrusting, an arm flung out in a display of self-abandonment.

I was desperately turned on, but not because I wanted her. No, I wanted to *be* her. I wanted to relinquish my pride, dignity and control, and have a man explore my body while other men watched. Worse than that, I wanted drunk, randy men encouraging my lover to keep at it; wanted a rowdy crowd on the verge of joining in and filling me with more cock than I could possibly take. A perpetual fantasy of mine, no more than that. Not a secret desire I longed to have fulfilled.

'It's cute,' said Misha. 'Very sweet.'

Sweet enough, I noticed, for Misha to have a raging hard-on. And, oh boy, that got my interest because I was somewhat shocked to notice that my polite, squarely dressed Russian friend was evidently hung like a horse. He lay propped on his elbow, making no attempt to conceal his arousal. In his jeans, his cock was a visible bar, its erect angle fitting neatly into the creases of his crotch, as if having a boner were such a frequent occurrence the denim had faded and shaped itself to fit.

I couldn't let the moment pass. I didn't know where I was going with it but I nodded at Misha's groin and said, 'Well, someone's enjoying the spectacle.'

He laughed crisply. 'Actually, the most arousing part was watching you watching them.'

Guh. Busted. My face burned.

'What do you like about it?' Misha shifted on his hip. 'Watching? Or the thought of being watched?' His features hardened, and his grey eyes settled on me. His upper lip lifted in a tiny smirk, and his gaze dropped to my breasts before returning to my face. I thought I caught a flicker of nastiness there. I felt as if he'd just put me in a different category of woman, and so I put him in a different category of men, the one marked 'potential misogynist; approach with caution'.

'Being watched.' My voice wavered, far less confident than intended.

Misha smiled as if he'd just won a private bet.

'Well,' said Sol, in a how-interesting tone. He tipped the beer bottle to his lips; then, hand around the base, rested the bottle on the kilim rug, looking from Misha to me and back.

Nothing happened. No one spoke or moved. Colours span around us, sliding over frozen faces. We were Manet's painting, *Le déjeuner sur l'herbe*. I'd made myself metaphorically naked for them, but no one seemed willing to pick up the baton. I guess none of us knew what to do. If you don't recognise the situation, how can you know the rules? I had no plan.

The prospect of a threesome was knocking around in my brain, sure, but it was a hazy, distant fantasy that had been lurking there for years. Me and two guys; two strong, muscular bodies working in harmony with my own dips and curves; me getting double of what I liked.

I used to discuss trying a ménage with Jonathan who declared he was willing to give it a whirl as a special treat for me. As I approached thirty-four, we went as far as emailing a guy on Craigslist who then sent a photo of himself wearing a white towelling bathrobe on a holiday balcony, an azure sea in the background. Jonathan got cold feet at that point, and offered to buy me a bottle of l'Heure Bleue for my birthday instead. I agreed, figuring perfume lasts longer than sex.

My only plan with Sol and Misha, if thinking two seconds ahead can constitute a plan, was to throw something out there and see what happened. Primarily, I wanted Sol – in me, on me, over me. But if he was going to play it cool, then the well-endowed Russian was worth investigating. I just had to hope I didn't embarrass him and lose a regular customer. But then you wouldn't call him a big spender, so no great loss.

Drawing a deep breath of courage, I said, 'So, what's a girl got to do to get laid around here?'

Sol looked at me steadily while drinking from the bottle. Misha smirked, glancing from me to Sol. Eyes still fixed on me, Sol set down his beer, smiling. A dusky purple light crossed his face, casting his eyes in deep shadow.

'You just gotta say "please",' he drawled.

I laughed. Damn, he was a bastard, the kind of guy I'd have gone nuts for in my younger days.

'Please,' I said briskly, before adding, on a surge of reckless daring, 'both of you.'

And it really was that simple. After a terrifying, uncertain pause when I feared I was about to be slut-shamed to high heaven, Sol addressed Misha and said, 'Well, I'm game.'

Misha shrugged. 'Sure, why not?'

They seemed so casual and at ease that I had to wonder if I hadn't mistakenly invited them to a hand of bridge, rather than a three-way. I looked from one man to the other. 'Heck,' I said, 'I wasn't expecting that.'

'Me neither but it's all good.' Sol pushed himself up from his relaxed sprawl, laced his fingers together and stretched out his arms as if warming up.

'Isn't it great to be modern?' I said, wondering how we move forwards from here. 'Um, I should maybe mention that ...' I leaned forwards, lowering my voice in an exaggerated play of secrecy, and beckoned them closer. They hunkered towards me, Sol grinning, Misha frowning. 'I like things on the kinky side,' I said. 'Nothing heavy, and if it's not your thing, that's fine. I just thought ...'

'I know no other way,' said Misha, sitting straight.

'Always happy to dabble,' said Sol.

'I'm a bisexual switch,' said Misha, his stern, matter-of-fact tone suggesting he was accustomed to presenting his sexuality to others. 'However, I prefer to bottom and I have strong masochistic tendencies, assuming the dynamic is correct.'

Sol smiled broadly, a touch nervous I thought.

'Heteroflexible,' he said, using a word I'd never heard spoken before. 'Been, ah, exploring my dom side recently. It's where I seem to be at.'

'Submissive,' I said. 'Bondage and mild pain only. A few humiliation fantasies. Spanking. That kind of stuff. Nothing traumatic.'

Sol nodded thoughtfully as if absorbing the information and then pointed to his bust lip. 'Listen, don't take it personally, guys, but do you mind if we don't kiss?'

I laughed. 'Prostitute's prerogative.'

He feigned offence. 'You calling me a whore?'

In low voices, we discussed a few more practicalities, our negotiation of boundaries doubling as a vehicle for flirtation and verbal foreplay. Our agreed safeword was Cinderella. I wondered how close we'd get to using it. By the time we stood, my skin was flushed with anticipation, the wetness between my thighs spiked by a fierce, insistent pulse.

We swayed a companionable path to the manor house, sniggering and whispering like naughty schoolkids. The dark lawn was illuminated by Chinese lanterns, ropes of LED lights, and gaseous yellow flames dancing in fire bowls. The tipis rose against the black sky like two witches' hats, poles crossing at their peaks, the canvas glowing in soft amber tones. The night felt magical. Everything seemed so easy, as if we were floating through life. I walked between the two men, my arms hooked in theirs, tottering on the grass in my impractically high sandals. I told them how, since separating from Jonathan, I'd built a small vintage and military-issue handcuff collection, primarily from picking up items online.

'Tell me,' said Sol. 'Do you have *any* flaws?'

I laughed. 'You got a couple of spare days?'

'If you own gear like that,' said Sol, 'I can overlook anything. Hell, you don't even need to know how to clean and cook.'

'And your flaws are?' I asked. 'Apart from unabashed chauvinism?'

'You got a couple of spare *lives*?' he replied. 'No, let's not go there. So you've brought some of these fancy cuffs with you this weekend?'

'Certainly have. German Clejusos. Among the heaviest and thickest in the world.'

Sol whistled through his teeth. 'Well I never,' he murmured. 'And you say your divorce has just come through?'

We laughed as we crossed a small, lamp-lit car park, feet crunching on gravel, to enter a rear door in the west wing.

'Give me metal over leather any day of the week,' said Sol. 'I can't wait to see these beauties.'

'They're incredible,' I said. 'They weigh over three pounds.'

My interest in the cuffs is related to sex, of course, but the objects fascinate in their own right. You'd think there might not be much variation in the design of an object comprising two linked hoops but there is. A lot of factors need to be taken into account so they suit both the jailer and the jailed, the cop and the robber. The perfect handcuffs should restrain without injuring but be easy and efficient to use. They're wonderfully contradictory, often elegantly simple and suggestive of grim, thrilling stories. They capture my imagination and I frequently find it hard to resist a purchase. I'd brought along the Clejuso 15s because I adore the weight of them pulling on my wrists.

I'd also figured their USP – heaviest cuffs ever manufac-
tured – might be a good talking point were I to meet
someone who shared my kinky proclivities. I appeared to
have struck gold with Sol.

Indoors, we dithered. 'Which way?' I asked.

'Man, this place is huge,' said Sol.

'Follow me,' said Misha, flicking a wall switch. Fake
candles in sconces lit our path down an oak-panelled corridor and up a gloomy flight of stairs. We emerged on a
floor with glinting crystal chandeliers, laughing when we
realised the door we'd closed behind us was camouflaged
in wainscoting and crimson flock to match the walls.

'I discovered this route earlier,' said Misha, checking
his watch. 'Excuse me.'

For a brief, hopeful moment, I thought he was about to
chicken out but instead he said, 'I need to return to my
room and then I will join you in your room in due course.'

'OK, cool,' I replied. 'West tower, turret room. The
highest one.'

He took the opposite direction to us, leaving Sol and I
to walk together down a grand, red-carpeted corridor
hung with gilt-framed paintings depicting chinless won-
ders from centuries past. I was pleased to be alone with
Sol.

'Fuck, marry or kill?' he said, indicating a portrait of a
chap in a tricorn hat.

'He's already dead,' I laughed.

'That's marriage for you,' he replied. 'How about him?
Fuck, suck or push over a cliff?'

The mood between us was light and friendly. I thought
how wonderful it was that we could all be so open and
straightforward about wanting to have sex together. The

lack of shyness, shame or game-playing meant we'd carved out a space for pleasure. We are three people, I mused, who know how to enjoy ourselves.

We took the spiral staircase to my turret room, me first, Sol behind with three empty wine glasses in one hand.

'I hope you don't mind,' began Sol.

I yelped as he swiped my arse with a swift, upward strike.

'Just checking out the goods,' he continued.

He landed a couple more smacks on my flesh, all perfect, sharp blows, despite coming from his left hand. Every hit made me squeal.

Inside the room, I handed him the Clejusos, leaving the door to the room half open for Misha. Sol bounced each thick, steel cuff in his cupped palms, the connecting length of chain drooping between them.

'Phewee,' he said. 'A real work of art.'

The cuffs were beautifully curved, the thickest part shaped like a comma, the hinged section a relatively narrow, elegant band. In the hazy lamplight, the nickel-plating gleamed, the curvature catching a tiny, convex reflection of the bed that looked too small for three people.

'Slip of a creature like you,' said Sol. 'Hell, these are going to pop your arms from your sockets, no?'

'I'm stronger than I look,' I replied.

'Well, I'll take that as my warning.'

I stepped closer and placed a hand on his hip. 'So can I trust you with the key?' I asked.

He turned to me, his hip swaying towards mine, and said, 'I think we should wait for your friend, don't you?'

The implication that I was being disrespectful to Misha

embarrassed me, although I noted Sol's body language belied his words.

'Yeah, sure.' I stepped back, taking the cuffs from him. 'But he's not a friend. I don't know him well at all.'

'Soon will do, I guess,' replied Sol.

I crossed the room and set the cuffs down on the dressing table, half wishing it was just me and Sol for the night.

'Damn, I wish I could place him,' he murmured. 'His face is so familiar.'

I took the key from my purse and lay it alongside the cuffs, ready for use. Then I poured three Belvedere vodkas into the wine glasses.

'So, do you go to fetish nights?' asked Sol. He strode towards the low, diamond-paned window, bending to squint at the darkness outside. 'Swingers' parties, that kind of thing?'

Without asking, he opened one of the windows, fixing the metal arm to a notch. I'd kept the windows closed during the day, to prevent insects getting in the room. Flying things bother me. They're like loss of control in material form. Laughter and music floated in from the gardens on the far side of the house. The cooler, fresher air was welcome.

'Swinging? Not really my cup of tea,' I said, handing him his drink. 'Maybe I'll try a club one day. Generally speaking, I prefer more intimate scenarios.' I raised my glass. 'You know, like this one.'

We clinked rims, grinning.

'So you do this a lot?' he asked.

'I wouldn't say that, no,' I replied. 'Not as often as I'd like. I don't meet the right kind of people. It's not that easy.'

'That's why you should go to clubs and parties,' he said. 'Put yourself about a bit.'

I moved away from him, slipped off my sandals and lay on the bed. 'Or I could just stay home and eat my own arm,' I replied. 'Sounds preferable.'

'What about Misha?' he asked. 'Is he on the BDSM scene?'

'I've no idea.' I sipped my drink and placed my glass on the bedside table. 'Like I say, I don't really know him.' I propped myself up against a mound of pillows, wishing he would join me without me having to ask. 'He just drinks at my bar once a week. Why the interest? Do *you* go to fetish clubs? Or do you want to?'

Sol laughed as if this were a silly idea. 'I'll pass, thanks. My gimp suit's at the dry cleaner's.'

Footsteps approached on the spiralling wooden staircase. Misha peered tentatively around the half-open door.

'Hi,' I said. 'Come on in. Close the door.'

He gave a curt nod and stepped inside, closing the door carefully. He wore his wire-framed glasses, his face now reassuringly familiar. Sol clicked into a different mode. He set his vodka on the bedside table with mine and leaned over me as if Misha's arrival were his cue to start. He smiled, fingers encircling my ankle. A shiver ran through me and I returned the smile. His tennis injury hung on his lip like a dangerous, tropical bud, his thick, dark hair catching curls of muted lamplight, and revealing a deep auburn tint.

'So, Lana Greenwood,' he murmured.

'So, Sol Miller.'

Misha watched from a short distance as Sol ran a strong hand up my bare shins to my raised knee. Spanning his thumb and forefinger wide, he began sliding down my thigh with exquisite slowness. My heartbeat quickened.

'What are we going to do with you tonight, I wonder?' said Sol. His warm hand nudged at the hem of my skirt, the blue fabric wrinkling like waves over his darkly haired wrist. I flexed my spine, pleasure rolling through my body, and smiled in encouragement.

'I really don't know,' I breathed. 'What do you suggest?'

Misha, his eyes still on us, unbuttoned his shirt.

'You say you like to be watched, huh?' continued Sol. His eyes were hidden in the shadows of his brows, and my nerves fluttered. Despite the sociability and humour, he had a remoteness to him, a suggestion of self-protection.

'It's only a small desire.' My voice had a gravelly catch. 'Not necessarily something I want to pursue right now. Or ever, to be honest.' I laughed quietly, hearing my own anxiety in the sound. 'Anyway, there's only two of you.'

He grinned. 'We could call for reinforcements.' His thumb ticked against the narrow bone of my inner thigh, back and forth. Inches away, concealed by sheer fabric, my clit throbbed, my arousal opening me out.

'Two's plenty, thanks,' I replied.

He smiled, nodding. 'Your call.'

With a maddeningly light caress, he ran his thumb over the plump crotch of my briefs. Inside my underwear, the repercussions of his touch prickled along individual strands of hair, shimmered in skin cells and slunk through my wetness, luxurious and wanton. I groaned and tilted my hips, searching for more.

A few feet away, Misha continued undressing as if alone, hanging his shirt in the closet before sitting on the dressing table chair to remove footwear and jeans. He placed his shoes inside the closet and then hung his jeans and boxers over another hanger. Moving in, are you? I thought. Finally, he removed his glasses, closed the arms, and placed them on the bedside table. Naked, he stood to face us, wrapping his fingers around a cock whose hard, upright magnificence proved my earlier assessment to be accurate.

Well, this was turning out to be quite a night.

Under the hem of my dress, Sol's thumb continued rubbing at my dampening briefs. I looked beyond Sol to Misha, basking in the joy of being attended to by one man while viewing another. Misha was athletically slender, his skin as pale as porcelain. His small pink nipples were encircled by wisps of light brown hair, each tip pierced by a silver ring threaded with a tiny ball. His fist shunted on his huge, ruddy erection, his posture bold and open, his expression slack. He didn't appear to have a scrap of reticence or self-consciousness about being the first to get naked.

In contrast, Sol and I were measuring the situation, taking cues from each other in a tentative build-up. Misha's fixed, confident stance caused a flurry of doubts to scramble my mind. I fought a wave of rising panic. I'd thought we were all singing from the same hymn sheet, but perhaps not. Something in Misha's attitude troubled me: implicitly demanding, infantile, as if he were entitled to his own satisfaction, his needs taking priority over that of others. A taker, I suspected, not a giver.

Sol leaned his thumb harder into my underwear, making my flesh squish and mould around the pressure. I groaned heavily, his gentle half-explorations making me want him so much.

'She's very wet.' Sol turned to look up at Misha. 'I can feel her pussy soaking through her panties.'

'Yeah?' Misha worked his cock with barely repressed eagerness. He gazed down. Without the assistance of spectacles or contacts, his eyes appeared to focus somewhere beyond us.

'Let's make her wetter, shall we?' Sol hooked his hands either side of my knickers. I lifted my butt to allow him to remove the scrap of fabric. My legs were loose and floppy with lust. I let my knees drop wide, baring my neatly trimmed split. I ached for someone to touch me there, to introduce shape and solidity where my body had swollen to nebulous sensation.

'You like to suffer?' asked Sol.

I cleared my throat. 'A little.'

'I do,' asserted Misha. His fist quickened on his cock. 'A lot.'

Sol chuckled. 'I can see I've got my work cut out for me tonight.' He gave my thigh a chivvying tap. 'Stand up.'

I did as told, enjoying his bossy confidence. My dress fell back into place, juices smearing on my thighs. Sol stood with me, the two of us on the opposite side of the bed to Misha. Sol glanced around the room and then swung the stiff-backed chair from the dressing table to where I stood.

'Sit down. What else you got?' he asked. 'Rope? Gags?'

I sat on the chair, facing the bed. 'Blindfold, vibrator, paddle,' I said. 'Nipple suckers, lube, a flogger. No rope, sorry. Oh, I have a scarf if you want. Top drawer on the right. In with my underwear. Everything else on the left. No gag, I'm afraid.'

Sol tugged open the underwear drawer, rummaged

briefly and retrieved my polka-dot scarf. After a quick inspection, he dropped the scarf on the dresser, clearly dissatisfied. He stalked into the bathroom, a man on a mission. Misha watched him, hand still pumping; then he looked to me with that slack, vacant gaze.

'Come here, Misha,' I said. 'Let me feel your—'

'Hey!' Sol emerged from the bathroom carrying a thin ribbon of pistachio-green silk, the belt to my dressing gown. 'You stay there,' he barked at Misha. 'She doesn't get what she wants *that* easily. And nor do you. Hands behind your back, Lana. Behind the chair. That's right.'

He draped the strip of silk over his shoulder and unlocked the hefty steel handcuffs on the dressing table. The cuffs clanked as he lifted them and he edged behind me, ducking to avoid the sloping wall. He clicked the manacles on to my wrists, and when he released his hold, their cool, hard weight settled around my hands, pulling on my arms and shoulders. I gave a faint moan of contentment, a pulse in my groin thumping with the pleasure of being anchored and bound. The Clejusos always make me feel that not only are my hands locked together but my body is pinned to its current location. A new centre of gravity holds me in place. I'm trapped as if in amber, enveloped by a gathering sense of submission.

Sol crouched by my feet and wound one end of the dressing-gown belt around my ankle before securing it to the chair leg. He repeated the loop on my other leg, tying me to the chair so my knees were forced apart.

I began to feel vague and malleable, aware I was slipping into a mild dissociative state where I could allow someone to take me over.

'That OK?' asked Sol.

I nodded, the day's alcohol making me heady and slow. Was this wise? Sol traced a hand along my jaw, observing me. His touch continued down my neck, past my collarbone, down to the low Peter Pan neckline of my dress. My cunt throbbed, aching for a heavy, deliberate touch.

'I'm afraid, Lana,' he said, 'I'm about to do something horribly cruel to you.'

'Be my guest,' I breathed.

He unfastened the top button of my dress. I swallowed, heat pulsing between my thighs. I glanced past him to Misha, who stood stock-still, eyeing us with his glazed expression, fist rising and falling on his big, solid shaft. His pink-white skin gleamed in the dimness, his muscularity glossy and taut. I half-fancied Sol and I were in the presence of a creepy, watchful statue.

Sol continued unbuttoning me until my bra was bared. Carefully, he pushed my dress onto my shoulders, exposing me more fully, smiling solicitously all the while. He cupped me through the fabric of my black satin bra, his hand easily encompassing my smallness. I tipped my head back as he massaged each breast in turn, my breath becoming shallow. What wicked delights did he have in store for me?

If Sol was a newcomer to kink, he was either a fast learner or strong on instinct. Already, I felt I could trust him to be neither too much nor too little; neither too aggressive nor too cautious. I've learned that getting the balance right is contingent on a tacit, ongoing negotiation; a game of guesswork and risk; of giving and reading signals; of checking in without destroying the flow. I respect those who respect me enough to trust that I want this. Sol's stated intention of being 'horribly cruel' made me deliciously nervous.

He nudged my bra straps down onto my arms and scooped a hand into one cup. He was warm and strong on my skin, and my tight nipple pressed into his palm as he freed my small mound. He repeated the action on the other side so my breasts were strategically exhibited, a display of objectification that humiliated as much as it thrilled. He stepped back to cast an eye over his arrangement and then gently adjusted one rucked-down bra cup.

His cool, scrutinising eyes made my blood race. Was this his way of appealing to my fantasy of being watched? If so, it was working. Having said that, Misha's dull-eyed observation from the far side of the bed unnerved rather than aroused me. He seemed removed from the scene, waiting rather than wanting, wanking patiently while biding his time.

Satisfied by the exposure of my breasts, Sol bent to unfasten the button by the hem of my dress. A shiver tickled along my spine as I mentally predicted his fingers' destination.

'Let's take a look at that sweet little pussy,' he said, working open a higher button.

'Pussy' made me wince but he was American so I forgave him. Besides, the thumping between my legs proved that my lust had no truck with semantics. With steady fingers, Sol unbuttoned my dress to my waist and tucked the parted fabric back. His eyes examined me where I was spread-legged and split. He nodded in approval, taking his time. Under his inspection, heat crawled over my face. My lower lips swelled, dense with sensation and thumping like a thousand heartbeats. Shyness made me draw my knees together but Sol pushed them wide again.

'Hold yourself like that,' he said. 'So we can see how wet you're getting.'

He stood, smiling. He shucked off his checked shirt; then, in a single movement, he whipped his T-shirt over his head, baring his muscular torso and the delicate botanical tattoo etched down one side. I almost sobbed with the need to be touched within, my longing exacerbated by the sight of him undressing while I was rendered immobile. His skin was flexed with shadows, his shoulders burnished by a patina of ruddy bronze where he'd caught the sun. His nipples were dusky brown discs just visible under the fur of dark hair across his pecs. He tossed his tee aside, unbuttoned his jeans while heeling off his trainers, then stepped out of his remaining clothes, kicking them aside.

Dear God, but he was beautiful: tall and powerful with long, hefty thighs meeting the taut globes of a lightly haired ass. His erection jutted from a thatch of rich brown pubes, a hard, handsome length topped by a smooth tip of deeply flushed flesh. Dents hollowed in his buttocks as he walked around the bed to join Misha.

Misha eyed Sol with greedy impatience, his hand frantic on his cock, his mouth parted. My arousal ran riot at the sight of the two of them standing naked together. Sol, darker and more heavily muscled than Misha, stood close to him but not close enough to touch. The bedside lamp washed their contours in a pale peach glow, and flecked their body hair with filaments of rose-gold. They seemed like a couple of prize specimens, two sleek, supple stallions. I wanted them both so desperately I found myself wiggling involuntarily in my chair.

Smirking, Sol clawed his fingers into the short sandy curls of Misha's hair. He gripped a handful and jerked

back Misha's head. Misha groaned, his Adam's apple bobbing once in his stretched neck. With his other hand, Sol
pinched a nipple ring between thumb and forefinger, and
then slowly pulled.

I flinched to see Misha's nipple stretching, his pectoral
flesh triangulating to a point. He uttered a low snarl of
pain, hand shuffling faster on his beast of a cock.

'You wanna play nasty?' asked Sol.

The question made my groin clench.

'Yes,' panted Misha.

'You sure about that, bro?' Sol released the nipple ring
and yanked at Misha's hair again. Misha grunted, neck
arched, eyes pinned on the ceiling.

'Yes! Yes, master!'

The words hung in the ensuing silence, unexpected
words that felt imported from elsewhere. No one had
mentioned any kind of formalised role-playing. Was this
Misha's way of doing things? Was Sol into that?

Sol shoved Misha forwards so he stumbled onto the
bed. 'You fucking piece of shit,' he spat.

I gulped, afraid. Misha crawled on the quilted coverlet, big
dick swinging below his belly as he turned to Sol, presenting
me with his pale ass and the low pouch of his bollocks.

'Get off there,' snapped Sol. 'On the floor, on your
fucking knees.'

Misha scrambled to obey, dropping to the floor by the
side of the bed, plaintive eyes looking up at Sol. For me,
forced into the role of onlooker, the scene acquired an
ugly, dangerous edge. I reminded myself this was simply a
game of power exchange. If I'd been less physically distant, I probably wouldn't feel quite so uneasy. I told myself
they knew what they were doing.

'You're a louse,' sneered Sol. 'A despicable fucking louse.'

I wondered if Sol really did know Misha from somewhere. Embarrassing if it later transpired he was Sol's bank manager or similar. But no, Misha was a pharmacologist and Sol was an ex-techie now working in construction, so this was probably OK.

'What are you?' Sol raised a hand and brought it swooping down onto Misha's face. I gasped as Misha's head reeled from the blow. He recovered quickly and gazed up at Sol, eyes still beseeching, jaw sagging.

'More,' he whispered. 'Please. I'm a louse, a despic—'

Sol swiped at him again, harder this time, his face clouding, brows pulling together. 'You motherfucking shit.'

Misha swayed but then returned to his upright kneeling position, one side of his face turning pink. Immediately, Sol hit him again. This didn't feel right. The expression on Sol's face concerned me. Impossible to know if he were flushed with genuine rage or if he were deeply immersed in the role of nasty bastard, his skin hot with exhilaration. I caught sight of the deepening flare on Misha's cheek as his upper body swung towards the bed. That was some heavy hitting.

'Sol,' I said, 'take it easy. He's been drinking, remember? We all have. You know, maybe this isn't such a great idea.'

Misha turned to me, his fine blond curls ghostly in the lamplight, his face haggard with shadows. 'Leave me alone,' he shouted, voice thin and angry. 'You don't know anything. I need this, I need it. So shut up! Don't interfere when you don't understand.'

I huffed in outrage. 'Well, excuse me! I was only trying—'

'Hey, dickwad,' said Sol, 'you don't talk to the lady like that.'

'She's no lady,' muttered Misha.

I swore, tugging against my bonds as Sol's hand crashed across Misha's face. His fist landed with a deep, resounding crack, brutal enough to knock the man sideways. Misha lurched and bumped against the mattress. He rested in that position, catching his breath, head on the coverlet. I was torn in two, half of me concerned for him, half of me thinking he damn well deserved it.

After a few seconds, Misha pushed himself upright, his smile smug, eyes raised to Sol.

'Oh, OK, I get it,' said Sol, stalking angrily away. 'You're trying to rile me, aren't you, you son of a bitch?' He turned his back to Misha, glaring at the wall. He raked his fingers through his scruffy dark hair, his chest rising and falling, his erection dipping.

'I need it, please,' replied Misha. 'I need to be hurt.'

Sol swung around. 'What am I? Your fucking pro-domme? Your Miss Whiplash?'

'I need to suffer, please, master! I need pain and abuse.'

Sol returned to him, fingers curled around his own cock, his stance confrontational. 'Well, what say this isn't all about you, dude? What say it's about my needs? What *I* want?' Sol worked his erection with a slow, intimidating shuffle, looking down at Misha with evident disdain. 'And what I want right now is to choke you with my dick, fuck it hard into your throat. Make you think twice before you go dishing out the insults, the demands. What about that, huh?'

Sol sprang forwards. He clutched Misha's head in both hands, fixing him at groin level. With his knees bent, he aimed his thick length at Misha's mouth. Misha opened up willingly, spluttering in protest as Sol slammed into him.

'I'll shut you up,' said Sol, lodging himself deep.

Misha kept his lips wide as Sol began to pound, his muscular buttocks indenting. He kept his hands clamped by Misha's ears, lunging to and fro, muttering and panting. Misha, eyes growing big, flailed for something to hold. He grasped the bed frame, tendons in his neck pulled tight as he fought, coughing and drooling.

I stared, uneasy but wildly aroused, my hot moisture sliding from me. The scenario looked so brutal. I was expecting Misha to call time any moment. But the two men kept up a mutual pace of aggressor and victim, and, before long, lust trumped my anxieties. After all, they were grown adults able to make decisions and look after themselves, just as I was. And as a grown adult, half naked and tied to a chair, I longed for a taste of the action. For several minutes, Sol kept at it, occasionally pausing for respite. My hunger to be involved escalated, my wetness seeping, but I was too proud to reveal my needs.

Eventually, Sol turned to me, his cock still stuffed in Misha's mouth, his hair wild and damp, his face red. 'You want some of this dick, Lana?' he gasped.

Oh God, did I ever. But I feared he was trying to catch me out. I tried playing it cool, not easy when you're held captive, burning up with need and lewdly exposed. 'When you're ready,' I replied.

'Well, tough,' said Sol. 'You ain't getting any. Because tonight it's boys' night.'

'Fuck you,' I said, refusing to believe him. If someone

didn't offer me some action soon, I fancied I might pass out from desperation. I wanted to be between them both, wanted their bone-hard cocks to shore up my hazy, horny, vanishing self.

Sol held his cock deep, looking down at Misha's imprisoned head as if testing the man's resilience. When Misha was at the limit of his breath, his face bright pink, he clawed and punched at Sol's thigh. Sol didn't relent so Misha thumped harder, his other hand pawing at the air, noises gurgling in his throat. Seconds later, Sol snatched himself free, leaving Misha doubled over, gasping and coughing.

'You Yankee bastard,' Misha rasped.

'C'mere,' said Sol. 'Crawl this way.' Sol clicked his fingers and moved around the foot of the bed, checking back on Misha's response. Misha followed on all fours until they were both beside me, both hard. 'How you doing, Lana?' asked Sol. 'Suffering yet?'

'Yes,' I said. 'You going to put me out of my misery?'

Sol laughed softly and bent low, his hand swooping between my open thighs. 'You wet for us, baby?' he asked. His fingers nudged at my folds then rubbed along my slippery groove.

I writhed and whimpered. 'I think I'm starting to hate you,' I said.

Sol laughed. 'So soon?'

'Do I get to join the party?' I asked. 'Or is it still a guys-only event?'

'One step at a time,' Sol replied smoothly. 'I want to see you come first. To be specific, I want to see our Russian friend make you come. With his tongue.'

'No, please!' I found the idea of a man being ordered to

lick me abhorrent, the instruction making the act seem like a distasteful chore.

'Yes. And within the next three minutes.' Sol stepped away to rummage in the pockets of his discarded jeans. He retrieved his phone and thumbed the buttons. 'You think you can do that, Mish? Gonna put you on stopwatch.'

'I'm more than happy to try,' replied Misha, shuffling into the gap of my open, bound legs.

I threw back my head, squirming in discomfort but wanting relief. 'No, please,' I said, less vehemently this time because the humiliation was twisting into a sultry, secret warmth. Being forced to come was very different to being forced to accept another's reluctant ministrations.

'Good man,' said Sol. 'You make her come in three, I'll buy us all a coke.' He addressed me. 'And don't even think about faking it.'

'No worries. I hate coke.'

Sol laughed. 'Pepsi?'

'How do you prefer your cunnilingus?' asked Misha, hands on my spread knees. 'Do you like direct clitoral stimulation or around the hood? And would you like me to use my fingers on you as well?'

I released a breath of exasperation. 'I prefer it when it's not like science class.'

'Two minutes forty-five,' said Sol, checking his phone.

Misha grinned, sly and confident. 'I cannot wait to fuck you,' he said. 'Is that something you'd like?' As he spoke, he eased two fingers inside me, curling them onto the fleshy pad of my G.

'Yeah, maybe,' I whispered, thinking of the prodigious cock rather than the nerdy man attached to it.

His skilful fingers moved. Sensation burst inside me,

quivering from my centre towards my head and toes. I gasped at the intensity of feeling and slid deeper in the chair, tilting my hips towards him. The chair back dug into my arms, the cuffs inhibiting my movement, but in the midst of such heady pleasure, the discomfort barely registered. Misha kept pressing on my sweet spot while his thumb roamed over and around my clit, exploring and frigging.

'You have a good cunt,' he said. 'Your clitoris is swollen and clear to locate, as is your Grafenburg spot.'

'Yeah?' I breathed. 'That's because I'm horny as hell.'

'Good,' he said. 'This makes my challenge easier.'

'Two fifteen,' said Sol. He transferred his phone to his left hand and grasped his cock with his right, jerking slowly. Misha canted forwards and enveloped the bud of my clit with warm, wet lips, fingers still hooked inside me. He sucked gently while his tongue swirled, bathing me in saliva. I groaned loudly, feeling as if my whole body were melting into his mouth. His juices flowed with mine and between my thighs I was a whirling mass of rising bliss.

'She taste good?' asked Sol.

Misha didn't reply, too intent on making me come and no longer playing the role of Sol's bitch.

'One minute left,' said Sol. 'Come on, bro. You can do it. Make her come.'

Sol moved closer to us, his hand sliding faster on his cock. Tremors of nearness darted within my thighs, growing stronger. Misha flicked his tongue around my clit, his touch deft but fleeting.

'No,' I gasped, feeling my impending peak recede. 'Harder, heavier. Please!'

He lapped at me with sure, wet strokes, returning to

the steady rhythm that was pushing me closer. I bleated, hips lifting, my breath shortening as tension bunched.

'She's gonna come,' murmured Sol. 'Good work. Keep at it. Any moment.' Sol released his cock and stooped to caress my breasts, his touch slow and confident. 'Look at her, look at that pretty little face. Come on, girl. Show us what you're made of.'

I whimpered, right on the verge. Misha's curled fingers slammed harder inside me and I felt as if my cunt were drowning, lost in the sloppy mobility of his clever mouth. Sol grabbed his own cock again, pumping harder, starting to groan. 'Eighteen seconds,' he panted. 'Go on, dude, you can do it. Nearly there. Fuck, you look good, babe. I'm gonna come on her when she comes. Come all over her tits, over her face. Over both of you. Ten. Nine. Ah.'

My abdomen crunched, the brink of my orgasm pitching me forwards. I released a series of squeaky, breathless cries.

'Six,' said Sol, wanking hard and fast. 'Five! Oh man, look at that. Beautiful.'

Misha's tongue pasted my clit in thick, wet stripes, the press of his buried fingers nudging the tension higher. I reached my limit and bliss held me on a plateau of impossibility.

'There,' gasped Sol. 'She's there.'

Ecstasy began cascading, racking my body, taking me over. I clenched my eyes shut, dayglo stars going supernova behind my lids, my core squeezing and spilling. The grips rolled over and over, holding me in their euphoric madness before they collapsed into a sudden fall. As the tremors faded, I gazed down at Misha, stupefied by shock. He kept his head between my thighs and raised his eyes, mouth and chin glinting with my fluids.

Next to me, Sol grunted, his noise rising to thin desperation. I turned to him, saw his hand blurred with speed. Then, despite all the vocalised aggression from earlier, Sol went rigid on a shudder and climaxed with barely a sound. His come jetted out in arcs, splashing on my belly and striping Misha's face.

Misha's tongue darted out to taste the liquid on his lips; then he leaned forwards to lap the pearlised streaks on my stomach. Sol tossed his phone onto the bed and grasped the back of my chair, panting.

'Whoa,' he said. I thought I detected a note of regret in his voice, a hint of 'what the fuck did I do that for?'

We were silent, the three of us catching our breath. I was weak and mellow in the wake of my orgasm but keenly aware we were all separate from each other, not united as is more usual when you've climaxed with someone. Only two of us had climaxed so perhaps this was an imbalance typical of threesomes between strangers. In a scenario like ours, the sex was always going to be recreational rather than emotionally charged.

Voices and laughter from elsewhere in the house heightened our strange, sudden silence. A nagging disquiet kept butting into my thoughts. Had the earlier hostility been part of sexual play? Or was it an indication of more sinister emotions? Misha's voice echoed in my mind: *She's no lady.* I wasn't sure I liked this man who'd just brought me to a head-spinning climax.

Some moments later, Sol said, 'So, you don't like coke?' I laughed. 'Nah. I'll have a Kir Royale, thanks.'

We all laughed, half exhausted but, it seemed, becoming more relaxed.

'We cool, man?' Sol asked Misha, his palm raised.

'Of course,' replied Misha, as if surprised by the question. He mirrored Sol's hand, meeting him with a sluggish high five.

Afterwards, the mood between us continued to lighten. Sol released me from the chair and we spent another couple of hours on the bed, fucking, sucking and exploring each others' bodies. We played with some of my kit but the point was sensation rather than powerplay. We didn't revisit the dynamic of earlier. Instead we were pleasant, considerate and relatively tender.

Cautious. Mistrustful.

Despite drinking a lot of the Belvedere and a handful of beers I'd brought along, we stayed in that zone of cold faux-sobriety, as you sometimes do when you've been drinking steadily for hours. We stopped when Sol declared himself whacked. 'Holy fuck, it's been a long week,' he said. 'You mind if we all bed down here tonight? Seems a shame to break up the party.'

'Sure,' I said. 'You're both welcome to stay. Misha?'

'Yes, thank you,' he replied. 'I'd prefer to stay a while longer.'

For the third time that night, Sol sat by the tiny leaded window, pushed the hinge wide, and gingerly placed a cigarette to his bust lip. From the bed, there was little to see of the outside world except an ink-black sky pricked with stars. I watched him through a haze of vodka and tiredness as he lit the cigarette, his hand cupped to the flame.

A warm golden flare tinted his skin and he inhaled deeply, head tipped back as he held his lungs at capacity. He sank at a low angle in the stiff-backed chair, one leg out-thrust, his damp cock curling on his pubes. I smelled nicotine and fresh air as he released a stream of blue-grey smoke into the night. A film of sweat gleamed on his torso, silvered by starlight. His dark body hair glinted with pale, bright threads.

In the distance, an owl hooted, reminding me how far I was from the mean streets of Saltbourne.

Gazing out into the dark, Sol appeared tranquil and relaxed, as if solitude were his preference. The night was startlingly quiet and fragile. When he inhaled, I could hear the crackle of cigarette paper as the edges burned.

I wonder how long it will be before I experience such peace again.

Part 2

Thursday 3rd July

The paramedics arrived first, calm, kind and efficient as they humped kit from their van and set to work on Misha, despite the apparent futility of doing so. We were ushered away, questions unanswered. 'Who found him?' 'Will he be OK?' 'Wasn't the poolhouse out of order?'

Half-dressed people clustered in the grounds, some distraught, others baffled, while Rose and her friends talked to the emergency services. I wondered whether to inform them that the dead man had spent the night in my bed along with some other guy I barely knew, but the fact seemed irrelevant.

When I learned the police wouldn't arrive for some time, and that the medics wanted people to stay put till then, I slipped away. I needed to dress and urgently talk to Sol. Surely the commotion had woken him?

It seemed to have done, but only just. In my earlier haste, I'd left the door of my turret room open. Sol sat naked on the bed edge, knees splayed, his head in one hand, fingers clawed into his dark, tousled hair. He looked up as I entered, giving me a pained, hung-over smile. His eyes were bloodshot, his jaw rough with stubble, and damn – inappropriate, I know – he looked beautiful: exhausted and bold, as if he'd been to hell and back for unknown, heroic purposes.

'They found Misha dead in the pool,' I said.

That roused him. He stiffened, eyes alert. 'Say again?'

'Ambulance is here,' I said. 'Police are on their way. I saw him lying there. He's … he's dead.'

Sol stood. He had an early-morning semi that I couldn't help but notice. He glanced around the room, searching wildly. He grabbed his jeans from the floor, back to the wall as he stepped into them, going commando. 'Holy fuck, he's dead? You sure?' he asked, buttoning up. His stomach was practically flat, jeans resting low on his hips, hair on his belly trailing down in a line.

'Stay here,' I said. 'Please. There's nothing you can do.'

He buckled his belt. 'I need to see what's happening.'

'Nothing's happening. They're trying to resuscitate him but … People are hanging around, just waiting. Everyone's sort of numb and shocked.'

He punched his arms into his T-shirt and shook out his hair, although it barely moved.

'When did he leave the room?' he asked. 'Any idea? Did you see him? Hear him?'

'No, you?'

'Nothing, no.'

He sat on the bed, fastening his big, battered trainers.

'I think they're trying to keep people in the garden till the cops arrive,' I said. 'Don't stay down there.'

'I'll be back in ten.'

I twisted in flustered half-circles. 'OK,' I said, trying to reassure myself. 'I'm going to get dressed and tidy the room. They might want to question us.'

'Why? What about?'

The harsh, demanding tone got to me and I snapped. 'Because we were the last people to fuck him!'

Sol stabbed his fingers into his hair. 'OK, I need to think.'

I seized my knickers from the floor and tossed them into the en suite. Sol grabbed his phone from the bedside table, checked it, and stuffed it in his front pocket.

'I won't be long,' he said. 'Let's stay calm, eh?' He edged past me, snatched his cigarettes from the window ledge and made for the bedroom door. But he doubled back before he left, returning to me. His dark brown hair stood in a skew-whiff quiff and his tennis injury hung like an obscene berry on his lip. He gave me a brief kiss on the cheek, his hand on my hip. He smelled of sleep and his bristled jaw scratched. We hadn't kissed during sex because of his wound. I wondered if we ever would.

'You cool about last night, Cha Cha?' he asked, poised to dart off.

The perfunctory concern pleased me: smart enough to be respectful but smart enough to know I didn't need sweet-talking. He had, however, clearly forgotten my name.

'Cha Cha?'

He grinned then winced. Carefully, he dabbed his lip, checking for blood. 'You got that whole...' He gave my body a cursory glance, making a brisk hourglass shape with one hand. 'Whole retro thing going on.'

'The name's Lana.'

'Sure,' he said, shrugging. 'I hadn't forgotten.'

'Liar.'

He began heading out of the room again, striding with loose, easy athleticism. At the door, he halted and turned to me. 'I'm Sol, by the way.'

'Yeah, I remembered.'

Alone, I didn't know where to begin. The room was a tip. I figured for starters I should flush the condoms. Ordinarily, I'd bin them but if there was a chance of the room being examined, then I wanted rid. I picked up a dry rubber, then another, clammy and pendulous. I recalled being young and naive, when sex was a one-condom affair, structured around his orgasm. During my marriage, with neither of us wanting children, I'd gone from pill to coil, but now I was back on the open market, so to speak, I was becoming reacquainted with rubbers. Most men worth their salt threw them around like bad confetti. We'd fuck, do something else, fuck again, stop. Ejaculation wasn't the centrepiece because sex was more sophisticated than fore-play then penetration. Kinkier too. Infinitely kinkier, as the items littering the bedroom floor testified.

In the en suite, I flushed the rubbers and dropped a few empty foils in the pedal bin. Immediately I thought better of it, retrieved the wrappers and put them in my make-up bag. No one would check there. The bathroom was com-pact and shiny: shower over a clawfoot tub, washbasin and toilet, but with the same twee aesthetic of the bedroom. Scalloped soap dish, gilt fittings, knotted bows on the tiles: that kind of thing. The towels were draped neatly over a ladder of gold rails, all apart from one, which lay crumpled in a corner.

I was puzzled. I hadn't dumped a towel there. I wouldn't do that. I'm a neat freak. I bent to retrieve it, a worn, coral-pink bath sheet, fishing among memories of the previous night. Had one of the men gone for a post-coital freshen-up? I couldn't remember either of them doing so but the sex was such a blur of bodies and vodka it could easily have happened. No biggie. I was about to drape the towel over the bath edge when I caught its smell. Chlorine.

I sniffed closer. Yes, definitely chlorine. How peculiar. Where had that come from? Misha hadn't returned from his swim so how could his towel be here? Was it even his? The colour was the same as the others in the bathroom, orangey-pink like factory-farmed, over-dyed salmon.

I pondered what to do: air the towel or add it straight to the laundry? Did guests have access to spare towels if they ran out? Should I have brought my own? Then I thought, no, this is not what I should be dwelling on.

Why was a damp, chlorine-scented towel here? Had Misha returned then headed downstairs again? Perhaps he was an insomniac. Or had someone else snuck into the room to return it? No, too crazy. Someone must have been at the pool with Misha. Sol. Sol must have been with him, the two men leaving me in peace as they continued socialising, or maybe fucking, outside.

But if Sol had been with Misha, why was Misha dead?

I admit, I panicked. I was bothered about the police crawling over the room, asking questions about what the three of us had done together. I like to think I'm old and wise enough to be immune from sexual shame but the prospect of the authorities prying into my private life in a quest for answers appalled me. Rationally speaking, I had nothing to feel guilty about. We hadn't broken any laws or caused any damage. But ours wasn't regular behaviour so I was eager to keep the encounter under wraps. I needed rid of the towel. Correction: I needed rid of all evidence. Flushing condoms wasn't enough.

So I took the damp bath sheet, laid it on the bedroom floor, and placed all the equipment we'd used in the centre. My hands began to tremble as the reality of my situation kicked in. The sound of sirens and of people moving on the floors below made me fear someone would come galloping up the stairs of the tower any second. What would I do? There's nowhere to run in a turret room. You can only fly or fall. I drew the corners of the towel together and twisted them to form a bundle. No, no good. It would come undone. Keep calm, Lana. Don't panic. Think.

I grabbed the polka-dot scarf from the contents and used it to secure the towel, making an enormous Dick-Whittington knapsack. Metal clanked against metal as I stood, cupping the lumpy package. The Clejuso handcuffs weighed a ton. I glanced about for somewhere to stash the item but figured the outcome would be worse if I was rumbled for having concealed something that could be construed as evidence.

I dressed quickly in a denim skirt and pastel-striped sun top, whisked a brush through my hair, cleaned my teeth and flicked on some lippy and mascara. Awkward in sandals and clutching the handrail, I clomped down the spiral staircase with my bundle and then along the west wing corridor to the room my friend, Nicki, was sharing with her partner, Ian. They'd been looking out for me since the start of the weekend, aware I'd arrived on my own and might appreciate the support. Plus, they were a broad-minded couple, which was going to help immensely.

Nicki was making coffee in a cafetiere. Ian was showering. Their room, larger than mine, was tidy and fresh, sunlight glossing the frame of a chintzy four-poster bed. The open windows gave on to a view of the gravel drive-way sweeping around the striped lawns to the front of the house. As I moved deeper into the room, I saw blue flashing lights winking in the morning's glare. The bright day, with its intimations of hope and joy, didn't suit the dark events unfolding.

Nicki didn't bat an eyelid when I asked if she'd store some bondage gear. I gave a brief rundown of the story, omitting the detail about the damp towel. Her main concern was for my emotional and psychological welfare. She understood my fear that the police, often mistrustful of non-mainstream sexualities, might get twitchy if they knew they were dealing with the death of a man whose proclivities were on the kinky side. And we agreed if the tabloids got hold of a story like this they'd be all over us, spewing out their judgemental adjectives: sick, twisted, perverse. I didn't want to be part of that narrative.

'I don't see why they'd want to search the room though,' said Nicki. 'He died in the pool, didn't he? Just a tragic accident from the sounds of it. You haven't done anything wrong.'

Tears burned my eyes because I felt as if I had.

'Hey, c'mere. Give us a hug.' Nicki stepped towards me, arms outstretched.

I stepped back in alarm, my hand raised. 'Don't, Nick. Please.' I blinked rapidly and dashed away a single tear. 'If anyone's kind to me, I don't think I could...I just need to hold it together here. Sorry. Don't be nice to me, please.' I dug my nails into the palms of my hands, creating pain to distract me from pain.

Nicki folded her arms, frowning. 'Well, OK then, bitch.

Have I told you how dreadful your hair's looking these days?'

A noise came out of my mouth, half laugh, half sob. 'Thanks, hun. Don't mention this to anyone, will you? That I was with him last night.'

'No, course not. Not if you don't want me to.'

I returned outside in search of Sol as a new wave of sirens became audible. In the pale morning sunlight, people sat on benches and walls, or stood in small groups. Some people held each other in casual, supportive embraces, looking numb and bored. Some were chatting, some smoking. Medics in high-visibility jackets and bottle-green coveralls talked to guests, or walked across the grounds with a reassuringly steady pace. Radios crackled. Nobody seemed to be panicking now.

Sol stood alone at the far end of one of the manicured lawns, his phone to one ear, his hand covering his other ear. He paced in short lengths, agitated, head shifting from low to high, looking anxiously around. When he spotted me, he raised a hand and beckoned me towards him with a flick of his fingers. As I approached, he turned his back to me, body hunched into his phone call.

Married, I thought. He's fucking married. On the phone to her now, making excuses as to why he didn't call last night.

He snapped his phone shut as I neared. 'Come on.' He walked ahead, nodding at a great froth of pastels and foliage edging the lawn.

'What's going on?'

'Cops are here. We need to make ourselves scarce.'

'Why? Where are we going?'

'We need to get our story straight. Just keep walking.'

We hurried into the dappled shade of a gravel path flanked with rhododendrons and azaleas. The blooms were on the turn but the candy pinks and whites still looked sugary enough to sweeten the air. Among the cloud of floral femininity, Sol was incongruously masculine and solemn. Dark clothes; dark hair; dark, perplexing Sol. He kept checking back to ensure I was following him. Each time, his gaze swept our surroundings as if he were expecting an ambush. He didn't once offer a glimpse of the wisecracking, cocksure man I'd met only the day before.

'You think he was on something?' he asked in a low voice.

'We were all pretty wasted.'

'Yeah, but there's drink and dope,' he replied, 'and there's dying. You sure you didn't hear him leave the room?'

'No, I was dead to the world.'

Ouch. Clumsy phrasing. Gravel crunched underfoot in our silence and the pump of my breath grew quicker. After a while, Sol deviated off the main drag and down a soil-stamped track set with flat stones. A tumbling rockery bordered the narrow path, patterned with alpines, ornamental grasses and lush, deep green ferns. Fronds wafted around Sol's ankles as he strode forwards, the feathery leaves springing off him to tickle my bare shins. Despite the early-morning warmth, the touch made me shiver.

'Do you know where you're going?'

'No. Guesswork,' he replied. 'Just want to get us away from the grounds. Man, this is such a ball-ache.'

The track led to a wooden stile in the gap of a dry stone wall furred with mustard-yellow lichen. On the far side stood a dark, tangled woodland, the canopy of overhanging trees casting mottled shade on the rockery's contrived chaos. Birdsong trilled in the leaves. The air was becoming cool, a touch clammy.

My mind returned to the damp, coral-pink towel in my room. How had it got from the swimming pool to my bathroom floor? Was it safe to go into the woods with this man? Did he want to get *us* away from the grounds? Or me? Was I a danger to him?

In one swift, easy movement Sol lunged upwards and over the stile, arms flexing as he grabbed the side posts. The muscles in his broad back shifted beneath his tee, the wings of his shoulder blades jutting. Fabric gaped above his jeans, flashing the crevice of his arse and a strip of two-tone skin, toffee dark and creamy white. No underwear. I'd seen him get dressed, battling urgency and composure in his eagerness to take control. The memory made me horny. I tried to push the feeling aside. A man was dead. Lust had no place here.

Sol thumped down onto hard soil and stood, gazing into the woods with a grim, preoccupied expression. Gold-green sunlight filtered in through the trees, patterning him in shifting, citrus colours. He checked his front jeans pocket and absently withdrew his cigarettes. I stepped onto the stile's narrow plank in backless sandals, clutching both posts. I hadn't banked on a country walk when I'd selected my footwear.

Sol turned, looking beyond me, face still pensive as he thumbed open his cigarette packet. Then he switched gear, instantly alert, as if seeing me for the first time in all my city-girl awkwardness.

'Hey, here.' He stuffed his cigarettes into his pocket and stepped close, offering a hand, his smile strained.

My fears melted into relief. He was pleasant and kind, not evil at all. I had nothing to be afraid of. I grasped his fingertips, reassured by their strength as I tottered over the wooden structure. I plunged down to the grassy path, shifting my weight onto his hand. His grip tightened in response, fingers curling into mine.

His fingers, oh God. That small moment of intimacy and support. Something broke inside me. Such a cliché, I know, but that's how it felt, as if a bar of steel which had taken up residence behind my sternum was shattering into a soaring fragility. A sob rose, too high and hard to contain, a tsunami of emotion. I made a sound, a strangled wail, my shoulders crunching, my eyes flooding.

Sol was motionless, still clasping my hand like a chivalric prince. To think that he held me so politely as I ruptured. To think it, oh God. So close. I heaved for breath and straightened my back, pinching my lips together. I made my eyes wide, fighting back tears as I shook my head. 'Don't be kind to me,' I wanted to say. 'Don't be kind.' But I couldn't speak. My constricted throat wouldn't let me form words.

Sol stared in bewilderment, the light of pale leaf-ghosts flickering over his face. For a second, we were worlds apart. I might have been on the other side of the stile, where order reigned. Then his face softened and he clutched me in a hard embrace, hiding me in his shadows. He nestled me in the crook of his neck, tilting his chin as he cradled my head, his other arm wrapped tight across my back. His chest was a solid wall of security, and the scent of his skin made me weak.

'Hey, it's OK,' he soothed. 'If you need to cry, go for it. I'm here, I'll hold you.'

I gazed into the blur of his T-shirt, tears falling fast as I fought to put the brakes on. If I started crying properly I might never stop.

'This sucks,' he murmured. 'Such a shock. He can't have been more than mid-thirties. And only hours ago we were all…

I gulped for calmer breath, digging my fingernails into my palms again as I quelled the tears. I could hear Sol's heart pumping steadily in his ribcage. Dark splashes marked his tee. I remembered his tennis-match sweat dripping from his torso onto the stone floor of the utility room, and the blood which surfaced on his lip when he laughed. All these liquids; all this life. Bodies which can't contain themselves.

How long ago that utility-room meeting seemed. How uncomplicated and innocent. If only we could rewind and do the day differently. I could barely comprehend how rigid the dividing line was, how this sudden death had fallen like a guillotine. There was a before and an after for us. For Misha, there was nothing, neither before nor after, unless you believed in heaven.

And right at that moment, across the world, were Misha's friends and family, oblivious to his death, unaware that a bomb was about to explode in the timeline of their lives. How could this man, who'd recently been so vital, now be cold and breathless? The heart behind his ribcage didn't beat, and yet Sol's was a dull, regular thud in my ear. How arbitrary life seemed. How prosaically fragile, when it was contingent on the functioning of this organ, on meat.

'You OK?' asked Sol, stroking my hair.

I tried to remember when a man had last held me so

closely. Probably Jonathan as our marriage nosedived and we didn't dare face it. Sol's embrace seemed to me the essence of humanity, the living comforting each other in the face of death, two bodies with heartbeats finding solace together. For an instant, I saw the chambers of the heart as four glorious, magical cathedrals, keepers of life in all its shimmering, painful beauty.

Maybe Misha was out there somewhere. Maybe he wasn't meat that had ended too soon. Instead, something of him was scattered across the cosmos in a manner we couldn't even begin to imagine. His strewn consciousness could be glittering among the stars, inexplicable fragments, transcendentally bright and far beyond knowledge.

I sniffed and nodded, easing back as Sol released his grip. I dusted the tear splashes on his T-shirt. 'Sorry,' I croaked.

'No need.' He smoothed my hair from my face and gazed down. Under his jutting brow, his once-twinkly eyes were now smudged with concern. The split on his lip sagged, a taut polished bead of bruises and blood. The injury seemed so decadent, a flagrant display of sensuality and excess bordering on the sordid. I wanted to kiss him there but doing so was forbidden. I might hurt him or open up the wound. And foolish to kiss where blood could spill into my mouth.

That his lips were off-limits made me desire to touch him there all the more. I raised my face higher, seeking and offering, my breath quivering with suppressed sobs. But I bottled out. Instead, I grated my lips over the rough, harsh stubble of his jaw, trying to inhale him. That was safer. I tasted my tears on my lips and I brushed harder, nibbling, kissing, smearing my saltiness against him, murmuring half-words of sadness. I couldn't stop. The scouring on my lips was addictive.

I liked to think I was shredding tender skin on the burn of his bristles; that he was ripping me at the molecular level so the kissing, murmuring wreckage of me would lodge with him unseen.

I edged closer to his lips. Wasn't it even more foolish not to kiss him there? A man was stone-cold dead. In the scheme of things, what did minor transgressions matter? Who cared about taking a chance on civility and health? So what if I tried and he was repulsed? Because wasn't this, right now, what mattered most; this seizing of messy moments undaunted by a wagging finger?

I gazed up at him, and I wanted to vanish into his eyes. The hand cupping my head coiled my hair into a gentle fist and, oh, sweet, dirty joy, his cock nudged against my hip. A thick, slow beat throbbed between my thighs, three distinct pulses that wetted and widened me. I opened my mouth as if I were about to eat thin air. With great care, I reached up to take his injury in a soft, moist hold. As tenderly as I could, I ran my tongue tip over the taut, cracked plumpness.

A noise snagged in his throat.

I pulled back, concerned. 'Does it hurt?'

'Everywhere.' His voice was a throaty whisper. 'But I can't feel it.'

His hand tightened in my hair and I whimpered. Mild pain prickled across my scalp. I felt so protected and safe, that hint of force affecting me more profoundly than any affection could. He understood me; understood that I didn't find comfort in the usual places. Slowly, he tilted my head back, his grip intensifying to prevent me moving my lips towards his.

'What is it you want, eh, Lana?' His voice was a low, sexy drawl. Evidently, he didn't find comfort in the usual places either. My arousal pulsed. I ached for his wound, his vulnerability. I tried to edge close again but his clasp locked me in place, pain nipping when I tried defying him.

'To forget,' I breathed. 'Just for a while. I want to forget.'

He nuzzled against my cheek. 'I can make you forget,' he whispered.

His voice carried a faint warning note and, oh God, that was it. Game over. I was demolished. I was a rag doll in his arms. A flood rushed to my groin. In my mind, those five little words whirled, dizzying me with their intoxicating promise. *I can make you forget*.

I eased forwards.

'I can make you forget who you even are,' he murmured.

My knees were boneless. I could barely stand upright.

We were in a twisted fairy tale, and his bust lip was the forbidden fruit waiting to punish us for our greed. But I didn't care. Today already felt like punishment of the worst sort. Sol didn't seem to care either. If he'd wanted, he could have stopped me from tasting him but he didn't. He just let me feel the stabbing burn in the roots of my hair, his fist following my movements with a tension that stung.

'You want to see if I'll trust you?' he asked. 'Is that it?'

I pecked and nibbled near his injury again. 'Do you?' I whispered.

'I don't know yet.'

Leaves stirred around us as if the forest were drawing breath. I nudged at the bruised bud with gentler lips. He didn't protest, so again I enveloped the lump as lightly as

I could. For a moment, Sol was stock still, allowing me to explore the texture of his hurt, tracing the hard smoothness here, the ragged cut there. Then he groaned and began tentatively kissing back. His body rocked into mine as his grip slackened on my hair.

The suggestion of abandonment made me melt even further. I grew loose between my thighs and my limbs were watery. I hooked a thumb into the belt loop of his jeans, needing the support. We kissed in fluttering, fleeting touches, the bump moving with his lips, a strange, solid intrusion in the flow of slippery sensuality. He pulled me closer, cupping my buttocks with his big hands. Overhead, a breeze rippled through the canopy and a couple of blackbirds sang merrily. From far away, the cry of sirens reminded me this was not what we should be doing.

Sol was the first to withdraw. His eyes searched mine, a frown deepening between his brows. 'We need to stick together on this, OK?' He ran a thumb over my lower lip. I nodded. 'Come on,' he said. 'Let's keep walking.'

Disappointment thudded. I was so horny that walking seemed an insurmountable challenge. Sol turned, reaching back for my hand as he began striding over compacted ground. My knees seemed not to exist and my senses were veiled, as if I weren't fully present. I hurried to keep pace.

'What should we do?' I asked.

We released hands. His legs were longer than mine and walking single-file was proving awkward.

'We just need to work out what to say and stick to it.' He threw me a backward glance. The track narrowed, sloping gradually into denser woodland of beech trees, their smooth, grey trunks rising to a high mesh of green brilliance. Sol tramped up shallow steps edged by thick twigs.

The forest floor was scattered with prickly husks of mast and dry, dun-brown leaf litter, friable and soft to walk on.

'I'm in stupid sandals,' I said irritably. 'Will you please slow down?'

He stopped and turned. I read impatience in his silence but I may have been projecting.

'I'm not dressed for this. Where are we going?'

'I don't know,' he said. 'Somewhere quiet.'

'If you ask me, this is pretty fucking quiet.'

'A little further on, that's all.'

He turned and continued marching along the low incline of the earthy, staggered path. I lagged behind, my breath quickening. Underfoot, the carpet of dead leaves muffled our tread and dulled the occasional crack of twigs. These makeshift steps hadn't been used in some time.

'You know that bit in *1984*?' I called. 'Where Winston and Julia go to the countryside? Is this like that?'

'Never read it.' He spoke loudly, turning to shoot me a fleeting look. 'I'm a Yank. We do Steinbeck. Why, what happens?'

I laughed, and the relief of doing so brought a wave of pleasure that made me laugh again. I felt feeble and giddy. My calf muscles ached.

'They go on a sort of date,' I yelled. 'And they have to keep walking through woodland, not speaking until they're...till they're past all the hidden microphones and bugs and whatnot.'

'Then what happens?'

I paused, panting for breath. The gathering hush blanketed our voices, our words seeming to linger in a realm unused to speech. I drew a deep breath and said, 'Then they sit down on the grass and have a lovely picnic.'

Ahead of me, Sol laughed. 'Get outta here!'

'OK, I lied.' I grinned as I strolled on. 'They fuck each other's brains out.'

Sol laughed again. 'Then yeah,' he hollered. 'It is like that. Because I totally forgot the picnic.'

The steps ended as the forest floor levelled out, the ground a deep bed of old leaves reminiscent of crumbled cigar skins. Sol stopped walking and surveyed our surroundings.

'Seriously, I can't go much further.' I stood downslope from him, gasping for breath. 'These sandals are useless. I'll break my ankle. Then you'll be sorry because you'll be the one carrying me.'

He smiled and began sauntering off the track towards a toppled beech. His trainers created small flurries of leaf litter when he picked up speed in a boyish scramble of pleasure. At the tree's base, a lattice of roots matted with earth formed a ragged wall, and the vast spread of dead, bare branches lay tangled on higher ground. Narrow sun-beams pierced the thinned canopy and saplings rose towards the patches of blue sky. Sol slapped the fallen trunk in a gesture of satisfaction; then he turned and leaned his backside against it. A bird rattled overhead before flapping away with a desolate cry.

Sol patted for his cigarettes, smirking as he watched me struggle over the lumpy terrain. I stopped a few feet from him, hands on hips, trying to catch my breath as I assessed our location. Ivy crawled over the horizontal trunk, the ground dipping in a small valley beneath the tree, thick with forest debris. Pale, filtered sunlight, dusty with forest air, gave the small clearing an atmosphere of reverence and myth.

Sol put a cigarette to his lips and tilted his chin. 'Take your top off, Lana.' The cigarette waggled as he spoke.

Lust slammed into my cunt. He cupped a hand to the cigarette tip, shielding his lighter. I laughed nervously, adoring his show of arrogance. A lock of his dark hair spilled forwards as he gazed at the flame. Smoke drifted up from his cigarette, swirling across shafts of light.

'Here?' I said. 'Do you think we're safe?'

He inhaled with long, luxurious pleasure, hard enough for me to hear the suck through his teeth.

'I figure so.' He released a slow trail of smoke, watching me steadily. 'Haven't seen any of those hidden microphones for a good while now.'

I laughed and caught a whiff of his cigarette. In the clean, fresh forest, it smelled illicitly industrial and modern. I could well believe we were the first to walk this way for years, that our voices were breaking an ancient silence. Secrets were secure here, the trees our only witness.

'Well? I'm waiting,' said Sol.

I faltered. Ordinarily, I'd have participated without a second thought. Sol and I had the hots for each other and seemed to be on the same wavelength. This was just a bit of fun, some casual sex at a weekend party. But we were fleeing a scene of death, so sex couldn't be easy and meaningless anymore. Indulging in pleasure seemed disrespectful to Misha. I knew too that, although we concealed it well, emotions were running high.

All these doubts flitted through my mind. But Sol looked at me and I looked at him, and my cunt didn't want to pay heed to my brain. And my overburdened brain, desperate for a break, wanted to relinquish control to my lust. I'm not sure what my heart was doing. Cowering in fear, most likely.

'So?' said Sol. 'You don't strike me as the shy type.'

He looked such a hot mess. Strong hips, worn jeans, cool way of smoking. I once read that women desire bad boys because they want to be the one who'll fix him and make him good. What are we? Zookeepers? I've never wanted to tame a man in my life. On the contrary, I've welcomed the excuse to become more like him, to have a bad influence foisted upon me. In my youth, I longed to be swayed off the straight and narrow. I'd wanted the dangerous, corrupting guys because they legitimised me acting like an archetypal man, reckless, hedonistic and selfish. I'd wanted Sol, care-free, randy fool that he was, because he made me believe I could fuck it all to hell. I wanted to join him for the ride.

But I learned the hard way that these are the guys who cause heartbreak and pain. I was quite certain I'd grown out of them. As an adult woman, I thought I preferred adult men who didn't fuck you about; who were able to take responsibility for their own lives and treat fellow human beings with respect and decency.

I thought I had it sussed. And then all of a sudden here was Sol, wild, intriguing, pleasure-hungry, and quite possibly implicated in a man's death. He was too much, way too much.

And at that moment, too much was what I craved. So, grinning, I lifted my top over my head and cast it to the ground. A faint breeze tickled my skin. Sol watched with wry interest but barely moved a muscle. All he did was stand there, cool as a cucumber, his cigarette tip glowing as he smoked. When I removed my bra, he gave a tiny smile, nodding to himself in approval. I dropped my bra to the floor and stood, shoulders back. The woodland shadows chilled, making sensation rise in my nipples.

'And the rest,' said Sol.

I glanced about. 'I'm not sure. Supposing someone comes?'

His shoulders hitched with a grunt of amusement. 'That's the plan, Cha Cha.'

Damn, I was starting to like this man far more than was good for me. 'Are you going to strip as well?'

He drew on his cigarette, his head tilted at a thoughtful angle. 'Probably.' Smoke streamed from his lips, making silvery patterns in the wooded low light. 'It'd be a shame not to.'

'You promise?'

'OK, I promise,' he replied, grinning. 'Just let me enjoy a smoke and a little floor show first.' He urged me to continue with an imperious flap of his hand.

'You cheeky bastard,' I murmured.

I unzipped my skirt, let it fall to my ankles and stepped free. Sol's gaze rolled up and down, slow, scrutinising and arrogant. His lips twisted in a smug smile and, damn, his attitude got me right in the groin. I glanced around, half expecting goblins and fae folk to be peeping from behind tree trunks.

Confident we were alone, I pushed my knickers down and stepped out of them. I stood proudly in nothing but my sandals, allowing him to see all of me as leafy air curled around my wetness. The thrill of misbehaving exhilarated, as did the thrill of Sol eyeing my naked body from several feet away.

He took another long draw on his cigarette. I felt awkward, just standing there. So I kicked back one foot, giving him jazz hands and a wide, cheesecake smile. He laughed. Smoke spilled from his lips and glittered across needles of light. Without a word, he tapped out his cigarette on the trunk behind him and dashed the butt to the ground.

Still watching me, he tugged his tee over his head. He vanished briefly in a stream of fabric and then emerged, torso bared, dark mop of hair askew. He shook his head as if to rearrange his hair and dropped his top onto the tree trunk. Even though it was mere hours since I'd seen him naked, the beauty of his physique was enough to stun. His muscularity was strong rather than sculpted, his chestnut-brown body hair clouding his pecs and running to a neat line down his belly. His skin tone was uneven, decades dark on his forearms, paler on his chest, reddish bronze on his brawny shoulders. The stem of the tattooed dandelion curled down the side of his torso, the seed heads drifting from the fluffy globe of the clock. I thought of him as an impossible forest creature, a grizzly bear or a satyr, who would eat me all up.

'C'mere, Cha Cha.' He unbuckled his belt with slow, deliberate menace.

I strolled towards him, cautious, the carpet of old, broken leaves springy beneath my sandals.

He removed his belt, brown leather whistling through the loops and finishing with a faint crack. Oh, jeez, that sound, that lick at the air. Arousal raced in my veins, the beat of blood pumping me to hot, desperate sensitivity. My heart rate skyrocketed. As I moved, I felt encumbered between my thighs, my flesh transforming into a thick, sloshing weight that was almost too heavy to carry. How could I even function when I was like this?

Sol unbuttoned his jeans and edged them down his thighs, baring his pale hips. His erection sprang out at a gloriously fierce angle, poking up from his wiry pubes. He paused, motionless, thumbs in his pushed-down jeans as if intent on showing me his hardness in all its implicitly threatening, flattering glory. He wanted me, and he damn well wanted me to know it.

He heeled off his trainers and shoved his jeans to his ankles. He tossed his jeans alongside his T-shirt on the crippled tree and stepped forwards, cock bobbing, leather belt in hand. Muscles curved and flexed in his powerful, hairy thighs. I stepped out of my sandals, the leaf-carpeted ground yielding beneath my feet while offering random little stabs as I walked. We were Adam and Eve but mutually wary, significantly hornier, and eager to grab that sweet, tempting apple.

Face to face, we stood without touching. Sol's eyes darkened with seriousness.

'I reckon we both need to forget,' he said. Tenderly, he hooked a strand of hair behind my ear.

I nodded, jolted by the pain of remembering why we wanted our escape. 'Do anything you want to me,' I said.

He pinched his eyes shut, raised his face to the canopy and then gave me a hard, direct look. 'Don't say things like that.'

He was dazzling to me, his jaw unshaven, his hair unkempt, his eyes deep in shadow. And at that moment, when he appeared to be wrestling with demons, he was more beautiful and dangerous than ever.

I shrugged without replying. I meant it. I didn't care. He was the beast, the poacher, the wolf in disguise, and I was small and defenceless, craving his destruction.

Sol took the belt in both hands. I almost forgot to breathe as he hooked the leather length over my head and positioned the strap across my back. He threaded the end through the brass buckle and pulled the belt tight below my breasts, trapping my arms by my side. The tug of the restraint forced a low grunt of need from me. Jeez, it gets me every time, that subtle imposition of dominance. It might be the press of bondage, the hint of bossiness in bed, the fist gripping my hair as we kiss goodnight in the street.

'That OK?' he asked. He ran a thumb over one taut nipple.

'More than,' I breathed.

He trailed swirls over my stomach. 'Good. Now kneel down. That's right.'

I obeyed, half mesmerised by his slow, sonorous voice, my tethered arms hindering my balance. Leaf matter and beechnut husks prickled against my knees. The air on my bared skin made me feel hyper-natural, as if I were turning into an animal.

'So beautiful,' said Sol. 'Now look up at me. Ah man, that's fucking hot.'

He bent close and brushed wisps of hair from my fore-head, drawing strands into a bunch behind my head. He continued with meticulous tenderness, his fingers soft on my face, until every fine, blonde hair was caught in his big, blunt fist. He straightened a fraction, still holding the ponytail he'd made.

'Open your mouth.' His voice was quiet, the volume suggesting gentleness, the delivery suggesting power.

I did as asked, or was it as told? Sol planted his feet wide, bent his knees, and eased his length into my mouth. I shaped my lips around him, pulling to and fro along his thick, solid shaft, my saliva turning his skin to satin-slipperiness. I explored with my tongue, finding a smooth dip where I was more accustomed to finding the crinkled band of a foreskin. My lips slotted neatly into the gap when I sucked on his end, and when I slid back and forth, his strength felt so good inside my mouth. Above me, he groaned lightly.

After a minute or so, he took my head in his hands and tested me with a couple of harder shoves. I took his thrusts, sucking firmly, and his groans deepened.

'That's good, baby,' he whispered, driving in a couple more quick, deep lunges. 'You think you can take me?'

I drew back for breath, nodded up at him, and then wrapped my lips around his thick shaft again. He gripped my head tighter and began sinking his cock into me with an increasingly nasty force. Before long, he was ruthlessly fucking my throat, grunting in gleeful pleasure and making a lie of the gentleness he'd exhibited earlier.

'There we go,' he cooed. 'You like that, huh?'

I coughed and spluttered, swaying unsteadily on my knees, eyes brimming. His fists clamped me in place, allowing him to steer my head as he wished.

'Are we forgetting yet?' he gasped. He continued to thrust violently until my eyes and nose were full of tears. My gag reflex kept clenching. Physically, it was unpleasant. Psychologically, it was hot as hell.

Above me, Sol panted and rasped. I began to fear I couldn't take any more. I wanted my hands back so I could shove him away. Then, as suddenly as he'd started, he snatched himself free. He held his dripping cock, gripping his length steadily as he gazed down, his chest lifting. I gulped for breath, dazed and dizzied.

After a few moments, my senses began to settle. I was fine; I'd survived his oral onslaught. I stayed kneeling below him, panting. I wished I could tidy up my face. A strand of hair lay stuck to my cheek, the tip of it tickling inside my lower lip. I tried to dislodge it with my tongue but it stubbornly remained.

'You OK?' asked Sol.

A breeze ruffled through the trees and a chirruping commotion of birds started up nearby. From above, a single yellow-green leaf fluttered down through the lattice of sunbeams, pirouetting prettily in its descent.

I nodded. 'Just about, thanks. You?'

He gave a grunt of amusement. 'You're too fucking cute, you know that? Here, suck me properly again. Show me what cock means to you.'

He edged forwards.

'You going to let me this time?' I asked.

'Hell, yes.'

I licked my lower lip, forcefully but to no avail. 'Sol, I have this really annoying hair. Could you?' I opened my mouth to show him.

Smiling, he bent close, eyes narrowed. He dusted my cheek ineffectually. 'Can't see anything. Ah, got it.' With sure but gentle fingers, he peeled away the stuck hair and hooked it behind one ear. He examined my face, swept back a few more strands, and wiped moisture from my chin.

'Better?'

I nodded.

'Good. Then go.'

He cradled my head in encouragement but used no aggression this time. Instead, he kept his hips static as I slathered my tongue around his bared end and slid firm lips along his shaft. I felt clumsy without the use of my hands, slightly penguin-y, to be honest. But the tight strap comforted me, its impact bigger than its inches. I was happy to be under orders and freed of the need to make choices. Soon, I was losing myself in the pleasure of cock, shoving shallow dips over his blunt tip and swooping to his base in long random strokes. Every now and then he groaned heavily, the rich sound rippling through the stillness of the woods.

'Harder on my end,' he said. 'I'm not so sensitive there.'

I wrapped the O of my lips to his uncapped head, forcing pressure back and forth. With my tongue, I fretted his underside, my mouth growing accustomed to the terrain of circumcision. He gave a long, low groan, a hand resting lightly on my head. His cries rose to a frantic pitch as I worked him. Then he pressed his fingertips to my forehead, stilling me, and withdrew so carefully his cock might have been made of glass.

'Fuck,' he breathed. 'You need to stop that.' He dropped to his knees in front of me and pulled me close, smearing kisses over my face while muttering words I couldn't hear. His body was warm and sticky against mine, his chest crushing my breasts. He nuzzled into my hair, kissing my neck. He gasped.

'Oh fuck,' he whispered as if to himself. He drew back and stared at me, gripping my trapped upper arms with harsh fingers. 'You—' His eyes searched my face. 'No,' he said, his voice weak.

'Sol?'

He shook my body, hands like thick claws, and pressed his eyes shut as if the contact were too much. 'We'll be OK,' he said, without looking at me. 'I promise we'll be OK.'

My mind hopped in all directions, memories of the

previous night's debaucheries jostling with today's sorrow and shock. And yet, despite the chaos of the bigger issues, I felt myself rooted in the summery forest. I gazed at Sol's closed eyes. I hadn't noticed how long his lashes were until then. Wasted on a man, people would say. But they weren't, not at all.

Then he threw me a pained glance and rushed to kiss my lips, dragging me close. The bump of his injured lip bobbed between us and I wavered on my knees, my pinned arms preventing me from returning his embrace. His stiff cock pressed against me; then I was falling backwards, bright green leaves spinning above me, a smattering of blue sky, a tobacco-brown explosion. For an instant, I was a rabbit trapped by the jaws of a snare.

He held me, pulling us both to the ground. Leaf litter rustled by my ear and spiny husks needled my flesh. His hand swooped between my thighs and he found me as wet as a river. I was on my back, helpless arms fastened to my sides, and his fingers were pushing inside me, making me crazy with rising need. He dipped between my spread legs and locked his lips onto my clit, sucking and sucking, no longer caring about his split lip. I cried out, over and over. Hot quivers within me swelled and rushed. He made me come in no time at all.

After a pause, he knelt up, his mouth and chin gleaming with my fluids. He looked as if he'd been feasting on greasy meat, gnawing on bones like a savage. He pulled my open legs onto his thighs, aiming his cock at my entrance.

'Condoms,' I gasped. 'We can't.'

'I need to fuck you.' He massaged my breasts with crude, heavy hands.

'I don't know where you've been,' I countered, hardly caring.

'I'm safe, I swear.'

'Don't come inside me.'

'I won't, I promise.'

He leaned over me on raised arms and I frogged back my legs to grant him access. His bulky tip nudged at my entrance and he glided into me, his thickness prising me open where I was hot and clingy. He threw back his head and groaned, holding himself steady before starting to fuck. His biceps bulged in strong curves, his hips lunging. Every thrust rubbed over my sensitive insides, my slick depths clinging to his girth. I scrabbled for purchase as my body was shunted away but my fingers found only brittle, broken leaves. He grabbed my hips, holding me in place, cock pounding high and hard.

After a while, he slowed, and that's when I felt him most, felt the shape of him, felt the bulge of his end, how he moved inside me, his cock fitting my spaces like a jig-saw. After a while, he sat back, and gazed down at our union, shoulders pumping. Sweat beaded his forehead, his messy dark hair floppy with heat. He stared, concentrat-ing, and brought a froth of saliva to his lips. Part of me recoiled. He allowed a line of clear fluid to fall from his mouth. The liquid landed in my pubes and he tried again, this time using his fingers to catch the wetness.

The action was crass, tactical and vulgar, making me wince in distaste. It was also shockingly hot. Some barely accessed part of me responded to this expression of base, icky intimacy. I imagined us becoming feral together, his roughness destroying my decorum until I was a grunting wolf-child in his custody.

He smeared his spit over my engorged clitoris, fingers circling me. Any misgivings about the nastiness of his deed vanished as lubrication swilled over my taut, tender bump, oiling the most sensitive part of me.

'I want to see you come again,' he said.

That eager, possessive watchfulness took my lust up another notch. He kept at me in a regular rhythm, slowing his fuck as he focused on me. Tension puckered within my thighs, my centre bunching, my clit thickening. High above me, lime-green leaves swayed over chequered patches of blue, while dust speckles drifted in fuzzy shafts of light. I closed my eyes, feeling as if I were melting into my surroundings, losing my edges, my definition. Sol picked up speed, his cock slamming harder into my greedy softness. Wooziness spread through my limbs. I became diffuse and insubstantial. I heard my own cries as if they belonged to someone else. Sol cried out too, his noises overlapping with mine like violent, tormented birdsong.

My orgasm tightened until I was at the point of no return. A few more nudges from his fingers then I was there, ecstasy pouring through me in billowing sensation, roll upon roll of wild, spasming pleasure. Sol reacted, getting off on my climax. He stopped touching me and began hammering harder, fucking in a growing frenzy. Tendons in his neck stood taut, lines of extremity under his sun-kissed skin. Droplets of sweat sprinkled onto me, landing on my skin in cold, wet shocks. I was so sensitised, so receptive to sensation. He was rainfall and I was earth.

He threw back his head, his face a grimace, then snatched himself free. He grasped his cock and cried out in four rising, visceral roars, his hand pumping. The last sound twisted into a howl, a raw, animalistic sound belonging to mossy forests and time immemorial. His body went rigid as he came. His liquid flew from him, beautiful white ribbons streaking through muzzy, golden air. Come splashed onto my stomach and breasts, and striped the leather belt strapping my arms to my side.

In the pause that followed, I could believe the world had stopped turning.

I recalled Sol's two orgasms from the previous night, each one accompanied by quiet, contained grunts. He might have been a different person.

'Ohhhh.' His noises slid on the downslide of his peak. 'Oh, holy fucking fuck!'

He stayed kneeling over me, the two of us frozen.

'Oh!' He laughed as if embarrassed by his cries. Visibly he sagged, shoulders slumping, body dropping towards mine. I let my legs fall astride him, bare feet on the forest floor, my arse on the crumbled, prickly bed of leaf fall. After a short while, Sol unbuckled my imprisoning belt and rubbed at the redness on my skin. I flexed my arms for the sheer pleasure of doing so. He lay down and rolled towards me, nuzzling into my hair. I flung my arm across him in a lazy embrace. His come slid on my skin. For a long time, we said nothing. I wondered who he was, what he wanted, and whether I would ever see him again. And if I did, under what circumstances. In court? In bed?

Eventually Sol spoke. 'We should go back soon. Don't want anyone getting suspicious about us.'

'Yeah, I know.' I flopped on to my back, gazing up at the high dense canopy pierced with vibrant blue. This place was like a huge, beautiful den. We fell silent again, nothing but birdsong around us. I let my hand drift over Sol's chest, enjoying the springiness of his hair beneath my fingers. 'I wish we could stay here,' I said. 'Wish we didn't have to face reality.'

He murmured in agreement, adding, 'Ain't that always the way?' He raised himself up on one elbow, gazing down at me with a resolute expression. 'So listen, this is what happened. We were chatting. We were all a little drunk. We decided to call it a night. The three of us walked back to the house then we went our separate ways.'

'Are you serious?' I pushed myself up on both elbows. Sweat and heat slid in the creases below my breasts, and his come trickled over my belly.

'Yes,' he replied. 'We have to make out we weren't with him.'

'We can't. I'd rather no one knew about my private life but…if we get found out… Fuck, we'll be in deep shit.'

'Then we mustn't get found out.'

I shook my head, fear and panic starting to clutch. 'People will have seen us! We were in the tipi together then we walked across the lawn, arm in arm. We were practically carrying a sign saying, "Yo, threesome ahead."'

'No we weren't.' He spoke through clenched teeth, a frown bunching his forehead. 'People don't think like that.'

'I do.'

'You're not everyone.'

'Is that a compliment or an insult?'

'Does it matter? The point is, we've got to keep schtum about this.'

'It's too risky,' I said. 'Anyway, why? We haven't done anything wrong. Let's keep it simple. We can scale down what we did in bed but—'

'Unusual death,' he said. 'There'll be a coroner's

inquest, at the very least. And a strong chance we'd get called to give evidence if we were the last people with him. And that's ugly and painful. Trust me, we don't want to go down that route. Let's just…just sever our ties with him right here.'

I sighed and lay down flat. I laced my fingers over my eyes, blocking out Sol so I could think straight. It was tempting to try and erase the night. I'd mentioned the threesome to Nicki, but she wouldn't tell anyone apart from Ian. And she'd understood when I'd explained I didn't want to disclose the encounter to the police. And no one else knew. Sol and I just needed to get our story straight and be consistent in our lies.

Lying to others was the easy part. I figured the best way to pretend something hadn't happened was by trying to convince *yourself* it hadn't happened. Get that part correct and the rest is easy. Then again, not so easy when you're sharing the secret with someone else. Did this mean Sol and I would need to sever our ties too?

I removed my hands from my eyes and looked up at him. 'It's too callous. Unethical. People will want answers, his friends, his family. We might be able to help.'

'How? Neither of us heard him after, you know, everything. He seemed kinda fine. A little weird maybe but we're not going to be able to offer anything that the toxicology report won't flag up.'

'Is that what will happen?'

'Yes, post-mortem. I imagine they'll test for alcohol and substance abuse. The police will submit their findings. It's not to apportion blame, just to establish the cause of death. Could be suicide for all we know. But if the police suspect foul play, that's a whole different ball game.'

'Fuck, this is awful.'

'So, let's keep it simple. We know nothing.'

'But me and you, we walked through the house. Lord knows what time it was but if someone saw—'

'Fuck, yes, you're right.' Sol clutched his hair, squeezing his eyes shut for a couple of seconds. 'So this is our story.' He sliced a hand at the air. 'We got hammered. The three of us walked back together. Misha said good night. You and me, we went back to your room. That was the last we saw of him.'

I wondered whether to mention the damp towel crumpled in the en suite, looking like cheap salmon and smelling of chlorine. Perhaps Sol would have an innocent explanation. 'But there might be stuff of his in my room,' I said.

'Then we'll tidy up.'

'I already did,' I replied. 'But I might have missed something.'

'Don't worry about it. Anyway, they're not going to search your room without a reason. And if we said goodbye to him in the corridor – which we sort of did, don't forget – then what he got up to after that is anyone's guess.'

I pinched my lips together, struggling to concentrate and identify the problems we might have overlooked. 'I don't like it. Supposing someone saw him coming up to my room?'

'Hardly anyone was around,' said Sol. 'Or sober enough to notice. And so what? He was just bumbling about looking for company. If he knocked on our door, we were too busy fucking to hear him.'

'You have all the answers, don't you?' My tone was unnecessarily bitchy. His attitude grated because I was tense and scared. I felt as if he wasn't taking this seriously enough, that he was skimming over problems in his haste to make everything neat and tidy.

Sol shrugged, not rising to my unkindness. He fell heavily alongside me and I turned my head away from him. 'Hey, it'll be OK,' he said softly. He ran his hand over my belly, where his come was still sticky.

At length, I said, 'I'm thirsty.'

'Yeah, a late night.'

'What time did we crash out?'

'Around two, I think. Maybe half past.'

'Not that late, really.'

'No. Must be getting old.'

I turned to smile at him. 'Let's stay here a while longer. I don't want to go back yet.'

He returned the smile. 'Sure thing. Works for me.'

We edged together and he wrapped his arm behind me, pulling me close. I lay sideways, my head on his chest, and draped a leg across his. He twisted a finger in my hair. I listened to his heartbeat pumping in his ribcage. The filtered sunlight was strengthening, dabbing my skin with warmth. Leaves stirred around us while birdsong fluted and fluttered. After a few minutes, Sol's breathing slowed. His legs twitched as he drifted towards sleep. He stopped toying with my hair. We dozed for twenty minutes or so. I slipped in and out of consciousness, tired but too uncomfortable to relax fully.

I'm remembering the scene as I write this, and it's as if I'm gazing down on a couple of time-travellers who've pitched up in another era, naked and lost. The woodland looks so restful, the sleepers so at peace. She's pale, blonde and slender. He's dark, broad and powerful, holding her close, even while he sleeps.

The woman lying there seems a different person to the woman writing this journal. It's late. I need to stop and try to get some sleep. I swam thirty-six lengths today. It doesn't seem to have tired me as much as I'd hoped.

Friday 4th July

I've made some good decisions in recent years. Today, I feel the need to remind myself of these as self-recriminations pile up in the wake of too many bad decisions. I swear I can feel Sol on me after Wednesday, still holding me down. It's been two days since he visited me. He's become a constant presence in my psyche. Everything I do, even this now, writing my journal in an empty bar, feels like an act of resistance against him, a fight to be free.

I do not want to be consumed by a man, to be lost in the chaos of lust and love. And yet the pull to abandon myself to such disruption is enormous and terrifying.

When my divorce settlement was finalised and the marital home was sold, I was faced with the prospect of buying a small apartment in London and continuing in the same job, or seizing the chance to pursue a radically different option. Jonathan and I were craft cocktail enthusiasts who'd long harboured a dream of quitting the rat race and setting up a bar. In idle moments, we'd muse on whether we'd prefer a beachfront shack in South East Asia, or a fancy establishment overlooking the Thames.

Castles in the air, we knew it, but always a fun conversation and one we had more infrequently as the years went by. The closest we got to our pipe dream was buying a kitsch, 1960s cocktail bar for the corner of our living room, complete with a pineapple ice bucket. Whenever we travelled, we bought obscure liqueurs and quality spirits, and then spent hours poring over recipe books and testing concoctions. We had some fabulous cocktail-fuelled arguments at that bar until it, and our marriage, began to gather dust.

Once I started to seriously contemplate a future without Jonathan, I began questioning everything I had and wanted. After we split, I knew money from the sale of our home wouldn't go far with property prices having grown so phenomenally high in London; but the trouble was, I needed to be close to Hyde Park for work, or at least on a good transport route. Unless, of course, I didn't. Unless I decided to downsize and steer my life onto another course. I could quit the job, relocate, and find a more fulfilling means of earning a living. I'd been working as an interior designer for over fifteen years and had begun to feel my creative flair was being stymied by the company's increasing focus on corporate clients. I'd been weighing up my options for a while. I wasn't sure what I wanted to do, whether going freelance and becoming my own boss was viable, or if I should quit the practice for a better one. I just knew I didn't want to design another sodding coffee shop for the Chinese market.

Eight months later, living in pricey rental accommodation in London, I was visiting Saltbourne, spending the weekend by the coast with Jenny, an old friend and fellow designer, when we spotted my cocktail bar for sale. That's how Jenny referred to it. We'd been out for dinner and, walking home, passed an inconspicuous building just off the main drag in Old Town. *For Sale/To Let*, said the board. 'Hey, Lana, there's your dream bar,' said Jenny.

It didn't look like a dream. At street level, a metal shutter concealed much of the building and only a small sign next to a door indicated the presence of a bar above. The bar was named *G8Crash*, a typographical play on 'gate-crash'. If it hadn't been for an intriguing stained-glass window next to the *For Sale* sign, we might have scoffed and walked by. Instead, we stopped in for a nightcap.

Upstairs, we found a small, cold, garish venue with, as Jenny said, all the personality of an airport lounge. Many of the original features were obscured in a misguided bid for minimalist modernity, and the stained-glass arch was nowhere in sight. The bartender was too hip to crack a smile, the range of drinks was limited, and you had to shout to converse above the music. Unsurprisingly, the place was empty. From that night on, Jenny and I referred to it as 'Car Crash'.

But, oh, the potential. My line of work had given me the ability to walk into the shell of a building and visualise how it should look.

'I can hear the cogs whirring,' Jenny had said as we sat with our drinks. 'You're putting together a design board in your head, aren't you?'

And she was spot on. If I'd known then how steep the learning curve ahead of me was, I doubt I'd have taken my dream any further. But I applied for full particulars; embarked on a course to gain an accredited qualification and a drinks licence; crunched some numbers; drew up a business plan; took out a loan and, after chewing off half my fingernails, sank the money I'd gained from the sale of the marital home into my new venture. The business came with an accompanying residence, the ground floor of a cute white-brick town cottage in the cobbled mews to the rear of the property. The place even had a garage. Car Crash became The Blue Bar. And I became happier than I could ever remember.

Saying goodbye to London and my friends was a wrench, of course, and the financial risk was enormous. But so far, no regrets. Moving here was a good decision, very good. As was transforming the bar's interior so that the style works with, rather than against, the architecture. My vision for The Blue Bar came together when I learned the building had been a funeral parlour in the nineteenth century. Inspired by that fact, I chose a Victorian gothic aesthetic with a muted, background colour scheme of black, silver and cream. I wanted the room to look like a fucked-up fairy tale, an antechamber in a palace of seductive dangers forever under threat of forest vines encroaching from outside. I think I achieved my goal.

The walls are cream satin with a faint shimmer of fleur-de-lys, and a sleek, stuffed crow in a tall, glass dome watches over events with black, unseeing eyes. A row of booths opposite the bar in dark oak and upholstered black leather are customised church pews, now reminiscent of open compartments on a macabre pleasure train. I like to imagine they once carried satanic day trippers to and fro along the blasted wastelands of an apocalyptic beach.

I don't make a big deal of the fact the bar is housed in a former chapel of rest. Sometimes, however, people enquire about the architectural features. Paradoxically, perhaps, given its potential for historic morbidity, the chapel's stained-glass windows provide a sense of respite and tranquillity. They were my starting point when I conceived the bar's design. The main windows, at the head of an alcove with a wooden, barrel-vault ceiling, are actually casement doors opening onto a small ironwork balcony. Directly above the two wings of the glass door is a matching stained-glass semi-circle, and the combined effect is of a saintly arch. The glass is formed of small leaded panes, a tiling of coloured squares. Daylight shines through the delicate blues, lilacs and the pale sea-greens, creating a hazy island of beatific calm that would have once fallen onto a gleaming casket or pasty-faced corpse.

That pool of soft, subaquatic light inspired the actual bar, a cubed LED counter inset with blue luminosity. The combination of enchanted gothic and industrial minimalism could have clashed horribly. Instead, the counter seems to hover like an uncertain mirage, echoing the stained-glass balcony doors and complementing the weird magic of the place.

I'd hoped to create a sense of the bar being a hub leading to other worlds. My table tops are clear glass while the chairs are reproduction Rococo in black velour and silver. I have an oval vintage mirror framed in cream and fixed at a wonky angle. It's a looking glass Snow White might have peered into after one gin gimlet too many. 'Mirror, mirror on the wall, who's the drunkest of them all?'

When I was researching the history of the building, purely out of interest, I learned that the Victorians would drape mirrors in the presence of death, out of fear that the reflective surfaces would trap the spirit of the dear departed. And so, because I am perverse, I decided there and then to incorporate mirrors, transparency and shininess into the design, mixing insubstantiality with the moody weight of leather, velvet and oak. Body and soul. Flesh and flight.

One of the bar's talking points is the bathrooms at the far end of the room: the wall of each toilet is inset with a two-way mirror. Once you're in there, you can see the room full of people and are struck with the conviction that they can see you; that they will turn and gawp when you hitch up your skirt or unzip your flies.

I still smile to see women returning wide-eyed to their friends, exclaiming, 'Oh my God, you've *got* to go to the loo! I'm not saying why! Just go! I almost couldn't wee!' The men are generally amused but less fazed. They're used to pissing in public.

These features add up.

The Blue Bar, I like to think, contains portals to transport people elsewhere, an ironic homage to its origins. It is, as a reviewer in the *Saltbourne Echo* said, 'a place that intoxicates before you've taken your first sip'. That review made me well up with pride.

So, all in all, a good decision. But on Wednesday, about fifteen minutes before opening time at five, the buzzer from the street-level door blared behind the bar.

'Not open yet,' I sang out to the empty room as I habitually do when someone wants a drink out of hours. The time I spend prepping is my favourite part of the afternoon. Daylight barely penetrates when the stained-glass windows are closed and the oak-dark, blue-tinged room is a world of stilled-gothic calm. I love the peace before opening when I'm queen of my domain, proud of my achievement and delighted not to be kowtowing to the whims of rich design clients anymore.

The buzzer sounded again.

'I said not open—'

I glanced up at the small TV screen relaying video from the security camera trained on the doorway. And there he stood, scruffy, sexy and smouldering. My bad decision. Sol Miller.

My heart raced. Without taking my eyes from the

screen, I wiped my hands, sticky from slicing lemons, on a cloth. I saw the ragged, digital image of him glance around the doorway; then he clocked the camera above his head. He gave a nod of acknowledgement. Stupid, I know, but my fingers shook as I called 'Hi' through the entry phone and buzzed him in.

I was already feeling edgy as this was close to the time Misha would habitually stop by for his weekly Long Island Iced Tea. My Happy Hour is from five till seven, and it's usually quiet to start with. I do the bar on my own for the first hour; then at six another member of staff joins me. I employ two wonderful, handsome mixologists, Raphael and Bruno, identical Italian twins sporting identical square beards. I also have an enormously talented catering student at the weekend, Sarah-Ann, who dyed her hair blue when she took the job. Good decisions, all three of them.

On Wednesdays after five Misha would often be the only customer. He would sit in one of the oak booths, tapping and swiping at a propped-up tablet while I pottered behind the bar, music playing gently. I was anxious about his impending absence that afternoon, fearing the sadness. Had I mentioned Misha's weekly routine to Sol or was his arrival a coincidence?

Sol's feet clanged on the iron staircase spiralling up to the bar. Below The Blue Bar, where, in the nineteenth century, the funeral parlour would have prepared the bodies, is a bookbinder's workshop. The two floors used to be connected by a shaft but not anymore. Katrina, the bookbinder, has become a friend. When she closes up at the end of the day, she sometimes pops in for a drink and a chat. I'd been wanting to see her since the weekend but she hadn't been around. I hoped she wouldn't choose today to drop by.

Katrina, this is Sol. I met him at the party.

Oh hi! How did it go? Can't wait to hear about it.

Yeah, great, thanks. We had a kinky threesome and the third person died.

I still hadn't decided what to tell Katrina, or anyone else, for that matter. I knew I should say nothing, should stick to the story Sol and I had given to the cops: we were drinking in the tipi with Misha; then we said goodbye to him indoors after midnight. Sol and I had gone up to my turret room. We hadn't seen Misha again.

But big secrets are a burden to carry. So far, only Nicki knew about the threesome. Which meant Ian was bound to know because couples share everything. But they knew my reasons for not wanting to relay details to the police and I trusted them to keep my secret safe. I knew I had to resist sharing the details with anyone else, no matter how bad I felt. Instead, I'd use my journal to offload my anxieties and try and bring some order to my whirling thoughts.

I selected background music just as Sol pushed open the door. My stomach somersaulted at the sight of him. Without a doubt, he was the filthiest, hottest creature ever to set foot in the bar, in part because ordinarily I would refuse to serve someone dressed as he was. Besides, people dressed like that don't generally want cocktails. He wore dusty workman's boots, battered, dirty jeans and a taupe T-shirt which had seen better days. When he'd said he worked in construction, I'd assumed it was at the higher-status end, as a site manager or engineer, not a run-of-the-mill builder. He seemed too educated to be a labourer and thinking such a thing made me feel like a snob.

But what the hell. He looked incredible. His tee hung from broad shoulders, his jeans hung from sturdy hips, and it was obvious that beneath the clothes was a fit, muscular body. His injured lip was now barely more than a patch of discolouration but he looked tired and tense. Stubble darkened his jaw and the skin below his eyes was heavy with shadows. There was hardness in his expression, his mouth set in a tight line.

I stepped out from behind the glowing blue bar, fighting my instinct to rush to him in a blaze of lust. 'Hey, how's tricks?' I said.

He shook his head regretfully and strode towards me, snaking among the dinky tables, his manner sudden and strong. His aggressive approach startled me and I froze, confused. When he reached me, he briskly steered me backwards with a hand on my hip bone, our feet shuffling awkwardly, his big boots versus my espadrille wedges.

'Sol, what's going on?' I asked.

A bar stool clattered into another as he shoved me against the blue counter, trapping me with his body.

Plaster flecked his dishevelled dark hair and he smelled like an animal, like dogs, semen, earth and multi-layered sweat. I could smell the salt on his skin, the pheromones in his armpits and the nicotine on his big, rough fingertips.

'All I want to do,' he said, in a low, threatening voice, 'is fuck you senseless.' He grasped my pencil skirt and yanked it up to thigh height.

'Wait!' I grabbed his wrists, trying to prevent him from raising my skirt higher. 'I've got to open up. Happy Hour starts at five.'

'C'mon, Cha Cha. Happy hour starts now.' He wrestled against my grip, fighting to lift my skirt.

'Sol!' I squirmed against him, half laughing, pushing weakly with my body. 'Mind my clothes. Come back later. I've got to—'

'Mmm, nice.' He pressed his chest to my breasts. 'Do that again, baby.'

'Sol, fuck off! I can't—'

He shoved his hand between my thighs. 'Yes, you can.'

'Sol!'

His fingers crumpled the silk of my knickers into my folds as he rubbed to and fro.

'You want me to stop?' His gaze was pinned on my face, his lips tilting in an eager grin as if he were watching for signs of my resolve collapsing. 'You going to call your safeword, Cha Cha?'

I tried not to breathe him in. He smelled so good. And I was reassured to know our safeword from the party still had currency. What word had we chosen, though?

'I want you to text first, that's all,' I said. My breath quickened as his fingers kept working. Our safeword came back to me: Cinderella. 'Not show up unannounced. I can't just—'

'Well, I'm here now,' he said. 'Too late for politeness.'

He leaned harder against me, his arm sandwiched between our bodies, and began smearing kisses over my neck and face. I tipped my head back, not wanting him to destroy my lipstick and leave my skin raw from the scratch of his bristles. The room swayed behind him, walls of cream fleur-de-lys tipping into oak booths and mis-hung mirrors.

His insistent fingers kept rummaging and massaging between my thighs. My hunger for him threatened to overwhelm my reason. I wished he would, or rather could,

ruin my make-up and lead me astray. Make me fuck it all
to hell. But I needed to prioritise my business, not sacrifice
it to some randy new guy who thought he could turn up
on my doorstep in the hope I'd drop everything for a fuck.
Sure, it was often quiet at five but that wasn't the point.
Plus, if the bar wasn't open and I had customers trying the
door, they might not bother again. You've got to be reliable in this game.

'Sol! I have to open up.'

'Don't worry,' he said darkly, 'I won't take long.' His
tone carried an edge of humour and I knew he'd back off
if I wanted him to. But I didn't. I was horny. I just wanted
him to note that I'd prefer advance notice. With one swift
tug, he yanked down my knickers, leaving them around
my ankles like loose shackles. 'Turn around.'

My groin flickered with a rush of pulsations. He dug
his fingers into my upper arms and spun me. He pushed
me face forwards over a tall bar stool and forced my skirt
higher. The skirt was tight so he had to ram it up over my
buttocks. 'Let's see this cute little ass again.'

I made small noises of protest but we both knew the
score. This was hot, if somewhat inconvenient. Or more
likely hot *because* it was inconvenient. When I was tipped
over the bar stool with my buttocks bared, knickers around
my feet, Sol swiped my cheeks with an upward cuff, once,
twice, three times. He sank his gritty fingers into my curve
and vigorously shook the flesh. 'Been dreaming of this ass.'

I glanced back to see him unbuttoning and heard him
tear a foil. Seconds later, his erect cock was pushing at my
entrance. He was too fast. I wasn't ready for him, wasn't
wet and open enough. I tried to wriggle away, wanting
more time.

'Hey!' I complained. 'Ever heard of seduction?'

He pressed a hand onto the small of my back, pinning me to the bar stool. 'Easy now,' he warned. 'We don't have time for that. You said so yourself.'

His cock nudged forwards, prising me apart and making me gasp. He pushed higher and harder, the angle awkward, until he was in me as much as my body would allow.

'You're so tight,' he breathed, pulling back. He began to thrust, my inner flesh dragging and holding him. He gave me two deep, deliberate shoves. I cried out, objecting to his attitude even as it swamped me with illicit excitement.

'Gonna wet you up,' he growled. 'Gonna fuck you till you give it to me. Till you give me your pussy, all wet for my cock.'

His pounding intensified, his hands still fixing me in place over the bar stool.

My body began catching up with my lust. I felt myself yielding, becoming wetter and wider.

'Ah, there we go,' he murmured. 'You're all mine now, aren't you, Cha Cha? Nice 'n' easy. Loving that dick.'

His hand pressed in the hollow of my back as he hammered with aggressive strength. Soon, he was slipping to and fro, my swollen flesh clinging to him. The stool scraped and rocked. I grasped a metal leg with one hand and gripped the edge of the bar with the other. The dark hardwood floor danced below me, the counter's LED blueness glowing by my side. Blood rushed to my head, making my face hot. My hair was a blonde curtain swinging around my vision. I heard Sol's breath pump faster, small grunts drumming in his throat. My cunt was so full of him, I felt as if he'd moulded me to his needs, had created my body to suit his cock.

His noises were contained and focused, as if his fuck was strategic. Which it was, of course. Strategic, selfish, all about what *he* wanted. And I found myself relishing that, loving the sense he was using me for his own gratification.

'Ah,' he exulted softly. 'Ah, yes.'

His slamming quickened, his cock swelling to its hard finality and pushing against my walls. His grunts rumbled deeper until, with a groan of relief which I swear sounded smug and amused, he came. I felt his thighs quiver against my buttocks as he anchored himself deep, letting his liquid jerk out of him. He sighed heavily, paused for a few seconds, and then withdrew. Exhausted, I peered over my shoulder as he snapped off the condom, knotted it and dropped it on the bar. He buttoned his jeans and I slumped again. Still gasping for breath, I stared at the oak-dark floor in a daze, vaguely aware of him moving in the corner of my eye.

'C'mon, Cha Cha,' he said. 'You gotta open up soon.'

I laughed softly. 'You sod.'

I stood, pushing myself up from my precarious position, and stepped out of my underwear. Lacking tissues to hand, I dabbed at my sticky inner thighs with my knickers which I figured were ruined anyway.

'Jeez, you're outrageous,' I said, smoothing down my skirt. 'What time is it?'

He grinned. 'Happy Hour.'

I went behind the bar, dropped the condom and knickers in the bin, and grabbed my make-up bag. Hastily I combed my hair back into a neat bob with my fingers and checked my phone. Three minutes to five. 'I'm going to freshen up,' I said.

'I'll wait.'

'Such gallantry.'

In the ladies, I watched him through the two-way glass while doing a quick touch-up of my face in the smaller mirror. Alone, he rearranged his crotch and withdrew a pack of cigarettes from his jeans pocket. He scanned the room with a sharp, rapid gaze, assessing rather than admiring. Alone, his manner was different. He leaned over the bar, one arm outstretched, and tapped blindly behind the counter. Was he planning on smoking indoors? Looking for an ashtray?

He stopped searching, perched his butt on a bar stool, flipped open his cigarette pack then closed it again. He continued surveying the bar while tapping his cigarettes on the counter, rotating the box. When his gaze crossed over the duplicitous glass behind which I stood, his eyes slowed. My heart froze. He looked quizzically at the mirror, skimming the edges before staring into the centre.

Logically, I knew he couldn't see me. From his point of view, he was seeing his reflection in one of the many mirrors in the bar. From my point of view, I was looking through a window and straight at him. And yet it felt as if my sneaky screen had been blown. Oh, he'd work out the trickery as soon as he used the Gents' and saw similar for himself but until then I had the upper hand. I could enjoy watching him unseen. But the way he focused on the glass made me fear I'd been rumbled.

But that's what my two-way glass was all about. It was a talking point and an object intended to unsettle, destabilise, amuse. I was in the position of a new customer, feeling observed and vulnerable. I thought I'd got used to that sensation, having been to the bathroom plenty of times while working, but Sol made it different. I felt caught out.

I saw him flip open his cigarette pack and stand, impatient. Damn, I wanted to continue watching but it was five and I needed to unlock.

I flushed the handle, waited several seconds, and returned to the bar.

'Nipping downstairs to get the door,' I said.

He nodded and I made my way down the ornate spiral staircase. My legs were wobbly, my head still reeling from Sol's sudden presence and the way he'd fucked me without so much as a 'Drop 'em, Blossom'. I clutched the metal banister, thinking of that phrase he'd used: 'Gonna wet you up.' Damn, he was so vulgar and nasty, so insanely hot.

I unlocked the street door, fastened it to the wall inside and put the A-board out onto the pavement. The afternoon was warm but cloudy, patches of blue sky peeping above the rooftops. Air breezed over my nakedness under my skirt. Funny how summer always progresses in fits and starts and yet every year I'm surprised when the temperature doesn't increase day by day.

I glanced up and down the short street, painfully aware that at this hour only a week ago Misha would have been minutes away. I imagined him strolling along, anticipating his Long Island Iced Tea after slaving over a hot microscope, or whatever he did on a typical day at work. I'd learned a little more about him at the party. He is – no, *was* – an industry pharmacologist doing clinical trials for a healthcare company with premises behind the railway station in Saltbourne. He'd lived a short commute away but liked spending time in Old Town. The Blue Bar had become a regular mid-week haunt for him because he enjoyed the quiet and the cocktails. He also said he appreciated my reliable Wi-Fi connection, a feature I regard as standard but remains a novelty for many of Saltbourne's pubs and bars. This town is somewhat backward.

The aluminium shutters were still in place over Katrina's bookbinding workshop. I remembered then that she was away for the week, trading at a craft fair in Belgium. I wished everything were normal and all the usual people were around. I returned upstairs to find Sol still perched at the bar, his gaze pinned on me as I entered. Behind him, the blue LED counter glowed, its light slicking the dark wooden floor with an azure pool. He looked as if he were part of a trippy illusion, a rough, rugged man rising from ghostly waters.

He smiled. 'Hey, barkeep, any chance of getting a drink? Service is kinda slow around here.'

I laughed as I crossed the room. 'So this is a social call, is it? What are you having?'

He shrugged. 'Surprise me.'

'OK. What do you like? Gin-based? Tequila? Whisky?'

'I like everything.' He gave me a wolfish grin. 'Go easy on the umbrellas though. Where can I smoke?'

I gestured to the casement windows in the barrel-vaulted alcove. 'Balcony that way. You'll need to unbolt the doors at the top. Here, take an ashtray.'

He took the ashtray I offered and strolled towards the alcove. Tiles of blue and green light rippled over him as he neared the stained-glass arch. I watched him reach up for the bolts, enjoying the chance to ogle how his worn jeans skimmed the strength of his arse. His broad shoulders flexed under his tatty T-shirt as he unlocked and pushed open both wings of the casement doors. I'm nervous of birds flying in so I don't always open the doors when I'm alone. Daylight flooded the wood-domed alcove, and the murmur of noise from nearby streets filtered into the music I was playing. The bar felt suddenly different, lifted by fresh air.

I turned to scan the array of liqueurs, bitters and spirits, wondering what kind of cocktail to make for a cheeky, horndog labourer. Something American and bittersweet. Something with a kick. I scooped ice into a shaker and poured in a stream of Kentucky bourbon. I glanced his way, my desire swelling at the sight of him. He rested his broad forearms onto the ironwork balcony, presenting me with his taut, scruffy rear. It's fair to say I'm an arse-woman. Opposite the bar is a bland, redbrick office block, its rooftop edged with pigeon spikes. Not pretty, but it means no one is ever gawping in at my customers. Sol gazed idly upstreet, smoke streaming from his lips. I noted his belt and my mind jumped back to us fucking in the woods, my arms trapped by leather. The countryside was a world away.

I added a splash of Kahlua to the bourbon and a dash of orange bitters. I screwed on the lid of the shaker and shook vigorously for a few seconds. Sol turned at the sound of clattering ice. I selected a martini glass, twirling it in the light to check it was pristine. He sauntered back indoors as I was straining his drink into the glass, bringing with him the grimy, sexy scent of cigarettes.

'Looking good.' He eyed his cocktail as he perched on a stool by the bar, resting a forearm on the counter. The LED glow cast a blue tint on the hair feathering his arm. I noted that the skin around his nails was ragged, and a crimson graze was scabbing one knuckle. He didn't, however, have the calloused, work-roughened hands of someone who'd been in the construction industry for years. What was his story?

I sliced a disc of peel from an orange and lit a match, holding it inches from the glass. I brought the peel close to the flame and when oil beaded the pitted skin, I squeezed. The spurting oils ignited, fire exploding briefly by my fingertips.

'Woah!' said Sol, impressed.

I rubbed the peel around the rim of the glass and dropped it into the drink.

'What's that all about?' he asked.

'Releases the oils.' I stood his drink on a black paper doily. 'On the house.'

'Why thank you, ma'am. So what have we got here?' He lifted the drink, his big fingers pinching the delicate stem. The bar's blue light gleamed in the coffee-spiked depths, contrasting with the bright coin of orange peel.

'I created it especially for you,' I lied. 'I'm going to call it… Utter Bastard.'

Sol laughed, threatening to spill his drink. He cast an anxious glance at his glass, steadying his hand to bring the liquid to rest. 'Thank you. I'm flattered.'

He brought the glass to his lips and took a long sip. 'Beautiful,' he said. 'You can't even taste the poison.'

Now it was my turn to laugh.

'You going to join me in one?' he asked.

'I don't usually when I'm working. Not until later, at any rate.'

He looked around the empty bar. 'This is working? Sign me up.'

'Ah, you're a bad influence.' I tipped ice into a tumbler,

gave it a swirl of chilled Dolin vermouth and glugged in a generous measure of Plymouth gin.

'So how've you been?' he asked as I stirred my ice and alcohol. 'You heard anything from anyone?'

'Not much, no.' I took a martini glass from the freezer, checked it, and strained in my drink. 'It's weird. Friends have been phoning to ask what I know, who he was, who was his next of kin, and so on. But I can't tell them much. He'd usually be in today. Wednesday, soon after five, week after week. And now, today, he's not. Never will be again.'

I pared off a twist of lemon and dropped it into my drink.

'Yeah, I remembered you saying,' he said. 'That's partly why I'm here. I'm working on site at the mall. New job this week. Thought I could stop by and help take your mind off things.'

'Well, you did that all right.' I raised my glass. 'Cheers. If that's not horribly inappropriate.'

Sol lifted his glass and we clinked rims. 'It's what he would have wanted. To the memory of our Russian friend.'

I took a sip of martini. My cheeks tingled at the taste, as cool and clean as Arctic moonlight.

'You haven't told anyone about…' he began.

'The three— No, not a soul. I never will.'

He nodded in approval.

'I still can't quite believe all this,' I went on. 'It made the local papers, did you see? Initial post-mortem results said he probably drowned.'

'Yeah, I think we'd figured that one out. Looks to be a late-night dip gone wrong. Never a good idea to go swimming when you're drunk.'

'Do you think he was alone?' I asked.

'Must have been.' He looked me dead in the eye. 'Or someone's lying to the police.'

I held his gaze, thinking of the damp towel in my en suite. I drank, the chill of gin turning to heat as it slid inside me.

'I think we did the right thing.'

Sol nodded. 'We did. But I've been thinking…Well, call it a hunch but I don't think this is as straightforward as it seems.'

My heart speeded up. 'Oh? How so?'

'Just a feeling I have, a bad feeling. There was something not quite right about Misha. You know what I mean? Hardly anyone at the party seemed to know who he was.'

I raised my eyebrows. 'Remind me again? You met, what was she called, Lou, through online dating? And she was a friend of Rose's? And that was your main connection?'

'Yeah, OK. But there's a reason for that.' He brought his drink to his lips, making me wait for his reason. The bar's glow, weakened by daylight, cast a blue star on the circular base of his glass. His Adam's apple shifted as he swallowed. He set down his drink.

'I'm new to the south-east,' he said. 'I don't have a long-standing network of friends down here. Me and Lou, we wanted different things from a relationship. We stayed friends, I met friends of hers, I got invited to the party. That's about the size of it.'

'You're quite guarded about your past.'

'Am I?' He looked genuinely perplexed and a touch wounded. 'I don't mean to be. Well, OK, perhaps I am. But it's not a pleasant story. Hell, and certainly not one I'd want to regale folks with at a party.'

'The party's over,' I said. 'Big time. And I'm all ears.'

He shook his head and gazed into his drink, fingers toying with the stem of the glass. 'I had a messy break-up with a woman, that's all. I needed to get far, far away. Start afresh. You mind if we hold off on this for a while? Things are dismal enough as it is.'

'No pressure,' I said. 'I was just curious. Sounds similar to my situation so I can sympathise. Anyway, go on. Tell me about Misha and this hunch of yours.'

'Ah, it's just…I think he did have strong connections at the party but nobody wants to own up to it.' He swirled his drink in his glass before raising his tired, dark eyes to mine. 'I think it's about sex. I think some people at that party are involved in something dubious, some weird kink, and he was part of it too.'

'Weird how? Illegal stuff? Oh Christ, he wasn't part of some paedo ring, was he? Please tell me he wasn't.'

'No, not kids. I'm not sure what. But I got the sense…it's hard to nail but a sense there was something *underground* about some of the people at Dravendene.'

'Underground?'

'Yeah.'

'What does that mean, exactly?'

'Secretive, dodgy. Not to be messed with.'

'You sure you're not misreading things?' I said. 'Some of Rose's friends were sort of alternative and sub-cultural but I didn't see anything sinister going on.'

He shook his head. 'No, not that. Darker than that. I felt people had connections that weren't being declared. Every now and then, I'd get this weird discomfort. A tension. As if people were afraid. You didn't get that?'

'No, not at all. What are you saying? You think Misha was bumped off?'

'Not sure. I just think there's more to this than meets the eye.'

I wondered whether to tell him about the damp towel. I'd been assuming Sol had dumped it in the en suite and was implicated in Misha's death. Or had at least been swimming with Misha. But maybe it was more complicated. Had a stranger entered my room to plant the towel when we were sleeping? Were they trying to set Sol up? Or was Sol now trying to throw me off the scent after realising I'd removed the towel without a word? I'd brought the towel home with me but it was of no use as evidence. I'd bundled it into the washing machine as soon as I could, eager to erase all traces of our lie. I'd washed and polished my items of kit too, ensuring no fingerprints remained. The threesome never happened. That was the story and that's what I had to tell myself.

'Will you do me a favour?' asked Sol.

'Try me.'

'Weekend after next, there's a big fetish night in Brighton. Will you come with me?'

I gave a half-laugh of surprise. 'Business or pleasure?'

'Bit of both. I reckon it's the kind of event Misha would have attended. I just want to snoop around a little, see if anyone knew him, that kind of thing.'

I shook my head. 'Why, Sol? He's dead. Can't we just leave him in peace?'

'Maybe it's guilt, I don't know. But I feel we owe it to him. If something's amiss about his death, it needs to be exposed.'

'If you suspect something, you should go to the police.'

'But I don't have anything, just this bad feeling. Plus, we've already lied to them. I'd rather leave it there and keep my distance. If I get something more concrete then, yeah, I'll need to reconsider. But until then...' He arched his brows in question.

'A fetish night?'

'Uh huh. Called Club Sybaris.'

'In Brighton?'

He nodded. 'We could stay at my place but it's kinda poky so I'll book us a hotel. I figured we could go along as experienced players. We're new in town, we've been living in New Jersey up until recently and—'

'But I don't know the first thing about New Jersey!'

'I do. And you'd be playing the role of my submissive so maybe you only speak when I give you permission.'

I laughed, finding the notion absurd. 'Jeez, Sol. If you want to walk me around on a leash, just ask. No need to cook up these convoluted amateur-detective scenarios.'

'So is that a yes?'

He reached out across the bar for my wrist, clasping me in a pinch of his hand. We froze for a moment on opposite sides of the counter, elbow to elbow as if engaged in an awkward arm wrestle. The possessive threat in the gesture aroused me. I adore having my wrists held. The bones are narrow and the skin on the underside is parchment thin. When a man holds me there, I feel he's found my weakest spot and has all the advantages. Sol squeezed harder, his thumb pressing into the delicate network of veins below the heel of my hand. Did he know what he was doing? Was he close to a pressure point that could knock me out or kill me? I imagined he was the kind of guy who knew about these things.

'Be mine,' he said, his tone deadly serious.

His thumb on my wrist moved in tender swirls, his

gentleness even more possessive than his force. My groin thumped in response. His manner suggested this was about more than bluffing the part to inveigle our way into meeting scene players. He meant it. He might be using our conspiracy to cloak his sincerity but he meant it. He wanted me in that role.

I've always regarded myself as a woman with kinky fantasies who likes to act powerless in a sexual domain. I'd never wanted to relinquish control to a man for more than the time it took to get off.

For the first time, I began to appreciate that playing beyond the bedroom simply made the bedroom bigger. I knew Sol would push me into dark places if I let him. He would blur the division that tried to keep sex separate, that tried to make it an activity which took place behind the safety of closed doors. When eroticism floods your veins and permeates your everyday, it's dangerous.

Be mine.

The words made me tingle. I wanted to be his, to feel both safe and afraid as he called the shots. Yet at the same time, I found the prospect horrifying. Having a fist in my hair and being roughly fucked was one thing. Being controlled, owned and protected was something else entirely. The prospect of him caring for me was the scariest of all. I could imagine him pushing me to my limits, breaking me down, and in the aftermath I'd become soppy and needy for him. I didn't want to be weak like that, didn't want to depend on a man to restore me back to wholeness.

When I spoke, my voice was a tremulous breath. 'OK,' I said. 'I'll be yours. But for one night only.'

He let his fingers slide gently down my arm. Sensation fluttered and throbbed in my groin.

'Good girl,' he said softly. He traced a single finger upwards to my wrist and drifted patterns over the skin where the pressure of his grip still lingered. 'One night only.' He smiled at me, his brown eyes level and calculating. 'I'll try not to abuse my power.'

Part 3

Monday 7th July

I've started to fear I might drown when I'm swimming. Before Misha died, I used to swim thirty lengths each morning at Saltbourne's municipal baths without a care in the world. I don't bother with private gym memberships because all I want to do is swim. I'm proud to say I haven't missed a day since Dravendene, although my first return to the pool troubled me greatly. When I pushed away from the edge and put my face in the water, I thought about him dying, about how it might feel to have liquid filling your lungs, crushing you from the inside.

I panicked. I had to stop and stand so I could put my feet on the bottom. I needed to reassure myself the depths weren't fathomless. I waded back to the poolside, acutely aware of the muffled echoes of other people around me. I'm a good swimmer, I reassured myself. I swim front crawl and have always loved the water. I can't run to save my life and most forms of exercise bore me. But I slice through the water, smooth and controlled, very low on splash. Every third stroke, I twist my head to breathe.

After a few lengths, I'm slipping into a meditative state, going back and forth, relishing the roll of my shoulders and the watery blue world visible through my goggles.

But last week, I clutched the tiled edge, taking long, steady breaths. Supposing that blue world were the last thing I saw? Heaving, coughing, unable to rise. Bubbles whirling like a snowstorm until all the bubbles were gone.

'Just one length,' I'd told myself. And I kept telling myself that – just one length – until I'd hit my requisite thirty and my mind was quietened. On the day after that, trying to fight the fear and prove I wasn't cowed, I swam thirty-two lengths. The day after, it was thirty-four.

Today, for the first time, I swam forty. It's a nice round number, and almost my age. From now on, this is what I will swim each day. I'll be stronger, fitter and more disciplined than I was before Misha drowned.

I won't go under with him. I won't.

Tuesday 8th July

Sol Miller. Solomon. A good Old Testament name, he'd said. I googled him, of course, but too many others shared the same name and I couldn't find him among them.

He'd opened up to me about his past though, despite saying he'd rather hold off. On that Wednesday at the bar last week, he stayed for a second drink when Raphael turned up for his six o'clock shift. We talked on the cast-iron balcony, the wings of the blue-green stained-glass doors gleaming in the high evening light. Sol gleamed too, the sheen on his brow catching the July warmth as he sat at the dainty table in his workman's gear, big, grubby and vital. The afternoon clouds had lifted. How apt, I thought. Sol turns up and the sun comes out. I was grateful for company from someone who knew the situation. I didn't want to be alone with thoughts of Misha and death, nor did I want to explain my mood to anyone.

Sol told me that his parents – his mother from London, his father from New Jersey – were killed in a car accident involving a drunk driver when he was eight years old and an only child. Mom and Dad had met as students in the early 70s, working as Kibbutz volunteers in Israel. They'd fallen in love; then had married and settled in South Jersey. Sol had dual nationality. After his folks died, he was raised by his father's sister and family in Queens, New York, but spent every summer vacationing with his mother's mother, being seriously fucking miserable in Hendon, north of London. His adoptive American parents separated when he was in his late teens and a few years later his adoptive mother died of cancer.

'I've always felt kinda rootless,' he said, taking a cigarette. 'The curse of my people, doomed to wander.'

'Do you still have family back in the States?'

He nodded, cupping a hand around the flame of his lighter, and inhaled. He glanced away towards Saltbourne's jumble of lichen-coated rooftops and its pink and gold Oriental domes. This place is such an odd mixture of magical and mundane. Like life, I guess.

'I've got family of sorts.' He released a stream of smoke. 'Two sisters and their kids. Well, my adoptive sisters. Cousins by blood. We're still in touch, still close in some ways. We have some distant relatives in Philly on my father's side. I don't have much to do with David, my adoptive father. It's a long story. Short version: he's a cunt.'

'And now?'

'I was living with a woman, Helena, in Manhattan, Lower

East Side. We split. Shit got ugly. I left town. Well, I left the
continent, to be accurate. Came back to Hendon, my second
home, partly because my grandmom was getting frail and I
wanted to spend time with her before she died. I needed to
take a career break too. I was working in IT, like everyone.
Data analysis. Half killing myself for a digital marketing
company. They described themselves as "bleeding edge".
Total nightmare. So I was feeling burned out. Needed a
change of scene. Anyway, my grandma passed after I'd been
here about a week. Sometimes, I swear I'm cursed.'

'Jeez, I'm sorry,' I said. 'You poor man.'

'Remember my tattoo?' He reached around himself
and touched his T-shirt under his arm, brushing down his
ribs. 'Every seed head represents someone or something
I've lost. Even Martha, the family dog, is on there.'

My heart ached for him. 'Show me,' I said gently.

He rested his cigarette in the ashtray and crossed his
arms, grabbing the hem of his T-shirt. I caught a glimpse
of his lean, dark-honey torso; then he halted, casting me a
sidelong glance. His shoulders dropped and that cheeky,
dirty grin curled on his lips.

'You're just trying to get me to strip, aren't you, Cha
Cha?'

I laughed. 'Would *I* do a thing like that?'

'I figure you would.'

'So go on then.'

'Promise you're not going to throw me off the
premises?'

'Cross my heart.'

He whipped off his tee and draped the garment, still
crumpled, over the arm of an empty chair. His beauty
made me catch my breath. His musky, salty sweat drifted

on the air. My groin thrummed with longing. He retrieved his cigarette, twisting fractionally as he did so to display the panel of his delicate, botanical tattoo. Dark hair flared in his armpit. Several inches below that was the inked image of a fluffy dandelion clock, its stem curving down his ribs to his waist. The seed heads floated away towards his chest, finely etched pictures of tiny parachutes drifting and twirling. Scattered among the seed heads were single strands of Sol's own body hair. It seemed as if he were physically emerging into the panel, his hairs becoming wisps of wind-blown meadow grass.

'That's a lot of death,' I murmured. Instinctively, I reached out, as if touching this representation of loss could soothe his pain. I stroked from one feathery seed head to the next and he kept still, allowing me to explore his personal history as embedded in his body. Smoke trickled up from the cigarette in his hand. A car horn honked in a distant street below. His skin was smooth and warm under my fingertips. The cage of his ribs lifted and fell with his breath. Two of the seed heads overlapped, their filaments connecting in a criss-cross patch. I lingered there, circling around the image without touching it.

'My folks,' he said.

I exhaled softly, stumped for words. I sat back in my chair and so did he, still shirtless. His dark chest hair glinted in the sunlight, and his lean stomach folded in small creases above his worn, low-slung jeans. The hair across his belly thickened at the centre, running like a seam towards his groin.

'Thank you,' I said. 'For sharing.'

'Yeah.' He drew heavily on his cigarette. 'Not something I do easily.'

I was flattered and pleased he'd opened up. Having to safeguard the secrecy of our involvement with Misha required strong bonds of trust. Together, we had to lie to the rest of the world. And our reasons for doing so were, I had to confess to myself, not honourable. We were lying to save ourselves, to make life easier and to keep others out of our sexual business. At times, I've tried to convince myself we're also doing it to prevent Misha's name from being dragged through the mud but, deep down, I know it's about us, the living. I feel guilty that we've distanced ourselves from Misha. We've effectively abandoned him, have turned him into a lost, lonely soul in his final hours, wandering friendless around Dravendene before going for that fateful swim, no witnesses to his activity. With our false story, we've made a restless ghost of him before he actually died.

I don't feel able to discuss this anxiety with Sol. Instead, I'm keeping my thoughts close.

'So what are you doing now?' I asked. 'Why Saltbourne?'

'I'm renting in Brighton.' He leaned forwards to stub out his cigarette and then sat back in his chair. 'My gran left me a lot of money. Crazy amounts. I'm in the process of selling her Hendon house. Well, it's a bit of hole so I'm renovating it. I used to do casual labouring as a student, learned some joinery and bricklaying, and I'd dabble back in the States. I was just going to work on the house but, oh man, after a few months, I seriously needed to get out of Hendon. Everyone my gran ever knew wants to marry me off to some nice Jewish girl they know.'

I laughed.

'It's not funny,' he said, grinning. 'I feel…*used*. Exploited. Can't even have a conversation without wondering if someone's got an ulterior motive. So anyway, I've put the renovation on hold. Might contract it out later. And now I'm signed with an agency. Had to take a couple of courses to update my skills and get on their books but I'm officially A OK. I'm just taking odd jobs here and there. It doesn't do to be idle. Bad for the soul. And I like the physical grafting.' He patted his taut stomach. 'Keeps me in shape.'

'Looks good to me,' I said. 'And cheaper than gym membership.'

'So do you work out?' he asked. 'Quite a body on you.'

'Good genes,' I said. 'And a tongue that favours sour and bitter rather than sweet and rich.'

He grinned. 'Tell me about that tongue. I like what I know of it so far.'

I laughed. 'You have a one-track mind, Sol Miller.'

He twisted in his seat and addressed me in a deliberately creepy voice. 'I do when it comes to you.'

'To return to my question,' I said. 'What are you doing here? Today?'

'The agency offered me some work yesterday. Bit of a schlep from Brighton but hey.' He shrugged, sitting back in his seat.

'I meant here. In this bar.'

'I wanted to see you.' His tone was casual and surprised, as if he were responding to a really dim question. 'That's not a problem, is it?'

'No, course not.'

I didn't know what else to say. I wanted to ask him what his feelings were; what this meant to him; if he had any hopes for this burgeoning relationship, or any fears and doubts. But engaging with those very issues entailed putting the relationship on another level, a more emotionally honest level. And that was what I wanted to know: what level are we at? The emotionally honest one? Where are we going, do you think? Are you as infatuated as I am?

The thing to be discussed was affected by the discussing of it. And that potential discussion might bring us to a more mutual understanding or result in us hightailing it in opposite directions. Broaching the subject was too great a risk to take.

'So are you seeing anyone else?' I asked. 'Early days, of course, but I'd just like to know...'

I trailed off. The phrase I'd been about to use was 'to know where I stand'. But that wasn't what I meant. Or, actually, it was, to my shame. But I didn't want him to realise that, as far as I was concerned, the cards were stacked in his favour. A forty-one-year-old divorcee with a cocktail bar might sound like a great catch, but experience had shown me otherwise. I'd tried online dating and had been open-minded when friends had tried to match-make. But it seemed the guys who found my status attractive were either feckless twenty-somethings who regarded me as a cougar with beer-dispensing boobs; men older than me who hadn't aged terribly well; or men around my age who wanted to cheat on their wives. Basically, all the good ones were taken.

'Not seeing anyone else, no,' said Sol. 'But, you know, we've only just met and I—'

'Oh, no, no! I wasn't expecting anything. Not at all. I just thought it would be good to be, um, transparent.'

I wondered if now was the time to raise the issue of our failure to use condoms in the forest. Sol reached for his cigarette pack and slotted his lighter into the box.

'I don't want to fall in love, Lana.'

'Nor do I.' My voice was sharp, panicked.

'Good. Then let's keep things light, shall we?'

I shrugged, turning aside. 'Not a problem. I think you've got the wrong idea. I was only asking.'

He sat back in his chair. The silence between us stretched. Jeez, did he think all women were out to snare him and needed to be warned off?

We acted relaxed, sipping our drinks, gazing downslope at all the mismatched rooftops. How do you keep things light when they've started off in darkness? Is there a switch you can flick?

At length, trying to make my tone neutral, I said, 'I need to get back to work soon.'

'Yeah, I need to head off, too.' He reached for his T-shirt and dressed. 'Thanks for the drinks.'

'Any time.'

We stood. I collected our two glasses in one hand, suddenly aware that, despite looking as if I were in professional bartender mode, beneath my nice, smart skirt I was knickerless and damp.

'Lana?'

As I turned, he drew me to him, his hand low on my back. He nudged my body towards his, pressing his hip into my belly while his fingertips skimmed the upper curve of my buttocks.

'Good to see you again,' he said, grinning.

'And you.'

I smooched against him. His sexual eagerness arriving on the back of his emotional distance confused me. But, no, he'd been fairly revealing about his past. This was a relationship distance, wasn't it? His other hand slid up to the nape of my neck. It bothered me that Raphael might see us from behind the bar. He didn't have enough customers to occupy him. Sol wound his fingers into my hair, gradually pulling harder. Sensation tingled between my thighs.

Keep things light. I needed to hold on to that, to not mistake one set of emotions for another. Our relationship had started off in tragedy. I mustn't import the intensity of feeling generated by Misha's death into the connection I had with Sol.

With my free hand, I reached around to encircle his waist, pressing into the slab of strength beneath his T-shirt. I thought we were going to kiss but, instead, he held my head in place as he scoured his rough jaw over my neck. The sandpapery caress fired up my pulses. His lips dabbed at me; then they were moving by my ear, his breath warm on my skin. The delicacy of his touch aroused me too. His hair swept against my face. I couldn't see anything except a jigsaw of near and far, the blur of his face, a seagull taking flight against a mellow blue sky.

'Come to Brighton,' he said gently. 'Mine for one night. My sweet submissive slut. That right?'

My heart went pitter-patter. I swallowed, closing my eyes. 'Whatever you want, boss.'

His lips brushed against my lobe. His voice was low, tender and approving. 'Good girl,' he whispered.

Oh God, how that phrase makes me melt. Delivered in that dirty, voluptuous accent of his, and I was practically a puddle.

'You know you want this too.' His thumb nudged under my top and stirred hard, tiny circles in the small of my back. 'And you know I'll look after you, don't you, Cha Cha?'

His promise to care for me made me weak with a surge of lust I couldn't comprehend. Hit me, bind me, make me beg for mercy. It made sense that these would turn me on, but lust sparked by protectiveness confused me. Don't dwell on it, I told myself. This apparent kindness is meaningless. Ours is a highly charged sexual relationship. That an expression of caring could excite me didn't mean I wanted more from him.

That was almost a week ago and I'm longing to see him again. The fetish night is this weekend. I'm not sure if I can cope till then. I am beyond horny, beyond sanity and reason. I feel as if I'm sixteen once more, utterly and absolutely consumed by thoughts of him and what he might do to me. I don't know what the weekend will bring but I'm quite certain it can't be as deliciously twisted as some of the scenarios I've been conjuring up late at night, fantasies so dark I can't even bring myself to record them in this journal.

Nothing is safe once it leaves the confines of your own brain. If you don't want anyone to know your innermost thoughts, say nothing and write nothing. After all, the only person you can completely trust is yourself. And even then, not always.

Wednesday 9th July
He emailed today and wrote:

Hey Cha Cha, this is the deal:
Wear a costume that disguises your face but exposes those cute little tits.
Be ready for me at nine, on your knees, in the Metropole hotel. The room's booked in my name.

Reception know you'll be arriving first. Bring along some of those fancy handcuffs you told me about.

Your safeword is 'blanket'. I figured we needed a fresh one.

Be mine until the morning. Then we'll take stock.

He included a link to the event but I'd already checked it out. The theme for the evening is uniform. Now, while I like a man in uniform, I don't much care for *me* in uniform so I've been racking my brains for an outfit. And I'm wondering what will happen when Sol walks into the hotel room and I'm on my knees in readiness, his until the morning. If I gift him with my submission, what will he do with that? Where will he take me?

I'm so ridiculously excited at the prospect of relinquishing control to him that I keep forgetting we're ostensibly attending on business. I didn't notice anything odd about the atmosphere at Dravendene so I'm not sure where Sol is coming from with his suspicions of 'underground' sex, whatever that means. But if he wants me to accompany him on an amateur sleuthing exercise, then it's Miss Marple at the ready. The roles we're playing here are layered and complex. Hard to say which is the most authentic, which is closest to our real reason for attending Club Sybaris together.

I keep hoping he'll pop into the bar again when he clocks off from work. Since we didn't use rubbers in the forest, and because I'm eminently sensible (except when I'm not), I recently took the precaution of getting checked out at the sexual health clinic and taking a pregnancy test. Going skin to skin is presumably atypical for both of us. I wonder if we should discuss it or just pretend it didn't happen. Probably the latter. People in the grip of passion can be relied upon to do dumb things. I figure we both understand that, so no point making a drama out of minor regrets. Either way, I'd happily spend more time with him before the fetish night. I'd invite him over for a drink but I keep replaying his knock-down: *I don't want to fall in love, Lana.*

As if I'd even suggested that! Anyway, I reckon it's generally best to play it cool. Don't want to scare him off. Jeez, listen to me! I really have turned into a schoolgirl. Next thing you know, I'll be writing his name over and over, and pouring out my heart in a diary. Haha! I am forty-one-and-a-half years old!

Sol Miller

Sol Miller

Mr Solomon Miller.

Lana and Solomon sitting in a tree, K-I-S-S-I-N-G.

I really must stop this and do some work! There are limes in need of squeezing and a floor in need of sweeping.

Saturday 12th July

Living by the sea thrills me. Normality has a sense of holiday excitement. Most days in Saltbourne, I only glimpse the sea but you can feel the buzz of excitement in the air. I get up late, I go to the bank, the pool, the shops; then my working day starts mid-afternoon and continues until midnight. If I have a delivery, I'll rejig things but, somehow, I always manage to swim. I still haven't skipped a day since Dravendene, and forty lengths is now my regular total. Fears are to be pushed past. I'm pretty good at doing that in order to regain control. If I weren't, I doubt I'd be here now.

I'm in Brighton, waiting for Sol, and feeling that rush of heady, seaside joy. The Metropole is swanky and, I assume, paid for by Sol's deceased grandmother rather than by a labourer's wages. I wanted to split the bill but he insisted not. His idea so his treat. I could get the next one. I have a bottle of white wine chilling in a sink of cold water in the en suite, two toothbrush glasses downed while I was getting ready.

I'm writing at the mirrored desk, dressed like a debauched, dip-dyed Marie Antoinette. I customised a ball gown from eBay to make a flouncy skirt from shot-silk taffeta. Its iridescent shimmer flickers between deep forest green and aubergine-black, the colour of bruises and a sea gone awry. An underbust corset would have been the obvious garment to complement the skirt but I figured I'd never be able to find a colour-match and, anyway, my tits are too small to carry off the look. Instead, I've opted to play to my strengths and gone for a hint of androgynous glam. I'm proudly bare-breasted and rocking a pair of braces. Or suspenders, as Sol would probably call them. And I'm not fully bare-breasted. I've bought sequinned nipple covers, shaped like stars. The packaging tells me they're called pasties, the word stemming from the adhesive paste used to glue them to the skin. This is a whole new world I'm entering here. I've wrapped a dark purple sash around my waist to conceal the clips of the braces. My concession to the theme is a medal on a ribbon pinned to my braces and a black beret in my hair.

I like the contrast of the huge skirt and minimalist top half. The skirt hem sways just above ankle length, exposing my Chie Mihara shoes with the Pompadour heels, so I'm hoping the skirt won't get trodden on and torn. Heck, I worry too much, I know. I need to learn how to go with the flow, to stop wanting to be so in control of things. In control of everything except when it comes to sex. But no, I'm in control of that too. In control of how I want to abandon control. Or I was until I met Sol.

I keep gazing out of the hotel room window to the charred black skeleton of the derelict West Pier, its frame hunched over the sea. The sky is a blaze of apricot and pink as the sun slips towards the horizon. Swarms of starlings swoop around the pier, making ribbons in the air. Low foamy waves ripple across the blue water. It's so peaceful.

When I catch sight of myself in the mirror, I barely recognise my own face. My eyes are smoky hollows, my cheekbones studded with sequins and glitter, deep purple swirls dotted with hints of emerald green to match the skirt. My lips are encrusted with silver and lilac. I've tonged my hair, too, so blonde ringlets hang from the black beret for that retro hint of land girl. It isn't a mask, but it's as good as.

I need to stop writing now. Sol will be here soon, and I've got to get on my knees, dressed in this crazy costume. I do love how weird this get-up feels. My wardrobe generally takes its inspiration from the classics, usually 1950s or 60s vintage. My clothes are either snug and tailored or cute and a little flippy. Dressed like this, I feel reckless and wild. I'm a warrior-witch-spider, emerging from the woodwork. I'm nervous too. Part of me wishes I were dressed in a more stylish, modest outfit and that Sol would swing by in Doug Hayward tailoring. And we'd go out for dinner to a fancy Brighton restaurant where we could be unknown and ordinary with a hint of swish. We'd finish up in a cosy bar, dimly lit but twinkling with our own tipsiness. We'd make eyes at each other over our nightcap of choice; then, hand in hand, we'd stroll along the seafront under a starry sky. Back at the hotel, body to body, we'd fall apart and together, over and over until we'd forgotten who we actually were. Instead, I'm going to stop writing and work out how to fix a pair of sparkly pasties to my tits. If anyone recognises me, I will die of embarrassment.

But I have to remember, this isn't about me. It's about Misha. We're doing it for him.

Saturday night or Sunday morning? Hell, I don't know. That was beyond anything I ever expected. I'm still not sure what to make of it or where it leaves us. I guess I should begin at the beginning to get my thoughts in order. Yes, that's what I need to do. Everything in order, Lana. It's Sunday 13th July, around 4.30 a.m.

Last night, shortly before nine, I knelt in the room, waiting for him, curtains drawn, lights dimmed. I'd brought handcuffs from my collection with me, as instructed, and had placed three pairs on the bed in case he wanted to use them as soon as he arrived. No point being shy about these things. He was approximately five minutes late. That might not sound like much but when you're on your knees in a hotel room, waiting for a guy you've got the hots for, every second is magnified. I listened to the sounds of the building, the odd murmur in the corridor or the closing of a door. Traffic hummed and rattled along the seafront road outside windows which wouldn't open. The aircon whirred. I wished I'd thought to put some music on. I contemplated slipping out of role to log on to Spotify. But he might arrive any moment. So I didn't. A tap dripped in the en suite. Jeez, it was torture. Should I risk moving to turn it off?

I'd like to say I knelt there, full of shivers and arousal, contemplating my submission, but in truth it was somewhat boring and awkward. Maybe I'm not cut out for obeying a guy in this manner. Maybe I like things on the more physical side. Fucking rather than waiting for him to turn up.

Then the door clicked with a key card, and my heartbeat whooshed. The doorway, backlit by the bright corridor, framed him. For the briefest instant, I thought I'd slipped back to a distant era. He stepped fully into the room, shutting the door behind him. He carried an overnight bag on one shoulder and he was broader and more powerful than I'd ever seen him before, a wide grin on his face, his dark eyes sparkling. He was dressed to the nines in a vintage military uniform in airforce blue, chevrons on one shoulder, gold detailing glinting in the half-light. His jacket bore the winged RAF insignia above one pocket, and the buttons and belt were unfastened, baring his hairy muscular torso. He wore a peaked cap at a rakish angle and he looked fabulously dissolute, an officer decidedly off duty. His grin was infectious. I wanted to leap up to give him a hug and a kiss, ask how he'd been, where he'd got the uniform from. Had he driven here, got a taxi or walked? Ordinary stuff.

He whistled between his teeth. 'Looking good, Cha Cha!' He tossed his cap onto the bed with a flourish, skimming it past the three pairs of handcuffs I'd laid out on the cover.

My grin widened as I raised my arm in a salute. 'Hey, handsome.'

'That's Squadron Leader Miller to you.'

He dropped his overnight bag by the bed, casting a glance at the cuffs. I'd brought along my reproduction medieval half-cuffs, my nasty Hiatt speedcuffs, and my beautifully elegant Marlin-Daley Bottlenecks.

'What have we got here?' he said, eyeing the goodies. He selected the speedcuffs, laughing. 'Man, where d'you get these?' he asked. 'You are something else, you know that?'

'Got them online,' I said. 'They're ex-police.'

He examined the object, rigid cuffs with black plastic moulding covering their thick stem. Not pretty but decidedly vicious. I hadn't even had the opportunity of wearing them since I'd bought them. I'd just fastened and unfastened them dozens of times, and, wow, they were fast to latch on to a wrist.

'They certainly look like the real deal,' he said. 'Still got the serial number on.' He rubbed the metal arm where the number was etched; then he picked up the cylindrical baton key from the bed. He turned the cuffs, frowning, and wiggled the key in the keyhole. He flicked the cuffs a couple of times, smiling as he explored how the pivot-hinged arm could turn round and round, slicing through itself. The scrape of metal and the jerk of his wrist made me thrum with anticipation. I love how the Hiatts seem to bite, like a metal beak springing wide then darting in for the kill.

'Neat,' he said. He poked the tip of the key into the hole of the double lock, fixing an arm in place, then unlocked it again. 'Ah, I get how they work. Cool.'

He dropped the cuffs into a deep jacket pocket and popped the baton key into his top pocket. 'For later. Because right now I'm going to collar you. Man, you're going to love what I bought for us.'

A twinge of disappointment at his failure to comment on the Bottlenecks, my favourite cuffs by far, was replaced by eager curiosity as he bobbed down to rummage in his overnight bag. Probably best he was opting to take the Hiatts if he had plans for later. The Marlins were genuine antiques and worth a pretty penny. I think I just wanted him to love what I loved, as if that might prove something. Prove he had class and good taste, I guess. Or that we were on the exact same wavelength and destined to fuck happily ever after.

He stood and crossed to me. In his hand was a large silver hoop, much bigger than any cuff, and split into two arcs. A metal collar. That was a serious object. I tried to get a better look but he approached too quickly.

I swayed away from him.

'Be still.' He stood in front of me, hands behind his back, crotch in front of me. 'You have to trust me.'

It wasn't a stance which inspired trust, given that scarce more than a zip fly separated his cock from my mouth. The uniform, too, added an extra edge to him, an authoritative manner that both unnerved and thrilled me.

'You OK?' he asked.

I nodded. 'Yeah, but don't you dare ruin my make-up.'

'Wouldn't dream of it,' he replied. 'Not yet, anyway.'

I remained motionless as he positioned the jaws of the silver choker around my neck. Three gold stripes circling the sleeve-cuffs of his jacket blurred in the corners of my eyes. I tipped my head forwards like a supplicant, allowing him to fix the clasp at the back. I gazed down at his boots, black and shining with a polish deep enough to hold a curve of bedroom light in their stout toes. Kneeling there while he fixed the collar stirred a sense of submission that was new to me. For a brief moment, I swear I worshipped him, this strong, cool, masculine lover with a past steeped in sorrow and loss. He seemed capable of carrying so much pain without the weight of it dragging him down. Bowing at his feet, I felt humbled and in awe of that emotional, psychological strength. Ratchets clicked lightly and then he turned the band so a chunky weight rested at the base of my throat. The metal was pleasantly cool on my skin.

'I'm the only person who can remove this now,' he said. 'Stand up. Take a look.'

My bruise-dark skirt hissed as I rose. I sat before the mirrored desk and my heart skipped a beat. The clasp of the silver choker was a combination lock, the sort you might get on a padlock or bike lock, nestled in the dip of my collarbone. The key, therefore, was a series of numbers encoded in Sol's brain; a key made of neural activity rather than metal; an abstraction lodged among his wealth of secrets and memories.

I swallowed nervously, touching the silver, barrel-shaped lock. Four tiny metal digits glinted in the display.

'Is the combination written down anywhere?' I asked, turning to him.

'Nope.' He tapped his head. 'It's safe in here.'

'When's your birthday?'

'I've not used my birth date, birth year, a pin number or anything obvious,' he said. 'It's a random number, unique to the collar.'

I ran my fingers around the silver band. I found the blend of hard physicality and cerebral fragility over-whelmingly hot, such a potent mix of opposites. If Sol forgot the combination, I'd be stuck in the collar until… Until what? Could someone crack the lock? Or would firemen need to saw off the band while trying not to decapitate me? Supposing Sol disappeared or died? Because people did that. People died unexpectedly, even young, healthy people like Misha. But then if history repeated itself, a locked collar would be the least of my concerns.

Sol had the number for my freedom and I needed to trust him to deliver.

'Well, I hope you've got a good memory.' I gazed at my unfamiliar reflection. 'It's beautiful, like a piece of jewellery.'

'Glad you like it. I hoped you might. Strong, elegant and clever. Like its wearer.'

I smiled. 'Flattery will get you everywhere.'

He moved to stand behind my chair, resting his hands on my bare shoulders. His fingertips massaged lightly. I couldn't see his face, just the strip of his torso where his unbuttoned uniform gaped.

'What's your safeword, Lana?'

'Blanket,' I replied.

'Good. Now, don't forget, we're putting on a show here,' he said. 'I want to get in with people who might have known Misha. Scope out the scene. The aim is to be a convincing DS couple. So tell me once again you're OK with that.'

'Yes, Sol, I'm fine with that. If Misha's death is dodgy, I want us to get justice for him.'

He leaned forwards, a hand sliding down to one covered nipple, and I met his gaze in the glass. Lightly, he traced circles around a black sparkly star, watching my response. Sensation tingled across my skin and I fought the impulse to arch my spine in pleasure. A smile curled on his lips, his gaze attentive and smug.

'And you're OK with public play?' he asked.

'Yes.' My reply was a faint breath. I cleared my throat. 'Makes me uncomfortable but if need be I'll go along with it for Misha's sake. Just don't push it too far or I'll safeword you and we'll look like a couple of novices.'

'I'll be gentle,' he replied.

His promise was like a dark caress. 'Yeah,' I said. 'That's how they boil frogs.'

He laughed and stood. 'And you're OK with me inviting other people to touch you?'

'Getting warmer in here,' I said.

'Are you?'

'Yes,' I replied. 'As long as they aren't gross or creepy. And if you promise to watch them like hawks.'

'I'll keep checking in on you,' he said. 'Let me know at any point if you're not happy with something. I want us both to enjoy tonight and I'm going to look after you. We want to find out what we can about Misha, sure, but we ought to aim for pleasure too.'

'Well, that shouldn't be too arduous,' I replied. I turned, reaching behind to stroke his lightly haired stomach. His skin was warm and I lowered my hand to give his groin a friendly, flirty caress. The wool of his trousers was rough against my palm, and a neat, swollen bulge pushed at the fabric.

He gave an amused grunt, took my hand by the wrist

and lifted it away from his body. 'Go easy there, Cha Cha,' he warned. 'Or you'll be reapplying all that make-up.'

'Come on,' I said, standing. 'Let's get a drink in the bar downstairs and then grab a taxi.'

He grinned as I swished towards the wardrobe for my jacket, taffeta hissing faintly around me.

'The collar looks beautiful,' he said. '*You* look beautiful. I'm tempted to take those…' He gestured towards the bed. 'The silver cuffs.' He crossed the room and picked up the antique Bottlenecks while I slipped on my jacket. The chain clinked lightly as he handled them with fascinated reverence. 'Man, I love these things, Cha Cha. They are something else. They curve like a sickle, don't you think? So graceful.' He studied them awhile, lifting and closing the narrow arm, before replacing them on the bed. 'And I bet they could tell a story or two. But I don't want to risk losing them so let's just stick with the cop cuffs, eh?'

I turned to him and gave a sharp salute. 'Whatever you say, Squadron Leader Miller.'

'At ease, slut,' he replied.

We left the room, laughing. Sol loved the cuffs that I loved best. I still didn't know what it proved but who cared? My heart was singing and that was more than enough for me.

Part 4

The venue was on three floors, a shabby affair smelling of plastic, rubber and beer. Laser lights slid puffs of colour over glossy latex and military uniforms ranging from chillingly severe to wildly theatrical. People laughed, drank and danced in an atmosphere quite unlike the one of posturing, moody angst I'd been fearing. Some of the costumes were glorious, some unimaginative and tacky, but everyone appeared to be enjoying themselves. It wasn't a million miles from your average nightclub except the head gear was taller and more flesh was on display.

Being half-naked thrilled me. Walking around bare-breasted, with no one batting an eyelid, was wonderfully freeing. I could only compare it to being topless on a beach except the aesthetic was inverted – dark, sexy and indoorsy rather than bright, healthy and spacious. Men didn't leer or encroach, although that might have been because Sol was by my side, implicitly doubling as a 'Hands off!' sign. Either way, I was pleased not be attracting too much attention. I felt Sol and I, in our guise of a long-term DS couple, fitted in nicely. You wouldn't know we were spies.

'I'll get us a drink,' said Sol on arrival. 'Wait there.' He nodded towards a column on the edge of the small dance floor.

'I'm not standing anywhere alone with my tits out,' I protested. 'Makes me nervous. Seriously, have you any *idea* what it's like to have tits?'

'OK. Stick with me.'

The bar was a crush and I gathered my skirt close, hovering behind Sol as he edged forwards to be served. Sol wouldn't allow me – and I'd allowed him to not allow me – to carry any belongings. I had a few items of make-up stashed in his vast RAF jacket pockets, which I could request to use, and nothing else; no house keys, phone, money or cards. Everything stayed back at the hotel. I wasn't even given my own cloakroom ticket. My lack of possessions, along with the collar around my neck, were a constant reminder of the part we were playing, rendering me dependent on Sol for the duration.

Surrendering to his guardianship created a peculiar sense of smallness in me that I liked. Small because he was big, masculine, competent and caring. I hadn't expected to feel anything quite so profound or affecting. On the outside, I was a blonde-haired woman in a nightclub, flamboyantly dressed in taffeta and sequins. On the inside, I was a defenceless dormouse curled in a nest of autumn leaves, and the leaves were Sol. He was all around me, his ownership of me supportive and benign as opposed to possessive and mean.

My sense of myself as strictly a bedroom player was wavering further. Jonathan and I used to kink it up, when we were hot for each other, although that very fact seems so alien to me now that I can only assume I was in the grip of demonic possession. There have been other men before and since, of course. But I'm fairly lightweight. I enjoy the physical and psychological pleasure of having sex a certain way and I adore handcuffs. And while kink had been a significant part of my sex life to date, without the sensory, without the cock, the concept of submission became too abstract.

Pleasure from being protected was new to me, as was that small rush of admiration for Sol as he'd fixed my collar in the hotel room. Both feelings contained a sexual element; they made me feel we were creating a space where I could trust him to push me past my perceived limits while ensuring I was safe, both physically and mentally.

'Vodka tonic!' I hollered as I gave his arse a swift grope. 'With a straw, please. I can't drink properly with these silver lips.'

When he'd been served, we stepped away from the crowd.

'Let's go find the dungeon,' he said. 'It'll be upstairs. They usually are.'

'Thought you'd never been to one of these events before?'

'When did I say that?'

'The night we met.'

'Ah, yes,' he said. 'I lied.'

We edged past a cluster of people, me apologising and asking people to accommodate my skirt. No one seemed to mind. I thought back to Dravendene and how Sol had quizzed me in my turret room before Misha had joined us. He'd wanted to know if I ever went to events like this and suggested I should if I wanted to meet fellow kinksters.

He'd also wanted to know if Misha was part of the scene too. Despite his apparent interest, Sol had mocked when I asked if *he* was involved in a kink community, or wanted to be. *My gimp suit's at the dry cleaner's*, he'd said.

'Why the lie?' I asked.

We began making our way up the dimly lit, busy stairway.

'Didn't want to put you off or scare you,' he hollered over his shoulder. 'Went to a couple of events in the States, that's all.'

His casual reply didn't convince. Why, after I'd suggested a threesome and been open about my sexual predilections, would he think I'd be put off by such an admission? I wondered if he was hoping to cover his tracks and obscure connections to previous partners. He was definitely keeping something from me.

At the head of the stairs, Sol ushered me aside and said, 'Now I want you to stay silent until I give you permission to speak.'

'Are you serious?'

'Are you challenging my authority?'

I laughed. 'Seems so.'

He gave me a warning glare. 'Shut. The fuck. Up.'

A smile twitched on the corner of his lips, threatening to undermine his attempt at nastiness, but somewhere under his heavy brows a darkness burned. And somewhere between my thighs a response tugged.

The dungeon was nothing more exotic than an upstairs bar in a smallish room. An anachronistic disco ball cast shattered light over people and rippled across pieces of equipment with a medieval aesthetic. A man in a terrible red thong stood strapped to a padded X-shaped cross, his back, butt and thighs striped with welts. A plump woman in a black PVC mini-dress thrashed him with a short whip. Two women sat on a peculiar leather-topped bench, drinking cans of Red Stripe. The other items of furniture, ominous pieces fashioned from wood, metal and leather, and adorned with clips and chains, remained unused.

Most people stood on the periphery of the dungeon space, chatting and drinking as if nothing unusual was going on. The whip cracked above the music and the man flinched whenever it landed, occasionally rolling his shoulders as if luxuriating in his painful pleasures. He'd clearly been fastened to the cross for some time. I wondered how it would feel to be subjected to such punishment. I couldn't imagine ever wanting to experience such an extreme degree of pain. Each to their own, but that was so far outside my comfort zone it was virtually in another universe.

'Let's hang out here and watch,' said Sol. 'Get the lie of the land.'

I turned to him with a deliberate open mouth, a visual comment on my enforced silence.

Sol grinned. 'You are so going to get it in the neck later.'

I raised my brows and smiled as salaciously as I could.

We found ourselves a corner to observe from. Sol held me close in front of him, an arm around my bare midriff, one hand under the strap of my braces, caressing lightly. His sweat-damp torso pressed into my back, the wool of his open uniform tickling lightly. We watched as a woman wearing plaits and a schoolgirl uniform took up position at a bench seemingly designed for spanking. She knelt on raised cushioned rests and leaned face forwards over the length of the padded bench. Her partner, a burly guy in military fatigues, lifted her plaid skirt onto her back and lowered her big, white knickers down to her knee-length socks. He rubbed at her exposed, dimpled buttocks, glancing up to see who was watching.

In my ear Sol said, 'You think you'd like that?' The caress on my waist strengthened. 'Ass in the air in a room full of people?'

I shook my head, closing my eyes.

'You sure about that, Cha Cha?' He pulled me tighter, holding me across the hips as he pressed into my buttocks, making sure I could feel the jut of his erection through my skirt.

My breath quickened, as did my heart. He wouldn't make me do anything so outlandish, would he? A dull crack sounded and I looked back at the couple. The woman's bottom wobbled with the impact of a blow. Her army guy stood behind her, leather paddle in hand. He swiped her other cheek, making the flesh shake. A woman in spike heels, a nautical bikini and a sailor's cap sashayed around the equipment, hands in the air.

Sol squeezed and rubbed my waist, cupped my breasts, and murmured filth in my ear. He could have been reading from a Chinese takeaway menu and the accent alone would have made me wet. I arched into him, rolling my head against his shoulder. He stroked my silver collar and drew fingertip circles in the hollow of my throat.

'That's where I wish my cock was right now,' he whispered, pressing firmer. 'In your mouth so deep it'd reach to here.'

He smudged kisses across my neck, behind my ear, until I was limp with lust.

'OK, Cha Cha,' he said. 'I want you to do something now. I'm going to give you some money and I want you to get us a couple of drinks.' He patted my arse sharply, changing the mood. 'And while you're at the bar, see if you can get into conversation with the guy dressed in black. The one with a goatee and a shaved head.'

I didn't want to move, wasn't sure if I could, but when I looked over to the bar, I couldn't help but laugh. 'You just described half the men in this room,' I said. I turned to embrace him and rubbed at his chest, his crisp, coarse hair springing under my fingers.

'Yeah, OK,' he conceded, grinning. 'The one on the left. He's with a woman wearing a green tutu and stripy stockings.'

I glanced their way as I slipped a hand under his blue jacket, caressing his warm, smooth back. 'OK, Squadron Leader Miller.'

'Don't get lippy,' he replied. 'Anyway, who gave you permission to talk?'

'Um, how else am I going to get into conversation with someone, Sherlock?'

'Here, take thirty.' He flipped open his wallet and handed me a couple of notes. 'Buy them a drink if you need to.'

'Who are they?'

Sol shrugged. 'Dunno. But they seem to know a lot of people so it might be useful to forge a connection.'

'OK, boss,' I said. 'Here's hoping they don't ask me about my years shacked up with you in New Jersey.'

I took a shortcut through the dungeon arena, careful to keep my distance from those wielding whips and paddles. Then I edged through the crowds, my skirt crumpling around me. I stood near the couple at the packed bar. I felt sorry for the harried guy serving but the chance to linger was useful.

'Is it usually so busy?' I asked the woman in the tutu.

She shook her head. 'First time they've had a night at this venue. There aren't enough staff on. It's mad. Bit shit as well, to be honest.'

'Where's it usually held?'

The woman's partner nudged closer to the bar, brandishing a folded tenner over other people's heads. I guessed he was her dom or master or top or maybe simply her kinky boyfriend.

'Best ones are in London. But here it's usually at Zangos. Down by the beach. You know it? Love your make-up, by the way.'

'Cheers! And I love your skirt,' I lied. 'Don't know Zangos, no. I live in Saltbourne. Only moved there recently. Just getting to know the scene down here.'

'Oh, a mate of mine lives in Saltbourne. Have to confess, I've got a love–hate relationship with the place.'

'Yeah, it's that kind of town.'

And we were away, chatting above the music while getting jostled by people eager to get served. She was called Emma, her partner was Mark, their friend was Tom, this was Declan, Veronica from Poland, and, oh and that was Merry Nell.

'You on your own?' Emma asked.

I was warming to her sweet, cheerful manner. 'No, with my partner. Seem to have lost him though.'

The group disbanded as people got served but I managed to keep chatting to Emma, Mark and Tom. We edged towards a square column with our drinks, because, when

I'd mentioned being the owner of a cocktail bar, Mark was keen to tell me exactly how to make a gin martini. I sighed inwardly because gin martini *is* martini. Vodka martini is a variation on a classic.

'I always say,' declared Mark, 'fill a glass with gin and wave it in the general direction of Italy.'

His friends laughed.

'That's a famous quote,' I said. 'Noel Coward, if memory serves.'

'Is it? Well, he had the right idea.'

To my relief, I spotted Sol threading a path towards us. I wasn't sure what I was meant to be doing, whether making friends with these people was enough or if I should be trying to establish if they knew Misha.

Sol had that dark, clouded look on his face, an expression suggesting he was either angry or mercilessly horny. Impossible to tell if he was pissed off or he'd fully stepped into his role as my dominant. Either way, he looked hot and mean, intent on business.

When he neared me, he clasped me lightly from behind and leaned close to my ear. His breath tickled. 'Put the drink down, baby,' he said.

His soft, authoritative tone sparked a liquid rush. He caressed my midriff, and between my thighs my lips thickened quickly. I swallowed nervously, placing my vodka next to his beer bottle on the ledge of the column around which we were clustered. He kissed and nuzzled by my ear then I felt him rummage in a jacket pocket. I half turned to see him withdrawing the Hiatts. With a quick, brutal flick, he snapped the cuffs on to my wrists, tugging my arms back so hard he jolted my shoulder sockets. I yelped, wriggling instinctively to be free. They were called speedcuffs for a reason but, nonetheless, the suddenness of his action startled me. I continued struggling, irked with him for slapping on the cuffs without warning.

From behind, he reached for my neck, half circling me below my chin with the span of thumb and forefinger. He titled my head backwards, stretching my neck taut. He held the cuffs around their rigid stem, twisting me fractionally, demonstrating how easily he could steer me. The metal edges dug into my hands.

'Hush now,' he murmured in my ear, lips brushing against me. 'Hush, there's a good girl.'

I calmed, his voice a swift, dizzying narcotic, and drew slow, careful breaths. Awareness of the eyes observing us made me burn with shame and dark, secret pleasures.

'That's better,' Sol whispered, removing his warning grip from my neck. I cast over my shoulder to see him take the baton key from his top pocket. I turned away from him and stood motionless, obedient, my eyes fixed ahead as he bent to lock the cuffs in place.

My three new friends watched, interested and amused. Cold, harsh metal weighed low on my hands, the angle of my capture causing my shoulders to jut, and my tits to thrust as if on offer to all and sundry.

I found my public vulnerability excruciatingly awful, my sequin-tipped breasts on display and devoid of protection. That inability to defend myself is what I love and loathe about cuffs. It's not simply about the restriction of movement; it's about the restriction of movement when you know damn well someone's keen to exploit that.

'You want to play with her?' asked Sol. He pinched my jaw with one hand, tipping my head back as if better to display me.

I winced, a wave of heat rising from my neck to my cheeks. A pulse pounded in my ears and my entire face throbbed with the upsurge of blood. Between my thighs, a burst of wet arousal made my folds swell and throb. I silently cursed Sol for pushing me towards my limit so early in the game. These people had accepted me without suspicion so the master/slave act wasn't remotely necessary. But Sol knew I couldn't protest without destroying the sham which wasn't quite a sham.

'I'd love to play,' chirped up Emma.

I heard chains rattle behind me and felt a slight tug on my cuffs. Cool metal touched my bare back and when I heard a click by the base of my neck I understood Sol had linked my cuffs to my collar with a length of chain. Jeez, he hadn't mentioned that his voluminous jacket pockets doubled as a portable dungeon. What else had he brought out with him?

'Excellent,' said Sol. 'Why don't you start by taking off her pasties?'

I jerked my shoulders in protest, complaining softly. Tears of humiliation stung my eyes. I wasn't sure I could tolerate being toyed with in such a public venue.

'Aw, but they're so pretty,' said Emma, sarcastically reluctant.

'What's underneath is even prettier.'

I closed my eyes as Sol stroked a finger around one nipple patch, lulling me towards receptivity, drugging me with lust. When I opened my eyes, Emma was studying me with an expression I'd never received from a woman before, cruel, mischievous and unpleasantly smug. Perhaps she wasn't the sweet, friendly creature I'd first taken her for.

With pinched fingers, she took the point of one sequinned star; then, her gaze pinned on my face, her tongue tip poking, she peeled down the sticky little shield to uncover my nipple. I felt my exposed tip begin to spike.

'Ooo!' She handed the pasty to Sol.

I was mortified at being treated this way in front of spectators; mortified too that my tormentor was a perky young woman wearing a cartoonish net skirt. With a brisk, workmanlike touch, Emma squeezed my nipple and then rubbed her thumb back and forth. She was erasing traces of adhesive and the confidence with which she handled me turned my cunt to syrupy warmth. I threw a glance at our onlookers. We had around half a dozen guys, presumably hoping for some extensive girl-on-girl action. But I'm not into women so I privately cast Emma as a sadistic slave cleaning me up for the approval of men watching me at auction. My imagination was evidently quick to get in role.

My nipple hardened fully. Smirking, Emma tapped with her fingertips as if dusting away flecks. She stepped closer, rested her hands on my waist, and leaned forwards.

Oh sweet Jesus, no. I squeezed my eyes shut, my face on fire. Heat and wetness flared around my nipple. A man laughed, a boorish thump of noise lifting above the music. Another jeered in encouragement. Someone whistled. Emma's tongue slathered circles around my stiffness; then she sucked tenderly as if trying to draw precious juice from me. I thought my knees would buckle. Her touch above my hips felt like a gigantic pressure threatening to topple me.

For several moments all I knew were those soft hands

on my waist and the wetness around my tip. I barely
breathed. My nipple felt enormous, expansive, as if Emma's
rippling, sucking, sloshing heat were spreading to over-
take my entire upper body and connect with the sensation
swirling in my cunt. And through all the dizzying bliss ran
the more dubious pleasure of knowing strangers watched
us, cocks getting hard. Their attention generated and
exacerbated the dark, stormy charge of my humiliation,
their enjoyment of my discomfort making my discomfort
worse than ever.

I kept my eyes shut tight, trying to block out my audience, until Emma pulled away. I released my breath,
gawping down at her in arousal and astonishment. She
gazed coquettishly upwards, grinning. She straightened,
flicked her thumb across my nipple. After a nod at Sol, she
turned her attention to my other, covered nipple. With
the same lingering pleasure, she peeled away my second
pasty, studying my face all the while. From behind, Sol
reached out a cupped hand and Emma placed the sparkly
black star in his palm.

'Aw, these shy little nips,' she said. 'Nowhere to hide
anymore, have they?'

Again she thumbed away the remnants of gum, and
then leaned forwards to bathe my hard nipple in wet,
sloppy warmth. This time, I couldn't help but groan as the
intensity of her oral caress swilled around my tip, obliter-
ating any attempt to keep my lust suppressed. With steady
luxury, Emma slurped and sucked, her small, gentle hands
resting on my waist.

I glanced around at my onlookers, seeing both smirking pleasure and slack-jawed captivation. Patches of
dancing white light dappled their faces as if I were in the

midst of a grotesque, monochrome forest. The sight made me close my eyes again. It was too much. Between my thighs, lust pounded, my wetness flowing into my skimpy underwear. I was sure my arousal rose, not from Sapphic delights, but from my subjugation in a scene orchestrated by Sol. But either way, I didn't much care. Deep down, I was lapping it up and yet at the same time, I was praying Sol wouldn't push this too far. I reminded myself this was for Misha, and I'd agreed to play a role. But now, in the thick of it, I began doubting my ability to stay in character because the character was too much like me.

Emma withdrew and stood, scuffing her thumb over my soaked nipple.

'Now what?' she asked, glancing from her partner to Sol by my shoulder. Without waiting for an answer, she slipped a hand between my thigh, crushing my skirt. The taffeta rustled as she sawed back and forth.

'Feeling good, sweetheart?' she asked.

I tilted my head back and gazed at the ceiling, shards of light twirling across its dark expanse. I fought to get a grip. I *was* feeling good, head-spinningly, cunt-thumpingly good. But I was also feeling uneasy, half wishing all four of us, Mark included, could explore this dynamic in privacy. If we continued, I didn't think I had the strength of mind to cope with the regret which would doubtless haunt me when I wasn't off my head on horniness.

'Here,' said Sol from behind. He reached out a hand to Emma, his fist bunched around an object. 'Put these on her, would you? Then I'm going to take her for a walk.'

Emma took the object. She laughed in wicked delight, holding up two nipple clamps linked by a chain. 'Now, let's see,' she said, edging closer.

'Oh God, no,' I breathed. Wetness sluiced through me. My heart fluttered wildly like a bird trying to escape my ribcage and the disco ball's light-fragments whirled at triple speed.

I held my breath. Emma bent to one nipple and cupped the underswell of my breast, lifting me for her inspection. She squeezed open the jaws of the clamp, bringing the object towards me. Glancing up at my face, she carefully closed the clamp on my tip, keeping the weight of the chain in her palm. The pain escalated sharply but then levelled out. I released a stream of breathy gasps as I adjusted to the sensation. She stroked around my breast with a consolatory gesture.

'You OK?' she asked.

'Yeah, fine,' I murmured.

'She'll let me know if she's not,' said Sol.

'Good to hear,' replied Emma.

She brought the second clamp to my other nipple. Again, she glanced at me before fastening the metal jaws onto my spiked, sensitive tip. Smiling, she watched my anguished face as the pain rose. When she let go, the chain hung slackly between my breasts. With one finger, Emma lifted the links, tugging lightly upwards so the clamps pulled on my nipples.

She leaned closer, speaking above the music. 'You're so responsive,' she said. 'Your face hides nothing. Your body shivers when I touch it. So gorgeous.'

She brushed her lips over mine, half mumbling, half kissing, then stepped away. Silver from my lips glinted on hers. I gazed at her with dumbstruck gratitude, not so much for the compliment but for such careful administration of cruelty.

In the corner of my eye, I saw Sol talking to Tom and Mark.

Emma tapped one of the clamps, smiling when I whimpered in response. 'Given half a chance, I could play with you for hours,' she said into my ear. 'Are you wet?'

I nodded, my cheeks burning with desire and shyness.

'If you and your guy ever want to join me and Mark, you'd be more than welcome.' She shoved my skirt into my groin again, rubbing hard through the starchy fabric. 'He doms. I switch. You think you'd like that?'

My throat was parched. I swallowed. 'I'd need to ask Sol.'

'You'd need to ask him if you'd like it?'

'No, if he was up for it.'

'Ah, I see.' She stopped rubbing me and unzipped the pocket of a belt around her waist. 'Here, take our details. We host private play parties.' She withdrew a card from her belt with a dramatic flourish and then slipped it inside the sash around my waist. 'Invite only. And I just invited you both. Or you alone, if you wanted. No single guys though.'

Sol and his companions laughed heartily; then Sol clapped Mark on the shoulder, saying goodbye. He moved to stand next to Emma.

'Nice work,' he said to her. Briefly he bounced the chain on a finger as if to weigh its length. He stepped behind me. 'Here, take this,' he said, his breath tickling by my ear. 'And this. Got them?'

He slotted our drinks into my cuffed hands, my vodka tonic and his bottle of beer. My fingers clutched the objects, glass clinking against glass. He returned to stand in front of me, raising the nipple chain again.

'C'mon, this way,' he said. He nodded at Emma and co. 'Nice meeting you guys. Maybe catch you later.'

Protesting, I followed Sol in mincing steps, eager not to allow him to exert too much strain on the clamps or to knock into someone who might dislodge them.

'You enjoyed that,' I said, mildly accusatory.

'Totally. And so did you from the looks of things.' He turned to grin. 'You OK?'

'Suppose so. Embarrassed though. And horny.'

'Cool. Let's go downstairs, find somewhere to sit. I want to spend some quiet time with you. Oh, hi!' He glanced back to acknowledge a woman we'd just passed. 'Lou! Hey, good to see you. Wow, you look amazing, doll! How's tricks?'

Doll?

He released my nipple-clamp chain and stepped away from me. Lou. Now, where did I know that name from? He embraced her, planting a kiss on her cheek while I stood there like a lemon. He chatted to her without introducing me. Then the penny dropped. She was the woman he'd once dated and his connection to some of the people at Dravendene. What had he said? It didn't work out, they'd wanted different things. Something bland like that.

I stood in silence as they talked, saw them nod and frown, becoming intense and tender. Doll! He'd called her doll. He never called me doll. A green-eyed monster began growling inside me. My jaw tightened. He touched her arm, his hand on her bare skin. Yeah, and he could do that, couldn't he, along with the hug he'd given her, because I was his mute underling, standing there with my tits in clips while holding his fucking beer.

The woman pressed her lips together, blinking hard in

a fight against emotion. Was she remembering how it used to be when he'd touch her with his fingers, inside and out? And was she the reason Sol had lied to me about his interest in fet nights? She gave a stiff-armed shrug. Sol reached out to squeeze a hand, lunging close to her as a passerby jostled him. She didn't retreat. She liked it, wanted him. My stomach plummeted. My blood turned to ice. They were practically holding hands in front of me. Christ, any moment now, they'd start fucking. They'd probably done it loads of times in places like this.

My instinct was to flounce off in a huff. I swiftly changed my mind.

'Don't I get an intro?' I said to Sol. I smiled so nicely that my hot, angry cheeks ached with the effort. 'Hi, I'm Lana. I'd shake hands but…' I turned to flash my cuffed wrists and the brace of drinks I carried. You get it, dollface? I'm his. He's mine. These cuffs? They're two-way, see, so keep your paws to yourself.

'Hey, sorry,' said Sol. 'Lana, this is Lou. We were just talking about Misha. Lou was at Dravendene Hall as well.'

My smile froze. Gah, how did I miss the most obvious explanation for their awkward intimacy? I was such a hot-headed, petty idiot. 'Oh, all so awful,' I said.

'Apparently the body's been flown back to his parents in Russia,' said Lou.

'Is it? Oh dear. That poor man. His poor family.'

'A mate of mine heard he had a head wound,' Lou continued. 'As if he'd fallen before he…you know.'

'Yeah, well, anyway.' Sol shrugged, hooked his arm lightly in mine and gave Lou's shoulder a squeeze. 'Let's not put a downer on the night. Might catch you later, Lou. Talk properly another time. Good to see you.'

Doll, I mentally added. I tottered alongside him, glass and bottle clinking by my buttocks, vodka tonic moistening my thumb as the liquid sloshed.

'I thought she might be here,' said Sol. 'She seems pretty cut up about what happened.'

Can't be that cut up if she's out on the razz, I thought bitterly. 'Did she know him?'

'Only by name,' he said. 'But she's sensitive. Highly strung. Enjoys a good drama. I'm glad I'm out of there, to be honest.'

I smiled to myself, pleased he'd made a point of distancing himself from her.

'Weird that no one seemed to know him very well,' he added.

But *we* did, I thought. Or, at least, we did temporarily. During that night, we saw a side of him that his friends and relatives would never see. Yet since then we'd become complicit in depicting him as a shadowy figure at the party, exploiting his mystery status to keep our bedroom door locked to a prurient public gaze. The more time went by, the more the secret Sol and I shared became one we couldn't even discuss together. We couldn't look our past in the eye. The threesome had never happened.

I'd begun to wonder if this calcification of our secret had a murkier rationale. Did Sol and I have different versions of events that night? Might that be the reason for our tacit silence? What else except guilt on Sol's part could explain that damp towel in my en suite?

Sol guided me towards the stairs, his hand nudging at the chain running parallel to my spine. One of the nipple clamps began to loosen, causing pain to throb.

'Sol! The clamps! Ouch, please!'

Instantly, he turned and pinched both clips wide open, freeing me. I howled and cursed as blood surged into the crushed tissue, flooding my nerves with pain. I threw my head back, half laughing and stamping my heel as I rode out the burn. My chain clanked behind me.

'Well done.' Sol thumbed around one sore nipple with a delicate touch. 'Over here. Let me unclip you.'

He ushered me away from the crowds and deftly freed me from the handcuffs and chain. He pocketed the objects and took his drink from me.

'You OK with your tits on show like that?' he asked.

'Why, do you have some pasty adhesive about your person?' I asked. 'Or maybe a bra I could borrow?'

He grinned. 'I love that attitude. Makes me want to spank you.'

'I think I've had enough public shame for one night,' I said. 'Come on. Tell me what you learned. We've been invited to a sex party, by the way.'

Downstairs, in the larger ground floor bar, we loitered until a space became free on one of the few squashy leather couches. A couple were kissing and groping on one half of the couch so Sol sat next to them. I straddled his lap, face forwards, my skirt ballooning around us.

I turned his peaked cap around. 'You're a Yank,' I said. 'You're meant to wear your cap backwards.'

He laughed. 'It's not a fucking baseball cap.'

I took a sip of vodka through my straw. 'Sol, is everything over between you and Lou?'

'Yeah, totally. We're just good friends. Not even good friends, to be honest. Just friends, part of a small group. Not even a group. A bunch of loosely connected people. You know how it is.'

Ludicrous that him bumping into an ex bothered me more than him putting me through the discomfort of being humiliated in front of a bunch of strangers.

Sol wedged his beer bottle between the seat cushions and slid his hands under my skirt. 'I reckon we could fuck like this and no one would even notice.' He grazed a thumb over my knickers, hand resting on my thigh.

I smiled down at him. 'I think they'd notice. Unless we were very, very still and quiet.'

'You OK about that little scene upstairs?' he asked. His thumb edged past the elastic of my underwear and my wet flesh parted in welcome. He stroked along my slippery groove but made no comment. Arousal thumped there, and I thought maybe he could make me come like that. If I buried my face in his chest and kept my cries low, we wouldn't attract attention. Not that anyone would care in this hedonistic atmosphere. But it wasn't about the place, it was about me. I'm too shy to orgasm in front of an incidental audience. Or possibly too concerned about maintaining self-control.

'Sort of OK,' I said. 'Although I would have preferred more notice, and I didn't feel the performance was warranted.'

His thumb nudged at my wet opening. 'No?' he teased, as if he didn't believe me.

'No,' I breathed, edging forwards for more of his fingers.

The kissing couple next to us left.

'Hey, quick!' said Sol. 'Grab that space.'

I protested, laughing, as he bucked me off his lap. Vodka splashed onto my stomach and I flung myself back onto the sofa, legs over his thighs.

'Perfect,' he said, grinning. He swivelled around and hunched over to lick vodka tonic from my belly. Desire pounded between my thighs.

'Listen,' he said. 'I'm going to the Gents' then slipping out for a smoke. Don't move, OK?' He stood, gesturing to the cushion he'd just vacated. 'That's some prime real estate we've got there, best seat in the house. Guard it carefully. I'll get us a couple of drinks if the bar's not too busy. Be good.'

I didn't move from the couch. I didn't move for the next thirty fucking minutes, and now I really wish I had done.

I'm tired. Sol's sound asleep in bed next to me. Sporadic early morning traffic is rumbling along Brighton's seafront road, the noise dulled by the hotel's double-glazed windows. A slit of dawn light gleams where the heavy curtains don't quite meet. A straw-gold glow from the dimmed bedside light cocoons me in the dark.

We visited some unpleasant places last night. At times, I thought it would be better if we went our separate ways. But we've come back from those places with a renewed understanding of each other. I think it's made us stronger as a couple.

I'll write more later. I can hear people along the corridor going down for breakfast, as if this were an ordinary day. Which it is, of course. It's always an ordinary day, for someone, somewhere.

Sunday 13th July. Again

I give up. I fucking well give up. Is it possible to be too tired to sleep? My mind buzzes and I know it needs to rest before I sleep. Then I start worrying my thoughts will never rest and frustration rises at the prospect of not being able to sleep. Which, of course, makes sleep even more unlikely. I can't get out of the loop. Tomorrow's going to be tough. No, not tomorrow, today. It's close to 9 a.m. Just as I was nodding off earlier, some bastard-little children went hurtling along the corridor followed by parental voices, yelling for them to be quiet. And that was that. Awake, alert, frustrated. And, next to me, Sol snoring gently.

Writing helps. I feel calmer when I've got my thoughts safely down on paper. Without that, my brain keeps tossing the memories about as if to ensure they won't be forgotten.

So anyway, at Club Sybaris Sol had been gone for around twenty minutes, leaving me stuck on that leather couch. I was growing bored, restless, and feeling vulnerable without any possessions. If I'd had my phone, I would have texted or called to find out where he was. When I craned forwards, I could see most of the bar. No sign of him there. I had to inform a couple of people who'd asked about the spare seat beside me that it was taken.

Might he have bumped into Lou again? Or someone else? I told myself not to get jealous and irrational; he was simply gone a long time. There was bound to be some innocent explanation. But, given that I was alone in a strange place with my tits bared and zero possessions, I began to wonder what that explanation could be. If Sol was going to play the dom and limit my ability to function independently, wasn't it his duty to take care of me as promised? To make sure I wasn't in need of anything? That I was safe?

He'd said he'd only get drinks if the bar wasn't busy. Why the delay? I felt abandoned and stuck. I didn't dare go looking for him in case we ended up losing each other

entirely. All I could do was sit tight and wait. I was no longer the contented dormouse basking in his protective
leaves; I was trapped in a cage of invisible bars.

My indignation began to burn. So, when a cute, out-of-
breath guy in rock 'n' roll leather trousers, studded belt
and an excellent bare chest strung with silver pendants
asked if he could sit down, I said, 'Sure.'

That'll show you, Sol Miller, I thought. Assuming you
do actually deign to return at some point.

The guy plonked himself down, and my seat cushion
lifted with the force of him. With him came a scented
wave of body warmth, sweat and a hint of patchouli, a perfume I detest. Doubly so when I'm in a foul mood. His
skin and trousers squeaked against the leather upholstery.

'Sorry!' he hollered. 'Phew.' He leaned back against the
seat and tipped a beer bottle to his lips. As he moved, his
damp skin juddered on the couch. The reverberations
quivered in my own body, the faintest vibration travelling
from him to me through our shared seat. I let my leg rest
nonchalantly against his, twisting briefly aside to disguise
the deliberateness of my action. I wanted to flirt and make
Sol jealous. I'd long thought I was too old and smart for
game-playing and yet, all of a sudden, I wasn't.

'Haven't danced like that for months,' said my neigh-
bour, calling out to the space in front of him rather than
addressing me directly. He gulped more beer and then sat
with his head back, knees wide, his shoulders rising and
falling. He clasped his beer bottle between his open thighs.
I forgave him the patchouli oil.

'You mind if I have a tiny sip of that?' I asked. 'I'm spitting feathers and my friend's got my purse.'

He sat bolt upright. 'Go for it! Have a big sip!' He

passed me the bottle and raised his arse from the seat to dig into his back pocket.

I took a swig as he withdrew his wallet. 'I'll get us both a drink if you save this seat. Need to chill out awhile. I'm fucking wiped! What's your poison?'

I laughed. 'No, really. I'm fine.'

'I'm not asking how you are. I'm asking what you're drinking.'

'Honestly—'

'You'd be doing me a favour.'

'You sure?'

'Yes! Quick, before I change my mind!'

'Vodka tonic,' I said, smiling. 'Ice and a slice.'

'Coming right up!'

'Thank you.'

As the guy wove his way through the crowds, I smiled and sat back, feeling myself relax. He was far too young for me; or, rather, for my taste. But he was cute and the distraction would be welcome. I gazed at people milling about, chatting and dancing. A woman walked by with another woman on a leash, the latter wearing fluffy bunny ears. I spotted a guy getting his cock sucked in an ill-lit corner. I wondered what Misha used to get up to at nights like this, assuming he attended them and we weren't barking up the wrong tree.

Moments later, I saw Sol, face like thunder, shoulders twisting stiffly as he side-stepped between people until he was there by my side.

I made a watch-checking gesture. 'Hallelujah.'

He bent and seized me by my upper arm, forcing me to my feet. 'We're leaving.'

'Oi! What the fuck? Do you mind?'

He ushered me forwards with a deft shake, fingers digging into the sinews of my arm. Was this part of our act? A staged row?

'Sol! What's the urgency? Where the hell have you been?'

'I saw you,' he said, teeth gritted.

'What?' I stepped back a pace, rotating my shoulder to escape his grip.

He glowered from under his peaked cap, his face ruddy with heat. 'He was about to buy you a drink. I saw you so don't try denying it.'

I gave an astonished laugh. 'I'm not denying anything! He was only—'

He made to grab my arm again but I recoiled from him, apologising when I bumped into someone.

'Don't you ever dare try and humiliate me like that again,' he warned.

'Humiliate? You don't know the meaning of the word. Where have you been? He was buying me a drink because I've no cash on me. You left me stuck on that fucking sofa—'

'Yeah, I leave you alone and you start hitting on someone.'

Incredulous, I laughed again. 'Don't be ridiculous!'

'Anyway, time to go,' he said. 'I'm done here.'

'Good! Because so am I.' I began walking away, skirt swishing grandly. He quickly followed. 'And I'm done with pretending to be your bitch for the evening,' I called, not caring if I blew our cover.

'Tough shit.' He grasped my wrist and I flung him off. 'Because I already threw you out of the kennel, baby.'

His insult knocked the breath from me. For a moment,

all I could do was stand and stare as he continued for the exit. My heart thumped, my face ablaze. Keep a grip, Lana, I told myself. Don't stoop to his level. Count to ten.

I glanced around, self-conscious and wondering if anyone was observing us make idiots of ourselves. Having a public row is bad enough but a public row when you're half-naked and preposterously dressed was the height of uncool. Thankfully, no one seemed aware of us. I drew a deep breath and headed for the exit, edging apologetically past people. I moved with deliberate slowness in a bid to regain my dignity and composure.

I felt bad for the guy buying me a drink but didn't want to risk a scene by seeking him out to explain, not when Sol had my cloakroom ticket. At the counter near the exit, Sol was being handed my jacket. As I approached, he tossed the garment into my arms.

'Here,' he said. 'Cover yourself up.'

That's when I saw red. That's when I lost it. His attempt to shame me for being sexual, when earlier my breast-baring liberty had been a delight to him, infuriated. I was so enraged, I became icily controlled. I was head-to-toe steel.

I tipped my chin high, looked him straight in the eye, and emphatically said, 'Fuck you, Sol Miller.'

I turned and left the building without a backward glance. Outside, I kept walking, pushing my arms into my jacket and wrapping it tight around me. The night was warm and the jacket was light. I wished I'd had the courage to remain defiantly bare-breasted but didn't fancy getting arrested for indecent exposure. On the street, the rules were different.

The venue was behind a main road and bordering a desolate patchwork of tarmac, cobbles, pavement and unused parking spaces. Ahead of me, the rear of a line of old stone buildings faced a block of squat, derelict warehouses. Streetlights were few and far between, each one breaking up the darkness of the broad, empty street with a feeble amber haze. Metal shutters covered the entrances to the warehouse units, all bearing layers of dense, elaborate graffiti. In recent years, I've come to regard Brighton as a hip, stylish resort for young, wealthy people; a place for clubs, cafes, music and art. London-by-the-sea is its nickname. If I'd had more money, I might have set up a cocktail bar in Brighton rather than down-at-heel Saltbourne. But as I stumbled out of Club Sybaris, I knew we were in an area that the town forgot.

I glanced back. At the nightclub doorway, Sol had stopped to light a cigarette. Damn him! Damn him for bringing me here and making me wear this stupid, fucking, disco-witch costume. I tugged at the hairgrips securing my beret and tossed them away. I flung my hat to the ground. Turning, I saw him inhale deeply as he frowned into the sky. Bastard. I kept walking, sticking to the centre of the road and avoiding the shadows. The road was marked for deliveries, the vestiges of paint defining old loading bays on the stony, broken tarmac.

When I next looked over my shoulder, I saw Sol snatch his hand from his lips, standing stubbornly stock-still, save for angry little twitches. His foot tapped rapidly and his RAF cap was tucked under his arm. Smoke rushed from his lips. I had no money on me. The hotel was probably a thirty-minute walk away. Reception would be unlikely to issue me with a replacement key card if I had no ID.

On the uneven road, my heels clicked, sharp and hollow in the derelict street. Sol wouldn't let me make my

own way back, would he? He wouldn't be such an irresponsible cunt. I wished I smoked, not that I wanted to
keep company with him but because it always looked a
great way to handle anger, all that furious sucking while
pointedly not talking.

*Cover yourself up. Cover yourself up. I already threw you out
of the kennel, baby.*

From the club exit came a muffled blast of music.
Voices and laughter spilled out on to the street; then the
noise of the club became a faint deadened beat again. I
could hear the people heading for the main road. I should
have done that. Much safer. Was he still smoking?

Behind me, footsteps grew louder and quicker. I knew
it was him but I wasn't going to slow or turn around. I
didn't acknowledge him until he was by my shoulder,
when I had no choice.

He grabbed my arm, swinging me to face him.

'Stop touching me,' I yelled.

'Hey, hey!' His eyes were wide, his face flushed, his hair
hectic. In his hand, he carried both our hats, my beret
stuffed inside his cap. 'What the fuck are you doing?'

I continued walking. 'Getting away from you. What's it
look like?'

'Who was he?'

'Christ, Sol! Stop being such a dick. He was no one.
Some guy. What's the big deal?'

'The big deal?' He reached for my arm. I lashed out,
fending him off. 'You're meant to be with me,' he said,
voice raised. 'That's the big fucking deal. I put a collar on
you. You're mine till I take it off. Mine, Lana!'

I whirled around to him. 'No, Sol! That's a game, an
act. It's fake!'

'No, it isn't! You know it isn't!'

We glowered at each other, his words hanging in the air, their meaning refusing to unfurl.

'And anyway, what?' He opened his arms, glancing left and right as if being sarcastic to a crowd. 'You think you can just stop playing when it suits you?'

'*You* stopped!' I yelled. '*You* stopped looking after me. Left me alone with no money, no phone. Nothing! Our deal wasn't unconditional, Sol. You've got to play your part too. I'm not…not subbing if you're not domming. And by domming, I don't mean acting like a selfish, arrogant twat who thinks he can do whatever he wants.'

I gathered my skirt and stalked off.

'I met someone who knew Misha,' he called.

'Whoopee fucking doo.'

'You're a smart woman,' he continued. 'I assumed you'd be able to work out what I was doing. Maybe have a degree of faith in me? I couldn't just leave. He's the reason we're here in the first place, remember?'

He strode after me. I spun around to him, my skirt hissing and swinging. 'Misha, Misha, Misha! Why are you so obsessed with his death? Who is he to you?'

He glared at me, jaw set tight, chest pumping. Lamplight lent his dark hair a fuzz of gold, and his face glowed warmly while his eyes were sunk in shadow. Flecks of my purple glitter sparkled on one cheekbone.

I stared at him, trying to read his face. Why so obsessed, Sol? Why?

Is it, I thought, because you killed him? Is that the reason the damp towel was in my room at Dravendene? Did you murder him in the pool and then sneak back into my bed? Or was his death, and that rumoured head injury, a result of an accident you were involved in? And now are you desperate to trace his friends to check no one's suspicious? Is that why we're here? Or are you trying to ensure my silence by encouraging me to collude in some ham-fisted sleuthing?

Sol shook his head as if to dislodge his thoughts.

'Tell me,' I snapped.

Frowning, he slotted his cap under his arm and clasped both my wrists, pushing them apart, forcing my arms straight, and making my jacket gape. The night air was cool on my stomach. I recalled how he'd caught my wrist across the bar several days ago back at my place. At the time, even though his grip had excited me, I'd wondered if he had the knowledge to kill me with pressure points.

'Be mine again,' he said, his voice much gentler.

I wriggled, trying to withdraw from his grip. 'Sol! Don't try and change the subject. Talk to me.'

He grinned. 'Show me your tits.'

I scoffed. 'Fuck off.'

'Come on, Cha Cha. Don't be mean.'

'Two minutes ago you wanted me to cover them up.'

'Because I want them for me,' he said. 'No one else. For my eyes only.'

'They're my tits, Sol. Not yours.'

I tried to yank my hand free but he gripped harder, edging me towards the pavement. He was stronger than me and wearing polished black boots. My Pompadour heels stuttered as I was forced backwards between his sturdy footsteps, my stiff skirt rustling against his legs.

'Sol, no.' I grabbed the back of his jacket as we shuffled over an exposed patch of old cobbles. 'Careful!'

'Come on, Lana,' he breathed. 'I'm getting hard for

you again.'

When I stumbled on the low kerb, he was quick to grab me around the waist and pull me close. His instinctive protection touched and thrilled me. I felt myself yielding to him, forgiving him like a weak-willed idiot. His swollen cock bumped against my silks, making arousal flutter low in my body. Still with his cap tucked under his arm, he manhandled me towards the wall of an abandoned truckers' cafe, its window boarded up alongside a sign featuring colour-leached photographs of bacon and eggs. I writhed, squealing in protest even while a dark excitement rose inside me. Had he fought with Misha by the poolside? Was he dangerous? How aggressive could he get? How aggressive did I want him to be?

He shoved me against the wall, grappling with my jacket. 'Show me,' he urged. He batted away my hands and flung open my jacket, baring my breasts. His cap fell to the floor.

'Get off me!' I snapped, tugging my jacket together. 'Someone might see.'

'Hey, come on, Cha Cha.'

Grinning, he tried to wriggle his hands onto my naked skin. I squirmed and slapped as he rummaged and groped. All he did was laugh softly at my efforts, mocking me. Before long, I began to laugh too, still fighting him but with decreasing energy. I felt light-headed and reckless, drunk with emotion, not to mention alcohol.

'What is it?' He glanced over his shoulder at the deserted, poorly lit road. 'You want an audience, Cha Cha? Is that the problem?'

He massaged one bared breast. I rocked my head against the wall.

'You're the fucking problem,' I said mildly.

'You telling me you don't want this?' He ground against me, dabbing kisses over my neck. The rigid collar jabbed me, the barrel of its combination lock pressing in the hollow of my throat. Sol's kisses moved higher, growing stronger and sliding over my skin. His stubble grated and he smelled of fresh cigarette smoke. I pushed feebly against his chest as my groin began to pulse with hammering urgency. Then his voice was by my ear, a low, tender taunt. 'Come on, Lana. Don't lie to me. We both know the score here.'

I bit back a moan of longing. He took my wrists and spread my arms wide, pinning them to the wall. I was trapped between him and the forgotten cafe, my jacket parted to reveal a stripe of flesh. Lust plunged to my cunt so fast and fierce that I groaned, a deep gravelly sound of capitulation. Sol gazed down at my face, lips twisting in victory. Specks of purple and green glitter shone where he'd rubbed against my make-up. I thought of the ways in which we become each other's bodies, how a punch becomes a bruise, how fluids mingle in kisses and how I take him inside me, the boundaries of our selves no longer sealed and whole.

'Is that a no?' he asked. 'Because it sure doesn't sound like one.'

Between my thighs, my lips thickened and throbbed. I turned my head aside, wincing at my body's treachery. I was so easy and pliant, so horny for him.

'Much better,' he murmured. 'No point fighting it, is there, Cha Cha?'

He released my wrists and I let my arms drop to my side. He slipped his warm hands into my jacket and caressed my naked breasts with a greedy, commanding touch. My nipples shrivelled and his dark eyes scrutinised me all the while. When I whimpered, he smiled and murmured, 'That's my girl.'

I wanted to sink to the ground, annihilated by lust. I love his tender condescension with all its abusive implications. It's such a crafty means of making me feel powerless, a victim of sly manipulation.

'Sol,' I breathed. 'Let's go back to the hotel.'

He looked over his shoulder, grinning. 'But I want you now. C'mere. This way.'

'What are we doing?'

'Being us,' he said. 'Doing it our way. No games, no show. Just us. Hot for each other. Needing to fuck. Hard, rough, messy. You've no idea what you do to me, Cha Cha. I want to fuck you all the time.'

Damn, but he knew how to push my buttons. So sleazy and romantic. That was a combination to demolish me, if ever there was one. He retrieved his cap and I allowed him to guide me into a small recess between irregular backends of buildings. Redbrick, Victorian blocks with window grilles and zig-zag fire escapes rose like tatty tenements around us. At street level, a short flight of concrete steps, bordered by spiky black railings, led to a featureless rear door. Grass and weeds sprung up between cracks in the uneven ground. It was classic murder-victim territory. But this was central Brighton near a nightclub, adjacent to an old, wide road, and I told myself Sol wasn't that kind of guy. If something had happened between him and Misha, it belonged in another realm. Violence and lies had nothing to do with me, Sol, and this situation now. We were fine. I was safe in the sphere of his protection.

He led me towards the steps, half holding me, the two

of us becoming conspiratorial in a spirit of giddy rebellion. Lamplight edged the recess, gilding the black, scabby railings and glinting on shards of glass near the opposite wall. A hard shadow divided the area into triangles of dark and less dark, the dividing line demarcated on the ground. Sol guided me past the foot of the steps until we were leaning against their staggered, concrete side below the highest railings. He posted his cap through two railings and placed it on a step behind me. He pulled the speedcuffs from his pocket, his lively, dark eyes flicking up and down. I could practically hear his brain whirring as he assessed our location, working how to take advantage of such a secluded, no-go area.

'Sol, we'll get arrested.'

He covered my body with his, rubbing his erection against me with firm, deliberate strokes. He glanced towards the dead road. 'You see any cops around here?'

I laughed lightly, pressing my hand against his chest. 'CCTV.'

He clawed around my knees, lifting my vast skirt in clumsy stages. I stalled him, fingers circling his wrist.

'What?' he asked, looking up and about.

'CCTV! There's always CCTV.'

'No there isn't.' He forced my skirt higher, and, again, I half-heartedly pushed back. 'Not in places like this,' he continued. 'C'mon, relax, Cha Cha. I bet you're wet, aren't you? Don't tell me you're not.'

'Yeah, but if we went back to the hotel we could—'

'We've got all night at the hotel,' he breathed. 'And a late check out. So...' He delved into a deep pocket, whipped out the speedcuffs and grabbed one wrist. I yelped and struggled as he flicked one cuff and then the other on to my wrists. Before I knew what was happening I was restrained, the inflexible stem keeping my hands fixed apart.

'Gotcha,' he said, grinning.

'You fucker,' I replied, smiling. I was enjoying these cuffs, their rigidity and ugliness making them harsher than those I'd worn in the past. They felt less like cuffs for kink, and more like serious players, the real deal. Which they were, of course.

Sol locked the cuffs in place with the slim point of the key and popped it in his top pocket. He took a step back, looking up, down and around. Then he unthreaded the blue buckle-belt from his woollen RAF jacket. My desire pulsed, memories returning of him stripping his leather belt from his jeans in the forest at Dravendene. It's one of the finest sights, a man with menace in his eyes removing his belt.

He looped the belt around the broad black stem of the cuffs, tightening the buckle, and then raised the length of fabric, forcing my arms upwards. His hands worked above my head and I wriggled for a show of protest. I caught the scent of his sweat on the cool night air and I longed for him. Distant traffic and occasional voices were the only sounds around us. When he withdrew, I was tethered to the railings, my hands above my head. I kicked the concrete wall of the steps and tugged at the belt; then I thought I shouldn't do that in case I made the knots too tight to loosen.

'You bastard,' I said, smiling. 'If anyone walks past—'

'Yeah, I know. I'm outta here like a shot. Because it doesn't look good.'

'You wouldn't dare.'

Smiling, he opened my jacket and tucked it behind me. He stepped back and observed my body, his gaze lingering on my bared breasts. The streetlight tinted him with amber-gold, bringing out the rust undertones of his scruffy, cocoa-brown hair.

'Don't go away now,' he said, turning.

'Hey! Sol!'

He walked towards the opposite wall, in the darkness of our concrete recess, and unfastened his flies. He angled himself at the corner, adopting a wide-legged stance, and began to urinate. I had to stay there in the light, exposed, uncomfortable and powerless while he relieved himself in the shadows, hidden, comfortable and powerful. I watched him, admiring the broad muscularity of his upper body and the strength implicit in his hips. I listened to his stream fade to a trickle, saw him shake. Then, with a hitch of his shoulders, he tucked himself away. As he stepped back from the gloomy corner, he ducked down to retrieve an object from the ground. He sprang up and swung around, grinning like a maniac. To my horror, he was brandishing a sliver of thick, green glass, curved and narrowing to a ragged tip. He swayed towards me, his gait slinky with threat. Hazy light from the adjacent street caught the glass, glinting on its chipped, crystalline edge. It was probably a piece of broken bottle. But I saw a vicious, emerald dagger.

'If you scream, Cha Cha…'

I screamed.

I screamed because I saw a murderer approaching. I saw a man with a weight of guilt who wanted to secure my silence to save his skin. I saw a stranger in a drunk, dishevelled uniform, gold chevrons on his sleeve, chest exposed.

I saw a timeless zone of a coastal town, and I was in it, trapped, about to meet my doom. So what if that zone contained modern materials, electric light and a nightclub just minutes away? It was timeless because it was neglected, a hole in society where events went unrecorded. I could lie there, bleeding to death, and the world would be oblivious. And here was a man I barely knew, looming in with a nasty, evil weapon, leering in sadistic pleasure. He wore a uniform to inspire trust, and delude people into thinking he was decent and good. He'd get away with his crime.

I kept on screaming.

'Woah, Cha Cha!'

He flung the glass to the ground as he hurtled towards me. He clamped a hand to my mouth, slammed his body into mine. My head hit the concrete wall. 'Shut up! It's fine! Shut up! Easy now, hush!'

His hand was hot, his eyes wide and fearful.

My screams wouldn't stop. His panic worsened mine, which in turn worsened his. He pressed harder on my mouth, glancing wildly towards the road. I tried to shriek and shout. Pain bloomed inside my skull where I'd bumped it against the wall. My breath was trapped in a pocket of humidity. My inhalations sucked on damp skin. I kicked and jerked, the cuffs slicing into my wrists. My teeth bit into my crushed lips, his weight compressed my ribs.

Had Misha died like this, running out of breath?

'Shut up, Lana!' He shoved my head against the wall. The edge of his hand squashed my nostrils. My frantic movements wrenched my shoulders, made me pant for breath. I could find only thin streams of air to draw on. My nose and mouth were blocked. Was this how drowning felt, as oxygen faded? Screaming made it worse but I had to scream to make him stop and he wouldn't stop because I was screaming. He wouldn't stop because he was a callous, pitiless killer able to maintain control until the life in his hands petered to a stop.

We locked eyes as we fought, our hair awry, sweat and breath thick between us. A fleck of black paint from the railings lay on one of his cheekbones along with the glitter from my face. His eyes were lit with terror and no doubt mine were too. What else had he seen in his years so far? What twisted memories were lodged behind those eyes? What sort of memories was he laying down for his future self as my lungs shrivelled within my ribcage?

Then, for a sudden instant, I could breathe. Air overwhelmed me. Clarity pierced my stuffy senses. I inhaled a night sky of stars and it was immense, too big for my body. My breathing function froze. So did my voice. I gaped at the dark, my lungs refusing to operate, my throat making tiny, desperate croaks. Then starlight shattered inside my head as pain exploded across my face.

Sol had slapped me.

I panted, a stunned relief rushing through me.

'Easy now,' he said, shoulders pumping. 'That's right.' He swept a lock of curled hair from my face and hooked it behind one ear. 'You were hysterical. Breathe easy. Good girl.'

I calmed, drawing in streams of free-flowing air, heat stinging my cheek. Our dingy surroundings were as flat and lifeless as a stage set.

'You're OK,' continued Sol. 'I'm here for you. I'm not going to hurt you. It was a stupid joke, that's all, and I'm sorry. You OK?'

I shook my head, tears stinging. 'Hold me. I don't know

what happened.'

He stepped close and wrapped his arms around my waist, his clasp firm and reassuring. He rested a hand high on my back, an embrace signifying safety rather than passion. And yet, unmistakeably, digging into my belly, was the blunt, rock-solid bar of his erection. That he could be hard after such a battle astounded me yet he made no attempt to conceal his boner. Had the fight turned him on? Did he get a kick out of terrifying women?

'Hush,' he cooed, rubbing my back. 'All OK now.'

'You're hard,' I said in an accusatory breath.

'Yeah, sorry,' he murmured. 'My dick can't distinguish between fantasy and reality.'

'Jesus Christ.' I recoiled from his embrace, trying to thrust him away, hampered by having raised, cuffed arms.

'Hey, but my brain can.' His voice carried a resentful note. 'And that's what I think with, Lana. Stiff dick doesn't mean I don't care. Doesn't short-circuit my critical faculties.'

I pushed again with my arched torso and shoved at his shin with one foot. 'Go away. Leave me alone. And get these cuffs off me.'

'Which one? Back off or unlock the cuffs?'

'Back off! I don't trust you.'

'Holy fuck, give me a break, Cha Cha!' He stepped away, palms raised in a gesture of peace. The paint fleck had gone from his cheek. 'Look, sorry I scared you. But don't try and claim this was about me getting my rocks off.'

I was jittery and hot. Sweat trickled down my back. 'I just don't want you near me right now, OK?'

'Because what? I'm a monster, a pervert? Hell, Lana,

get some perspective.'

'You just scared me half to death,' I yelled, tugging at my tethered wrists. 'So, yes, my perspective is probably shot! How about we factor that in and make this about *my* pain, not yours. Jeez, cut me some slack, Sol!'

He withdrew his cigarettes, cool as can be. 'Ah, the guilt trip.'

'What?'

He didn't reply, lighting a cigarette instead. The flame cast a reflection on his profile and glowed in the tips of his messy, dark fringe. He inhaled, stepping back and turning aside, purposefully ignoring my presence. Smoke drifted from the cigarette in a thin, blue-grey stream.

'Why did you do it, Sol?' I called. 'To punish me?'

He released smoke as he turned to address me, frowning. 'What?' he asked in a quiet, baffled tone.

'For talking to that guy? You wanted to scare me to get revenge?'

He made a noise of exasperation, half twisting away again. He pulled on his cigarette, exhaling before answering. 'I get it,' he barked. 'I screw up, make one tiny mistake, and you start laying into me.' He swung around, poking the air with his cigarette, emphasising his point with an angry gesture. 'Listen, sweetness, I'm done with those kinds of relationships. If you think—'

'No!' I pitched forwards, furious and frustrated. 'Don't go projecting your baggage on to me.'

'*My* baggage?' He gave a hollow laugh. 'Mine? So what in hell's name was that about? Kicking off when I'm just fooling around with a bit of glass? What's your story, huh? What's your excuse, Lana?'

'Oh, that's rich!' I said. 'So now you attacking me is *my*

fault?'

'I didn't attack— Oh, man, this is insane! In-fucking-sane.' He stalked away, sucking hard on his cigarette, his back to me.

'Unfasten me,' I demanded. 'Get me out of these cuffs.'

He whirled around. 'You mean it this time?'

'Yes!'

He threw his half-smoked cigarette to the ground. 'Happy to oblige. Your freedom is my freedom, Cha Cha.'

He fished around in his pocket, withdrew the key, and then reached above my head to release the cuffs. I stepped away from the wall, rubbing my raw, grazed wrists while he untied the belt from the railings. I pulled my jacket over my breasts and turned to address him, chin jutting in defiance.

'And the collar.'

He gazed at me, stuffing the cuffs and belt into a pocket. His eyes were wet black pebbles in the depths of shadows, his frown dragging his brows together. He glanced at the collar and back to my face, his expression softening. 'Lana...'

I shook my head, lips tight. 'Remove it, Sol. You don't have my submission anymore. I'm not yours.'

'Lana, please.' He reached out a hand to me. 'Why are we doing this?'

I stared at him, confused, and didn't take his hand.

'Why are we fighting?' he continued.

'Because you're a prick?'

His lips twitched with a hint of amusement. 'Apart from that?'

'I don't know,' I said, folding my arms. 'Enlighten me. Why *are* we fighting?'

'Because we're starting to care about each other?' he

suggested. 'And we're too afraid to admit it?'

I recalled sitting with him on the balcony of The Blue Bar, trying to make tentative enquiries about his feelings, and being curtly rebuffed. *I don't want to fall in love, Lana*, he'd said.

'No,' I replied. 'It's definitely because you're a prick.'

He laughed. 'OK, you win. You still want me to take the collar off?'

'Yes.'

He stepped closer, so his body was only an inch or two from mine. I stood my ground, proudly raising my chin and wishing I could kiss his stupid, smoky, sexy lips. He took the barrel of the combination lock in both hands, his arms jutting like wings either side of me. A lazy shiver of pleasure rolled down my spine.

'You sure this is what you want, Cha Cha?'

'Yes.'

His lips moved towards mine and my skirt hissed as his feet edged closer. I was stock still. Stones grated under his boot soles. Other than the purr of distant cars, the night was quiet. I fancied I might be able to hear waves breaking on the shingle beach if I listened hard enough. The ratchets of the first number clicked faintly as Sol's fingers twisted the wheel. Overhead, a lone seagull wailed, its cry fading as it passed. I put my arms by my side.

Sol's breath warmed my cheek. The voice in my ear was deep, languorous and seductive. 'Eight,' he whispered.

Desire sunk to my groin and pulsed there. I swallowed nervously. That single word was so rich and sexy. Sol's slow articulation made the innocent number sound like a delicious warning. My mind returned to our first encounter, when he'd ordered Misha to lick me while he'd

counted down to my climax. That seemed so long ago
now. I pushed the thought aside. I didn't want to dwell on
the past.

His fingers edged along the barrel. His lips brushed my
cheek in a half-kiss. His hips swayed towards me and his
crotch bumped lightly against my belly, a fleeting touch
but enough to indicate he was still hard.

The second metal wheel clicked below my chin. Tiny
vibrations rippled in the hollow of my throat as his fingers
moved.

'Five,' he breathed.

The word slid into my consciousness like an enchant-
ment, tempting me towards blissful oblivion. I felt as if he
were relaying a heavily guarded secret which would put
me in mortal danger. His manner, intimidating and indolent, made me dizzy with longing. He was teasing and
testing, refusing to unlock the collar in a manner that
might imply deference to my demand.

In the aftermath of my crazy screaming fit, I was suddenly tired. His fingers worked on the third wheel. My
sluggish brain churned, processing the implications of
him revealing the next number. If he told me the third
digit, the fourth, final number could be only one of ten
options. I would practically have the combination, rendering the collar as good as useless. The key to my freedom
would no longer be safe in Sol's brain, nestled among
unknown dark thoughts. I would share the number. I'd be
able to remove the collar as and when I wished. It would
become a meaningless ornament, a piece of jewellery and
no more.

His fingers slowed, his lips moved towards my ear. He
was about to give me the third number, to hand over his

symbolic power, but I couldn't let him.

'No!' I gasped. 'Stop! Don't tell me.'

He paused but didn't retreat. His warm lips fluttered silently against my ear; then he leaned his body closer, cock still erect. 'No?'

'Stop,' I breathed. 'I don't want to know.'

His voice was low and amused. 'You don't?'

'No, please.'

'Why not, Cha Cha?'

I pressed my lips together, embarrassed that I was asking for this; that I was having to admit my hunger to submit was stronger than any need to win a fight.

'It's yours,' I whispered. 'You have it.'

'It?'

'The number.'

'Uh huh. And what else do I have?' He held still, fingers poised on the lock, lips by my ear. 'What else is "it"?'

I slumped, tension leaving my body in a sigh of relief. 'Me.'

He spun the digits on the barrel lock and released his grip on the collar. 'That's what I like to hear.'

Oh, that soft, solicitous tone again. He slid a broad, warm hand onto my bare waist, nudging under one strap of my braces. 'So you want to wear my collar,' he said. 'Until when, Cha Cha?' He caressed firmly, his hand sliding up towards my breast, teasing me. My groin swayed towards his.

'I don't know,' I said.

He thumbed my tight nipple. 'She doesn't know. I like that too. C'mere. Let's sit down. You feeling better now?'

He led me towards the steps and I was grateful for the breather. The stone was cool and hard beneath my

costume. Sol sat by my side, midway and on the step below
me. He rubbed my thigh through my big skirt. In the half
light, the shot silk flickered between blackish purple and
green, the street light gathering in its dips like pools of
molten gold.

'Let's stay here awhile,' he said. 'Take a moment.'

He pushed my skirt higher, baring my shoes and shins
as he bunched folds of iridescent fabric around my knees.
Between my thighs I was swollen and heavy, thumping
with need. Having only recently rebuked Sol for mis-
placed lust, my own arousal made me guilty.

'The collar looks good on you,' he said.

'Feels good,' I murmured, touching the chunky lock.

He dipped his hand under my skirt and grasped me
above the knee, his touch sliding inwards.

'You sure we can't be seen?' I asked.

'Positive.' His hand glided towards my crotch. 'You
disappointed?'

I laughed and leaned back, letting my knees flop open.
The steps' corners dug lines into my back. I felt like a
Victorian whore, voluptuous and easy, and I liked it.

Sol grazed his thumb back and forth over my knickers.
My plump, wet lips filled the dampening gusset. I clasped
the railing, the thick paint blistered and scabby in my fist.

'Let's take a look at that pretty little pussy.' He hooked
his fingers high into my underwear and tugged. I raised
my butt from the step so he could ease the garment down.
Night air on my bared, wet crease made me shiver with
the thrill of misbehaviour. He wriggled my knickers off
and stretched them in both hands, pulling the gauzy black
fabric taut.

'Give me your ankle,' he said, grasping it. He nudged

my leg sideways then wrapped the silk and gauze around my ankle, fastening me to the railing, my foot on the step. The corroded metal scratched unpleasantly on my skin. Sol cursed under his breath as he pulled the delicate fabric tight, fumbling over a double knot. I tried not to think of how much the knickers had cost me. When he was satisfied with his handiwork, he nudged my other foot towards the wall of the steps so my legs were spread, one forcibly, the other willingly. He sat in the gap of my thighs, leaning against me so my free leg was no longer quite so free. He murmured appreciatively as he pushed my skirt up to my hips, taffeta rustling into corrugations, leaving my swollen split bared to him, surrounded by a froth of shimmering skirt.

'If they could see you now,' he said. Gently, he trailed a finger over my pouting lips, watching my expression as he teased me. 'All those people from the club, standing around, wanting to fuck you. But they can't because you're mine, aren't you?'

My flesh tingled beneath his finger. He continued stroking me awhile and though the night was warm, goosebumps prickled across my skin. He parted me, gliding gently along my slippery centre, and smiled to see me arch and whimper. Finally, when I thought his leisurely caress might send me mad with horniness, he eased a single finger into me. I groaned in pleasure-tinged frustration. I wanted so much more. My cunt ached with emptiness and I craved a thick, solid, rough penetration. He stroked within me and I bucked against his hand, frantic to be pushed open and filled.

'Greedy,' he reproached. 'Keep still or you get nothing.'

I moaned, fighting the instinctive rise of my pelvis, and

allowed him to continue with his tease. He inched higher up my body, half kneeling so he was closer to my face but not close enough for kisses. He brushed his thumb over my clit, his gaze still fixed on my reactions. I gasped lightly as his thumb swirled circles over the tender nub. Hot, fierce blips leaped to meet his touch.

'I wish they were all here now,' he murmured. 'All watching you, their dicks getting harder and harder. I'd tell them they could fuck you but they'd need to form a line and be patient. Because I'm first.'

With a measured pace, he drove a second finger into me, curling both onto my sweet spot. The thumb fretting my clit grew firmer. Tremors flared and faded along my inner thighs as he continued speaking, his words stimulating my imagination while his hand did likewise to my body. Although I was sprawled on a flight of derelict, weedy steps, his words transported me. I was wherever he said I was, and with whomever he conjured up.

'It's not that I'm desperate to fuck you,' he went on. 'I just want to ensure all my nice, new friends have a first-rate experience with you. I'm a generous guy, see, and I like to impress. So I need to prep you first, loosen you up, make sure you're wet and easy. Make sure you're gagging for cock, even though you won't admit it. So I'd fuck you hard, checking you were good enough to be offered up for use. Then, once I was done, I'd step back from you and I'd say to the guy at the head of the line, "She's ready for you, dude. If she complains, take no notice. I'll gag her if she gets annoying." And I'd zip up while my friend unzipped. Then he—'

But I never learned what happened next because I drowned out his voice with my groans, tension tightening at my core, lifting me. I started to come, my body crunching and jerking, my senses scattering in the delirium of bliss. I wailed as quietly as I could while orgasmic ripples seized me, my leg tugging at the restraint around my ankle. In my mind's eye, Sol's new friends crowded around us, populating the grimy recess where I reclined on concrete steps, tethered to the railings, my thighs spread open. Their presence shamed me because their lechery caused my pleasure. The circle looped in vicious infinity, pleasure causing shame, and shame causing pleasure.

Sol's real-life voice drifted into my imaginary scenario. 'Hot little bitch,' he murmured, his fingers still inside me.

My peak ebbed away, leaving me reeling in its aftermath, depleted of strength.

'I could feel your pussy gripping my hand,' said Sol. 'You liked my bedtime story?'

I nodded, glowing with contentment and experiencing a huge rush of warmth towards him. I felt recognised and understood. No man had ever done that before, had taken the seed of a fantasy I'd owned up to and spun it into a bespoke narrative for my enjoyment. Away from the bustling theatricality of Club Sybaris, we'd found a dirty, secret space of our own where we could conspire and dream, beyond the pale. It seemed an intimacy greater than fucking. The secrets we shared were mounting: the threesome, the lies, the pretence, the sex.

Sol withdrew his fingers and half stood to unzip his flies. We froze simultaneously at the sound of a car rumbling along the adjacent road. My heart skipped a beat. Sol turned, watching over his shoulder.

'Unfasten me,' I urged. 'We'll be spotted.'

'Wait,' he said, eyes on the section of road running past

our hideaway.

'Sol, please!'

He rummaged in his trousers and his cock sprang free, jutting at an angle and gloriously hard. He grasped my hand, making me let go of the railing, my anchor, and pulled my fist onto him. He was thick, warm and resilient in my grip. As the purr of the car engine grew louder, I laughed, realising Sol was getting a kick from the risk. So I played along to accommodate his pleasure, trusting him to judge the situation. Gently, I worked his length, relishing how his smooth skin slipped over its bone-hard sub-structure. The beam of headlights shone onto the dark road ahead. The car moved closer as my heart beat faster. Seconds later, a taxi crawled past, its driver a dark silhouette in the grey interior. I slowed, fearing the man would turn and see us, me wide-legged and jerking off a guy. Then the cab was gone, engine fading.

Sol gave a quiet laugh. 'Phew.'

'Let's go back to the hotel,' I said. 'Get comfy.'

Sol turned, knocking my hand from his boner.

'But I don't want comfy.' His voice had a sudden edge to it. 'I want you here on these steps. Want you in this skanky part of town. Want to treat you like the greedy little slut you are.' He pulled a foil from his pocket and tore it open with his teeth, spitting out the strip and tossing the wrapper to the ground. He rolled the rubber onto his cock. 'Sorry there's only one of me, Cha Cha. But, trust me, I can make it feel like ten.'

He raised himself over me, his cock bumping at my entrance. He grabbed my wrist, pinning my arm awkwardly above my head as he drove into me. His bulky shaft pushed me open, my heavy, wet insides clinging to his thickness. I cried out, as thrilled by the hand squeezing my arm as I was by the cock surging into me. He shoved high and hard, his fingers tight around my wrist.

'There we go,' he said. 'Nice and gentle to start with, huh? Build you up to it.' The steps dug into my shoulder blades as he fucked me in long, slow thrusts. His blunt end bumped at my inner flesh, seeking the furthest reach of me. He shifted the angle of his strokes as if determined to rub himself into every slick, pulpy millimetre of my enveloping grip. His jacket gaped, baring his broad hairy chest, and its weighted pockets bashed into the steps.

'You want it harder, slut?'

'Yes. God yes.'

He built up speed, hips pumping, fast, aggressive, greedy. My head bumped against the uppermost step. I gasped, swamped by pleasure. A nagging voice told me I should be wary of him but I didn't listen to a word. I raised my head, grabbing the railing with my free hand. A step grated against my lower back, rubbing my skin raw. I didn't care. My breasts bounced as he pounded into me. Sensation overwhelmed me, his driving cock hitting my most sensitive, tender depths, turning me soft inside. And throughout, he held me spread open beneath him, my leg tethered to the railing, my opposite arm pressed into the steps.

I was his, splayed. I was my fantasy and so was he. He'd arranged my body to suit his purposes, and I had no choice but to let him fuck me however he wished. For the first time in a while, I felt safe with him. He might be dangerous, yes, and a man not to be trusted. But the very elements that ought to have frightened me made me want to be taken under his wing. Because, sure, if you were on the wrong side of him, this man was trouble. But if you were on the right side, and he wanted to protect you, then the fear belonged to other people. I was safe within the sphere of his dubious power. Safe getting ruthlessly fucked by him in a neglected part of town.

'You want it harder, Cha Cha?'

The question was rhetorical. Harder wasn't possible. Tremors bunched in my thighs, my swollen clit responding to every fleeting touch of his body. In the quiet night, my gasps were loud and incongruous. Above me, he grunted with rising urgency, his noises like knots tugging in his throat. I could tell he was close, oblivious to how he sounded, not caring where or who or when he was. The noises had to come out; he couldn't keep them down. I remembered his inhuman howl when we'd fucked on the forest floor, far away from everyone. As he thrust into me, his cock banging deep, I felt we owned the world. We *were* the world. We were there at the beginning of time, emotionally overwrought in a hellish, leafy paradise, and now we were here at the end in this decrepit dystopia, fearful of cameras, cars, people and each other. We were everything. We were infinite. And it was as tragic as it was beautiful.

Then I was coming hard, memories of his primitive cries mingling with his presence. He responded with high, thin groans of breathy disbelief. His grip tightened around my wrist and he arched his neck. He groaned, slowing, then he came, his staccato cries prefacing his spurts and shudders. His noises dropped to silence. For a moment he was poised above me like a half-fallen statue, his head bowed. Sweat gleamed on his collarbones, and the military squareness of his shoulders filled my vision. After a short moment, he withdrew and slumped towards me with a grunt, releasing my wrist. He nestled into my neck, his breath streaming over my skin, and rested his hand on my stomach.

'Lana,' he breathed.

I said nothing.

'Lana,' he repeated.

I toyed idly with his hair. 'I'm listening.'

He didn't reply and we lay there, sprawled on the grubby steps, me with my leg still attached to the railings, his collar still fixed around my neck.

At length, he said, 'Lana, do you feel guilty?'

'All the time,' I replied quietly. 'It's a woman's lot. You?'

'Yeah. All the time.' He gave a soft laugh. 'It's a Jew's lot.'

For a long while, we didn't speak. We were motionless on the steps, my hand in his hair, his hand on my belly, the two of us feeling guilty but unable to say why.

I stopped writing there to look at him, lying peacefully beside me in the hotel bed. He sleeps as if he hasn't a care in the world while I'm anxious and restless, unable to fall. Dawn has slid into mid-morning, and all I've managed to do is nap. When I was gazing at him just now, thinking we'd need to check out in a couple of hours and wondering how things would be in the future, his eyes flicked open. He looked directly up at me, expression unchanged. I think he'd sensed me watching him, as if I'd filtered into his dreams.

'You doing, Cha Cha?' he mumbled.

'Writing.'

'What you writing?'

'My diary.'

He gave a sleepy half-laugh, eyelids dropping shut. He rolled towards me and slotted his hand between my thighs. 'All your secrets,' he murmured.

No, I thought. Not all of them.

Part 5

Monday 4th August

I haven't written here for a few weeks, and for a good reason. Very good! We are an item, a couple, exclusive and monogamous. I refer to him as my boyfriend, amused to be forty-one and using the language of giddy teens. I feel inappropriate and vulgar; mutton dressed as lamb; woman being girl. Girl. His girlfriend. He's thirty-eight. I joke that he's my toyboy. It feels as if we raided a sweetshop and ran off with all the Haribo. We're gorging on rainbows and nobody else can share; nobody can understand what it means to be this alive.

Logic tells me I've been here before. This is infatuation, in love, insanity. It's a common chemical imbalance and I've no reason to feel so goddamn smug, as if he and I are the only ones ever to take this path, hand in hand, tongue around tongue. But logic can go fuck itself because I'm eating all the rainbows, and sweet, succulent colours run riot in my veins. Now we've made this commitment to each other, there's no stopping us. The game playing's off. Caution's sulking in a corner. My knickers are in shreds. My heart is bursting. We are drunk on our desire.

Most week nights, Sol swaggers into The Blue Bar straight from work, hot, sweaty, dirty, stinking of building site and as randy as a bull. I'm neat, petite and blonde, and he wants to mess me up. He drinks bottled beer, grins mischievously, and for the next hour or so, we chance it. If no customers are in, he'll paw and grapple, nuzzling close or landing a swipe or two on my butt. I play at being nervous and disapproving, wriggling away because it's fun to do so, and, anyway, I truly am nervous.

But my man, my strapping, sexy, hungry bastard, he won't take no for an answer. Before long, my skirt's around my hips and his cock's inside me, fat, urgent and thrusting. We'll fuck over an oak table in one of the church-pew booths or up against the bar. Sometimes we fuck behind the bar, pretending we have customers in and he's humiliating me in front of an audience. I do my best to keep an eye on the monitor relaying images from the street-level doorway. The stained-glass doors open on to the balcony, catching glints of sunlight in their leaded blue-green tiles. August heat fills the room. We're grateful whenever a breeze steals in to trickle over patches of damp, bared skin. Sometimes, when I'm dazed with bliss, I lose sense of where I am. The LED counter casts its sapphire blue haze and the glass doors sparkle like gems made of tropical seas, a glitter of turquoise and jade. I swoop through my surroundings, flying into cerulean skies or swimming in subaquatic depths. When I come, my world turns watery and I float in its etherised blur.

I can't get enough of us. In the late afternoons, it's mainly fucking, maybe a little spanking, or the type of cocksucking he refers to as 'service provision' where he holds still while I work him, careful not to spoil my make-up for my evening behind the bar. Invariably, he tops me with his attitude and his muscle. It's embedded in the way he moves and holds me, in the half-hypnotic words he mutters in my ear. He likes to claw my buttocks as we fuck, and my skin is flecked with scarlet marks. When I go for my late-morning swim, I sport the evidence of aggressive, reckless sex. The younger Lana would have been embarrassed but not me, not any more. I'm proudly, defiantly happy. The wounds put an extra wiggle in my stride as I make my way to the poolside. Can they see? Do I care? Hell no. And, best of all, the wiggle's still there when I'm fully dressed and no one's in the neighbourhood to see me.

One time we fucked in the Ladies' loo, watching the empty bar through the two-way mirror, the sensuous oak, leather and lapis lazuli blues contrasting with the tiled white sterility surrounding us. He had me bent over the sink, inches away from a streaming tap, threatening to stick my head in the water to show me who was boss. I had to make a dash for it when three young women entered the bar, glancing warily around in search of life.

'Hi, ladies!' I breezed into the room, straightening my clothes and caressing my wiggle. 'It's Happy Hour till seven!'

I fiddled about behind the counter as they pored over their menus, praying none of them would need to powder their nose. I knew Sol would be watching me through the glass, probably finishing himself off, his big dick in his big fist, but what could I do? How could I get him out without any of them noticing? A few minutes later, Sol sauntered from the bathroom, grinning as if he hadn't a care in the world. Two of the women glanced at him. I repressed a smile as I searched for something to say, concerned they'd realise we'd been up to no good.

'All fixed, ma'am.' He raised his pinched fingers and stuffed them in his jeans pocket. 'Your washer needed replacing.'

'Oh, great, thanks.'

His grin broadened as he headed for the exit. 'Any time, Cha Cha. You call me if things get wet again.'

My hidden smile turned to laughter.

Damn, I adore his cheek.

Raphael or Bruno clock on at six as usual. Then, depending on how busy we are, Sol and I will take the rear stairs and head across the cobbled mews to my flat for a couple of hours. I tell the guys we're going to eat and sometimes we do, but sometimes we just fuck again and then I wolf down some cheese and crackers. I'm sure the twins know what we're up to. Their grins are bigger than ever but they're polite so they act oblivious. I've given Sol the code for the gate to the courtyard so he can park his car if there's space but I haven't given him a key to my flat. I'm not quite ready for that yet. My home is still my own. Most nights, I'm back at the bar for nine, where I'll work until midnight, full of the joys. Sol stays at the flat, watching TV, cooking, napping, reading, or playing video games. He's brought his Xbox over and he puts his laundry in with mine. I bought him an ashtray but asked that he smokes out of the windows or on the back patio, and he said he does that at his own place, anyway.

He's a fairly tidy guy but, during the day, I find evidence of his presence strewn around the flat, and the reminder of him warms me. He devours thrillers, leaving fat curling paperbacks with gold embossed covers splayed open, their pages folded, their spines cracked. I feel a certain amount of identification with those books: well-thumbed, well-read, sought out with a robust, compulsive hunger. Neither I nor those paperbacks are held at a distance, and nicely preserved. Our physicality is incorporated into his because he's greedy to have us, his possessions. We get his attention, one hundred percent, and he treats us with a rough carelessness born of wanting. He lays waste to us in his cherishing. His fingerprints are everywhere, and he's dog-eared my heart.

He wears glasses to read, and he looks seriously sexy and sexily serious, a debauched evil genius. He's generally in bed by the time I'm home, occasionally reading but usually not because it's late. The windows are raised and the blinds are angled to allow air into the room, slats of white light from the mews striping the bed. If he's awake, he'll give me a dozy, welcoming smile as I join him and I know he's getting hard under the duvet. If he's asleep, he'll stir and instinctively roll over to embrace me. Invariably I manage to wake him fully because his nearness makes me horny and I'll never get to sleep if we don't fuck each other senseless. We have sex when I've got my period too. I'm pleased he's not one of those guys who are prissy about blood. Far from it. He revels in the slippery chaos, and he likes making, as he calls it, 'a butcher's shop' of the bed.

I know I ought to be more concerned about what might have happened between him and Misha at Dravendene Hall but the more I know him the more I trust him. I don't think he's capable of inflicting deliberate harm. Accidental, perhaps, but aren't we all? If he has a secret, I'll guard it with him should he need me to do so. But he's not asking me, and I'm not quizzing him. I'll wait until he's ready, even if he's never ready. And, in the meantime, I'll try and forget that I ever found a horrible, damp, chlorine-scented towel in my turret room. The threesome never happened. That worn, salmon-pink towel does not exist.

After midnight, in the depths of dark, we often take sex to the next level. Considering he claims to have only recently begun exploring his dominant side, he appears to know what he's doing and certainly isn't reticent about expressing his desires. I suspect he's been practising this for longer than he's letting on. He told me he'd been to a couple of fet nights in the US, after initially claiming he'd never been to such a thing. He was quick to suss out how my speedcuffs worked, and he knows his way around knots too. Sexually, he's able to strike the perfect balance, ensuring I'm OK without letting that detract from our nasty games. Is the latter an instinct or a learned skill, I wonder?

He hasn't told me much about his long-term ex, Helena in New York, but I wonder if perhaps their relationship had a DS dynamic. Maybe he doesn't want to talk about it. Maybe he wants to make me feel special by having me believe he's never shared anything so depraved. Mind you, I've had more than my fair share of twisted, dominant lovers, and I've never known anything as good as this. Even so, I'm pretty sure there's something Sol's not telling me about his life to date. But, again, if he has kinky secrets, I can wait.

When it's late, he often cuffs my wrists and shoves my head into the pillows, refusing to fuck me until I've begged for what I want. He makes me debase myself; that's the worst and the best of it. *He* doesn't do it to me. I do it to myself. Sometimes, he makes me select the handcuffs I'd like used on me from the drawer containing my collection. He makes me bring my choice to him by holding it in my mouth, crawling to him on all fours, like a dog fetching a toy for its master. Other times, he uses rope to truss me in all manner of configurations, his favourites being the ones where I'm stripped of my dignity, ankles by my ears, belly in folds, my arse and cunt on view. He uses a vibrator as a cruelty, shaming me for coming and for enjoying his perversity.

I usually remove my make-up before getting into bed. Some nights he'll ask – no, *tell* – me not to because he wants to fuck my throat while I'm nice and neat, and I refuse to let him do that at the start of an evening. Which, of course, makes him want to do it all the more. But I make him wait. Then, at night, he shoves with rough, crude strokes till mascara streaks my cheeks and my mouth is a smear of Pleasure Me Red or Ruby Woo. Then he comes on my face, ruining my public self. He'll grasp a fistful of hair, insisting I take a look at my reflection. Bars of lamplight from outside slice through the blinds and fall raggedly across my body. The image in the mirror is of a broken whore, a defeated clown, her lips bleeding into a blotchy face, his cream sliding into her inky tears.

All my outlines are gone, and it feels the same on the inside too.

'That's how badly you want it,' he once said, addressing the mess of my face in the glass. 'That's how low you'll stoop for it. Greedy little slut. What are you?'

Afterwards, he holds me close, soothing me when I'm broken and sore, making me whole again.

'You're so strong,' he once said. 'I couldn't do what you do, Cha Cha. Couldn't risk falling apart like that. I've got to stay in control.'

But I can only risk falling apart because he makes it safe for me to do so. He'll catch me if I fall. He'll piece me back together. We're co-conspirators, and ours is a beautiful, complete cycle; a process of abandoning ourselves to dark, erotic pleasures then returning to the light, sharing and understanding, adoring each other for wanting to play this way.

And then I sleep. Finally, I can. After so many restless nights since Misha's death, I sleep a deep, sound, restorative sleep. I seldom even wake when Sol gets up at seven. He's gone by half past. We see less of each other at weekends because I'm busy with the bar and he returns to Brighton, further along the coast, joking that his dick's had it and he needs some sleep. He usually observes the Jewish Sabbath, too, despite identifying as an agnostic Jew, so Friday nights and Saturdays are his. 'An ethnic habit,' he said. 'I don't light candles or go to synagogue. I just chill the fuck out.'

I'm considering offering the twins some extra hours to free up more of my time. I'd like to visit Sol's flat, see him in his own space, but he claims it's too cramped. Instead, he says we should take a trip to his London house some time.

'Don't you have family there?' I said, flattered but horrified.

'Distant family.'

'And you'd introduce me?'

'Sure, why not? You think you could act Jewish and get them off my back?'

He is sexy, irreverent, charming and smart. With him, I've remembered the joy and rootedness that sexual, emotional intimacy can bring. I look back on my life pre-Sol, when I was single and dating, and I see a woman who doesn't realise she's living with a void, oblivious to the scar tissue that's hardened her heart. I wasn't looking for love. I'm still not. But I think it's trying to find me. And, to my surprise, I'm not running scared.

All this has happened since we decided to put the riddle of Misha's death behind us. After fucking on the steps near Club Sybaris, we had a heart to heart in the hotel room, lying in bed in the curtained dark, spooning loosely, the aircon whirring and clicking. Without the aircon, the room was stuffy, its windows locked tight, but the aircon was noisy so we kept it on low.

'I was out of order, I'm sorry,' he said, his voice low, croaky and regretful. 'But I hated seeing you with someone else. Made me think I might lose you. Jealous, possessive. Ugly emotions, I know. But I've had so much loss in my life that I'm in constant fear of more.'

'Everyone fears loss.'

'Yeah, probably. But not everyone acts as if they've the right to demand reparation.'

Behind me, he sighed heavily and his breath stirred my hair. I was still wearing the collar, enjoying the mild discomfort and the sense of him resting around my neck, encircling the route between my heart and my brain. Guarding it with his combination lock.

'I'm not trying to make excuses,' he continued. 'I just want to tell you how it is for me. How I feel as if can never trust anything. Can never enjoy happiness without fearing it's going to be snatched away.'

I felt him shift higher up the bed and prop his elbow on the pillow. He stroked from my waist up to my shoulder blade and down again. My skin was moist with sweat.

'It's one of the reasons I like to keep moving,' he said. He rubbed my hip, his touch distracted and familiar. 'As a kid I got used to being between two homes, Queens and London. Now, not settling means lower risks. Keep ahead of the game, ahead of surprise and tragedy. Change, move. Try and outwit the future that wants to ruin your belief you're in control of your life.'

'None of us are in control,' I said. 'We just keep trying to convince ourselves we are. Because the reality of our powerlessness is too much to bear.'

'Yeah. And I need to let go of this. Of this dumb idea I can find out why Misha died. Accept it was a tragic accident. Move on. I shouldn't have left you alone in the club like that. I'm sorry. But I wasn't thinking straight. My priorities were fucked. I thought I'd got a lead on Misha and, suddenly, that was all that mattered. Selfish. Irresponsible. I know. I don't want to harp on about this, Lana. Don't want to make you my shrink. But like I said, there's been so much death in my life. It's as if that's compelling me to find a reason to explain it all, to make sense of it. Truth is, shit happens. I'm not to blame for these deaths. Mustn't feel guilty. Don't need to hunt for a reason to let me off the hook for something I'm not even responsible for. Sorry. About tonight. About this. About me being a prick.'

I wriggled around to lie on my back so I could see him. In the room's heavy darkness, his face was pale and indistinct. A shoulder was angled above the bed covers like a listing ship, a film of sweat glossing its muscular curve. He gazed beyond me into the middle distance. I slipped my fingers under the cover to stroke the side of his torso where the drifting seed heads were inked, one for every loss.

'It's OK,' I said. 'Your life hasn't been easy.'

'No. But I mustn't let that ruin the life I've got ahead of me.' He looked down, a hand rubbing my stomach, his smile tired. 'I like you, Lana. You're hot, smart. Fun to be with. You don't take any shit. I love what we've got together. Love spending time with you. I don't want to spoil it by sending us on some wild goose chase that's basically all about me and my fuck-ups. I want to keep this, us, going. I like it.'

'Yeah, I like this, us, too.'

'So how about we try for a fresh start?' He snuggled down closer to me and pulled me tight, edging me back to spooning, his arm beneath my breasts. He kissed my shoulder and his ever-hungry cock poked at my buttocks. 'Forget about Misha,' he said. 'Quit playing detective and hanging out in dungeons. Focus on us instead.' He stroked my thigh, his caress tender and comforting. 'I'd like that. What do you think?'

'Yeah, maybe. We could try.' I rubbed my backside into the crook of his groin, suddenly worn out and eager for calm. His cock twitched higher, hardening. He draped an arm around my waist, holding me with tenderness, and printed tired, fond kisses on the slope of my neck.

For a while we lay in comfortable silence.

'We could go out for dinner,' he said softly. 'Or I could cook something for us.'

'Mmm,' I said, drifting towards sleep. 'Sounds nice.'

His hand stroked my stomach, cock poking more insistently. We rubbed and nudged, encouraging each other to continue while equally too wrecked to take the lead. The room was hot, even with the aircon on, and we were sticky beneath the thin sheets. Eventually, we fucked as if we'd been fucking for years. One of those lazy, domestic, Sunday-morning fucks, far beyond the place where you feel the need to impress or put a bit of effort in. He fucked me from behind. I wriggled to get a better penetrative angle. He came. I didn't. So I masturbated, because I knew how to bring myself off better than he did. He kissed and caressed me as I fretted myself. Then we broke apart and fell into a deep, exhausted sleep.

Except, of course, I woke before too long, roused by the shadow of a shadow, or a gull opening its eyelids, or a crab scuttling in the shadows. When I'm awake, that's it. I struggle to go back. Instead of sleeping, I write, recording events and thoughts in these pages.

Or I used to. Since Sol and I have started spending so much time together, that's altered. We've stopped chasing Misha's ghost. I sleep soundly now and I neglect my journal. But I don't mind. Maybe it needs neglecting.

Thursday 21st August

I'm so happy, I'm almost sad. Strange, I know, but my days have a melancholy pleasure to them. The change Sol has brought to my life allows me to see the bigger picture, and with that comes an inevitable tinge of loss. How long will this last for? How long will we live for? Will our world end with a bang or a whimper?

I guess I've caught some of Sol's anxieties, the difference being I accept loss as part of life, and see mine as a wise happiness. I'm not scared or brooding. Rather, the awareness of loss makes me grateful for my present joy.

I've created a new cocktail using a French violet liqueur described as having an 'endless finish'. I want to develop a blue menu for the bar featuring blue-coloured cocktails, some old favourites and new twists, all without relying too heavily on blue curaçao. The range will span the seasons with, at one end of the spectrum, summery drinks reminiscent of Caribbean beaches, and at the other end deeper, gothic numbers evoking darkness and midnight skies. Inevitably, the blues will bleed into indigo, violet and the black raspberries of Chambord. A touch gimmicky, I'll grant you, but I need to get the punters in and it's good to have something they'll remember you by.

Sol was having a night off from me – his words, not mine – and I was feeling in need of company. It was a Wednesday, Misha's former hour. It's been almost two months since he died but Wednesdays haven't yet become ordinary, each one marking another week that's passed since his death. The coroner's inquest was held just over a week ago. Prior to that, Sol had been fearful we might get called as witnesses or be required to submit statements but nothing came of it, thank God. Some other people from Dravendene had to give evidence, the ones who'd found him and tried to save his life. But not us. Because the threesome never happened.

So it's all over. He drowned. He had high levels of alcohol in his blood and a head wound but he was alive when he was submerged. Water in his lungs. Death by misadventure. He must have slipped on the poolside and fallen into the water, possibly unconscious. Sol got the details from Lou. We've been lying low for the most part.

Once or twice, I've wondered if Sol knew Misha. The night we met, he kept saying he recognised him from somewhere. Was there unfinished business between them that got wrapped up at the pool with Misha's death? Since I wrote my last journal entry, I've been thinking more about Sol's unconvincing claim that he's new to DS. Sure, there could be a perfectly innocent explanation behind it: he's a fast learner, an instinctive dom and a skilled, imaginative lover. Or it could be he's hiding something about his past with Helena and others. I wonder if something about his secret, sexual self links him to Misha. For the most part, I regard Sol as a man who wouldn't set out to hurt someone. And yet sometimes, when sex is getting hot and nasty, I see a dark, cold look in his eyes and I'm forced to ask myself: who is this person? Where do his limits lie?

Yesterday, when I went downstairs to open up at five, the sky was crouched and murky, the air oppressively humid. The prospect of a storm added to my Wednesday wobbles so I cupped a hand to the window of Katrina's bookbinding workshop, hoping she might be free. The window features a display of her work, handbound books in a range of styles from rustic brown leather threaded with matching thongs through to vintage-lace wedding albums and ornately stitched journals backed in Indian silks. She does restoration work, commissions, supplies gift shops and sells from the premises too. She waved at me from the murk of the workshop. I see less of her since Sol's been on the scene. She used to pop up for a drink every couple of weeks, or we might chat on the doorstep until my first customers arrived. Now she keeps a respectful distance, and I've failed to carve out time for her.

'Hey, come in!' she called.

I checked no likely customers were approaching, locked the street door of the bar, and joined her. She has a wonderful antique bell above the door, which jangles to announce visitors. The smell of the workshop always enthrals, a mix of old paper and earthiness. I inhaled as I entered, goosebumps lifting on my skin. The equipment puts me in mind of medieval dungeons. Frames and presses both large and small, in cast iron, brass and oak, are dotted high and low, their screws and clamps sadistically suggestive. I could almost taste the stories which seem to hang in the air like a magical mist of secrets.

Kat had a large bag on her shoulder as if she were about to leave.

'You got time for a drink?' I asked. 'I'm about to open up and I have a new cocktail that needs test-driving.'

'Love to,' she replied. 'Got to dash to the post office before it shuts though. Back in ten.' She flicked a switch behind a small serving counter and the shutter outside began to rumble down over the window.

'Excellent, see you in a bit.' I stepped outside again. Shadows darkened the street and the clouds were lined with an ominous anthracite glint. A few fat, warm raindrops fell, each one printing a splodge on the hot, dry pavement. A couple touched my bare arm, and one my face.

I ducked back into the workshop. 'You might need a brolly, Kat!'

'Bollocks, I don't have one,' she said.

We both stepped out onto the street, Kat hastening to lock her door as I opened mine.

'Well, I *might* make it back before it pisses it down,' she said, glancing skywards.

'Hmm, good luck with that.'

I didn't bother setting up the A-board on the pavement. It would only get soaked. I returned upstairs just as distant thunder grumbled. It grew gloomy enough to warrant me turning up some of the evening lights. Despite the muggy warmth, the bar felt cosy and winterish. Leather, oak and glass gleamed in the half-light, and the cream satin walls took on a luxurious sheen. The row of church-pew booths along the wall opposite the bar looked as if they were in a creepy train station, waiting for the undead to board. Pale light glossed the floor in front of them, puddles of poisonous mercury on the train-station plat-form. The stuffed crow in its glass dome gazed dead-eyed into the freaky emptiness. This bar, I thought, relishes a good thunderstorm. It's almost as if its moment has arrived and all the ghosts of the Victorian funeral parlour will be joining us for drinks.

I was less keen on the prospect of a storm. Takings would be low. I left the stained-glass balcony doors open, hoping to feel the rush of a cool breeze descending with a downpour. The back of my neck was clammy so I scraped my hair into a ponytail before selecting my bottles to mix the cocktail with no name. Maybe Kat could help me christen it.

I took down gin, Cointreau and the crème de violette from Provence or, as I think of it, romance in a bottle. For a long time, crème de violette had been a bitch to get hold of, even in France, where it's made. Jonathan and I had once traipsed around half of Nice in search of a version from Benoit Serres containing hints of vanilla. And, oh God, it was worth every blister. My nameless cocktail was a twist on the classic Aviation and called for mathematical precision in its measures to achieve the perfect mix with a colour that was just so.

Beyond the balcony, rain started to fall as I tipped jig-gers of liquor over ice. Minutes later, Kat came rushing into the bar with a whoop, hair dripping, as I was shaking my shaker, ice clattering. 'I love it when you do the maracas,' Sol had once said. 'Makes your tits jiggle.' Even though he wasn't there, I felt him watching me, smiling lecherously.

'I'm fucking soaked,' cried Kat, holding her hands out as if to dry. 'You got a towel?'

Water fell from her, sprinkling the varnished floor. Her hair seemed longer and blacker than ever, thick strands plastered to her head and clinging to her shoulders.

'That way.' I laughed, nodding to the galley kitchen adjoining the bar. 'Cupboard to the left of the sink.'

She followed my directions, leaving a trail of wet footprints and continued exclaiming about the awful weather through the open door. Lightning shuddered, making the bar flicker. After a pause, thunder grumbled and then rose to a bang. I glanced at the rain pouring down on the balcony, droplets hammering on the glass-topped tables, splashes jumping. If I didn't get any customers in the next couple of minutes, I probably wouldn't get any all night. I wondered where Sol was. Probably in his car and heading westwards to Brighton. I hoped the coastal road was safe.

Kat emerged from the kitchen, cheeks pink, her hair wrapped in a bulky turban.

My stomach fell away.

'What?' She frowned, touching the heap of towel perched on her head.

The towel was the colour of cheap, supermarket salmon, threads straggling from its edges.

'You look as if you've seen a ghost,' continued Kat. 'What is it?'

'Nothing, it's fine,' I said, forcing a smile. 'Just the storm. Makes me edgy. I reckon it's going to be quiet tonight.'

Kat returned to the public area of the bar, rubbing lightly at her wet hair beneath the turban. She sat at a glass-topped table in a silver and black Rococo chair. 'Can't believe how fast it came down,' she said.

My hands shook as I strained the mixed drink into a martini glass. I bent close to ensure I didn't spill, wishing I could hide somewhere safe. How had the towel ended up in the kitchen? It wasn't a towel I ever used. It didn't match my bathroom, for one thing. I recalled bringing it from Dravendene, packing it in my luggage with the bondage gear bundled inside. Back at home, I'd washed it twice, and then stashed it somewhere out of sight and out of mind. I couldn't even remember where.

I strained the second drink into an identical glass, upended the shaker in the washer, and went to join Kat at a table on the other side of the counter.

'Wow,' said Kat as I stood our drinks on black cocktail doilies. 'Gorgeous colour. What's this one?'

'My new creation,' I said, returning to the bar with my tray. 'Currently nameless, so if you have any ideas, share.'

'Oh, that smell. Takes me right back. What is it? No, don't tell me!'

I sat at the table and watched her. She gazed at our cocktails and leaned forwards to inhale, holding on to her turban. The liquid was a dusky lavender grey, sitting in the glasses like a eerie, twilight-hued smoke. The colour hovered on the edge, in the zone between overcast skies and an unearthly luminescence.

'Parma Violets.' Kat sat back in her chair, triumphant.

That towel on her head was such a dreadful colour. Too much orange in its pink. I must have brought it across from the flat with the other cloths and towels. I do the bar's laundry at my place, tumble drying it as well because there's no room for hanging, indoors or out. At some point in the process, the towel must have made its way into the load.

'Lana?'

'Yes?'

'Parma Violets. Is it?'

'Yes sorry.' I sat upright and drew a sharp, head-clearing breath. I could smell the rain, the wetness of hot concrete and the freshness of drenched trees from further along the street. 'Crème de violette. But only a smidgen. Don't want it to be too perfumed and sweet.'

Kat raised her glass, examining the contents. I raised mine. The room flared with lightning and for the briefest instant, the flash was caught in our drinks. The after-image was branded in my mind, the liquid lit like the final colour of the rainbow, about to vanish beyond the visible spectrum and become an apparition. Ultraviolet, a dangerous, hidden light.

'To stormy weather,' said Kat. 'And to being stranded in a top-notch bar on a wet Wednesday evening.'

Carefully, we clinked rims and sipped. Thunder rolled and boomed as if careening around the room. Glasses tinkled behind the bar.

'Beautiful,' said Kat. 'I'm feeling better already.' She set down her drink and unwrapped her hair, draping the towel over her shoulders as she rubbed her ends. 'So how's life? Haven't seen you for ages. Mr Macho still around? Business booming?'

We chatted about this and that, and all the while questions about the mysterious re-appearance of the towel clamoured for my attention. I could only conclude Sol had found it somewhere, had presumably used it, then added it to a bag of towels and cloths, not realising the contents were bar laundry as opposed to domestic. It would have been easy enough for me to miss it in the mix of other items. Then if one of my bar staff had unpacked the bag of laundered linen, I'd have been none the wiser to the towel's presence. But where had Sol found the towel in the first place? He was getting too comfortable in my space if he thought it was acceptable to go rooting around in bottom drawers and backs of cupboards.

And I was getting too careless, too casual.

'Purple Haze?' said Kat.

'Sorry?'

'The drink,' she said. 'I'm trying to think of names.'

I laughed. 'Would you order a drink with the word purple in the title?'

'Good point.' She twirled the stem. 'Ghoul in a Glass?'

'Maybe for Halloween.'

'Stormy Sunset?'

'Too naff.'

'This is difficult.'

'The more you drink, the easier it gets,' I replied.

'It reminds me of stone. No, of marble. Medusa!'

'Already taken.'

'Damn.'

'Opals, that's it,' declared Kat. 'That's what I'm reminded of.'

'Ah, I see what you mean.'

'With an edge of pearly moonlight,' Kat continued. 'This is fucking good stuff, Lana. It's turning me into a poet. What about Opal – Opulence!'

'By Jove!' I cried.

We clinked glasses. 'To Opulence.'

'I'll fix us a couple more,' I said, standing. Lightning shimmered, eerily silent.

'That weather,' said Kat, as thunder began to roll.

Behind the bar, I scooped ice into a shaker and selected the same set of bottles. I glanced out at the rain, still pouring down and leaping from the tables on the balcony. In the barrel-vaulted alcove, water was pooling on the floor. Health and safety. I'd need to mop that up if any customers arrived, although I doubted they would.

'Oh, I knew I had something to tell you,' called Kat. 'There was a guy looking for you the other week. One afternoon. He had the most amazing colour of eyes. Sort of blue-green, and kinda dark but bright. Yeah, that's helpful, isn't it? Anyway, he wanted to know when you were around so he could catch you.'

'Who was he?'

'Dunno, didn't give a name.'

'But, what? Here to read the gas meter. Deliver post?'

'No, no, nothing like that. He was…good-looking guy. Early forties, maybe. He was…hard to explain. He had something about him. An edge. Something mean. Not overtly aggressive. Just…coiled.'

'Sounds intriguing.'

'Description doesn't mean anything, then?'

I shook my head. 'I'm sure he'll find me if it was important.'

'Yeah. I think he will.' She swirled the last of her drink. 'Actually, you know what this colour reminds me of? Cock.'

I laughed, already able to see where she was coming from.

'The head of a cock,' she continued. 'White guy. You know what I mean? Sort of mauve and blue-ish and a sort of non-colour. Cock has more pink tones than this but, yeah, that colour.'

'You're obscene,' I said.

'I vote we re-christen it. Knobulence!'

A clatter at the foot of the spiral staircase made me glance at the wall clock. Six p.m. already, and still tipping it down. Bruno entered, soaking wet and wearing a sinister black trenchcoat.

'Pig of a night!' He shook his head vigorously, scattering droplets. He removed his coat and underneath he was as neat as ever in black shirt and charcoal grey waistcoat, his clothes perfectly complementing his boxy, black beard. He headed for the galley kitchen to hang his coat. I silently congratulated myself for employing hot, handsome, well-dressed twins.

I twisted the top on my shaker and shook. 'You want a drink, Bru?' I called over the rattle of ice. 'I've created a new goodie. Don't think we're going to get many in tonight.'

Bruno emerged from the kitchen and clapped his hands together, rubbing eagerly. 'Cool, let's make it a mixing night. I could give Raf a ring. He'd hate to miss out.'

I closed the bar at ten, by which point the four of us were seriously hammered. And still we continued. We created some excellent new cocktails and some real horrors, most with filthy names thanks to Kat. I texted Sol a couple of times and sent a selfie in which I was wide-eyed and sipping a bourbon-based cocktail through a straw, telling him he was missing out. Unusually, he didn't reply. He hasn't been in touch today either. Maybe his phone's on the blink. I wonder if I should mention the towel. I'm not sure how to. Not sure I want to, either. I should probably bin it, put everything behind us.

Anyway, it was a great night but I'm paying for it today. My head's woolly, and my tongue is thick.

I'll feel better after a swim. I always do.

Monday 1st September

Sol's been evasive and distracted recently, and a few days ago I learned why. I'm not sure how I feel about it yet. Concerned, at the very least, and while he told me not to worry, I remain unconvinced because he was less than emphatic in his reassurances. Breezy, almost. Dismissive. And since then, he's begun to fade on me like a ship going out of range.

It was last Thursday. He texted in the afternoon, saying, 'I'll be over later.'

Because he hadn't been spending as much time at mine as usual, and because when he was with me he'd seemed preoccupied, the text acquired greater significance than it might do ordinarily. Difficult to read between the lines when there's only one, but, nonetheless, that's what I wracked my brain trying to do. That curt, cool sentence contained so much silence and my anxious imagination is prone to feed on these things. Was it a silence born of coldness, indifference, laziness or any other of a number of issues to which I was blind? Was his interest in me waning? I hadn't seen him since Monday and that was a long time for us.

I couldn't identify any problem in our relationship, except perhaps that we'd quickly become full-on. But the tacit understanding was Sol spent a lot of time at my place because he was working at the construction site in town and staying over was handy. Acknowledging that convenience didn't trivialise our feelings for each other. But we benefited from the emotional safety net of such a set-up as it meant our apparent transformation into Romeo and Juliet, diving headlong into foolish love, was actually a considered choice based on pragmatic decisions. We were in control. Sure we were hot for each other but we weren't behaving like reckless teens, throwing caution to the wind. No, we had the measure of this thing.

So what else might be the problem? Easily bored? Maybe he did this kind of thing all the time, rushing in then rushing straight out again. But that wasn't the picture he'd painted of himself. He seemed solid and reliable, even in his wild, greedy eagerness for me. I'd thought we were evenly matched in that sense: mature enough to embrace our feelings for each other but smart enough not to over-invest.

But perhaps we weren't evenly matched and the scales of our desires were starting to tip. What did he mean by 'later'? Later but at the usual time? Or later than usual? And why no 'x' at the end? He usually signed off that way. Usually or always? I couldn't say. I might not have noticed a previous omission if it hadn't felt like one. Should I torment myself by going through hundreds of old messages?

By half five, he still hadn't shown up at the bar. No text either to say he was en route. By that point, I'd practically convinced myself that when he did arrive he was going to finish it between us. 'It's not you, it's me,' he'd say, and I'd try not to reveal my pain as we agreed to part as friends.

I recalled sprawling on the steps after Club Sybaris,

post-coitally languid, and he'd asked me if I ever felt guilty. 'Do you?' I'd asked. 'All the time,' he'd said. I'd thought it was a covert reference to Misha, to our denial of the three-some or to whatever had happened at the pool. Or perhaps it was deeper than that, a reference to his family members who'd died before their time, leaving him with the guilt of being alive. Or maybe it truly was the Jewish guilt he'd half joked about.

But recently I've been thinking I'm barking up the wrong tree on all those fronts. He has something else he needs to hide, and it's about sex. When he'd talked about sensing a peculiar atmosphere at Dravendene, something 'underground' about the people, was he actually project-ing what he felt about himself? Perhaps this change in his behaviour has something to do with his past. And I'd never find out because there was a side to him he'd always hide. Maybe he'd met someone else and I'd soon be joining his ex, Helena, and nameless other lovers who were part of a kinky history he wanted to perpetually erase. Was he ashamed of what we did together? Could he only sustain DS relationships for a limited amount of time before mov-ing on and presenting himself as a newbie?

All this speculation was buzzing in my head as I mixed drinks and put on a happy face. I had a birthday party in, around a dozen lively people, evidently fresh from the office, so I was fairly run off my feet. I didn't immediately notice him; he was just a newly arrived customer in the corner of my eye. I was carrying a tray of tiki cocktails over to one of the tables, sparklers, umbrellas, big hunks of fruit, and so on, when I noticed this figure enter the room. The customers were oooing and wowing as I glided over to them, balancing a mini Mardi Gras in my hands. They'd asked for 'the works' so I'd obliged by going overboard on the gimcrackery. I swear I nearly dropped the tray when I realised the newcomer was Sol.

Crazy, but I started to shake. I lowered the tray to table height, resting it on the edge, and very nearly spilled as I set down a Mai Tai on a black paper mat. I glanced over my shoulder at him. He was full of smiles, proud as fuck, and barely recognisable in a well-cut, brown, herringbone suit and fat, floral, burgundy tie. His authoritative stance unnerved me. Who was he, all of a sudden?

'Hey,' I called, grinning. Then, turning back, 'OK, so, who's for a Painkiller?'

My heart thumped, and the sight of him was seared in my mind: tall, cool and sexy, with his hands thrust in his trouser pockets, his collar undone, his tie loose. He stood motionless, all cocky and expectant as he watched me work, waiting for me to spot him in his whistle and flute. You didn't turn up with that attitude if you intended to dump someone. We were safe: safe as houses, solid as a rock.

I wanted to rush over to embrace him, tell him about these awful fears I'd been having, and listen to him soothe me back to security. 'Get a grip, Cha Cha,' he'd say. 'I'm going nowhere.'

When I'd set down all the drinks, I wove my way back to the bar, tray by my side. He came towards me, a cool, ironic grin on his face.

'Hey, how's it going, barkeep?' He pressed a mildly salacious kiss to my lips, his hand sliding onto my arse, groin nudging at my thigh.

'Looking good, mister,' I said, giving a tweak of his tweedy lapel. 'What's the occasion? You in trouble?'

I withdrew and returned behind the counter, selecting bottles for the next lot of drinks. Sol perched on a stool and leaned his arms on the bar's radiant blue surface.

'Nope,' he said, gaze lingering deliberately on me. 'But *you* might be, the mood I'm in tonight.'

'Is that a threat or a promise?' I poured a stream of rum into my shaker.

He grinned and sat back a fraction, glancing about the room. 'We'll see. Busy in here.'

'Yeah,' I said. 'Not sure when I'll get a break. You OK to stay awhile?'

'Sure.' He shrugged. 'I'm happy if you're happy. Always.'

I selected a bottle of beer from the cooler, flipped off the top, and placed it in front of him. He drank about half in one go. I love seeing him drink when he's thirsty. The bob of his Adam's apple in his bristle-speckled neck stirs my desire. I don't even know why, except that it looks so…*him*. And he's drinking so I can't touch him and he doesn't know I'm watching. For a moment, he's like a moving image. Seeing him in a suit was a curious pleasure. He was simultaneously familiar and unknown, the clothing creating an enticing distance. He was a mysterious stranger, a villain, tycoon, man-about-town or lord of the manor. Who knew? But whoever he was, he was an adventure I wanted to go on. I imagined he would come on strong and do unspeakably hot, nasty things to me because we'd only just met and would never see each other again.

'Listen,' he said, setting down his bottle. 'You mind if I pop back to the flat? You got your keys handy?'

'Oh, don't leave.' I pouted childishly. 'I haven't seen you for—'

'No, I'll be right back. Just want to grab my book. Need something to occupy me while you work off that cute little butt of yours.'

'OK, cool. They're in the—' I stopped. I'd been about to direct him to the keys in my bag in the adjoining kitchen but, recalling the incident of the towel in the laundry, I thought it might be advisable to observe some boundaries. 'Hang on.'

I went to retrieve the keys and then placed them on the bar. Sol scooped them up as he stood and slotted his beer bottle in his jacket pocket.

'Do me a favour, cowboy,' I said, unable to contain my smile.

He raised his brows, ready to oblige.

'Don't change.'

He frowned, perplexed, his amusement fading. 'What do you mean?'

'Out of the suit.'

He laughed and wiggled his tie. 'You approve?'

'Damn right, I do. And I'm itching to know what the occasion is.'

He grinned then tossed and caught the bunch of keys. 'Got me a swish new job, Cha Cha! Things are on the up.'

'Yeah?'

'Start next week. Back to the whizzy world of IT. Data analysis, doing what I do best. Working for a mobile phone company but then you can't have everything.'

I smiled and smiled, and though I acted excited and intrigued, all I could think was: I knew it; it's over between us; he has no reason to stay here now; I've lost him. There are no swish jobs in Saltbourne. Our feelings for each other are no longer convenient.

'So are you going to be rich on your own merit?' I asked.

Before he could reply, a brash young woman from the birthday group approached, wanting to know how much the snacks cost. *Which snacks?* I thought irritably.

'Back in five,' said Sol, whirling my apartment keys around his finger.

I worried about him snooping, poking around in corners where towels the colour of dead salmon were hidden. But he returned swiftly, still suited and booted, and sat at the corner of the bar. He draped his jacket over an empty bar stool, unfastened his cufflinks and briskly rolled his shirt sleeves to the elbow. His shirt was off-white and threaded with a faint caramel check. He looked damn good, and accustomed to the clothes he wore. He put on his stern, heavy-rimmed glasses and swigged from the bottle as he read, apparently unbothered by the music and chatter. More friends joined the birthday party and we didn't get chance to talk properly until a while after Bruno had arrived for his shift.

Sol removed his specs and folded them onto the counter. He leant across the bar and I tipped forwards so we could exchange a short kiss of greeting. 'Wish we could go someplace and celebrate,' he said. 'I want to wine, dine and fuck you.'

Those simple words made my clit spark up. 'So go on. Tell me everything.'

And he did as I listened, my arms resting on the lit, blue counter. He claimed he hadn't wanted to jinx the interview by mentioning it to me. The work entailed travelling around the south-east initially and then he'd probably be doing more work from home. He didn't need the money, he said. The inheritance from his grandmother would see him good for several more years. And if he invested wisely, longer than that. But he missed doing a job that gave him satisfaction, a sense of fulfilment and personal pride. He didn't want to be a bum or a builder. He wanted to work. And on Sunday he was off to the Midlands to attend a week-long training programme. Training. More like trying to indoctrinate him in the company ethos. In at the deep end but they needed people urgently so he just had to suck it up.

As he talked, his thick paperback lay spread open on the bar, a bird poised to take flight, its wings patterned with gold.

I began to wonder when our last night together might be, and would I even know it was our last? Supposing it was now, tonight? What if he met someone in the Midlands and never returned?

'What are you thinking?' he asked.

'Oh, I'm just excited for you,' I said.

'Liar.'

'Am I that obvious?'

'Yes. What's wrong?'

'I *am* pleased for you,' I said. 'It's just that…it means we'll be seeing less of each other, doesn't it?'

I saw him blench, I'm sure of it, a look of horror so brief my perception of it was practically subliminal. 'Course not,' he said, grinning. 'Once next week's over with, we'll work something out.'

'It's happened so quickly,' I said.

'It's a fast world out there, Cha Cha. You know what would help slow it down?' He reached casually across from where he sat, elbow propped on the bar, and brazenly, firmly, ran his hand down the side of one breast. He didn't even attempt to disguise his action.

I grinned, glancing around to ascertain if anyone had seen us. 'You'll get me sacked.'

'Ah, I'm sure your boss will understand. I hear she's a bit of a goer.'

'Yeah, but she's not too keen on me shagging the customers.'

'Come on,' he said. 'Let's quit this joint. I need to fuck your brains out.' He stood and upturned his book, folding the corner of a page to mark his place. Then he slotted his specs in his shirt pocket.

'Hey, hang on,' I said. 'I can't just leave. We're busy.'

'Then phone the other one. Tweedledum. See if he can work. People love seeing double in a bar.'

He took his jacket from the nearby stool and slung it over one shoulder, finger crooked in the collar, book tucked in his armpit, waiting. His erection pushed at the fabric of his crotch. I adored how he was momentarily trying to take over managing the bar so we could fuck. Not that I'd let him. My bar. My business. I was the one in charge here. And yet I wanted what he wanted.

'Ack. I dunno. I'm always doing this. It's not fair to keep asking—'

'Then close the goddamn bar, Lana. Or I will. Holy hell, I'll turf them out on to the street with their drinks, and I'll say, "I hope you don't mind, folks, but this hot little piece of ass needs fucking."'

He tossed his jacket onto the stool again, dropped his book on top of it, and reached across the bar for me. He grabbed my hair at the nape of my neck. My entire body was instantly his, my nerves zinging, my heart palpitating,

my cunt swelling; and all because he'd immobilised me
with such a swift, sexy action. To an observer, his gesture
might have seemed vaguely affectionate but it was the
opposite. It was hot, controlled and threatening. My scalp
stung as he clenched his fist tighter, inching me closer to
him. I smiled, loving the challenge. Sensation thickened
the tissue of my cunt, pulses slamming. I slanted across the
counter, trying to avoid the drip tray by my legs, and doing
my damnedest not to wince as heat crawled across every
millimetre of my skin. I gazed at his open collar, and the
fat knot of his loosened tie. Wisps of chocolate-brown
hair curled around the hollow of his throat. My face
burned but still I smiled.

He dropped his voice to a low, slow whisper. 'And this
hot little piece of ass is going to do everything I say. Isn't
she?'

He tipped my head back, forcing me to look at him
directly. We held the stance, silent for a moment. Between
my thighs, arousal pounded in a liquid flood. I swallowed.
'Yes. Yes she is, you bastard,' I said. 'I'll phone Raf.'

He released his grip and stroked a finger along my jaw-
line. 'Good girl,' he said tenderly.

I swear, my legs nearly gave out. I turned to see Bruno
studiously tidying the jiggers, his face bright red, his body
tense. When I asked about his brother's availability, he
acted surprised, as if I'd jolted him from a daydream.

'Oh, yes! He might be free,' he said eagerly. So I phoned
Raf, wondering if they talked to each other about us. I was
so horny I was prepared to pay them double-time but for-
tunately didn't need to. Raf was happy with the extra
hours.

'So now we have to wait for him to show up?' exclaimed

Sol. 'Jeez, Cha Cha. I could club a baby seal with this boner. Now what? How about I fuck you over that table in full view of everyone? Because I'm not sure my dick's prepared to wait any longer. I've missed you. Did I tell you that?'

Bruno came to stand next to me behind the bar, face ablaze. 'Lana,' he said. 'I can manage till Raf gets here. Please go home.'

Sol raised his hand, and the two men high-fived each other, Sol more enthusiastically than Raf. 'Good man,' he said. 'One day I'll do the same for you.'

'Do you *mind*?' I said, failing to conceal my amusement through my show of disapproval.

We grabbed our gear and left, taking the kitchen's rear staircase leading directly to the mews. The mews, a cobbled L-shape of terraced, white-brick cottages and garages, was as quiet as usual. Bedraggled pink and purple petunias spilled from the hanging basket at number two, the blooms looking weary in the pale dusk of a summer evening. A smudged pearly glow haloed the wall lanterns. I thought how lucky I was to have found a place as charming as this to live. I don't miss London at all. I wondered if Sol would remember the peace here when he was number-crunching in some over-lit office in Birmingham.

As we crossed the cobbles, I fished around in my bag for my door keys. Inexplicably, I felt uneasy. There was a sudden stillness, a silence, and I was struck by a vague sense of dread. Weird, I know. With a little distance from the situation, part of me puts the peculiar feeling down to my anxieties about our relationship changing. But at the time I felt as if a sixth sense were trying to warn me of something. I felt we were being watched. I glanced over my shoulder, checking the street beyond the courtyard's broad, metalwork gate, but saw nothing untoward.

Before we reached my door, Sol hooked an arm around me from behind, dragging me into a backwards embrace. The paperback tucked under his arm jabbed at my shoulder.

'You feel that?' He rubbed his hefty crotch against my buttocks. 'You feel how hard you make me, huh?'

His reached down for me, crushing my skirt into the juncture of my thighs. I tried to wriggle free, laughing.

'So hurry up then,' I said. 'Let's get inside.'

'My thoughts exactly.'

I grappled with him, tried to slap at and prise away his arm. 'Sol!' I said, playing at primness. 'What will the neighbours think?'

He butted close to my ear. 'They'll think you're a greedy little bitch who can't get enough cock.'

'Let me go!'

He released me and I tottered, laughing. I turned to flick a reprimanding tap against his chest and, as I did so, I saw the figure of a man at the gate, looking in through the ornate iron bars. Immediately, he stepped back and out of sight, on to the street. Tall and dark-haired, that's all I saw.

Sol followed my gaze, frowning. 'What?'

'Oh nothing. Just...a cat.'

As I unlocked, Sol ground himself against my arse, muttering dirty talk into my ear. Were we still being watched? I scanned the courtyard as I closed and locked the door but no one was around. I'd barely turned the key when Sol tossed his jacket and book on the hallway floor and slammed me against the wall. I gasped, the breath knocked from me. His hands mashed my breasts as he bit and kissed my neck. I laughed, rocking my head against the wall, trying to shove him off me so we could do this more comfortably.

'I'm already scared of how horny you're going to be after a week away,' I said.

'So you should be.' He began tugging up my pencil skirt.

'Slow down,' I urged. 'Let's get into bed.' I pushed at his chest, and felt his specs in his shirt pocket. 'Sol! You'll break your glasses if we carry on like this.'

'I'm gonna give you something to remember me by tonight,' he said in a low growl. He jerked my skirt harder and up over my hips, past my thighs and knickers. His cream-and-caramel shirt sleeves were rolled to the elbow, baring his strong, hairy forearms. The flex in his muscles as he grappled with my skirt made my stomach flip. I love it when he has to force my clothes off, his touch determined and strong. He makes me want to wear figure-hugging skirts forever.

'Gonna put some marks on that pretty little ass of yours.' He hauled my gusset aside and drove two fingers high and hard into my cunt. I gasped and he gave a small victorious grunt. 'Sopping wet,' he said. 'Just as I thought.' He began finger-fucking me, banging urgently so my juices squelched and poured onto his fist. I gasped over and over, sensation escalating so fast it dizzied me.

'You going to promise me you'll be good when I'm gone?' he panted. He rested his forearm across my chest, pinning me to the wall, and squeezed a third finger inside me. 'Are you, Cha Cha?'

He used no technique or finesse, offered no clitoral stimulation. He just trapped me there, using three fingers to fuck me nonstop while he watched my face. I couldn't speak, couldn't do anything except wail, and plead for mercy.

'Are you?' he snarled.

'Yes,' I managed. 'Yes.'

'Can't hear you,' he said. He snatched his fingers from me and grabbed my hair. 'This way,' he said, jerking my head. 'I can see I'm going to have to beat it out of you, aren't I?'

'Oh God.' I tottered after him, crouched and wincing in pain, as he led me into the kitchen by a fistful of hair.

'Here we go,' he said. 'Over the table for me.'

He tipped me forwards onto my reclaimed, oak-beam dining table, steering me with my head. I lay across the unvarnished surface, arse jutting, the wood cool on my face. He shoved my skirt higher onto my back; then he yanked my knickers to my ankles with one sharp tug. I winced at the indignity of the position. The kitchen, separated from the living room by a breakfast bar, isn't overlooked but I was still bothered by the uncurtained patio doors.

'Sol, the curtains,' I said.

'Ain't nobody watching, Cha Cha,' he said. 'Maybe next time, if you're lucky.'

He crossed the slate-tiled kitchen floor, eyes darting around the room. I lay still, greedy lust pounding between my legs, my thighs drenched. He rifled through a pot of bamboo utensils and plucked out a slotted spatula. He slapped it on the heel of his hand and laid it on the granite worktop. To my consternation, he began flinging open drawers and cupboards, peering in and bending down. With his shirtsleeves rolled back, he looked as if he owned the place. Is this what he did when I wasn't around? Was that how he'd found the towel?

'Ah ha!' he cried, squatting before a cupboard I barely used. He stood, and in his hand was a baguette board, a slender piece of wood with a short handle. 'Perfect.'

I tensed as he stood behind me. 'I'm not even going to warm you up,' he said. 'You going to be good for me, Cha Cha?'

Before I could reply, he brought the makeshift paddle down onto my buttocks, swiping low across the fleshiest part of two cheeks. The contact smacked dully and I yelped, although the blow sounded worse than it felt.

'Are you?'

'Yes!'

He thwacked me on the left cheek, then the right. A burn began to rise. 'Yes, I promise!' I gasped, half laughing.

He hit me again in the same places, the whump of contact loud in the quiet cottage. The heat intensified. My laughter faded. I stared at the blur of grain and knots on the table below my face.

'Because I know what you're like,' he said. 'A cock-hungry slut. Not sure I can trust you to behave while I'm gone.'

He landed two more blows, one on each cheek. My flesh was starting to smart, the skin turning tender.

'Please,' I wailed. 'I'll be good.'

He swiped at me again, harder this time, the force of him jolting me. The wooden table legs grunted on the slate tiles. I cried out in agony, banging a heel on the floor as I tried to ride out the spreading pain.

'Consider this punishment for something you haven't even done,' said Sol. 'Preventative medicine.'

Again, he slammed the board onto my rear. I howled,

my skin sizzling, pain pushing deeper into the tissue. I heard him panting lightly behind me.

He followed up with another strike. 'I'm going to colour this ass,' he said. 'Mark my territory. So if anyone comes near it, they'll know it's taken.' The paddle banged onto my scorched cheeks, catching me on the upper thighs. 'Used goods. Someone else's property.'

'Please,' I gasped.

'What's that, you want more?' he said. 'Wanna make sure these marks last all week?'

I screamed as he landed a series of pitiless blows on my inflamed backside.

'Because you don't trust yourself to be good,' he said. 'Is that why you want it?'

He stepped away from me and slid the baguette board onto the work surface. I thought he was releasing me from my torment but instead he crossed the kitchen and returned with the bamboo spatula. His face was flushed, his hair chaotic, and one shirt flap had come untucked from his waistband. His burgundy tie was askew and his erection pushed a great, gorgeous lump in his trousers.

'Got to layer it up,' he said. 'Make sure my bitch remembers who she belongs to.' He pressed a hand into the small of my back, holding me to the table, and cracked the spatula onto my burning flesh. It hurt like hell. The board had landed with dull thuds. This vicious little implement stung, air whistling through its slats.

I yowled and writhed as he swatted me with sadistic relish. He didn't pause, didn't make me anticipate the next blow. He just thrashed me harder and harder until I thought my skin would break. My skin didn't break, but the spatula did. The bamboo cracked, its impact immediately weakened. Sol tossed the tool to the floor, where it landed with a clatter.

'Look what you did,' he said. 'You broke it.'

He dropped to his knees behind me and parted my buttocks. His broad, strong hands were cool on my blazing flesh. I cringed to feel his perusal, shame streaking through me as his fast, warm breath breezed into my cleft. He held me splayed open for a seeming eternity, and with every passing second my mortification grew. I longed to be whisked away from his intrusive inspection and have a soothing, cold compress applied to my cheeks. Then he dived into me, his tongue latching on to my hole. I whimpered as he slathered me in wet, squirmy attention. The pleasure was excruciating; delightful, awful. Beneath his sloppy caress, my crinkled rim became something else entirely, silky and soft, tender and tingling. He wiggled his tongue tip into the pinched circlet, probing and teasing. My flesh seemed to rise to him, swelling with sensation, greedily seeking his touch.

'Oh God,' I breathed. 'Please, please.'

I felt I was vanishing there, the velvet sensitivity almost too much to bear after the flesh-heavy ferocity of his beating. He drew back a fraction and his tongue was replaced by the press of a digit, his thumb, at a guess. He eased into me, breaching my tightness.

I moaned in distress and bliss, woozy with lust.

'Ye-es,' he said in a low, exultant tone. 'I'm taking total ownership of this ass, inside and out.'

He screwed his thumb back and forth and I bleated constantly. He withdrew after a short while then inserted two fingers, harder, bulkier, and deeper. My opening stretched to take him, and he worked me, twisting and pumping, loosening my muscles, making my body relax for him.

I groaned, engorged with gathering ecstasy, aching with need. When he pulled free of me, I was slack with pleasure, so slack I thought my flesh might slip from my bones. I couldn't move. I was powerless, broken by desire. Through my dazed perception, I heard Sol head into the bedroom. All I could do was lie sprawled on the table and wait, a stream of booming pulses surging through my body. He returned, naked, rolling a rubber onto his gloriously stiff erection.

Usually, that's the point when I tense up, concerned penetration might hurt, but I was so doped up on horniness I felt anyone could shove anything into any orifice, the bigger the better, and I'd gladly take it. Sol spat into his palm and moved behind me, shunting his cock in his wet fist. He stood on the knickers shackling my ankles together.

'Spread yourself,' he instructed, his manner cool and smooth.

I stamped and wiggled one foot until I was free of my underwear.

'Good girl.' He widened my stance with a soft kick and held my cheeks apart. I cried out as his blunt, solid end pressed into the creased pit of my butt. My instinctive resistance locked him out but he nosed in deeper, prising me open.

'Come on, Cha Cha,' he said, voice a touch strained.

He grunted as my grip encircled him, my muscles nipping as they stretched to take his girth. He advanced steadily, and I wailed constantly as I took the slow, inexorable force of his cock. When he was lodged to the hilt, he held still, the two of us groaning through our ragged breath. I clasped the table edge, needing something to hold. I was stuffed to the brink, packed with Sol's meaty weight. When he withdrew his stroke, my narrowness clung to his shaft, desperate not to lose him.

He pressed his hand into the dip of my back near my rucked-up skirt, stabilising himself while trapping me.

'Here we go, baby,' he breathed.

He drove forwards again, and my passage expanded around him. He eased back and deep again, picking up speed, starting to thrust. The table edge bumped above my clit, sending tremors through me. Ordinarily, I'd need more than that to get off but my orgasm began to bunch, a thousand and one shivers amassing in my thighs.

I cried out, complained, begged for less, begged for more. I was an incoherent mess, full of contradictions.

'This should keep you going for a week or two,' said Sol, huffing and grunting. He hammered into me with ruthless excess, his cock slamming high, his hips battering my raw, bruised buttocks. 'You going to remember this, Cha Cha? Remember who you belong to?'

My breaths rose to a pitch, the tension inside me becoming too dense to contain. I wailed as he banged away until I climaxed with an intensity that shocked. My orgasm flung itself out from a deep, hidden part of me, taking possession of my body. I pitched, jerked and shuddered, sobbing with bliss.

Sol grabbed a bunch of my hair, making me arch my neck backwards. 'That's my girl,' he cooed, slowing his thrusts. 'Coming from my cock. Taking it like a whore.'

He released me and I slumped against the table, my
nerves simmering, my calf muscles tingling. With a harsh,
mean grip, Sol sunk his fingers into my buttocks, exacer-
bating my soreness as he began fucking with increased
brutality. The table legs dragged against the slate floor
and Sol's noises grew loud and wild. He gave a long roar, a
pained cry, and then his body was spasming against mine,
fingers clawing me.

His roars dropped to groans and then a final gasp of
pleasure puffed from his lips. He stayed there awhile,
catching his breath. His size dwindled inside me, the
movement sending out little pulses.

'Oh God, Cha Cha.' His voice was quiet, loaded,
remorseful.

He withdrew from me and I twisted around on the
table, fearing he was upset. He heaved me to him so I was
perched on the table edge and he held my face in both
hands, staring into my eyes. I was confused.

'Sol?'

He shook his head and leaned in to kiss me. His lips
were warm and pliant, his mouth wet, and all the time he
held my face in his cupped hands. When he broke away, he
said, 'I'm going to miss you.'

'It's only a week,' I replied. 'It'll be over before we know
it.'

Since then, I've been thinking about that kiss, how he
held my face in his hands and looked at me, his eyes
clouded with emotions I couldn't decipher. I thought I
saw desire and tenderness there but also sorrow. I can't
recall if the kiss troubled me at the time or if, only now,
I'm perceiving it as a goodbye because he's barely been in
touch these last few days. When he left early the next

morning, he woke me with a kiss on my lips. He was travelling on Sunday and had a ton of stuff to organise so I wouldn't see him until he returned. He stroked my hair from my forehead, smiling affectionately. I gazed up at him through sleep-bleary eyes.

'Shalom, sweetheart,' he said gently. 'Catch you on the other side.'

'Safe journey,' I murmured.

He texted a few times over the weekend and said he'd phone before he left yesterday but didn't. And all I've had since then is silence. He's only been away one day, I know, but it's unlike him. I've called, I've texted, I've emailed but no reply so far. Technology is my only means of reaching him, and the connection feels fragile and tenuous. He'll be in Birmingham now but I have no details of where he's staying or working. I know the name of the road he lives on in Brighton so I could drive over there and loiter. That might make me feel a degree or two closer to him but it's of no practical use. I try telling myself he's been too busy to get in touch but I'm fooling no one. He used to be reliable but then he changed, grew erratic and cagey. If it weren't for that change, weren't for my growing suspicions he harbours a secret, I might have been more worried he'd come to harm.

I can only conclude he wants out of the relationship but doesn't have the balls to tell me. So now we're going to go through a fraught painful period where he treats me badly in a bid to make me finish what we had. Perhaps his inability to bring this to a decent close is related to his history of bereavement. He's unable to instigate a break-up after suffering so much from death imposing loss upon

him. Or perhaps he's a callous, lying bastard, and I've
been fooled.

Safe journey, Sol Miller, whoever you are.

Shalom.

[PAGE MISSING]

Tuesday 2nd September

There's a page missing, I know. I wrote something I
shouldn't have done but it's OK now. It's gone.

This journal's looking ragged and worn. The spine's
broken from me leaving it splayed open too often, and
some of the pages are coming unglued. It's a cheap thing.
If I'd known I was going to record so much, I would have
thought more about the object in which I was writing. I'm
considering asking Kat to bind it in leather, although I
wouldn't want her to read any of the content. Perhaps she
could mend it while I was there so I could ensure my
words were safe from her eyes. A cover with a lock would
be good. If Sol's going to go rooting around in my drawers
looking for towels, who knows what else he might stumble
upon. Well, assuming he ever comes back, that is. But I'm
starting to think he will. I over-reacted yesterday. He
probably forgot his phone charger, that's all. And the hotel
Wi-Fi is down.

The digital era makes us expect constant communica-
tion, making modern silences louder than those in the
past. I'm glad I decided to record my thoughts longhand.
This journal has a reassuring physicality. Nonetheless, its
shabbiness is a reminder too that paper is vulnerable.

I'm drawn to the idea of having my story contained in
a sturdy binding, whole, neat and orderly. No looseness,
no words escaping, no narrative slipping its moorings and
coming undone.

Wednesday 3rd September

Something's desperately wrong, and I'm scared. I think
Sol's in trouble. And I think I might be too.

Today, just after five, a guy walked into The Blue Bar,

tall and broad-shouldered, looking like trouble. His dark, silver-threaded hair was swept back in an oriental-style bun, scruffy, silky wisps framing his face. Salt-and-pepper bristles shaded his jaw and neck. Mid-forties but aging well despite the hard look of cynicism on his face. I see a lot of customers. Some strike me, some don't. I'm always pleased with myself when I remember a previous customer. If someone appears familiar, I'll usually opt for a friendly, 'Hi, how are you doing?' in a tone that suggests I know them but, if they're newcomers, doesn't sound too weird.

I'd never seen this man before. I would have remembered him.

He wore good, lived-in jeans, and his black T-shirt hinted at the contours of a powerful chest. His arms were athletically strong and his skin had the deep olive tones of someone from a country where it seldom rains. On his feet were dulled army boots and the overall effect was of a guy so brutishly masculine that I had to wonder if The Blue Bar had been recommended in a gay listings magazine.

He approached the bar, glancing quickly about the empty room, and ordered a bottle of Czech pilsner. His eyes dazzled. They were a deep turquoise-green, of such dark, compact brilliance it felt as if they could cut into you like a laser. Their colour, like the iridescence of petrol and peacocks, wouldn't quite settle. Bluish-greenish-blackish eyes under jutting brows heavy enough to cast shadows.

At a guess, I would have said East European. His cheekbones were high, his nose was on the beaky side and his lips, as if in defiance of those angular features, were full and rich, their colour comparable to the ruddy-purple skin of plums. His stubble was heavy, bordering on a beard, and around the chin, greyish, angular patches gave the suggestion of an unkempt goatee. As I flipped the lid from his beer I mused that if he were an actor, he'd always be cast as an alien or a replicant, a creature from other worlds. I practically had to brace myself to look at him again.

I noticed then, on one side of his face, a scar running near enough parallel to his jaw. The stubble broke apart in a jagged line, giving a glimpse of a seam of shiny, pinkish, puckered skin. Wow, I thought, that's taking the rough-trade look a little too far.

Ordinarily, I'd exchange a bit of chit-chat, especially for the first customer of the day when the place was empty, but something told me this guy didn't do small talk.

He withdrew a wallet from his back pocket, paid with a note and then, with a slow, precise gesture, placed a pound coin in the silver tip saucer on the bar. He allowed his thumb to press on the coin for a moment too long, fixing me with those glimmering eyes and a cold smile. Then he strolled away onto the balcony with his bottle of beer.

I couldn't help but feel insulted.

He stood between the open wings of the stained-glass doors, glancing up and down the street. His man-bun was loose and artless, strands dangling and tufts sprouting from the knot at the back of his head. The fine silvery tones in his hair were pure and bright, off-white and platinum swirling in soot-black richness. His wide shoulders tapered to slender hips and his jeans hung from a backside I could barely take my eyes off. I told myself I wasn't being disloyal to Sol; I was simply appreciating a man's arse as I might do a piece of art. I admired the suggestion of muscularity beneath soft denim, and the carelessness of having one pocket made bulky by the square of his wallet. I fiddled needlessly behind the bar, sliding my eyes towards him or glancing at one of the wall mirrors reflecting the side of his head and the curve of his nose when he turned. Slung on one shoulder was a small rucksack, a cheap nylon affair in black with garish flashes of electric blue, and a nasty, orange, net sidepocket. I figured a gay man wouldn't be seen dead with a bag like that.

He stepped fully out onto the ironwork balcony, stood his bottle on the table, and took a pack of cigarettes from a rucksack pocket before dropping the bag on a chair. The packet was gold. Benson and Hedges. He was becoming less gay by the minute. He turned aside, head low, and cupped a hand to the flame of a lighter. An amber-rose reflection lit his profile. On the building across the road, sunlight glinted on the rows of pigeon spikes, making them seem as sinister as prison walls. I wanted to say, 'Hold it right there, mister,' so I could whip out my phone camera. He looked iconic, his stance and attitude putting me in mind of Brando's urban swagger and sexiness.

He smoked with a leisured pace, standing solidly with his feet apart and gazing out on to the street, sometimes left, sometimes right, sometimes at the redbrick offices opposite. I kept glancing his way and not just because he was hot. He unnerved me. Why was he here? Why come to a cocktail bar for a beer? Was he meeting someone? A woman, perhaps?

When he'd finished his cigarette, he dropped the end to the balcony floor and briefly rubbed his boot over it. He took a swig of beer and returned indoors, his stride slow and threatening. My heart rate galloped as he approached the blue counter. I had one of my occasional

thoughts where I wondered if it was wise for me to staff
the bar when I'm alone.

What had Kat said? 'Something coiled about him.' Was
this the guy who'd been looking for me?

He stood his bottle on the bar and perched his cute
butt on the edge of a stool. 'I'm wondering if you can help
me,' he began. 'I'm looking for a guy who usually drinks
here around this time. Russian guy.'

My heart skipped a beat and sweat stabbed like needles
under my arms.

'The chemist?'

He laughed. 'Yeah, the chemist.'

I looked at him, considering how to phrase my reply
and where this was leading. His gaze was anchored on me,
and I fought the instinct to recoil from his scrutiny. I
noted a purplish tint in the shadows beneath his eyes, and
how they picked up the deep pigment of his lips. His
colouring made it seem as if bruises were beneath his skin,
waiting to surface.

'He's dead,' I replied.

The flinch was barely perceptible. He raised his craggy
brows. 'Oh? What happened?'

My heart was thumping so hard I felt dizzy, my head
thick with expanding fire. I cleared my throat. 'He drowned
a few months ago. An accident in a swimming pool.'

The man nodded to himself and made a 'how interesting' sort of pout. Evidently, he wasn't too upset. He lifted
the beer bottle to his lips and drank the remaining liquid.
I watched his Adam's apple bob in his stubble-dark neck. I
thought of Sol, and wetness pooled between my thighs
but, even now, I can't say who the desire was for. He placed
his empty bottle on the counter and pulled his wallet from

his back pocket. He flipped it open and removed a business card.

'Do me a favour, will you?' he said. 'If anyone comes in here asking for him, let me know.'

He set his card on the blue counter. I didn't pick it up because why would I if he's not going to give me the courtesy of handing it to me directly? I looked down. The card was blandly minimalist, low on style. It read: Ilya Travis, Consultant.

I laughed. 'Consultant what?'

He gave me a twisted half-smile. 'Just consultant.'

With that, he gave the bar a goodbye tap and walked towards the exit, rucksack on one shoulder. I was captivated. I didn't want him to leave.

'I was with him the night he died,' I called. I'd hoped to sound casual but I heard my voice, frantic and eager.

He stopped in his tracks and turned. In the ensuing pause, I wondered if I'd just made the biggest mistake of my life. Sol and I had agreed to put this behind us, to stop playing detective and let Misha rest in peace.

'You knew him?' he asked.

God, but my heart wouldn't regulate. My palms were moist and I was struggling to think straight. 'Kind of,' I began. 'But not really. Initially as a customer here.'

Ilya Travis took a step closer. 'Go on.'

'He'd visit every week, every Wednesday.' I gulped. 'Then we were at the same party and well, you know, that night...' I knew what I was about to say, and even though my rational self was begging me to shut up, to say no more, some idiotic compulsion urged me to throw caution to the wind. I wanted to draw this stranger into my world. As far as everyone was concerned, everyone, that is, except

Sol, Nicki and Ian, the threesome hadn't happened. We'd lied to the police, had concealed the fact the three of us had been fucking in my turret room. All I needed to do was perpetuate that lie and I was safe. And Sol was safe with me.

'At the party, before he died,' I said. 'I was *with* him.'

He nodded contemplatively and strode back to the bar. 'So you're one of those?' He rested his darkly haired forearms on the bar, scanning my face, a slight, smug smile on those plump, dusky lips. The knot of his hair made him seem sinister and cruel; villainous rather than Hollywood hipster.

I tried to swallow. My mouth was bone dry. My throat was a desert. 'One of what?'

'One of those women who like to see men crawl.'

My pulses soared. Jeez, who was this guy? I felt as if he wanted to strip me naked and, worst of all, I wanted to let him. I battled against my nerves and my good sense but maybe it was already too late. I addressed him, my chin tipping in defiance.

'No,' I said, voice cracked and throaty. 'I like to do the crawling.'

His smile broadened and he stood straighter. He gestured to the business card on the counter.

'Then you should definitely call me,' he said.

My legs turned to jelly. I gripped the edge of the bar.

'And who knows,' he continued, 'if you're good to me, I might have some news for you about your boyfriend.'

He hitched his bag onto his shoulder and stepped away.

'Wait!' I cried. 'What do you know? Where's Sol?'

But he didn't reply.

'Tell me!'

Again, silence. He sauntered from the bar without uttering another word. I listened to his boots clanging on the iron staircase spiralling towards the street entrance. I didn't even have the presence of mind to go onto the balcony to check which direction he took. Instead, I stood behind the bar, clutching the counter for support, shaking and on the verge of tears.

Something's happened to Sol, I know it has. It's three in the morning. I cannot sleep. I've triple-checked the doors and windows are locked. I don't know what I need to do next. I'm trying not to panic. Trying and failing.

I wish I could swim. Right here and now, I wish I could get out of bed and slip into cool, comforting waters and swim, swim, swim in the middle of the night. Swimming empties out my brain and gives me clarity of thought. It's as if the thinking takes care of itself, churning away at the subconscious level, while I flow, back and forth, up and down, swimming. I wish I was in the zone, becoming nothing but swimming.

Oh God, where is he, where is he? Have I said too much?

Thursday 4th September
I woke this morning from another restless night, and knew I couldn't go on like this. Every reasonable explanation I came up with to account for Sol's apparent disappearance I trashed within seconds. He's lost his phone. Well, he could email. He's been too busy. How long does a text take? He can't get Wi-Fi or a phone signal. He's in Birmingham, not Antarctica.

My wilder theories had no answers: he's been injured, he's left me, been kidnapped, lost his memory. He's dead.

I had two potential points of contact: the building site in Saltbourne where he'd been working (and from there I might be directed to his agency, who might know more about his new job because maybe they'd provided a reference); and Lou, the ex, and her friends, who'd been the reason Sol was at the party at Dravendene in the first place. I could call Zoe, ask her to get Lou's contact details from Rose, and then drop Lou a line. Would she think I was acting like a needy, possessive girlfriend? Did I care? Supposing he'd gone back to her? No, they were over, I was sure of it. Hooked up with one of her friends, maybe?

The construction site seemed my wisest starting point. I made my way to Castlegate Plaza after swimming this morning. I've been swimming less in recent days because I can't bear to be away from my phone in case he calls. But today, shivering and dripping wet in the changing rooms once again, I'd retrieved my phone from my bag as soon as I'd opened my locker. And, once again, nothing from Sol or from a hospital or a mortuary.

I was scared of visiting the building site because it implied he truly was gone and that this was looking serious. I was conducting my own missing person's enquiry. The temptation to stay in denial was strong. Maybe I could go tomorrow? Just one more day of hoping?

Now I almost wish I hadn't gone because I'm even more confused than ever.

The white hoardings around the site were emblazoned with signs: DANGER KEEP OUT. CAUTION CONSTRUCTION AREA. HARD HAT REQUIRED.

I had no hard hat. Couldn't even find an entrance for a while. When I finally spotted a doorway in the hoardings, I entered the site, feeling altogether too feminine and quite the trespasser, even though I was making no attempt to hide. The terrain was alien to me, a noisy, volcanic landscape of scaffolding, bricks, wheelbarrows, rugged yellow vehicles and workmen in reflective jackets. Planks swung from cranes high above and concrete mixers whirred. For the first time, it occurred to me that Sol might still be working here. Maybe the new job was a well-intentioned lie. His stint in manual labour was supposed to be a break from his geeky norm, a chance to kick back and take a breather from the stresses of data analytics. As he'd said, he didn't need the money so could quit the building work anytime but enjoyed routine and productivity. We're very similar in that respect.

Of course, I'd never judge him for his choices, and it was fun to have him acting as my bit of rough, but a steadier, more respectable job might suggest we had future prospects. I'd never said anything but perhaps he guessed at times I was concerned I might be scarcely more than a complement to this casual, temporary lifestyle. *Living by the sea, working on a building site, a fuck-ton of inheritance money, knobbing this chick who owned a bar, yeah, that was a great summer, man.*

Was he trying to convince me things were about to change while, in reality, he was still slogging away here? My eye was caught by a guy in protective earmuffs, drilling some distance away, and of a similar build to Sol. My heartbeat ricocheted. Could it be? But the very next second he was nothing remotely like Sol. If it had been, if I saw him here in his hard hat and dusty boots, I'd run to embrace him. I'd tell him I didn't care what he did, that he didn't need to lie to me, and there were no problems on earth that we couldn't work out together.

Hope can take us to some desperate places.

I approached three guys in discussion near a heap of lurid, orange sand.

'Hi,' I called, picking my way across rubble. 'I wonder if you could help. I'm looking for a guy who worked here recently. Sol Miller.'

The three men all looked at each other, confused and a touch alarmed.

'What's she say?'

'Sol Miller,' I said. 'Do you know him?'

Again, they glanced blankly from one to the other. What was the problem? Didn't they speak Vagina?

'Members of the public shouldn't be in here, love,' said one. 'Not without a hard hat.'

'Well, could you get me a hat?' I said. 'Or if I stand outside, can someone help with my question?'

'What's she want to know?'

A shrug.

Were these hard hats translation devices?

'Sol Miller,' I called. 'Do you know him?'

'I'll go and fetch John,' said one to the other. 'If you could wait outside, love.'

I traipsed out and stood by the open, makeshift door in the hoardings until John turned up with a clipboard. No, he told me, no one of that name has ever worked here.

'You must be mistaken,' I said. 'He was working here less than two weeks ago.'

'Not this site,' said John.

'Yes, it was. He told me.'

John gave me a pitying smile. 'Maybe he had his reasons.'

He gave me a card, told me to phone the switchboard

and check with Human Resources. 'But I know who's on site,' he said, 'and we've had no one of that name, I guarantee you.'

Despondent and baffled, I drove home, scouring my brain for an explanation. I had the right site, I knew I had. Castlegate Plaza was getting a facelift and the work was only taking place in one area. Had Sol given a false name? Was it a tax dodge? Theirs was presumably a legit operation so how could he even do that? Had he stolen someone's NI number? Perhaps he didn't have a work permit, couldn't get one for some reason. Was he working cash-in-hand elsewhere in Saltbourne? Had he concealed the truth because he was aiming to trick me into falling in love so we'd marry and he could settle here as a UK citizen?

My thoughts were a blizzard of increasingly implausible theories. Nothing made sense. I was starting to wonder who Sol was. Previously, I'd thought he might have a kinky secret, a past life he was protecting. I'd thought he might be involved in Misha's death. Now, I didn't know what to think.

I didn't bother contacting Human Resources, partly because I didn't want to risk landing Sol in trouble but mainly because I know John was right. Sol had never worked there. Instead, I got in touch with Zoe and tracked down Lou's contact details. I texted her, explaining who I was, and asked her to give me a call when she was free. I explained I was worried about Sol.

She phoned when I was sitting at the table in the kitchen adjoining the bar, cashing up takings from the night before.

'Is he OK?' she asked.

I gazed at the towers of coins before me and they blurred as my tears welled. I silently reproached myself: *For God's sake, Lana, don't cry on the phone to his ex.*

'I'm not sure.' I blinked, allowing two tears to roll, and flicked them from my face. I briefly moved the phone away and sniffed. 'He's gone quiet on me. He's in Birmingham on a training course and I haven't heard from him. All my calls go to voicemail. Just wondered, well, if you were still in touch.'

'No, not really. Haven't even bumped into him for a while. I emailed him about the inquest but he didn't reply.'

I was relieved even though that gave me no further clues as to Sol's whereabouts or his thinking. 'Do you know anyone who might know?'

'I think he goes out for a beer with Ryan and Eddie sometimes. I could ask.'

'Would you? I'd be so grateful. I just don't know what to think or what to do.'

'Leave it with me,' she said. 'I'm sure there'll be a simple explanation.'

I didn't have her confidence. Unless, of course, the simple explanation was: he's left you.

Lou texted an hour later: *Ryan says they haven't seen Sol for weeks. Says he's spending all his time with a woman in Saltbourne. Good luck! Maybe he's just having a wobble?*

I was out of options. I needed to stop fooling myself. Whatever was going on was bigger than a relationship wobble. It involved Sol, Ilya, Misha and God knows who else.

Yesterday, I stashed Ilya's card in the safe in the kitchen. Tonight I retrieved it at the end of the evening when I was putting the cash box away. It's here now on my bedside table, still mocking me, still calling.

Ilya Travis. Consultant.

It's too late to phone him now. I'll do it in the morning. I've been wondering whether to leave a message on Sol's voicemail telling him about Ilya. But what if he's held hostage somewhere and the message causes problems? The wrong person may hear the wrong name. No, I'll find out what I can from this Ilya guy before doing anything risky. I'm probably better off keeping a distance, playing the part of the innocent girlfriend.

I hope I can sleep. I have a large brandy with me. I remember when I started this journal, I'd drink brandy and soda, a mix of darkness and sparkle. I don't bother with the soda these days. The darkness is plenty.

Saturday 6th September
The cliffs along this part of the south-east coast are whiter than their cousins at Dover. I heard they're sometimes used as a substitute in films because they look more like Dover than Dover does. The chalky cliffs peak and trough for miles, topped by grassland and occasional patches of development. Below, waves of the English Channel crash on narrow shingle beaches where boulders sulk and rock pools glisten. The cliffs are bone white because erosion keeps the surfaces free of plant growth. But not at Dover, where the cliffs are protected. Strange to think these mighty structures are crumbling away, and the very outline of the south-east is mutable.

Solid as a rock. I'd used that phrase to describe my relationship with Sol when he'd turned up at the bar in his suit. But rock can be deceptive. Rock can be fragile. Rock can crumble to dust.

The wide cliff-top road follows the coast for the most

part. The drive to Ilya's was westerly, towards Brighton and, therefore, towards Sol's empty flat. My mind kept tempting me to keep my foot down, to speed past Ilya's house, beyond all the cliffs and sea and into Brighton's bustling, narrow streets. I could park in Sol's road and try to guess which flat was his. I could use the time to clear my head, to work out my best course of action. Should I be going to the police instead of to Ilya's? No, a foolish thought. We didn't want police involvement, and anyway what did I have? *'Scuse me, Officer, my boyfriend hasn't called and he's usually quite reliable.*

In my car, I was in a cool bubble of aircon but my hands were clammy on the wheel. When my concentration drifted, I felt protected and in control; then I'd remember where I was heading and my stomach would drop. Ilya had information on Sol and I wanted it, be it good or bad. My mind wouldn't rest. It searched for a reason, constant and frenzied, still churning over a range of theories from 'he's dead' to 'I've been dumped'. In my blackest moments, I've had to wonder which of those two extremes I'd prefer. The thought that he might have left me voluntarily, not even caring enough to explain himself, tore my heart to shreds. If silent desertion explained his absence, I'd be forced to re-write the entirety of our past. But, no, I had to keep reminding myself this wasn't about us. It had something to do with Ilya and Misha. Or was that wishful thinking?

My desperation to know more had spurred me to contact Ilya. But, I had to confess, I was also motivated by a desire to know more about this brooding, smirking stranger. My imagination had been working overtime ever since he'd pressed that pound coin into the tip saucer at the bar and had given me a look that said, 'I can turn you inside out and you know it.' I felt guilty about my curiosity in him but that's all it was, curiosity. I'd no intention of going anywhere near him, not in that sense. Deliberately, I'd dressed in sober clothes: grey pencil skirt, crisp white shirt. I might have been attending a business meeting.

Ilya appeared to be a guy who wouldn't give much away, so meeting at his place seemed to be my only option. When I called him yesterday, he'd mocked my suggestion we sit down and talk, as if sitting down and talking wasn't something he did; or, at any rate, not with women. He'd talk to men, probably in some smoky poker den until 3 a.m.; whereas women – he'd just fuck them till they were sore. The thought of such casual misogyny aroused me. Yeah, that one again: fucked-up, I know. But some fantasies, like my fantasy of being watched, aren't made for reality. I'm happy just using them to get off; I don't want to act them out; nor do I want to endorse some lunkhead's view of the world by appearing to conform to it.

I knew my guilty thoughts about Ilya and what he could do to me ought to belong in that category of 'not for real life'. But the boundaries were blurring already. I was driving along the coastal road to his home, mulling over how I might respond if he came on to me. And he would, wouldn't he? I reckoned he was luring me to his place with Sol as bait, confident or arrogant enough to know I was also attracted to him. But luring me for what purpose? It had to be more than sex. He didn't strike me as someone who'd be going short. So what else might he want? He wasn't going to reveal all about Sol from the goodness of his heart. Was he toying with me? Toying with Sol? Was I being set up? Used?

When I'd phoned Ilya, he'd claimed to be busy. 'If you want to know more,' he'd said, 'take down this address and drop by at noon tomorrow.'

My satnav told me to take the next exit on the left, the automated female voice so reassuringly calm I felt as if I had a friend along for the ride, offering moral support and encouragement. I heard my indicator click and realised I'd acted without dithering. I told myself I could still turn around, could return to the main road and head west to Brighton or east to Saltbourne. But it wasn't happening. I was sailing coastwards through smooth, wide roads of an estate of bungalows; then the estate was behind me, and I could see the sea again, glorious and timeless. The narrow road rose to a cliff-top peak, the angle obscuring the view further along the coast. Ahead of me were three clifftop villas, isolated from one another, bordered by white walls at the rear. Each villa resembled a stack of sugar cubes, as white as the coastline stretching ahead. Deliberately, I hadn't looked on Google Earth before setting out. Doing so had felt like too much of a commitment. Without the image of my destination, I could pretend to myself I was just taking a leisurely drive along the coast.

Now I wished I'd checked. Ilya Travis had money, that much was clear, and I was certain the money was dirty. I might have thought more about the wisdom of this trip had I been aware how ostentatious and isolated his house was. I parked on the narrow road near a pair of ornate black gates opening on to a sweeping gravel drive. When I got out of the car, a smaller side gate opened with smooth slowness. I glanced around, spotting the camera trained on the entrance. He was watching me, waiting. I crunched along the edge of the driveway into a treeless garden.

The surrounding walls obscured any view of the sea but you knew it was there. I could hear remote waves crashing on the shore far below, and the breeze was fresh, salty and exhilarating. Gulls wheeled overhead, white wings spread as they floated on currents of air. Around me, Ilya's garden was large, bland and flat, an expanse of patchy, landscaped grass broken up by gravel side paths and stone statues of the kind you might see in a garden centre. The plot seemed well kept but unloved and soulless. I was reminded of holiday lets whose low-maintenance gardens try to offer hints of magnificence, but succeed only in looking bleaker and cheaper for the attempt. I had to wonder if this was his home or just a temporary stay.

I took a surreptitious photo of the garden on my phone, just in case. In case what? In case it was the last photo I ever took?

No, people didn't openly give you their address if they were intending to bump you off. My imagination was getting carried away with itself. With my heart in my throat, I crunched along the final few metres of gravel and rang the bell of a door whose frosted glass panel was decorated with an ironwork grille of swirling leaves. Rude of him, I thought, not to be at the door for me. Presumably, he was the one who'd opened the gate, so he knew I was here. But then he hadn't struck me as the courteous type.

A dark blur formed behind the glass panel, growing into a shape too short and bulky to be him. Hell, I wasn't expecting other people. I must have got the wrong end of the stick. How embarrassing. A stout, middle-aged woman opened the door. She had a large plastic tote bag on one shoulder and a jacket draped over one arm. She was obviously about to leave. She gave me a polite smile and greeted me in a northern accent.

'Mr Travis is waiting for you in the main room,' she said, beckoning me indoors.

I entered a white, spacious entrance hall, archways left and right. The floor was tiled in fake sandstone, the buttery yellow gleam lending a warmth to the cavernous whiteness. Ahead, three broad steps rose to a wide corridor, a dun-coloured Persian-style carpet running along its length into the distance. Small display alcoves in the white walls featured vases, plates and vessels in copper and pewter. The woman pointed down the corridor and, with strong, eager hand gestures, directed me to turn left after the third door, through the arch, go down that corridor and take the first door on the right. She hitched her bag on her shoulder and nodded goodbye.

His staff, I thought, as she closed the door. Maybe his cleaner.

I stood for a moment in the silence, hesitant to leave the safety of the door. Then I remembered I was doing this for Sol and needed to be brave and selfless. My heels clicked on the shiny tiles of the hallway. I called 'hello' but doubted I'd get an answer. I kept walking, heels tapping, until, beyond the steps, the Persian runner softened the sound. Why the drama? Was anyone else here? Couldn't he have just answered the door like a regular person?

My blood quickened as I walked deeper into the villa, further away from the safe entrance. Archways gave glimpses of other archways, of pale, glossy floor tiles and polished pine door frames, some empty, some heavily curtained in brocade. Regular wooden doors didn't seem to feature here. The place was light and airy, its cool minimalist interior studded with objects of rustic texture. High windows and occasional skylights brought the bright, sparkling air of the coast indoors. The whole place looked as if it had been teleported in from the Mediterranean. It would be bitterly cold in a Sussex winter. Did he live here throughout the year? Did he even live here? It didn't feel like a home; more like a status symbol.

I could hear the faint crash of the sea, a slow rhythmic pulse as if the house had a heartbeat. The sound grew louder as I neared the arch I'd been directed towards. When I turned the corner, I was feet away from the entrance to the main room. A reflection of water cast silver ripples high on one wall as I walked into an expanse of whiteness. I half expected to find John and Yoko seated at a piano. Three steps, the width of the room, so long they were more akin to rock stratifications than interior architecture, took me up to the main arena. Half a mile ahead, or so it seemed, and beyond a huge stretch of sliding glass doors, was the pale blue sky, puffed with cloud, and the deep, glittering blue of the sea. The doors were open at the centre, and warm briny air had already settled in the room. Standing on an angular, white balcony, gazing out at the horizon, was Ilya, hair drawn up into a messy bun again.

My adrenaline soared. Heat prickled on the back of my neck and my veins felt tight, as if my blood was trying to surge beyond the confines of its narrow channels. He wore black sweatpants and his nut-brown shoulders were bared in a snug, grey vest, his biceps tautly contoured. The neat wedge of his back, shadowed with the latent strength of muscle at rest, was so beautiful that I couldn't help but mentally strip him down to a pair of bathing trunks. In my mind, he became one of those arrogant sods I'd encounter in the pool; a spectacular butterfly swimmer who'd hog the fast lane, his big shoulders powering his stroke, blades like wings, stunning to see but a pain to share a lane with.

He didn't acknowledge me as I crossed the white room, my heels clicking on the pale gold tiles. Either he was ignoring me or was oblivious to my presence. Our worlds didn't overlap. I recalled covertly eying his arse when he'd stood on the balcony at The Blue Bar, gazing out at nothing in particular. For a moment, he was a man always staring out of windows, a lonely guy looking for something he'd never find, lost in his own dreams.

'Hi there,' I called. 'It's Lana.'

He turned around and walked barefoot into the room, smiling faintly and pinning those unusual dark teal eyes on me. The bun and the clothing made it look as if he practised martial arts, the style with flick-knives. Even when he smiled, a cold cynicism remained in that strongly-boned face with its hawkish nose and plum-dark lips. His semi-beard was handsome, greyer than his head and not overly clipped to neatness. I fancied he didn't need to put much effort into looking good.

'Nice place you've got.' My mouth was dehydrated, my cheeks tacky against my teeth.

'So you found it OK, then?'

'Yes, no problem.' I laughed nervously. 'Just needed a satnav once I was indoors.'

'You want a drink?' He raised his brows.

I shook my head. 'Actually, yes. Water would be nice. Tap water's fine.'

'I'll be right back,' he said. 'Make yourself at home.'

He turned towards an archway and jogged down a short flight of steps into a shadowy room. I crossed to drop my handbag on a sofa of chrome and black leather, debating whether to sit down. How do you make yourself at home in a place devoid of homeliness? I glanced around, noting an enormous TV screen on one wall, and a middle-eastern style carpet hanging from a thick wooden pole on another. Anxious not to appear to be scoping out his place, I strode towards the open glass doors, inhaling deeply. I was feeling infinitely more relaxed than I had done a couple of minutes ago. Ilya seemed ordinary, at ease, no longer the sinister stranger with dubious intentions. Perhaps this was just going to be some awkward attempt at a date. But what did he have to tell me about Sol? And how did he know about me and Sol? Had he been watching us? Why?

I wanted to ask outright but thought it wiser not to push him. I got the impression he liked to be the one running the show and setting the pace, doing his best to keep people on the hop. Well, if that was what he wanted, let him have his fun.

I stepped beyond the glass doors and laughed from the peculiar joy of being on a cliff. I was on a raised patio bordered by a white wall topped with boxy crenellations, as if this were a modernist castle. A bedraggled potted palm stood in one corner and an onyx ashtray on a ceramic-tiled table was cluttered with cigarette ends. The breeze ruffled my hair and the sea roared, the brown palm tree leaves rustling dryly. I thought how pure and clear the light is on the south coast, as if it carries the essence of diamonds, silver and that ancient bright, white chalk. I was grateful I'd moved out of London after my divorce. I might have less money these days but, hey, I lived by the coast, owned my own bar and possibly had a hot, horny boyfriend. I wouldn't trade back for anything.

I filled my lungs, gazing down towards a sunken half-garden and the distant cliff edge. To the east, the land dipped and I watched waves smashing chaotically at a rocky outcrop at the base of the chalk-white cliff. Foam leaped and sprayed, water rolling this way and that in glorious, violent swells. A gull flew below the cliff edge, lower than me, and I was reminded of how high up we were, higher than the birds.

When I heard Ilya approach, I returned indoors. In his hand he carried a shallow bowl. He bent and placed it in the centre of the tiled floor.

'There you go,' he said, standing.

'What's that?'

'Your water.'

I stared at him, lost for words.

'On your knees,' he said.

'Are you fucking kidding me?'

'Get on the floor,' he said, 'and drink.' His voice was slow with threat, and a sneery antagonism lined his face.

I swallowed. 'You know what? I'm suddenly not so thirsty.'

I moved towards the sofa to retrieve my handbag. Ilya took a sidestep to block my path. I paused and we stood several feet apart, facing each other. I caught sight of that silver-pink scar on his jaw, gleaming through his short, scruffy beard. I thought my heart might explode.

'I want to leave,' I said.

'So soon?'

'Yes. Coming here was a mistake. I'm sorry to have wasted your time.'

'Don't you want to know the truth about your boyfriend?'

I tucked my hair behind my ears, straightened my spine, and drew a couple of deep breaths, trying not to freak out. 'Where is he? What do you know?'

'Drink, Lana. On your knees like a cute little puppy. Show me how much Sol means to you.'

'You tricked me,' I said. 'This is tantamount to blackmail.'

He grinned. 'I'm capable of far worse.'

I didn't doubt him for a moment. 'I wouldn't have bothered coming if I'd known you were going to play games like this,' I said. 'Why am I here?'

'Because I have answers to your questions about Sol. Answers that could change your life.'

'And what's in it for you?'

'The pleasure of seeing you squirm,' he said, smiling. 'Of having you in my power.'

I shook my head. 'If you'd wanted a kinky date, you could've just asked. And then I could have turned you down.'

'But I don't want a kinky date,' he replied. 'Too tame for my taste. Drink, Lana.'

For a long while, I didn't reply. I struggled desperately to find a solution to my dilemma. In the silence, the sea beyond the glass crashed against the foot of the cliff, as rhythmic and hypnotic as the sway of a lullaby.

'I don't trust you,' I said, finally. 'I could do what you ask. Could drink from your stupid bowl of water and you'd give me nothing in return.'

'Wise not to trust me,' he replied. 'But there's one thing I am, and that's honourable. Unlike, say, your boyfriend.'

'Who is he to you? What's your connection?' My voice was sharp with frustration.

Ilya glanced at the bowl of water. 'There's a good little puppy,' he cooed.

'You're trying to humiliate me.'

'Damn right I am.'

'Why?'

'Because it makes my dick hard.' He took a step closer. 'Even now, just picturing you on the floor, burning up with shame, is making me hard. You wanna feel?'

'Fuck you,' I breathed.

'I'd love it if you did.'

'I want to leave,' I said. 'Let me pass.'

'You sure about that?'

'Never been surer.'

He stepped aside, giving me free access to the sofa. Straggles of hair from his top knot hung around his face and neck. He looked like an evil overlord from another world, albeit an extremely attractive overlord. I crossed the room, head high, fearing he might pounce. But he didn't. He watched, smirking, as I collected my bag.

'I'll see myself out,' I said. 'Thanks for your hospitality.'

He laughed gently. 'Any time.'

My heels sounded louder than ever as I retraced my route. I felt his eyes on me as I descended the three vast steps and left the room, entering the labyrinth of archways and passages. Tears burned my eyes. Disorientated, I faltered, and headed in the wrong direction before I got my bearings. I turned the correct way, heart hammering as I found the corridor I'd walked along earlier. The door by which I'd entered stood in the distance like a vision of hope, daylight glowing through the frosted glass and iron-work leaves. All I needed to do was keep walking along the Persian runner. The carpet dulled the noise of my heels. I felt as if I were sailing along a white tunnel towards a bright light of freedom. The door wouldn't be locked, would it? Might I end up stuck in this building like a lab rat running around a maze? Keep walking, I told myself. Don't think about Ilya. Don't think about Sol. Just look after yourself.

I would go back to Saltbourne, to my empty flat in the cobbled mews, and I'd forget about them both. But, oh God, where was Sol? Why had he vanished? Was he in danger?

If I left this villa now, I might never know the truth. My pace slowed and I grappled for reason and sense. Supposing Sol came to harm because I'd refused to drink water served in an unconventional manner? Because I'd prioritised my pride over his welfare? It was only water from a bowl. And a regular soup bowl, not a dog bowl or anything similarly vile.

I paused and leaned against a whitewashed wall, press-ing my head against stone. The faint pulse of the sea surrounded me, soft and peaceful. That crystalline coastal light hung in the broad corridor. In a shelf cut into the wall, a pewter vase gleamed like a holy relic. For a while, time stood still. I was held in a limbo of indecision, in a place of worshipful calm, distant waves murmuring like an incantation.

Do it, Lana. Do it.

Don't, Lana. Don't.

I told myself you only experience humiliation if you buy into the context. There was nothing intrinsically demeaning about drinking from a bowl. The problem arose from the fact that animals, lacking digital dexterity, drank on all fours and we believe ourselves to be superior to animals. Ilya wanted to force me lower, make me less than human. But if I drank willingly, happily, as if it were no big deal, I could thwart his attempts to debase me for his personal kicks. I could spin the situation to suit my needs, not his. Or I could try.

Besides, it wasn't as if these kinds of games were anathema to me. In a different situation, being shamed and humiliated would have been right up my alley. But this wasn't a game. Ilya had something I wanted and that gave him authentic power. Even while that imbalance was infuriating, a small part of me thrilled to it because I found him attractive and excitingly dangerous. But I knew it was unwise to pay heed to that part.

Could I walk away? Was staying such a big deal? What would Sol want me to do?

What did *I* want to do? I withdrew my compact from my bag and checked my reflection. My skin was shiny so I blotted and powdered. I looked and felt calmer. 'For Sol,' I told myself as I snapped the mirror shut.

I strode boldly down the corridor, shoulders back, and returned to the sea-view room.

'OK, I'll drink,' I called breezily. I took the three broad steps up into the room. 'Bring it on!'

Ilya lay sprawled on the chrome and leather sofa, knees wide apart, as if he'd been expecting me. His posture was lewd, indolent and menacing. He grinned and nodded to the bowl of water. 'All yours.'

I fished about in my handbag for a hair elastic, set the bag aside, and briskly pulled my bob back into a tail.

I smoothed stray strands from my face, hooked threads behind my ears and knelt. The floor was cold and hard against my shins, as smooth as ceramic to the touch. The big rectangular tiles spread out around me like a weird football pitch, their soft honey sheen mottled and lightly veined. I tipped forwards, my clammy hands flat to the floor, and pursed my lips on the water's surface. Immediately I realised I didn't know how to drink on all fours. I didn't have the tongue technique to lap.

'Drink,' said Ilya. 'Don't pretend.'

I made a little slurp and dipped my head up and down, hoping to give the impression I was drinking. I tried to ignore the pulse ticking between my thighs. In the corner of my eye, I saw him stand.

'Don't stop until I say so.'

His bare feet moved closer. I kept pecking and sucking at the water, trying not to feel like a fool. His footsteps made small sticky noises on the polished floor; then his feet were by my head. I slotted my eyes sideways. Even his toes were handsome, the nails neat, ivory squares. My heartbeat quickened. I suppressed the urge to put myself at a safe distance from him. Just keep drinking. It's a means to an end, no more than that. The water cooled my lips and I concentrated on the sensation, hoping to block out the fear and the desire. I sensed him bend closer and then felt his hand on the back of my head. It was the first time he'd touched me. I feared he was about to push my face into the bowl but, instead, he deftly removed the band from my hair. A fine, blonde curtain swept over my face. Lust bolted to my groin. Dear God, that he could get to me so quickly, could make me so weak and soft in the cunt, was beyond my comprehension. The tips of my hair dipped in the water and filaments swirled in the liquid, tangling with my tongue. Before long, wet hair was clinging to my cheeks and lips, ruining my bid to stay tidy and crisp. Embarrassment heated my face. I prayed I could conceal my arousal from him.

'Put your hands behind your back,' he said. 'As if they're cuffed.'

I did as told, the pulse drumming between my thighs as I continued to drink.

'Now we're talking,' said Ilya, and I heard amusement in his voice. 'Sit back.'

I obeyed, perching on my heels, cheeks flushed. My hand instinctively rose to my messy, wet face. Quick as a flash, Ilya grabbed my wrist, preventing me. His grip was warm and firm. More than firm. Severe. Think of Sol, I told myself. Things were bound to improve once I'd seen this through. Ilya leaned close and I glared at him. I caught the faint hint of his scent and I wanted to snuffle all over his neck, breathing in his skin's oil, his sweat and his fragrance, eager to get the maximum amount of him.

'Your hands are cuffed,' he said. 'Remember? Keep them in place until I say you're free.'

He released me and I pressed my wrists together as required. My lips and chin were uncomfortably damp. Water dripped from the ends of my hair onto my shirt, cool droplets tickling uncomfortably below my clothes. Ilya removed the bowl, feet squeaking on the tiles. I gazed directly ahead at the parted doors and the line of the horizon above the stone balustrade of the patio. The sky was cornflower blue, the vapour trail of a plane slicing a fluffy line behind the glass.

Ilya returned to stand in front of me. 'Look up at me.'

I did, noting that his sweatpants were bulky at the crotch. He towered above me, and his height and strength versus my reluctant, kneeling obedience made my groin flood with a yearning for submission. Not for servility and obedience but for a forced, whorish submission.

'It's very touching,' he said, 'that you'd abase yourself to this extent for the sake of a man.'

'I'm not abased,' I replied coolly. 'Just slightly damp.'

He laughed. 'Nice try. So Sol means a lot to you?'

I shrugged. 'I guess so. Are you going to tell me what this is about? Or are you just going to keep tormenting me?'

'The latter. For a while, at least. Because I'm interested, Lana. Interested to know whether you're making a genuine sacrifice here, in doing what I ask. Or getting pleasure from it. I said, "Look up at me."'

I'd let my gaze drift. I returned to my meek, doe-eyed pose, on my knees in my invisible handcuffs. 'Why?' I said boldly. 'Would it ease your conscience if you thought I found this exciting?'

He squatted on his haunches so we were eye to eye. Carefully, he thumbed wetness from my chin. I held his gaze, refusing to be cowed. 'Yes. Yes, it would,' he said. 'More than you'll ever know.' He tipped his head, sarcastically tender and concerned. 'But, either way, it's not going to stop me.'

He brought his hands to the top button of my shirt and unfastened it. I let him. He glanced from my cleavage to my face, trying to read me. I was doing my best to give nothing away, to deny him the comfort of my consent. Despite the late summer warmth, goosebumps crawled across my skin. He undid a second button, continuing to watch me. My face was stone. Ilya's smile curled in triumph as he opened a third button, widening my shirt enough to push the cotton over my shoulders and down my arms, symbolically trapping me. Water dripped from the ends of my hair, cool droplets rolling down my skin.

He eyed my bra. 'Sol's a lucky guy.' He placed a broad hand over one lacy cup and gently caressed, scrutinising my face.

I knew I was reddening, and could do nothing to stop it. Between my thighs, arousal throbbed, my flesh becoming plump and open, my wetness seeping. He kept massaging my covered breast while observing me, driving me half-mad with lust. Anger simmered alongside my desire but the latter was stronger. At length, he tucked a finger behind the lacy cup and firmly stroked my nipple. A small sound escaped my lips as my tip crinkled under his touch. I closed my eyes in regret.

'Don't fight it, Lana,' he breathed. 'I'm not going to tell anyone. This can be our little secret.' He pushed more of his hand into my bra, squeezing. My nipple was as hard as a pebble. 'We can have a good time together, you and I. Don't make this difficult for me.'

He withdrew his hand and methodically nudged my bra straps aside. He stroked across my collarbones and swirled a finger over my bared shoulders, as if covetous of my skin. I did my best not to react, knowing he'd see that as a victory, but between my thighs I was a storm of need. He pushed the straps further down my arms and then slipped a hand into one cup. His broad, confident touch made me groan.

'That's better.' He lifted my flesh from the fabric. 'Try and enjoy yourself, Lana.'

I pinched my lips together as he scooped me free of the bra. He wriggled both cups lower, leaving me exposed and half-dressed, hands still clasped as if I were in bondage. My skin was streaked with dampness, occasional drips falling from my hair. I kept trying to clutch at rationality, at a fragment of good sense that might urge me to stop but my resistance was low. Lust consumed me. I was greedy for him and couldn't bear to break away.

'Tip your head back,' he said. 'Imagine your hair is tied to your wrists.' His voice was soft and soothing.

I obeyed, arching my back and gazing up at the bright, white ceiling, knowing the position made my breasts jut.

'Pretty as a picture.' He ran a hand down my neck and along the valley of my cleavage. 'I assume you have a lipstick in your bag,' he said. 'Do you?'

'Yes,' I whispered.

'May I?'

'Yes.'

I listened to him stand and root around in my handbag. I wanted to direct him away from the Mac lipstick and towards the Boots 17 but was loath to complicate matters by giving him instructions. I winced to think of how weak I was. I wanted to know about Sol, yes, but this was a long way from heroic sacrifice. I liked it. Liked being on my knees and at the mercy of a man I should be running ten thousand miles from.

I glanced aside as Ilya approached with the lipstick. I was held in invisible bonds, head back, wrists tied to ankles, and I didn't want to move. I wasn't sure if he would use actual, physical force if I declared I wasn't prepared to go any further. I didn't think so. He got off on the fact I was acquiescing to this, and ostensibly doing so out of concern

for another man. Ropes and handcuffs might be hot, yes.
But Ilya's greatest pleasure was in seeing me fix myself in
these psychological snares. He wanted to see me doing it
to myself. That was the worst of it. I couldn't escape him
because I couldn't escape myself.

'Head back, Lana,' he said.

He crouched and wiped my chest and breasts, removing traces of moisture. I flinched at the first touch of
lipstick there; then I held still, breathing shallowly to
give him a steady canvas. He wrote on my skin, but it was
impossible to track the letters. All I felt was the cool,
waxy press of lipstick moving across my chest and skimming the upper swell of my breasts. He clicked the top
back on the tube and rolled it across the floor, away from
us. He stood.

'Beautiful,' he said. 'So beautiful that I want to stick my
cock in your mouth and fuck your face. Fuck you like a
cheap, dirty cumslut. How about that, Lana?'

I said nothing although my heart boomed. I hated him
but, even so, a dark, sultry lust uncurled within me, steal-
ing through my veins. He bent close and pinched my jaw
in one hand, squishing my lips into a duck shape. 'I said,'
he continued sternly, '"How about that, Lana?"'

I jerked my head free of his grip, a grunt of annoyance
snagging in my throat, but I kept my wrists locked
together.

'Is that a "no"?' he asked, straightening.

I didn't reply.

'So, is that a "yes"?'

Again, I remained silent.

'Yes or no, Lana?' From the corner of my eye, I saw
him whip off his grey vest and fling it to the ground. 'How

do you want to take this? The easy way or…forgive the pun, the hard way?'

I cleared my throat, eyes still fixed on the white ceiling. 'Do what you need to do.'

'I wish Sol could see you now.'

'You're such a cunt,' I breathed. I glanced towards him, catching a glimpse of his crotch, his black sweatpants tenting with swollen cock. His thumbs were hooked in his waistband. My groin thumped harder.

He laughed darkly. 'I know, I know.'

The red lipstick letters were a blur across my body but I couldn't make out any words. Didn't even want to try. In my peripheral vision, I saw him stretch the waist of his sweatpants over the thrust of his cock, slow and threatening.

'And still she waits,' he taunted as his thick length sprang out, hard, handsome and snaking with veins.

I did wait, it was true. I waited as he lowered his sweatpants and stripped. He tossed his clothes across the floor. I tilted my head a fraction. His thighs were powerfully curved, his flushed erection bobbing from a patch of thick, black hair. His dark skin faded to paleness around his hips, accentuating the privacy of cock. I longed to sit up straight so I could drink in the sight of his nakedness but I held still. He wrapped his fist around his length and stepped closer, hand shunting with intimidating steadiness.

'All this dick,' he said. 'And it's all for you.'

He stood by my shoulder and then swung one leg across me so he was straddling my upper body. I tried to breathe steadily, aware I was failing. His thighs rested against my shoulders. I caught a waft of his scent – body scent not aftershave – and though I wanted to close my eyes and block him out, I couldn't. Slanting above my face, his big, broad cock dominated my field of vision, a lattice of blue veins flowing beneath stretched, satiny skin. I gazed past his length to the hair on his taut stomach rising to thick black curls cloaking his chest, and higher still to that cruel, fascinating, gleeful face.

'Stay like that,' he said, meeting my eyes. 'Arms behind you, head back for me.'

He reached down and cupped my jaw in his hands, shuffling closer. His velvety balls brushed against my chin; then he re-angled us so the blunt head of his cock was nudging against my lips. When I didn't open to take him, he laughed and swayed left and right, lightly swatting my face with his erection.

'Open up, Lana,' he said. 'Stop acting as if you don't want it.' His end butted at my lips again and, when I failed to oblige, he cradled the back of my head in one hand and pinched my nostrils together with his other.

I made a muffled squeal of complaint but kept my lips tight.

'Come on,' he urged. 'Give me that whorish mouth. Show me what you're made of.'

My breath burst out in a rush and Ilya seized his chance. He lunged forwards, driving his hardness into my gasp with a smug, triumphant grunt. He clasped my head in both hands, tipping my arched body backwards as he slammed towards my throat. I coughed, gulped and spluttered but he showed no mercy. My saliva spilled from my mouth, sometimes erupting in bursts. I squealed in wet protest but all the while, and much to my shame, no matter how viciously he thrust, I kept my hands locked behind my back exactly as he'd instructed.

'I knew you'd like it,' he gasped. 'Knew you were a dick-hungry bitch. I bet you'd drop to your knees for anyone, wouldn't you? Let anyone use that greedy little mouth. That cunt, that arse. All of you. All of your holes for anyone and everyone.'

Moments later, he withdrew and inched backwards, cock in his fist. He pumped hard, groaning, his end aimed at my face. 'Open your mouth,' he snapped. 'Now.'

I complied because there was no use pretending anymore. He edged further back, eyes darting from my face to my breasts as he jerked himself off, face tight with focus, noises snagging in his throat.

With a loud, broken groan, he came, his liquid jetting out in spurts. I flinched and blinked. Deliberately, he marked my face and chest, targeting the last of his come at the lipsticked words on my skin. I tasted only a droplet of him. My tongue darted out, searching my lips for more.

Ilya gave a soft, satisfied grunt. I looked up to see him grinning. 'Don't move,' he said, walking away. 'Party's not over yet.'

I was motionless save for the heave of my ribcage and the swivelling of my gaze. I eyed the flex of his narrow buttocks as he slid open a high white door camouflaged as a wall. Inside was a floor-to-ceiling jumble of shelving and boxes. I heard him rooting around and then he returned to me, carrying a large white object on a cord. I strained my eyes to identify the object without breaking from my position. As he neared, I realised it was a heavy-headed massage wand, a toy I'd previously been curious about but had rejected for being too cumbersome, noisy and ugly. He knelt by my knees, crumpled my skirt high and pushed my thighs further apart.

'Let's see what we've got here.' He ran a finger over the fabric of my crotch. 'A greedy, wet cunt,' he said. 'Just as I expected.'

He flicked the switch on the wand and the motor whirred loudly.

'You look a mess,' he continued. 'You look used and cheap but it's obvious you love it. Love being treated like a filthy whore. And now I'm going to prove you love it by making you come. If you want to know about Sol, keep your hands behind your back.'

He guided the wand towards the juncture of my thighs and I pressed my wrists together.

'Don't try and resist,' he said. 'There's no point. Because one way or the other, I'll force it out of you.' He moved the juddering head of the massager onto my underwear and let it drift over my damp, silky crotch. I gasped at the intensity of the vibrations, a fast, heavy rumble that stirred the depths of my flesh, even with a delicate touch.

'That good?' Ilya brought the weighty head of the wand to rest on the gauzy fabric covering my pubis. He nudged downwards, and the tremors reverberated through my groin, seeming to caress my clit from all angles, inside and out, without even making direct contact. I gasped over and over, shivers of nearness clutching in my thighs already. I wished I could touch him, could clasp his magnificent, naked body, and then bend over and have him fuck me from behind while this beast of a machine stimulated my clit. I suspected he wasn't about to give me the satisfaction.

'Let's take a look at that dirty, wet cunt.' With careful fingers, he edged aside my knickers, baring my split. My flesh tingled under his fleeting touch and I craved penetration, ached for him to fill my hollow, pliant body with the clumsy, aggressive thrust of his hand.

'Sol's cunt,' said Ilya. 'So this is what he gets to fuck, is it?' Still holding my underwear to one side and focusing on what he was doing, he let the wand hover on my clit. 'Nice work if you can get it.'

I wailed, my orgasm rushing close. He laughed gently and moved the tool to a less intense spot, allowing it to throb against the swollen outer folds of my labia.

'Go on,' he said, glancing from my exposure to my face. 'Come, Lana. Come while you're covered in spunk after being face-fucked by a man you barely know. You can act as if you hate being used but I know the truth. That you'd drive miles to a stranger's house to get what you know you deserve.'

I squeezed my eyes shut, panting for breath as he released my knickers, keeping the wand inside the elastic so it throbbed within my underwear. Shame and humiliation blazed on my skin. I was wretched with lust. Seconds later, Ilya held the wand to my clit again. My thighs were crammed with urgency, arousal shooting across synapses, my flesh quivering. I snapped my eyes open, howling and swearing, feeling as if my lower body were melting while vibrations poured into me, churning me into a new form. Ilya looked different. No, he'd changed position. His fist was held high. My heart lurched. He was filming me on his phone. Oh fuck.

I glanced at him. 'No,' I whimpered.

He had one hand on the wand, the other raised with his phone tipped towards me. He grinned, looking from the little screen to me. He rolled the hammering wand-head away from my clit, taking the edge off my closeness.

'Sorry, I didn't hear that,' he mocked, nudging towards my clit again.

I panted and gasped. After the jolt of shock, I didn't even care. I was too far gone to protest any further. All I wanted was to come. My body started to buck, tiny jerks rushing along my spine as my peak bunched tighter. My groin was a tumult of sensation, the strength of the vibrations unlike anything I'd ever experienced. Being recorded made me feel objectified and insignificant. Just a porno woman coming. A slut for unknown viewers to get off on. My fantasy of being watched, a reality I'd shied away from, was made manifest in Ilya's cold, controlled, intrusive recording.

I teetered on the edge of ecstasy, afraid of how hard I was going to climax. I was spaced out, floating, breathless, debased. Then I started to tumble, screaming as the first wave of my orgasm ripped through me. The looseness of bliss surged, my back arching, my inner muscles clutching as wave after wave lifted and lowered me. My calf muscles clenched and my feet twisted. I unclasped my hands to steady myself, dropping closer to the floor, knees splayed.

Trails of silver stars swirled behind my eyes. I heaved for breath, cursing in incredulity. I felt wrung out and my clit was still pulsing hard. Ilya removed the wand and silenced it. He brought the phone camera in front of my face then downwards for a final shot.

'That's who she is,' he said, holding still before lowering his arm and switching off the camera.

My ragged panting merged with the rhythmic beat of the sea, warp and weft, water and breath. I felt cocooned in a soundscape, glowing with bliss, my mind stunned into unthinking. I could barely feel my legs. Ilya fiddled with his phone, paying no attention to me. He laughed to himself, watching the small screen. I heard my own groans of pleasure, remote and small.

'Looking good, Lana.'

I pushed myself forwards, wiping wetness and damp hair from my face. Ilya, kneeling beside me, had a semi, his stretched curved length resting on his wiry black pubes.

'And my reward?' I asked through gasps and gulps. 'Where's Sol? Or are you going to keep spinning this out?'

'You want to see?' He turned the phone screen towards me, inches from my face. I saw myself in miniature, head thrown back, face twisted, crying out as I climaxed. I looked pained and shocked. My cries sounded as if they were trapped within Ilya's phone.

Naked in front of me, as if he were my friend and lover, Ilya kept the phone steady, watching me watch myself. The shaky camera angle panned down from my face to my chest, to three bold, bright words written in red on my pale skin, rising and falling with my breathlessness. Moisture and come had smeared some of the lipstick, and pink dribbles trickled towards my breast, but every letter was legible. Inside the phone, Ilya's recorded voice said, 'That's who she is.'

The words on my body read: SOL'S DEAD WHORE.

I recoiled, shuffling on my buttocks across the glossy tiles. 'No, no!'

My blood was ice. Ilya gave me a predatory grin. My heel skidded on wetness as, half-seated, I tried desperately to push myself away. I wanted to stand, to flee, but my body was useless, stripped of strength. My orgasm had left me trembling and now fear made me shake. 'No! Don't hurt me. Please.'

Ilya crawled after me on all fours, his pace heavy and

plodding, lips tilted in a sick smile. 'I'm starting to like you, Lana,' he said. 'It almost pains me to have to do this.'

'No, please,' I begged. I scooted backwards on my butt, making feeble progress. 'I'll do anything. Don't hurt me, please.'

'You'd do anything, anyway,' he said coolly. 'So your offer doesn't count for much.'

'Please,' I sobbed. One arm gave way and I slumped to the floor. Quickly I propped myself up again.

Ilya followed with deliberate, lumbering slowness as if emphasising the hopelessness of my situation. His lengthening cock swayed by his thighs. I kept trying to power myself away but my arms were as wobbly as my legs, my elbows made of sponge.

'Where's Sol?' I cried. 'Who are you?'

With a grin and a controlled lurch, Ilya grabbed my hair at the nape of my neck. I screamed. He crouched above me, big shoulders blocking out the room's whiteness, and I froze. His knuckles dug into the back of my head. His cock twitched higher.

'You want to know what I've got for you?' he asked.

I couldn't speak, couldn't move except to tremble.

'This is going to hurt, Lana.' He watched me intently, eyes sparkling with cruel glee, brow hunching in a frown. His expression darkened and the fist gripping my hair tightened.

'Your boyfriend's a cop,' he said. 'He's a spook, an undercover officer, and you've been taken for a ride, sugarplum.'

I stared at him. Impossible. This was another bad dream. I needed to wake up and get a grip. 'No.' I was melting into the floor, turning into the tiles. 'No.'

'Yes.' His voice was clipped and firm. 'Sol's used you, Lana. But not in the way you enjoy.'

'No. Not true. Can't be.'

'And I want him off the case,' continued Ilya. 'Off my fucking back. You hear?' He pulled on my hair, arching my neck backwards. He leaned towards me and, with the wet tip of his tongue, licked a line across my throat, left to right.

I wondered if I were dying. Had already died. This reality wasn't possible.

'And if you don't make that happen,' he said, 'then that's what you'll be. Sol's dead whore. They'll find you in a ditch one day with those very words carved into your pretty, white flesh.'

The damp track of his tongue cooled on my skin.

'I don't care how you make it happen,' he continued, 'but you make sure it does. OK?'

I couldn't do anything except sob and shake beneath him, stuck in the cold grip of horror. Because I knew it was true. All the pieces began slotting into place. Sol's patchy backstory, his interest in Misha, his recent disappearance.

Besides, Ilya had no reason to lie to me. I wondered what Sol's reasons were. Why me? I didn't even care that my life might be in danger. Sol had deceived me, betrayed me. That appalling knowledge made me realise how much I cared for him, even at the point we were unravelling and he was turning into someone else.

'I'd really like to fuck you now,' said Ilya, 'but I think you're traumatised enough so I'll spare you.'

'Who *are* you?' My voice was a shivery whisper.

'I help people out,' he said calmly. 'Make sure business transactions go smoothly. That kind of thing.'

'What kind of thing? Who's Misha?'

'*Was* Misha,' he corrected.

'Who was he?'

'He was a grasping, double-crossing cunt,' said Ilya, his voice perfectly level. 'He was supplying certain chemicals to, let's say, a different pharmaceutical industry to the one he legitimately worked in. Then he got greedy and started supplying to a rival company. It's quite fortunate he died, really. I was about to have a quiet word in his shell-like on behalf of some associates.'

'And you were going to do that in my bar?' I asked. 'That's why you were looking for him? Is my bar some kind of drugs den?'

Ilya gave me an icy grin. 'I wasn't looking for *him*, Lana. I knew he was dead. I was looking for you.'

'Why?' My voice fractured into a sob.

'So you can steer Sol and his merry men away from me.'

'I don't know anything,' I said, my words tumbling in a panic. 'I swear. I don't know how I can influence Sol. I have no money, no connections. I don't know what I can do. Please, please! Don't hurt me, please.'

'You'll think of something.'

'How? What? Sol's not going to listen, is he?' I cried. 'Not if I don't mean anything to him. Not if it was all a sham.'

Ilya released my hair and stood. 'And that's the greatest tragedy,' he said. 'I've seen you together. It's obvious he adores you. But, trust me, he can't have it both ways. Now tidy yourself up and leave. You've served your purpose.'

I couldn't move. 'You're vile,' I said. 'Despicable.'

'I know,' he said, grinning. 'But you enjoyed it.'

Dressing and trying to make myself presentable was the worst humiliation. I wanted out of there, fast. I made a cursory attempt to clean myself with tissues but the lipstick remained as a stubborn red blur across my chest. I gave up and grabbed my bag. I tried to fasten my shirt to the neck as I hurried from the room but my hands wouldn't stop shaking.

'I'm watching you, Lana,' he said as I left.

I fled down the white corridor, following the enormous Persian runner to the entrance hall, where light glowed in the glass panel of the door. Outside, in the strange, sudden ordinariness of the sun, I ran down the gravel driveway, trying not to sob. The central metal gate parted as I approached, the large gate for vehicles rather than the side gate for people, as if Ilya wanted to emphasise I truly was free to go. The gates swung open, ironwork arms welcoming me on to the empty avenue, where my car stood like a small sanctuary. Evidently, he was still watching me. I imagined him smirking at my image on a screen, the damsel in distress fleeing the ogre in his lair.

Even now, hours later and safe at home, I feel as if his eyes are on me. I've bathed twice since then. I can't get rid of him.

For the first time in years, I didn't swim today. I must swim.

I need another lipstick too. I left mine at his, discarded on those buttermilk, fake-stone tiles. He won't return it, will he? Maybe he'll bin it or keep as a souvenir. Maybe he'll use it on some other poor woman. I'll never be able to wear that colour again.

I can still feel the line of his saliva on my neck, as if its coldness has been soldered there. I don't know what to do.

How can I influence Sol if I can't even contact him? I contemplated leaving a message on his phone, telling him what has happened, but I'm too scared. His phone could be tapped. I don't know who's watching who, or how to distinguish lies from truth.

My head's spinning as I sit here, propped up in bed, writing. My brandy is enormous. I'm going over and over the past, analysing Sol's behaviour from my new, darkened perspective. Everything makes a sick kind of sense and I wish it didn't. I wish I could roll back time so I could unmeet him, unsleep with him, unknow him, unlove him.

And if he knew the truth about me, if he knew what I'd done, he'd probably wish for much the same.

Part 6

I close the journal and switch off my Maglite. There are no further entries after that. I feel guilty as hell for reading her inner life. But, as I peel off my gloves, I'm also thinking I am seventeen different kinds of fucked. My cover's been blown. Travis is on to me. I need to get off the case, pronto. Worse, after all I've put her through, Lana's going to hate me to high heaven and I can't say I blame her because now I hate me too. I fucking hate me. Have done for a long time, doing a job like this. Right now, the hate is spiking.

I drop the gloves on the bed beside the journal and remove my glasses. A noise startles me. I turn. She's standing in the bedroom doorway, so petite and fair, my English rose. I didn't hear her come back. Too absorbed in my reading. Hell. A rookie mistake. Her blue eyes are wide, a hand's clamped to her mouth, and she's just staring at me. Staring and staring like I'm a monster. And I think, no. Now I am eighteen different kinds of fucked.

But so is she. Because this account of events isn't a diary. It isn't her truth. It's a lie, a trap, an alibi, or something else I can't begin to wrap my head around. My

English rose, she isn't without her thorns. Meaning she's screwed too. We are both damned. We're going to hell in the same handbasket or to jail alone.

I want to haul her into my arms because, holy fuck, this woman blows my mind and I've missed her. But now we're strangers to each other because I've read her shit and I'm busted and we can't get near. Besides, if my suspicions are correct, I'm concerned she might be dangerous. Petite and fair can be deceptive, especially to dumb schmucks like me who allow their dicks to get the better of them. But, no, who am I trying to kid? It wasn't my dick, it was my heart. Still is.

'I didn't know you swam every day,' I say, feeling nervous.

She drops her hand from her mouth. 'Is it true?' she asks. 'Are you a cop?'

'Yes.'

'Oh fuck fuck fuck.' Her voice is so soft and thin, so devastated. 'Are you wired up now?' she asks. 'Or bugged or . . . or whatever the terminology is?'

'No, I'm clean. It's just me and you. Always has been.'

She shakes her head. 'I don't believe you.'

'I don't blame you,' I reply. 'Listen, sit down. Let's talk this through.' I pat the bed and immediately regret it. That must have looked pretty skeevy.

Wisely, she ignores my suggestion. 'Sol Miller?' she says. 'Is that even your name?'

I shake my head. 'I'm Sol Revivo. Solomon Revivo.' And in my mind, my wisecracking alter ego pipes up, 'Hey, good to meet you!'

She covers her mouth again, arms wrapped across her front, and goes back to doing the stare thing.

'Lana—'

She lowers her hand from her mouth. 'Who are you working for?'

I breathe as quietly as I can. I feel like a stabbed coffee bag, life whistling out of me. 'London Met.' I try a smile. 'So I can get you all the police-issue handcuffs you want, Cha Cha. Upgrade those old Hiatts.' The joke falls flat. That's understandable.

'I don't know who you are,' she says, voice shaking. 'You are made of lies.'

'No,' I say. 'Not made of, I swear. I've lied to you, yes, and from the very bottom of my heart, I am sorry for that.'

Hell, I can't say anything that doesn't make me sound like an asshole. I decide to shut up. Almost. 'Ask me anything you want,' I say, and a voice in my head goes, 'Gee, that's big of you, Revivo.'

'How did you get into my house?' she asks.

Straight for the jugular. 'I made a duplicate of your key.' I have never felt shame as bone-deep as this.

'You bastard,' she breathes. 'How? When?'

I clear my throat. 'I took a clay impression.'

These sordid truths of my profession feel like a tawdry gift. I can't offer much to excuse my behaviour but at least I can expose how we work. Keep on giving her one hundred per cent truths. Not that I can ask her to believe them. But she's not exactly Mary Poppins herself. Lord knows what her story is. I have to remind myself that, much as I want to hurl myself at her feet and beg forgiveness for my deception, I need to be on my guard. Because Lana Greenwood probably ought to be begging for forgiveness too. Unless, oh fuck. Unless this relationship means jack shit to her and I'm a bigger fool than I thought. My self-loathing reaches new heights. What world do I inhabit?

'What are you doing here?' she asks. 'Are you back from Birmingham for good?'

My heart breaks a little. 'Lana, there was no Birmingham. The new job doesn't exist. It's part of my exit strategy.'

She shakes her head as if trying to clear her thoughts. 'Your *what*?'

'I'm being pulled from the operation,' I say. 'I have to withdraw from you without arousing your suspicions. I'm meant to dick you about a bit, make you mistrust me. Then I vanish.'

'Withdraw?' The word is pure contempt.

'I'm too involved with you, Lana. And my superior officers know it. We're not meant to get romantically attached to people we're—'

'Romantically attached?' She's sneering at my choice of words again.

'It's the Met, Lana.' I'm trying not to raise my voice but I'm so fucking frustrated. 'We don't use the phrase "fall in love".'

I want to show her the truth, to unpeel my outer self and say, here, take a look, this is me. But I can't. We can't. None of us can ever completely know another person but this is a different ball game altogether. My line of work amplifies the basic tenet of human existence, the unknowability that leaves us locked in our own meat, clawing to get out in search of another's unreachable soul. Trying to stave off the isolation. Not that they mention that on any training course.

'This fake IT job was going to land me a contract in Spain,' I continue. 'I'd make out you could come and visit.

I'd send you a postcard from Europe. Just one. Then you'd never hear from me again. That's the plan. I'm meant to be executing it now.' I crimp my lips together, trying to stay tough on the outside. 'But I can't do it, Lana.'

My voice thins to a squeak. It's pitiful.

I cough and draw a breath. 'If it helps any,' I say, 'you could get me hauled over the coals. Sue the ass off the Met.'

'Every cloud,' she says bitterly.

'I'm sorry.' The word will never suffice but what else do I have right now?

She takes a step into the room, arms curled around herself as if it's cold in here. 'So is my life in danger?' she asks. 'From Ilya Travis?'

'We can get you police protection.'

She looks at me, aghast. I feel bad that it's about to get worse.

'Why did you kill Misha, Lana?'

A sob erupts from her, a snatch of a wail that chills me to the marrow. She tries to swallow it, clamps a hand to her mouth again, and staggers back against the bedroom door. Bump. Her noise falls to whimpers and sniffles. I know I've guessed correctly. It's some time before she has the composure to speak. But that's OK. I can wait.

Eventually she says, 'Are you spying on me? Is this why we were together? Have you known all along?'

And that breaks me, that totally fucking breaks me. I'm half off the bed, about to run to her, to scoop her up in my arms and squeeze the pain away. And the words are there, formed, ready to leap from my mouth: *No, Lana, no! I love you, you crazy fucking bitch. I love you, and this isn't about that.*

But I freeze and I don't speak because sanity kicks in. I realise those aren't appropriate declarations to make to a suspected murderer, especially not when you're a cop. Besides, she's kinda in the ballpark with those questions of hers.

'I smelled chlorine in your hair,' I say. 'At Dravendene. When we were fucking in the forest.'

She nods heavily. Comprehension's dawning, for one of us at least.

'The way you cried out,' she says. 'When you came, you howled like...'

'Like I was in pain,' I offer. 'Like I was shattering into pieces. Like I'd just realised this woman I was fucking, who I was really getting to like, realised she was my enemy. And I should back off if I knew what was good for me.'

'I'm not your enemy.' Her voice is soft as velvet.

There's a lump in my throat. 'Why did you kill him, Lana? That's the part I can't figure out.'

'It was an accident,' she says, quiet as a mouse.

'Care to tell me about it?'

Maybe my tone is off. She's suddenly angry. 'Why the fuck should I tell you anything?'

I have to concede she has a point.

'For a long time,' I say, 'I had you pegged as working with Misha. Thought maybe the bar was a business front. But I'm pretty sure I'm wrong on that score. If I'm not, then you're damn good, Lana. And I take my hat off to you.'

'I didn't know him,' she says. 'Just a customer. It was an accident.'

'So you keep saying,' I reply. 'You wanted me to read this journal, right?'

She's silent, just looks embarrassed.

'Because you're always leaving it lying around the place. Hell, Lana. One night you left it open on the coffee table.'

'Why are you in my home?' she asks.

I sigh. We're back to me being the one in the wrong. I figure I have to take it. This isn't the time to discuss who has the moral advantage here, who's committed the worst sin.

'I came back to continue reading your...story,' I say. Man, I didn't meant that to sound quite so sarcastic. 'I started reading before I made out I was leaving for Birmingham,' I explain. 'Couldn't leave it hanging. Thought the truth might start to emerge if I wasn't on the scene.' I check my wristwatch. 'I thought you'd be at the bar till late.'

'I'm in no mood for it tonight,' she says. 'Raf's with Bruno. They're going to lock up. I'm exhausted. I came back to sleep. I saw you through the blinds so I crept in.'

Ah, yeah. Those blinds I'd left open so I could spot her if she came back early. Hoist by my own petard.

'So what are you trying to convince me of with this?' I say, gesturing to the journal. 'Your innocence?'

She nods.

'But you're not innocent,' I say.

'And neither are you,' she replies crisply. Her shoulders stiffen and her chin tips up. 'So tell me, Mr Revivo. Why did we have a relationship? What did I mean to you?'

I note that she keeps using the past tense. 'Sit down, Lana. Please.'

She shakes her head. 'Tell me.'

I draw a deep breath. I can't sugar-coat any of this. But I wish she'd sit down with me. The way she's standing in the doorway like that makes me edgy. As if she's on the verge of walking out. I'm on her bed with her diary. She's looking in at me, and I'm looking in at her life. It's not good, really not good. I am the lowest of the low. Even if she meant for this to happen, I should have been a bigger guy. Infiltrating a bunch of crooks to get intel on them is one thing; reading the heart of your lover is another. If this *is* her heart. God, but I hope it is.

'As part of an ongoing investigation,' I say, 'we had to gain access to the social circle of a number of people. We had Morozov and others under surveillance. We knew Morozov went to fetish clubs in his personal life so I tried to get involved in the scene. Met Lou via a kinky dating site, Brighton-based like him. And then I was in. Or on the outskirts. Turns out she didn't know him that well. No one seems to have done. Kept himself to himself. Then I got an invite to Dravendene with Lou's crowd. And he was there. And you were all over me and you knew him and it was a gift, a total gift dropped right in my lap.'

She nods. Her face is tense. She's remarkably calm, considering. It bothers me.

'That night,' she says, 'you kept saying you thought you knew him from somewhere.'

'An act. A way to forge a connection. Make him think we moved in the same circles.'

'You used me to get close to him.'

And here comes the wrecking ball, smashing into my dreams.

'It's not that clear cut,' I say. 'Sure, this was a covert, intelligence-gathering operation but—'

'Bullshit.'

'I swear, Cha Cha, I didn't—'

'Don't Cha Cha me, you treacherous, fucking cunt. You used me!'

'Lana, please! Let me explain. Give me a chance here.' God, I sound like such a cliché. I wouldn't blame her if she tried to punch me in the nuts.

She glares at me, lips pressed tight, shoulders rising and falling. 'I need a drink.'

It sounds like an accusation. She leaves the bedroom. I listen to her moving in the other room, bottles, glasses and ice clinking. Will she fix me a drink? Do I deserve one? Should I ask? Should I join her? I could kill for a smoke but I'm holding off a while longer. It's self-indulgent and rude. I'm walking a tightrope here. I need to not fuck up any more than I already have done.

Minutes later she returns, a balloon glass in one hand, a tumbler in the other. Brandy for her, bourbon for me. Over ice. Two cubes, the way I like it. It's the little kindnesses that kill you. Bourbon on the rocks and I want to weep with gratitude. She passes me my drink and stands by the bed.

'So why don't you tell me who you are,' she asks, 'and I'll tell you what I've done.'

I raise my glass to the air. 'Quid pro quo.'

She sits on the edge of the bed with me, not too close, and she takes a sip of brandy. Then she lies back on the duvet, feet still on the ground, and gazes up at the ceiling. One hand clasps the balloon glass to her stomach, the other is tucked behind her head. Lamplight from the courtyard shines through the window, throwing stripes across the lower half of her body. She's wearing this sky-blue dress, an ordinary, straight-up-and-down number which probably cost a whack because she always looks so damn good in it. Her knees peek out the bottom. She has great knees. Her posture is open, as if she's lying on a river-bank and dragonflies are dancing around her, but there's a stiffness in her body. Everything about her says, 'Don't you dare fucking touch me.' So I don't. I value my balls.

'I'm listening,' she says.

I inhale deep and hard. I figure it's best to start at the end because that's of most relevance to us. 'Like I say, you seemed a useful link to Morozov,' I reply. 'That was the start of it. Plus, you know, you were cute, so that helped.' She doesn't smile. Failed again. 'Then suddenly he's dead,' I continue, 'and when I smelled your hair, I knew there was something you weren't telling me. So, forgive my language, I decided to cultivate the connection and monitor you off the record.'

'And they say romance is dead.'

I ignore the barb. She has every right to fire them.

'You know, we ought to have been at his inquest the other week,' I say. 'But my unit had words with the right people and we were let off the hook because it could've gotten complicated. What else? Hell, so much to fess up to. I faked the building site job. Used it as an excuse to be in Saltbourne. With you. I've been briefed on the building trade. I'd work from home, writing up reports, checking in with HQ. Then I'd go for a run, stick on these dirty clothes and smear a little grime and plaster here and there. Then I'd drive over to the bar for...for Happy Hour. And I *was* happy, Lana. You made me happy, so fucking happy.' My throat tightens. I wait for it to pass. 'Can't fake happiness, Lana.'

'No,' she says sternly, still lying there, eyes fixed on the ceiling. 'Tell me who you *are*, Sol Revivo. What makes you tick?'

The pause that follows seems to go on forever. Tumbleweed practically rolls across the silence. And I'm thinking I am a man who, right now, would peel off his own skin and dive into salt if it would take away your pain. But, instead, I tone it down, stay matter-of-fact, and I say, 'I'm a regular, middle-class Jewish guy from New Jersey. Been living in London these last twenty years. I have dual nationality. That part was true. Joined the police force in my twenties and gradually moved up the ranks.'

'Why did you leave the States?'

I give a hollow laugh. I can't help it. This stuff's so petty. 'Quiet, toxic family dramas. The usual. Wanted to get away from my mother. Ironically, my mom swapped continents for the same reason. It's a family tradition.'

She sits up next to me, frowning.

'So your parents weren't killed in a car crash when you were a child?'

Ah, hell. It's hard to keep track of what matters when you fabricate a life. 'No,' I say. 'Alive and well.'

'There was no Little Orphan Sol?'

I wince. 'No.'

'And your grandmother with the inheritance?'

I shake my head. Man, this is harrowing, and it's all my fucking fault. I want to reach out and hold her hand as she sits there, stunned, but I don't think the gesture will be helpful.

'It's useful to have money and no job when you're undercover,' I explain. 'Wins you friends, keeps you free to roam. I played up my Jewishness. Claustrophobic relatives with cash. That kind of thing. Easy to convince people of your credibility when you tap into their . . . their preconceptions.'

'So your tattoo?' she says. 'Those seed heads? One for every loss.'

I shake my head. 'Just a tattoo, Lana.'

Her face flushes, a darkening rose. She takes a large, steady sip of brandy. She stares at the wall opposite us.

'You made me care about you,' she says. Her voice is so tiny, as if she's having to eke out every word. 'With your tales of loss. Your talk of fear. Guilt. I thought – stupid, stupid me – I thought it meant we were close.' Then she turns to me and, with a vicious little jerk, hurls the remaining contents of her glass in my face.

It's cold, it's wet, it's a shock. For an instant, I can't see. Alcohol stings my eyes. She's on her feet and so am I. She's running from me. The room is blurred, but I follow. I hook her around the waist and pull her back. She shouts but she lets me restrain her. I'm damn certain she lets me.

'Lana, forgive me, please. Please! I'll do anything, I swear to God, I'll . . .'

Tears well in my vision. A reaction to brandy in the eyeballs. I'm holding her against the open door of the bedroom. No, not holding. Let's face it, I've trapped her. My arms are either side of hers, my hands are flat to the door. She's motionless apart from the faint pump of her shoulders. I blink and the tears spill. I expect her to knee me in the cojones. She doesn't. Another wave of tears rises. I'll admit it, that's not the brandy weeping anymore.

She reaches up, face moving close to mine. She presses a sucking sort of kiss to my cheek. Ye gods, but it's impossible to second-guess this woman. Her lips pulse. It's like a sea anemone's got suction on my face, and it's beautiful.

Fucking beautiful. She's slurping on her brandy and on my tears. I can taste the mixture when it dribbles to my lips, salt and sweet and warm. Part of me's wondering if she's about to bite a vengeful chunk out of my face, and part of me's getting hard. I hope to hell she doesn't notice.

Well, she notices. Too late. Her hand is on my dick, rubbing me through my pants. Immediately, I'm a good deal harder.

'Make me forget,' she whispers.

Oh God, Lana, Lana! I'm right back in the forest at Dravendene. 'I can make you forget,' I'd said, and I had meant it. Or I'd wanted to. I'd wanted us to get lost together, lost in each other, to forget everything for a while before facing the fray. Because we were both reeling from the death of Morozov. But, yeah, for different reasons. I get that now.

She raises her arms, inviting me to take off her dress. So I do, and she's there against the door in her bra and panties. I'm not sure if this is good medicine for either of us but, right now, I'm risking it.

'You OK?' I ask.

'No,' she says. 'Are you?'

'No.'

I reach behind her to unhook her bra and she lets me. She makes slopes of her arms so the bra slides to the floor. The responsibility I'm being given here terrifies me. I rub the indent of her waist, hands either side of her. Her skin is so soft. Sometimes I worry I'll break her. She's so slender and I'm such an oaf. But I know that's dumb of me. She's not a porcelain doll. She tips her head back to the door, eyes closed. She's giving me her surrender. I'm not sure I can take it. Not sure I deserve it. Well, no. No,

I don't deserve it. But, oh God, the things she lets me do to her. It's always been this way.

By now, I know what she likes. It chimes with what I like. The second-best aspect of this job has been learning about a world that caters for people with marginal desires, people such as me. I've gained skills and understanding. I've put my new knowledge to good use with Lana. Sure, I've still plenty to learn but, for the first time in my life, I feel I can be the sexual person I've never dared be before. I'm thirty-eight years old. That's pretty freaking major. And I have Lana to thank for giving me that freedom. She loves what I love to do to her, and that makes me love it all the more. It was supposed to be a role ordained by the Met. They reckoned I looked the part, could carry it off. I guess you could say I've gone native on that score.

Meeting Lana trumps any BDSM training, of course. Although right now, I've hurt her so badly I'm wondering if it would've been better if we'd never got involved. Had never known happiness. Her voice echoes in my head: *Make me forget.*

What does she want to forget? Us? Our past together? Please, not that, Lana. The past might be all we have.

I tug off my tie. The bedroom door has this row of hooks slotted over the top. There's often something hanging there. Clothes, towels, bags. But not tonight. I glance at the hooks. I think we both know where this is leading. I take her wrists, raise them in front of me and cross one hand over the other. Briefly, she closes her eyes and gets that dreamy look of hers. She holds the pose I've put her in, offering her softly clenched hands. Then she watches me as I wind the tie around her wrists.

'Is this OK?' I ask.

She nods.

I lift her hands, raising her arms above her head, and catch the sound of a tiny mewl. My dick throbs. Her arms are so pretty. So graceful and strong. That'll be the swimming. How did I miss that? I fasten my tie to one of the hooks and run my hands down those pretty arms. Then I stroke down further to her waist and her panties. I tuck my thumbs in the band and slide them down her legs. She steps out of them willingly. She uses her toes to edge off the flats she's wearing. Naked, pale and vulnerable, tied to the door. I guess she's thinking I have a plan, something in mind I want to do to her, but I don't have a notion in my head. Well, there's a lot I want to do to her, there always is, but none of it is appropriate right now. So I touch her and look at her while I'm mulling it over, and my cock's hard as rock in my jockeys. Her bush is dark gold. Her tits are two perfect handfuls. Her nipples are pink as shells.

I think of Ilya Travis and I want to kill him.

I stoop for a mouthful of nipple. She goes from soft to stiff in no time at all. I suck and tongue her, my hands spanning the curve of each tit, nudging into her flesh. I want to devour her. I edge up to kiss her neck. I lick and kiss, nuzzle and nibble. I want to erase every dread and every memory that Travis planted in her mind when he sliced his tongue tip across her slender neck, left to right. I'll get him one day. And I'll have him strung up with his own vas deferens.

They say something soured him, that he lost a woman he loved when he was bartering with some low-lifes. I'd wish him sorrow till the end of his days but I figure he long since cut his heart out.

Lana whimpers when I drop to my knees. I am a drowning man. She is my air. I don't care what she's done. I press my hands to her inner thighs, pushing her apart. She tips her hips as I move in. Her pussy melts into my mouth and I'm all over her, in, around and through, lapping and slurping, wet on wet. She floods my tongue, brine running fast and fresh. Her flesh is warm on me and she smells ripe. I mean that in a good way. Seriously good. Above me, she's making tiny gasps and cries, quieter than usual, as if she's loath to give me anything. After a while, I shove two fingers inside her and devote my mouth to her orgasm. She's hot and pulpy around my fingers. Her fat clit rolls beneath my tongue, glossy and taut. I fuck her with my fingers, curving them the way she likes it, and she fucks right back, grinding into my lips with eager little thrusts. Soon, she's coming in a series of jerks and shudders, small, focused and violent, as if her loins are having a seizure. She barely makes a sound.

I sit back on my heels and then I stand. Her juices cool on my face. Her cheeks and chest are mottled with heat, her mouth slack. She looks at me. Her eyes are far away. Vacant. I sweep a strand of blonde hair from her forehead and lean in for a kiss. She turns her head aside. Ah, hell. What's to become of us?

'Thank you,' I say. Man, that sounds awful, as if I'm thanking her for her pussy, but what I mean is, thank you for not hanging me out to dry. I release her raised hands and unwind the tie from her wrists. As she steps away from the door, I slip off my jacket and hang it from one of the hooks.

I want to squeeze her to my chest but instead I say, 'You want me to fix you another brandy? Then you can tell me about this accident?'

'Take your clothes off first,' she says. 'Quid pro quo.'

Well, I'm good with that. So I strip and hang my clothes on the door hooks. I don't want to assume I'm staying the night but, at this point, I'm hoping. And so is my dick because it's bouncing around like this is party time. Hush, I want to say. There is no party.

I take our glasses. In the other room, I top up my bourbon and pour her a hefty measure of brandy. I'm about to return but she comes to join me. She's got this dark brown blanket over her shoulders and it trails behind her like a poor man's version of a regal cape. Without a word, she drops onto the sofa. She tucks her knees under her chin, and flicks the blanket around her like a tail. Her hand emerges from the heap when I pass her the glass of brandy. She looks like whipped chocolate.

'At Dravendene, afterwards, you fell asleep fast,' she begins. 'You always do. I was still alert. So was he. We were chatting. You were snoring.'

I take a seat on the opposite end of the sofa. 'Yeah, sorry about that.'

'I told him I was disappointed the pool wasn't open because I'm a swimmer. I feel ropey if I don't swim every day. Misha said he'd heard there was some problem with the heating so they'd had to keep the poolhouse closed. Then he said if I had a hair grip, he could try picking the lock. It just seemed a fun thing to do. Rebellious. Silly. Drunk. He got dressed, saying he'd probably go back to his room after our swim. I was pleased about that. The bed wasn't big enough for three people. And I liked you the best.' She blinks hard, looks away for a second or two before continuing. 'So I fished out a couple of bobby pins from my make-up bag and wrapped a towel around me. Couldn't see the point of wearing my bikini when we'd been fucking for the last couple of hours. And swimming naked is glorious. Water flowing over every inch of skin. Like silk lapping at your body. Blue silken liquid. Trying to slide into all your openings, sneak into your secrets. I wanted that. So soothing.'

I see a hint of pleasure in her eyes, the suggestion of a smile on her lips. Then her expression hardens and she takes a sip of brandy.

'We went via that secret stairway he showed us,' she goes on. 'We didn't see a soul. He twiddled with the poolhouse lock for ages. I could hear a few people still in the garden on the other side of the house. I was starting to worry he might damage the lock but then we were inside, and it was fine. He opened the panel to a little alcove at the back, flicked switches until we had just a couple of spotlights underneath the water. The surface was perfectly flat, not a ripple, and the beams were sharp. You could see the tiles of the pool. It looked so inviting. Everything else around us was dark. We didn't want to attract attention. The statues on the poolside looked kind of spooky. As if they might move when you weren't looking.

'The place was hot in the morning when we found him, so hot and stuffy. I'm not sure what dials and knobs he messed with, but I guess he demonstrated their heating system was screwed. Anyway, I dipped my toe in the water and it was cold. Really cold. Colder than at the swimming baths. But you just have to get in and swim, and you're warm in no time. So I tossed my towel on a plastic lounger and I dived in. As soon as my head hit the water,

I realised I was drunk. Knew I shouldn't be doing this. The cold was fierce, like a slap in the face. Everything had this hyper-clarity to it. Bubbles streaming from my lips, splashes jumping with every stroke, spotlights wobbling in the water. I swim front crawl, I'm fast. I did six lengths in no time but it was exhausting. My muscles ached. So I climbed out. I was heading for my towel. He was naked by now and half erect. He grabbed me.'

'Ah, hell,' I murmur. Now I'm the one with a hand clamped to my mouth, horrified.

'I laughed, pushed him off,' she says. 'I was breathless. "I want to fuck you more," he said. He grabbed me again. I pushed back again. My foot skidded on the wet tiles. Just a little but enough to make me wary. I elbowed him away and I was heading for my towel when he grabbed me again. Harder this time, nastier. I could feel his cock against my hip. We tussled. I was slippery, he was dry. And stronger than me. He said crass, scary stuff. "I know you want it." "Just one more time." But I didn't want it. Then we were close to the pool edge and I wriggled and pushed. I was shouting at him. I saw him fall into the pool. Heard the splash. I grabbed my towel and left. Didn't look back. Just assumed he'd be OK. Lesson learned for him. Customer lost for me. But, yeah, not so simple. Because in the morning he was dead. '

'Holy hell,' I say. 'I'm so sorry. So sorry for all you've been through, Cha Cha.'

That self-loathing I mentioned? It's back with bells on. Because these last couple of months I've been wracking my brains trying to work out if she'd killed him and, if so, why. Never even occurred to me it might be in self-defence. My blindness shames me.

I want to haul her towards me for comfort but she's still bundled up on the far side of the sofa. Whipped chocolate with brandy. Untouchable.

'Who was he?' she asks. 'Why were you spying on him?'

'He wasn't a particularly nice man,' I reply. 'If that helps any. Or, at any rate, he was involved in a business that isn't too nice. It's much as Travis said. He was supplying pharmacy chemicals, pseudoephedrine to be exact, to a gang of local methamphetamine cooks. Or two gangs, according to Travis. That was news to me. As far as we can work out, Morozov wasn't visiting your bar for any underhand reasons. Just liked a drink there. But, yeah, he was a key figure for us. We've been working to bust a major drugs ring that's been gaining traction in the south-east. Crystal meth, Lana. It's nasty shit. Generally requires a big hidden space to manufacture on a large scale but somehow, as far as we can tell, they're managing to do it down here, not too far from London.'

Her eyes are glassy. 'I killed a man,' she says.

'No you didn't,' I reply. 'A man assaulted you. You pushed him. He died. It wasn't your fault. You had every right to push him.'

'But I killed him all the same.'

I shrug. 'Maybe you did everyone a favour. Maybe some people are alive now, now and in the future, who wouldn't be if he were still around.'

She shakes her head. 'But it's not for me to decide who gets to live or die, is it? Which lives are worth more than others.'

'It was an accident, Lana. You didn't decide. Try not to torment yourself with guilt.'

She sips her brandy and stares ahead at the wall. She looks numb.

'Listen,' I say. 'Let me tell you about this drug. It destroys the brain's dopamine receptors, makes it impossible to experience pleasure. Turns people into shells of themselves. A substance you take to get high ends up robbing you of the very thing you want. The very thing that makes life worth living. I don't mean hedonism. I mean pleasure, joy, love. You get the absolute opposite of what you signed up for. Don't know about you, but that makes me sick to the pit of my stomach. The drug's abhorrent, totally fucking abhorrent, and so are those bastards getting rich off it.'

After a while, she says, 'Thank you. For trying.' Her lips tremble.

'So do I get a hug for trying?' I ask.

She gives a spluttering sort of half-laugh and sets her glass on the floor. I set down my own glass and hold out an arm to her. She scoots along the sofa towards me, tugging all that whipped chocolate mousse with her. She nestles into the crook of my arm and tucks a corner of the blanket across my lap. A tear smudges on my chest where she rests her head.

I hold her close and print a kiss on the top of her head. Her hair smells of apples.

Eventually she asks, 'Who's Ilya Travis?'

I keep my sigh as shallow as I can. 'Real name Ilyas Zarakolu. Turkish born. Gun-runner, money-launderer, hitman. Or, at least, he's adept at putting the pressure on when required. Has a couple of property businesses. Notoriously hard to pin anything on him but we're getting closer. Or we were. And there's a whole host of dubious characters we've been watching, trying to get the measure of the network. No point going in too soon.' I sweep my fingers through her silky hair, drawing it back from her face, hooking it behind her ear. 'I'm so sorry for what he...what he did to you.'

'It was my choice.'

'But not a free one,' I say. 'You were doing it for me.'

She strokes my chest, fingertips moving through hair in light little circles. 'It's like you're my crystal meth,' she murmurs. 'I got the opposite of what I signed up for.'

Moments later, my face is wet and I'm shaking.

She twists in my arms and looks up at me, surprised.

It's a while before I can find my voice. 'All I ever wanted was to be the hero,' I say. 'The good guy who brings the bad guys down. But not at this cost. Not with these sacrifices. I'm sorry I got you involved in all of this. So fucking sorry, Cha Cha.'

She wipes away my tears with the flat of her hand.

'I wasn't going to leave you, I swear,' I say. 'Didn't know what I was going to do but I knew I couldn't walk out on you. We can get it back. We can make it work.'

She smiles stiffly and shakes her head. 'No, we can't, Sol.'

'Lana, please!'

'You're a cop,' she says calmly. 'I've confessed to a crime.'

'And so?'

'So you have to arrest me,' she says. 'Report me. Or something. We have no future, Sol. We're on opposite sides of the divide.'

'Are you fucking serious?' That she thinks I'd snitch on her makes me appreciate how little she feels she knows me. How little she trusts me. 'I'll take it to my grave, Cha Cha,' I say. 'It never happened. Like the threesome, like the towel. It never happened.'

'Except it did. It all happened.'

'We can move past it,' I say. 'Besides, the inquest's been held. Finito.'

'Unless there's new evidence.'

'There is *no* new evidence,' I reply. 'I didn't hear a word you just said. Besides, it was a coroner's inquest. There's no police investigation going on. It's over. Signed and sealed. Death by misadventure.'

She lies on my chest again, arm wrapped around me. We say nothing for a while, just hold each other. I rub her shoulder through the blanket.

'How much of the diary is true?' I ask.

'All the important parts,' she says. 'All the parts about you, my feelings for you. That's true. It started as a lie to myself, to make myself believe I hadn't killed him. That someone else had been with him because of the towel. I had to explain the towel. Then I started to think I needed to convince you as well. And if I'd made out I suspected you of being with him when he died, then obviously it couldn't be me.'

'It's a little crazy, Lana.'

She shrugs. 'It's not easy keeping it together when you've killed someone.'

'And the page you ripped out?' I say. 'Was that about the accident?'

She nods against my chest. 'I started to write about the night at the pool after I thought you'd left. I was losing it. Losing control. Of myself, of my journal. Some nights I hardly sleep at all. You'd found the towel in my flat. I thought you might start putting two and two together. Realise I'd killed him and the diary was a lie. I wasn't sure if you were reading it but I hoped you were. But then I thought I'd made it worse because I'd never told you about the swimming. Then when I thought you'd left me, thought maybe you'd realised the truth. And I couldn't save myself or us. So I started to write about what had really happened. Then I stopped. It wasn't helping. So I ripped out the page and burned it.'

'You sure you burned it?'

'Yes. It's gone.'

'Good.'

I lean over to pick up my glass of bourbon from the floor. She rolls with me in my lap, allowing me to squash her a little; then we ease back. Inside the blanket, her hand drifts across my chest, back and forth, round and round.

'Was the towel a sign?' she asks. 'A way to tell me to be careful? Or a warning or something?'

I laugh. 'I guess I found it when I was looking for something else. Before I'd read any of your journal. I don't even remember it. I'm a guy, Lana. I'm not going to notice if a towel doesn't match your bathroom. The point of a towel is to dry a wet person.'

There's a faint laugh from her. She twines her finger in my chest hair, making a tiny whirlpool between my pecs, just idly playing with my body much as she used to.

'I thought you might have spotted it at Dravendene,' she says. 'When I came to tell you about Misha you were sitting on the edge of the bed. I didn't wake you up. You were awake already. I was worried you might have gone to the bathroom before I arrived. Seen the towel, smelled the chlorine. I just dropped it on the floor when I got back from the pool and climbed into bed. I was like a hurt animal, wanting to hide and lick my wounds. I'm usually tidy but I wasn't that night. That discarded towel's cost me a lot of sleep since then.'

I shake my head. 'That's your guilt, Lana. It's gotten you a bit obsessed about the towel. We should have a burning ceremony one day. Get rid of it for good.'

'I'd like that,' she replies. 'I keep meaning to throw it out.'

It's my first sign of hope, like a green spear in wintry ground. Spring. Growth. Renewal. Life.

I knock back my bourbon and set my glass on the ground. Inside the blanket, she ruffles the twist of hair she's made on my chest, erasing it, and rubs across the breadth of me. She butts into the crook of my arm and her hand sweeps lower. She tips her head back, looks up at me, and cups a hand over my groin.

'Make me remember, Sol,' she says. 'Make me remember how good we are together.'

Present tense. Present fucking tense.

I twist around and clasp her face, staring at her, at those China-blue eyes. I can scarcely believe what she just said. I'm getting another chance here? The blanket tangles around us as we shift position, and I'm patterning her face with kisses. I grab a handful of hair by the nape of her neck. Instinct. Habit. She groans deep and low. Her body slumps as if my strength depletes her of energy. Her reaction makes my cock jump. She closes her eyes.

Briefly, I wonder if I should be touchy-feely and tender. It's been a tough night, after all. Then I remember what she wrote in the beginning. *He understood me; understood that I didn't find comfort in the usual places.*

I'm on my knees on the sofa and she's leaning back against the padded arm. I tighten the fist in her hair, arching her neck, and I shove her thighs wider with one knee. Her foot drops to the floor. She wriggles and whimpers but she's wide open and glistening for me. I cover her mouth with my hand. Her hot breath pulses in my palm. Her eyes are locked on mine and she's looking a touch alarmed. I lean towards her face.

'You might regret asking for that,' I say, putting on a dark, snarly voice, 'when you can't walk tomorrow because I've fucked you to hell and back.'

She moans into my hand, wriggling more violently, but her eyes are playful, hungry. I'd recognise that glint anywhere.

'Sshh!' I murmur. 'There, there. Just try and block it out till I'm done.'

My dick is bone hard. I release her mouth and her hair. She pants for breath beneath me. I grab her arms, push them higher, one behind her head, the other squashed against the cushions. She squirms, hips lifting. Greedy, greedy. God, how I love that about her. I straddle her hips, half off the sofa. When I release one of her arms, it stays in position, flung back against the sofa as if I've moulded her into that pose. I slap her tits a little. She flinches, writhes, gasps. I take a nipple between thumb and forefinger, and I squeeze as slowly as I can. I keep one arm crushed into the sofa. I watch her face, and I realise I'm grinning. I increase the pressure, loving how her cries increase too. When I think she's at the limit of her pain tolerance, I squeeze a little harder.

'Please, please,' she wails, head thrashing, legs kicking behind me. 'No more, please.'

That's the part I love, when it slips into the real. She'd safeword me if she meant it. I hold the grip a while longer, pull her tit higher.

'No!' she gasps.

Coolly, I let go. I smile down as if I'm bestowing a great kindness upon her. 'You remembering yet, Cha Cha?'

'You bastard,' she breathes, and there's the snatch of a shocked laugh.

I edge back and hoik her ass in my direction. Then I change my mind and flip her over. She's very flippable, always is, and, hot damn, how I love that ass. I slam her upper body against the sofa arm and paste a couple of blows on her pale cheeks. Well, OK. I apply *more* than a couple of blows. Enough to make my palm sting. When she's nicely reddened and leaping like a landed fish, I guide my cock towards her pussy. Her wetness pretty much pulls me in, and her heat is wrapped around my dick.

The sound she makes is music to my ears. Her flesh hugs my shaft as I ease back and deep again. We're fucking without rubbers just as we did in the forest. It's like being licked by a choir of angels. Dirty, horny, cock-loving angels. I figure skin to skin is safe since we're not fucking anyone else. I plunge harder, faster, keeping her crushed to the sofa. I look at her ass, rosy pink and split, and below that my dick shunts in and out, glossy with her milk-white juices. I wish I could get closer than this, could get past the membrane separating her from me. And then we'd know each other wholly, the way you never can.

But, yeah, even though we can't get to that place, I thrust harder and harder, as if fucking her might make it so. Below me, she starts strumming her clit. Still makes me wild to see how frantically she goes at it. When she comes, I feel her ripple around my shaft like rivers of velvet. I can't take any more. Warmth's rising inside me and I'm too full of pleasure. The pressure valve needs to blow. I pull out, whack off like a madman, and then I'm coming all over her back and ass, showering her perfect skin. And I'm euphoric. It's as if all our time together is distilled in this moment of coming, all the bliss we ever tasted compressed into the here and now. I'm complete and I'm boundless. My come is on her body in stripes and splatters, no longer inside me, clamouring to get out.

I mark her in so many ways. Because she lets me.

I gaze down at her, at the dip of her spine, the curve of her ass, the breathless lift of her ribs. I'm dazed. I swear, I just touched the stars.

I am instantly fucking wrecked, exhausted. Gasping, we collapse into each other, clinging tight because the sofa's as narrow as a life raft. I burrow into her hair from behind, kissing her neck as we spoon, and she reaches back to fondle my thigh. My come smears between us, wetting my chest, and I wish it were glue to bind us together.

At length, she murmurs, 'I remember. I remember everything.'

'Damn right you do,' I say. 'And I'm going to make sure you keep on remembering.'

She wriggles her butt against my tingling cock. 'That a threat or a promise?' she asks. It's one of her cute lines.

'Both,' I say.

She laughs gently. 'Thank God for that.'

We kiss and caress with lazy tenderness. I drape my arm around her, cup one of her breasts, and simply hold her there. It's deeply comforting. Before long, we're drifting off together on our cushioned life raft. I listen as her breath slows, feel her body softening in my embrace. And as I slip towards sleep, I picture dangerous waters lapping at our edges.

Dream logic tells me to hold on tight to her, to keep her safe from harm. And that the wisest thing we can do is stay here forever, taking care of each other as best we can.

Part 7

Wednesday 12th November

Ilya Travis came to the bar today, shortly after five. My hand hovered over the panic button we've had installed behind the counter.

'I'm not going to hurt you, Lana,' he said, strolling towards me. 'I just wanted to thank you for getting lover-boy off my case. And I wanted to return this.'

He placed my lipstick in the silver tip saucer on the hazy blue bar. Fairy lights strewn around the oak and leather dimness cast reflections on the little dish. I picked up the lipstick.

'You shouldn't have,' I said, and I dropped the tube into the nearest bin.

He grinned. 'Guess I won't stay for a drink, then.'

'I guess not.'

He turned and sauntered out. I wasn't even interested in looking at his arse. Well, not much.

Sol clattered in the adjacent kitchen and staggered into the bar carrying two crates of bottled beer, biceps taut. He lowered the crates to the floor and slid open the glass door of the cooler.

'You OK, Cha Cha?' he called cheerily. He squatted by the fridge and began removing bottles from the top shelf. 'Thought I heard a customer.'

I smiled down at him as he restocked, pushing new bottles to the back of the shelf.

'No such luck,' I said. 'Some guy just popped his head round the door. Wanted to know what time we close.'

'Uh huh.' He lined up the chilled bottles along the front of the shelves. 'Going to be another quiet night,' he said.

'Yeah,' I replied. 'Bad time of year. Cold and dark. Christmas on the horizon.'

He stood and sidled towards me, wrapping an arm around my waist from behind. He dabbed kisses on the back of my neck. 'So what say we warm it up?'

I laughed, pressing my buttocks against his crotch. Sometimes I feel as if I can't say anything without him twisting it into an opportunity to seduce. I adore his deliberately heavy-handed approach, the way he acts like some cheesy throwback with terrible chat-up lines. I'd wondered how much of the old Sol would remain when we decided to give it a shot, and thankfully, it's quite a lot. As Sol said, a lot of what I got was him all along. He's good at compartmentalising, sure, but he's human. He leaks. The divisions aren't hard and fast. So there were lies, yes, but a lot of truths, too. If he'd been made of lies, as I once accused him of being, I'd have seen right through him. He was pretty much like my diary. A few lies. Many truths. Sol Miller is part of Sol Revivo, and vice versa.

'It's gone five o'clock,' I said, a mild reproach in my tone. 'Happy Hour's here and we're open for business.'

'Mmm.' He ground himself against me. 'I wish *you*

were open for business.' He started hitching up my skirt, a wiggle skirt, so he had to force the fabric over my thighs in the way that excites me.

'I could always put a note on the door downstairs,' I said. 'Saying we're opening at six.'

He stepped back from me, surprised. 'Yeah?'

I shrugged. 'Why not?'

He raised his brows. 'Hell, so what are we waiting for?'

I moved to fetch paper from the back room, smoothing out the wrinkles in my skirt. Sol grabbed a bar towel and cracked it across my buttocks, making me yelp.

'I said,' he continued, '"What are we waiting for?"'

I laughed and jabbed a finger in his direction. 'One day,' I replied, 'you'll push it too far.'

'In your dreams, Cha Cha.'

I scribbled a note on a sheet of A4 and headed downstairs. On the leaf-strewn, lamplit street, I glanced left and right, wondering if Ilya might be lurking. But, no, he'd gone. He had better things to do with his time than intimidate me. Besides, he has no need to trouble me anymore. Sol's quit the force. His undercover colleagues have been pulled off the job, and the operation's being scaled down. For a while, at least. Either way, it no longer has anything to do with me or Sol, and Ilya is well aware of it. The unit suspect they have an informer in their midst. Ilya knows more than he should. 'Everyone's twitchy,' said Sol. 'Who can you trust?'

I brought the A-board in from the street and taped my notice to the street door: OPENING AT 6 P.M. DUE TO STAFF SHORTAGE. APOLOGIES FOR ANY INCONVENIENCE.

I locked the door and returned upstairs, where the blue counter's glow illuminated the soft-lit, satin-walled room.

The balcony doors were closed, the stained-glass arch catching chips of brilliance in its leaded blue-green tiles. I put on an American accent as I entered, shoulders back. 'Hey, barkeep,' I called. 'Why don't you fix me a beer?'

He flipped the lids off a couple of bottles and poured mine into a glass. Having him around is a joy. We're a great team. He lost the Brighton flat when he quit the Met, and lost a damn good salary too. He's renting out his London home and living with me till we work out our plan. We've talked about buying a bar together, somewhere far away and hot where I can swim in the sea each day. 'We'll go skipping off into the tequila sunset,' he quipped.

I sleep well these days and my dreams are rich, dreams of snorkelling in vivid blue oceans and sleeping under cotton sheets, sweat-salt on his skin, sea-salt in my hair.

He's never going to read this journal again. I got Katrina to bind it in leather and secure it with a lock. A combination lock. I took my inspiration from the collar Sol once fixed around my neck. He can't see in my mind to get the number. I'm not going to tell him that Ilya turned up today. Sol feels he can never do enough to make up for the past and win back my trust. But the last thing I want is a man crippled with contrition, a man who feels he's in my debt and needs to be permanently on his best behaviour.

Letting him believe Ilya might still be a threat seems a good compromise. Sol gets to feel useful by looking out for me, ensuring I'm safe, and I enjoy the sense of security he brings. If he ever becomes suffocating, I'll rethink.

He stood our beers on the bar and came to join me on the other side. In the aquamarine haze of the counter, we clinked a toast, bottle to glass. 'Here's to Happy Hour,' he said.

He swigged from the bottle and yanked me close with his free hand. He kissed my neck, his lips cold and wet.

'To Happy Hour,' I said, laughing. I set my glass on the counter.

He placed his beer next to mine and inched my skirt higher, struggling against its tightness.

'You stop my clocks, Cha Cha,' he said. 'You stop my fucking clocks, you know that? This Happy Hour's going to last us quite some time.'

'That a threat or a promise?' I said.

'Both.'

He gave my skirt a hard, upward jerk. I heard a tiny rip. I'm hearing it again in my mind as I write in this journal, and I'm in the blue of the bar again, reliving the magic.

With the rip, I melt. My knees weaken. My limbs are loose. He slides a hand between my thighs, where I'm swimming with desire, liquefying. Oh, Sol, how you break me and make me. I am coming undone at the seams.

Acknowledgements

My thanks, as ever, to the Black Lace team for keeping the erotic flag flying; for making the process seamlessly smooth for me; and for giving me the chance to play at the darker edges of this genre.

Thank you to all the friends (too many to mention and I may have forgotten your names) who, inadvertently or otherwise, have helped me with my cocktail-drinking 'research' over the years; and to Chris Seggerman for infectious cocktail nerdery and for directing me to the best virtual bars from across the pond.

An enormous debt of gratitude to my wonderful sister who came charging to my rescue when my laptop went belly up.

Massive thanks, love and respect to Lorelei for understanding when I was taking mental notes at the grimmest of times; I wish that story could have been different.

And to Ewan, so much to Ewan, for finding extra days in the week to read the ms with insight and enthusiasm; for boundless support, encouragement and inspiration; for putting the tequila in my sunrise; and for being in this glorious sandpit with me where we get to make stuff up in our heads and tell each other about it first!

Also by Kristina Lloyd:

THRILL SEEKER

'I'd never set out to snag Mr Right but I'd veered so far off that
track I was now at the mercy of Mr Dangerously Wrong...'

Betrayed by her lover, Natalie Lovell finds herself
exploring the world of internet dating.
    Then she meets a dark sexy stranger online who prom-
ises all the danger, excitement and dominance she craves.
But how far will Natalie go to get the ultimate in thrills...?

**A sexy and controversial erotic thriller –
Fifty Shades Darker than E L James and Sylvia Day.**

BLACK
LACE

Also available from Black Lace:

DIAMOND

By Justine Elyot

*Her name is Jenna Diamond. She is about to
meet her match…*

Since the painful breakup with her famous musician
husband Jenna has returned to England and bought a
crumbling old house back in her hometown.

But Jenna discovers a mysterious stranger hiding out at
Holderness Hall. Logic suggests she should alert the
authorities, but when she looks at her sexy, young house
guest Jenna finds it all too easy to let her heart rule her
head…

**Book 1 in the Diamond trilogy, a glamorous erotic
romance, from the bestselling author of *On Demand***

BLACK
LACE

Also available from Black Lace:

WRAPPED AROUND YOUR FINGER

By Alison Tyler

A story of submission

Samantha is loving her 24/7 BDSM-lifestyle: costumes, erotic toys and role-playing fulfill her dirtiest dreams. And Jack, the ultimate dominant's Dom, pushes Sam's boundaries to the limit, making her do things she'd never thought she could do.

Yet can she manage to stretch her love for Jack to incorporate his carnal need for his male assistant, Alex, as well?

Take the ride with this deviant trio. This diary of a submissive ups the ante with intense sensuality that will have you hanging on by your handcuffs!

BLACK LACE